RESERVATIONS

KINDLE ALEXANDER

T R A D E M A R K
A C K N O W L E D G E M E N T S

The author acknowledges the trademarked status and trademark owners of the following trademarks mentioned in this work of fiction:

007: Danjaq, LLC
Advil: Wyeth, LLC
America's Next Top Model: Pottle Productions, Inc.
Armani Code: Giorgio Armani, SPA
Beavis and Butt-head: Viacom International Inc.
Bluetooth: Bluetooth Sig, Inc.
BWI: Maryland Aviation Administration
Cheshire Cat: Disney Enterprises, Inc.
Collin Street Bakery: Collin Street Bakery, Inc.
Corvette: General Motors, LLC
Doc Martens: "Dr. Martens" International Trading GmbH
Dr. Phil: Peteski Productions, Inc.
El Pollo Loco: El Pollo Loco, Inc.
Escalade: General Motors LLC
FaceTime: Apple, Inc.
Ferrari: Ferrari S.p.A.
Froot Loops: Kellogg North America Company
Google: Google, Inc.
GQ: Advanced Magazine Publishers, Inc.
Grey Goose: Barcardi & Company
Grindr: Grindr, LLC
Heineken: Heineken Brouwerijen B.V.
HSN: HSN Holding LLC
Hush: Danxiao Information Technology
Iron Man: Marvel Characters, Inc.
Keurig: Keurig, Inc.

La-Z-Boy: La-Z-Boy Incorporated Corporation
Lifetime: Lifetime Entertainment Services, LLC
Mack Truck: Mack Trucks, Inc.
Marvel: Marvel Characters, Inc.
MTV: Viacom International Inc.
Passeggiata: Black Ankle Vineyards, LLC
Realtor: National Association of Realtors
Reddit: Reddit, Inc.
Sherlock: Conan Doyle Estate Limited
Speedo: Speedo International
Sprite: The Coca-Cola Company
The Marlboro Man: Phillip Morris USA, Inc.
Tinder: Tinder, Inc.
Toyota: Toyota Motor Corporation
Tropicana: Tropicana Products, Inc.
Two Hearted Ale: Bell's Brewery, Inc.
Viagra: Pfizer Inc.
Whole Foods: Whole Foods Market IP, L.P.
Williams-Sonoma: Williams-Sonoma, Inc.
XT5: General Motors, LLC
Yelp: Yelp, Inc.

SPECIAL THANKS

Marie Ullrich
Thank you for stopping your life to help us.

Steve Wiscaver
You've become such a great friend. Thank you for everything.

Ted Hayes
You're a BOSS! You've taught me to love a comma.

Ryan Wilson Foley
You just make us smile all the time.

Melissa McEntyre
We could never do this without you.

Karen Jones
You're a dream. Thank you, thank you!

Jenna Underwood
I still don't have my bowl.

DEDICATION

Kindle, you are forever in our hearts.

Perry, you're missed every day.

"Sometimes you will never know the value of a moment until it becomes a memory." ~Dr. Seuss

In memory of my beautiful friend and incredibly talented author, **Sandrine Gasq-Dion**. You will be missed.

Find Sandrine's books:
https://www.amazon.com/Sandrine-Gasq-Dion/e/B006WNHN04

CHAPTER 1

June 2016

Thane Walker's tires squealed as he rounded the corner, barely touching the brakes before pressing the gas again. The small digital clock on the dash flipped a single digit, making him officially late for his two o'clock meeting.

"Are you listening?" Erin asked, drawing his attention back to the phone conversation just as the impressive sight of the newest Escape property in Coronado, California, came into view.

"No, I wasn't. Say it again." Thane held back the growl as a red light forced him to stop at the intersection. So close, yet so far from his destination.

"When are you gonna be home? Brock's best friend from high school's coming to stay for a few days. He's six-one, blond hair, nice body, good job. He's interviewing for a position in the State Department…" Erin trailed off as if she were dangling a carrot, but he could only half listen to her as he nervously drummed his fingers on the steering wheel, willing the light to change. "He's twenty-nine, your age, and I want you to go out with him."

That caught his full attention.

"I'm not interested," he said and took off when the light turned green, following way too close to the car in front of him.

"Thane! I've told him all about you and he's interested and his name is Noel. I love that name. It fits him so well."

"I've told you this before: no blind dates, no friendly dates, no Erin insisting upon dates."

Erin and her husband, Corey, were his neighbors…and some of the best friends he had. Erin watered his plant while he traveled—yes, a plant she gave him for his last birthday, but Erin had a way with keeping plants alive, a trait he didn't share. But Erin insisted on trying to set him up with all available bachelors in hopes he'd fall in love.

Since Erin was as close a friend as he'd ever had, Thane was comfortable saying, "You need to build that bridge and get over it. Like I've told you over and over, it's never gonna happen."

Though the Escape resort hadn't been far from the traffic light, it took a veritable eternity to turn onto the short drive leading to the front entrance.

"You're frustrating. What am I gonna say to him now?" Erin's eager anticipation had changed to crestfallen in a matter of seconds. Her pout at being shot down came through the car speakers loud and clear, even if she should be used to his turning down her setups by now.

"Crochet him a scarf. One like you made me last year. It'd be a better deal for him anyway," he said, giving a grin at her frustrated sigh. "I gotta go. I'm here."

"Good luck on whatever you're meeting about!"

Thane grinned at her encouragement and reached over to end the call as he swiftly pressed the brakes, coming to an abrupt stop in the middle of the covered drive. He threw the vehicle in park then grabbed his laptop bag from the passenger seat before sliding out of the rented SUV. He slung the packed leather case over his shoulder and began patting his front suit coat pockets to find the keyless remote key fob. About halfway between the valet stand and SUV, the vehicle brought him to a forced stop as it began going nuts with all its alarms warning him he might be walking too far out of range to keep the engine running.

"Mr. Walker, you're back," a valet said, vaulting away from the stand, jogging the few steps toward him with a big toothy grin. "How was your flight, sir?"

Even being late for this meeting with Arik Layne and Tristan Wilder, and with an anxiety level of about a nine point five, Thane returned the grin. He stuck his hands in his slacks pockets when his initial search for the key fob came up empty. "Be honest, how do you always know who's getting out of these cars? You can't possibly remember all these people," Thane asked, finally locating the device and handing it over.

"Well, sir, I do remember you. You own the best restaurant here and our employee discount extends there. That makes me real happy, so I'll let you in on the secret." The kid lifted both his forefingers up to the awning as he started moving around Thane toward the driver's side of the vehicle, which immediately silenced the alarm as the valet got closer to his still open door. "That Wilder dude, he's going nuts here. We have cameras and all this artificial intelligence that feeds information to the monitors at the different valet stands. If you've stayed here before and pull under this canopy, we know who you are and the front desk is notified of your arrival."

Thane shook his head in amusement. Of course an Escape property would have the best of the best technology. Arik Layne and Tristan Wilder concepts were the hottest things to hit the hospitality industry in years. That dynamic duo had made some explosive accomplishments. Luckily for Thane, those two men had taken a liking to him, and he wasn't going to mess up the opportunities that afforded.

On that thought, he quickly tipped the valet and went straight for the front doors of the hotel. No reason to be any later than he was. "I have luggage in the back."

"Yes, sir. I saw you were staying the night. I'll get 'em to your room."

Normally, he'd take the minute to appreciate the over-the-top, magnificently decorated lobby, be proud that his own accomplishments had led him to do business with the likes of people who created such beauty, but not this time. Instead, he headed toward the sweeping staircase leading to the second-floor conference area and took those steps up two at a time.

A few years ago, right out of college, Thane had been working for an investment banker. He'd stumbled on a failing small chain of family-owned restaurants. They'd had three locations, and out of nothing more than Thane's love for food, he'd made the declining company an offer. At the time, he'd been naïve and completely full of himself, but that had turned out to be the winning mix for his newly acquired business. After replacing the entire staff, including the management team, and putting some strict policies and procedures in place, Thane had those under-performing restaurants turning a profit within a couple of months.

In five short years, he'd rinsed and repeated the same concept with more than two hundred restaurants spread out across thirty-three states. To the delight of his taste buds, his restaurants offered every type of cuisine.

From that humble beginning, he now rubbed elbows with the likes of Arik Layne. It was almost unimaginable. He could feel his heartbeat increase with his excitement. Today was the day Arik was either going to sign on to his newest venture or bail. All indicators signaled the first option's likelihood, which meant his dream project would truly come to life.

Thane hit the top step and came face-to-face with Arik who must have been notified of his arrival, proving again, the Escape team was damn good at what they did. Thane was attempting to tie his newest project to the best of the best in his industry. He extended his hand. "I'm sorry I'm late. I ran into some traffic on the way from the airport."

"It's not a problem. I just arrived myself," Arik said, shaking his hand. "I've got a conference room reserved. Tristan's teleconferencing in. I hope you carved out the remainder of the afternoon. We have a lot to go over."

"I did. And I've also arranged to stay the night. One of my restaurants downstairs is having a big celebration this evening," Thane replied.

Thane had spent quite a bit of money trying to get ahead of the diversity trends in food. When he had gotten the call he'd been approved for two restaurant spaces here at Escape Coronado, he'd jumped in. One he'd kept conservative: an American grill. The other he'd splurged on. He built Castelli's from the ground up, and the somewhat fine-dining, Italian slash

Asian fusion cuisine restaurant had taken off like a dream, beating even his wildest expectations.

"I heard Castelli's made top sales this quarter. Is that correct?" Arik asked, sticking his hands in his slacks pockets.

"Yes, it won our internal corporate contest. They came out of nowhere and took the prize. I have a Tex-Mex restaurant in Texas that thought they had it in the bag. Of course, Castelli's has the popularity of the resort to thank. It seems all anyone's talking about is the magnificence of this place. You've outdone yourself."

"That's nice to hear, but I think Castelli's holds its own. Come this way." Arik started across the long catwalk above the front desk, and Thane followed, keeping Arik's casual pace as they walked side by side. "I noticed you have a signature brand of infused oils and vinegars. They seem to be a big draw to your customer base. Chef Ferico explained you're taking your oils to merchandise."

If Arik knew so much about the oils, he had to have spent time in the restaurant, which gave Thane a tremendous sense of pride. As much as Arik was known for his resorts, the two of them had bonded over their mutual love of food. It pleased him that Arik enjoyed his restaurant, but that didn't stop the warning bells that began to ring. Mass producing his blends was proprietary information only a handful of people knew anything about.

Thane slowed until he came to a stop just steps away from a door that automatically opened as they approached. He cocked his head in Arik's direction as the man came to a stop to face him. Arik was a bold one; he stared straight at Thane while trying to hide his knowing grin.

"We are taking them to market," Thane finally said and nodded.

"Don't worry. I can be very persuasive when I want to be, especially when it comes to delicious food. One night I was alone, Kellus wasn't with me, and I finagled my way into the kitchen where I stayed quite a long time. I sampled all the flavors of the oils and vinegars Chef Ferico had freshly fused together. They're outstanding. That's when I discovered some of the plans you have. And honestly, he kept the secret until I tried to get him to go into business with me." Arik laughed now, lifting both hands in the air in some sort of truce offering. "I'll confess that my intentions weren't completely honorable. I didn't necessarily include you in my plans, but in my defense, it was after an entire bottle of wine. I'm sure I would have done right by you in the morning."

"Okay, well, I'll confess that it was only after a bottle or two of wine that Ferico and I began blending the unusual flavors together," Thane replied, still not entirely sure how he felt about his chef revealing their trade secrets.

Arik again chuckled and turned, heading into a small conference room. "Some of my best ideas come at the end of a bottle of wine."

Just like the rest of the resort, everything flowed in the theme of over-the-top luxury. There was a table that sat no more than six people, the chairs looking like scaled down versions on La-Z-Boy recliners, a monitor extended downward from the ceiling to hang just above the edge, and a small food and drink cart was parked nearby.

Arik grabbed a cookie off the tray, passing on the sliced fruit, and took a hearty bite before grabbing a water bottle and heading around the table to his seat. "Have a cookie. Kellus watches my diet so closely; he worries about my health. I take my treat days when I travel alone."

Thane did take a bottle of water and began to mentally tick off the number of times Arik mentioned Kellus Hardin. The last time they'd spoken over the phone, Arik had used Kellus's name eight times in a twenty-minute conversation. Arik was a man utterly in love and let anyone who might listen know. The guy seemed insanely proud that Kellus wanted to take such good care of him. For Thane, it seemed a bit smothering, but he never said a word. Instead, he let Arik have his moment.

"So, I want in."

That declaration startled Thane as he put his leather case on the table, taking the seat directly across from Arik. He wasn't expecting to hear those words so early in their meeting. He would have thought the man would need a little more convincing. He looked over at Arik, hoping to hide the shock even as he began to realize something wasn't exactly right with the statement. "In on what?"

Arik's eyes lit up like he'd just gotten an extra free dozen cherry iced box cookies from the famous Collin Street Bakery in Texas. "On manufacturing the oils and balsamic vinegars. I've taken the liberty of drawing up a possible proposal. I've delved into manufacturing, gotten my toes wet. I could add value to the process. Of course, I have no idea how far you've gotten."

"Not very. I have estimates out, that's all."

Arik tossed an envelope across the table. It landed with a thud a few inches in front of Thane. He picked up the package and peeked inside at the stack of stapled pages. What had kept him from jumping right into producing the oils was the load of capital required to start a project like that. He'd invested a chunk of change into Castelli's, and more recently, he'd covered all of Julian Cullen's medical bills after Julian, a man he'd regularly spent time with, had been found badly beaten and abused, and those expenses had been extensive. Then factor in this new project, and he wasn't sure it was the time to drop so much cash on something as avant-garde as infused oils and vinegars.

Absently, Thane pulled the pages free of the envelope and thumbed through the contents. He noted several sections outlined in the document, from start-up through delivery. Arik had done his work, and this information proved he was dead serious in his desire to invest and be involved. "Thank you. I'll look this over."

"Thank you for allowing me to insert myself in your business. I figured since we'll already be partners, you might consider extending that relationship," Arik said, reaching for a remote control nearby. The monitor at the end of the table lit up, showing Tristan Wilder with his head bent, working on something at his desk. The screen's position and size made it feel as though he were sitting in a chair with them rather than hundreds of miles away.

"Hey. Give me a second," Tristan said, before looking up, giving a cheeky grin. "You're late."

Again, for the second time in a matter of minutes, Thane was thrown off balance. Arik's words caught up with him, and he cut his gaze between Arik and Tristan. "You've agreed?"

"Tristan and I want to hear from your mouth exactly what you're thinking," Arik started.

"Not all the legal crap you sent over," Tristan continued for Arik who nodded his confirmation.

"But we also don't want you to be long-winded. Just touch on the highlights." Arik finished off the thought, proving what was being said about the two—that they worked well together, exactly on the same page.

Thane took a deep breath and began to mentally scale down his prepared presentation while pulling his portfolio from his leather case. "For me, this is more of an emotional venture. I don't see it raking in large profits. It'll be costly to start and maintain, but I believe it's necessary to those it helps protect," Thane began, looking down at his notes. He had so much written there, nothing easily pared down, so he went off-script and decided to drive the points home with the facts. "Tristan and I have a mutual acquaintance named Julian Cullen…"

"The man who was attacked the night before this resort's grand opening, correct?" Arik asked, turning serious.

"Yes," Tristan answered for Thane. "Have they found the attacker?"

Thane shook his head. He remembered the night with clarity. He had flown across country to be in Coronado for not only Escape's grand opening but also Castelli's. Tristan and Arik appeared to enjoy their marital and monogamous statuses, but Thane had the complete opposite mindset. He exclusively enjoyed the company of escorts, and whenever he had reason to be on the West Coast, he'd give Julian a call. And that trip had been no different. Thane had pre-booked Julian's time for the entire grand-opening weekend.

When Julian hadn't shown, hours after their scheduled time, Thane had gone in search of Tristan. When Tristan agreed Julian wasn't the type to be a no-show, Thane had enlisted Tristan's help in tracking down Julian. Through measures Thane wasn't sure were legal, Tristan had used his hacking skills to locate Julian, lying broken and beaten in a hospital bed in Los Angeles. It had taken months to get Julian strong again, and even then, the man was nowhere close to being the same as before. Thane shook his head again, this time to refocus on the question that had been asked.

"No, Julian isn't remembering much. They're saying he's blocked it out." Images of Julian's beautiful face, swollen and bruised, his body covered in burn marks with strips of flesh torn from his skin… Thane would never forget that horror.

He had voluntarily covered every expense for Julian. Thane had also tried to be a friend to the guy—as much of a friend as he could be from his home in Maryland, which happened to be just about as far away from San Diego as a person could get and still live in the same country.

On that somber note, Thane continued his presentation. "The idea is to create a safe place for men to meet. I'm looking to open an exclusive, members only, upscale gentlemen's dinner club slash nightclub. We'll have two types of memberships. One will be our primary customer base. We refer to them as the Gentlemen. I see them as the majority of our clientele. There'll be a significant annual membership fee to join. Gentlemen will agree to undergo a comprehensive application process and pass a thorough and extensive background check."

Thane paused to make sure Tristan and Arik were following. When both stayed quiet, patiently waiting, he continued with the more complicated part of the membership process. "The second type of membership will be a much smaller group of men, and they'll be referred to as the Companions. Escorts will fall under this category. They'll also have a background check performed to gain entrance. Their fees will be much smaller. The goal is to have a safe environment for men to meet one another. So, if a Gentleman's looking for an escort, or just to meet another man, they'll have the added security of knowing these background checks have been performed, protecting all parties, keeping them as safe as we possibly can."

"Let me make sure I've got this straight." Arik's brow furrowed as he pushed back in his reclining chair. "Outside of the requirements you've mentioned, the restaurant and bar will operate as any do?"

"Absolutely. Maybe once or twice a month, we could host a social event. We could encourage theme parties, sponsor cheese and wine afternoon meet-ups. Make it a place where someone feels comfortable knowing the men they're meeting and hooking-up with have had a background check performed. That everyone involved will keep things discreet and no one expects anything other than their agreed upon arrangement, whether that includes compensation or not," Thane explained.

"Will you handle the payment for sexual transactions?" Tristan asked.

Thane immediately shook his head. "Absolutely not. No sex on the premises. Hard rule. I'm not pedaling ass, merely facilitating an environment for men to meet as safely and discreetly as possible. In this phase of my life, I've chosen to live with the services escorts provide. That's a better option for me. I don't have the time, nor do I want to spend my energy in cultivating a relationship when it's only going to end in a miscommunication of feelings, and I don't believe I'm alone in my philosophies, but I also acknowledge that not everyone feels that way."

He let that sit there a moment, knowing both Arik and Tristan had lived much of their lives in that same way until they'd settled down. "Plus, I'd like to give these escorts as secure a place as we can provide to meet potential and existing clients. Had Julian had something like this, he quite possibly wouldn't have ended up being so badly abused. I understand his process of checking out potential new clients was nothing more than calling his buddies and asking around. That's unacceptable and entirely too risky. We can do better."

"Mmm. It's an interesting concept. And I agree it's very much needed. I'm not sure if I've ever heard of anything quite like this before," Tristan said, and a noise on Tristan's end caused Thane to focus more closely on the monitor. Dylan Reeves,

Tristan's husband, had come inside the room and taken a seat beside Tristan.

"I'm sorry I'm late. Keep going. I'll catch up," he said, encouraging them to continue. Thane glanced at Arik who looked deep in thought. Dylan's presence made Thane a little unsure. The few times Thane had ventured into short-lived relationships, the guys had become super possessive; yet here Dylan and Tristan were, working on this together. A project inspired by Tristan's past lover.

"I'd probably have enjoyed a place like this before I met Kellus," Arik said and pushed up in his seat to reach for a calculator, still seemingly lost in thought.

"I've got the restaurant portion down. We'll be a fine-dining establishment with a nightclub attached. One that offers entertainment and dancing, things along those lines. Where Arik comes in are the rooms. If I have someplace nearby that always has rooms available, with a security guard stationed on the floor and the needed amenities waiting, it'll just heighten the safety factor."

"I agree. Do you have any idea how many rooms we'd have to block out?" Arik asked, picking up a pen, starting to jot down notes.

"No idea, but to make this work properly, the members will need access to a room. For purchase of course."

Arik nodded and continued writing on a stray pad of paper.

"My struggle's going to come during peak season and on the weekends, but I'll deal with that," Arik added, absently.

"How do you keep undercover police out?" Tristan asked.

"I don't. Entry requires membership, and that's a lengthy process, but if they set up an undercover operation, and we don't catch it, that's on members. I can't stress this enough. We're not *selling* sex. I sell booze and food. Arik sells rooms. I truly believe these safety measures would have helped Julian. I'm not suggesting every man that steps inside our club will pay to have sex. Many won't, but if we're ever again subjected to something as horrific as what happened to Julian, we'll be able to find the man and make him pay. That's where Tristan comes in," Thane explained.

"Our contribution'll be setting systems in place for background reports and the surveillance security in both the club and the hotel. They'll ideally work together to provide a complete security trail," Tristan added.

"Yes," Thane confirmed, "Exactly."

"Who do you have in mind to run such an operation?" Arik asked.

"I'll take care of that. It won't be much different than any restaurant site I have, but once everything's in place, I thought Julian might be a good fit. He's got the companion connections down. I'll get him some training, and he can handle personnel. It'll be a tough transition for him, but if he adapts well, I'll move him up. He needs legitimate employment. He's not progressing in his care as much as we might have hoped. He's got some disfigurement, not anything noticeable unless you knew him before. He's also on a cane; he's got a limp that's frustrating him, but the main obstacle seems to be in his head. He's started counseling recently." Thane tapped his temple with his forefinger as he spoke those last couple of lines.

"Mmm, I'm sorry to hear that," Tristan said.

"Me too," Arik murmured.

Silence ensued while they all stared at one another. That wasn't unusual, negotiations always needed a minute to sit and, what he liked to call, marinate.

"Do you have a name for the club?" Arik asked, still sounding somewhat distracted.

"My initial market research shows favorability toward the name Reservations."

Dylan nodded. "That's clear and to the point. Makes it obvious a person can't just walk in," Dylan added. "I like it."

"All right. Well, is Wilder in?" Arik asked, focusing on the monitor.

"We've got the software ready. It's relatively easy on our end, and we've agreed to the financial commitment," Dylan answered instead of Tristan.

Arik nodded and turned back to Thane, looking at him for several long moments, not saying a word. Thane turned his uncertainty toward Tristan who just shrugged. "I thought maybe the screen had frozen," Tristan responded cheekily. Thane snorted, but Arik didn't acknowledge the joke.

"It's very important to me that we're clear from the beginning: we don't operate in the sex business, no more so than any other legitimate club where people meet and possibly leave together. It's just our people have been vetted. I like the idea of being somewhat remote from major urban areas so men have a place to come and relax. My initial thought is that I'd like to see this restaurant slash club open in my exclusive adult's only section of this property. It's a quick walk from the restaurant to a room from that location of the resort. We have remote check-in; rooms can be booked through a mobile application. So that's all discreet and efficient," Arik said, making notes as he spoke.

When Arik again turned silent, Thane said, "I wholeheartedly agree with everything you've said."

"We can do a trial here in Coronado. If this works without blowing up in our faces, I might even want to talk about expanding. I have forty properties across the globe, and all have adult's only sections."

"I honestly believe this'll work," Tristan added his encouragement.

"It's been a while or, more accurately, not ever," Arik amended his sentence rather cheekily, "since I've done business for the sole purpose of giving back. My husband was in a bad situation..." Arik paused.

Thane hid a smile as he counted either the third or fourth reference to Kellus since he'd gotten there. Arik held up to his reputation as dick-whipped to the extreme, and he didn't even seem to care, proud, in fact, of his deep infatuation with Kellus. Thane was determined to never let that happen to himself.

"I like the idea of working with someone of your integrity, Thane. I like to have a purpose accompanied by a clear vision," Arik continued.

Thane appreciated that compliment and nodded. "Thank you." Grinning like a Cheshire cat, he added, "So, you're all in?"

"Yes, with some very defined protocols, and an out-clause if things go south, but yes, Wilder's in," Tristan said.

"We need to work out the details; let legal make themselves crazy preparing for every conceivable outcome. It'll be difficult to keep so many rooms open, but we can work that out. I don't know Julian, but you and Tristan have vouched for him. I'm willing to bring the guy into the Layne family fold and get him some management training and experience. We'll know quickly if he can cut it or not. Have him contact me in the next day or so," Arik offered.

Thane nodded, knowing Julian wanted to work, provide for himself, and needed a change of scenery. "I'd appreciate that. Thank you."

"Hey, ask Julian to tell you both about the three-way he had with us."

Arik and Thane swung their heads toward the monitor in unison, staring at Dylan who had turned five shades of red before he reached over and pushed at a laughing Tristan's shoulder.

"I'll never live that down," Dylan said and tossed a disgusted hand in the air as he rose from his seat and started to leave the room. That had Tristan laughing even harder as he stumbled over the chairs in his fit of humor, going after Dylan.

"Babe, don't be mad. I was teasing."

A door slammed outside the monitor's view. Tristan came back to the screen, his face large in the camera. "Really. Ask him about it. It might cheer him up. Ciao." The screen went dark.

"Okay, well, there you go." Arik pushed back from his chair and grabbed his notepad and iPad before picking up the remote and pointing it at the monitor. "When you find out about that three-way, I want the details." Arik came around the side of the table and grabbed another cookie. "Why don't you take me downstairs and buy me dinner? I have the evening free. If you're game, we can start with dinner, then come back up and go over the finer details. I have a lease space opening up out back that might work well."

"Perfect." Thane followed Arik until they were trotting down steps toward the first floor. "This was much easier than I thought."

"Says the man who hasn't met my legal department," Arik quipped.

CHAPTER 2

February 2017

Past exhausted, Levi Silva willed the hands on the old clock above the condiments bar to magically race forward and put an end to his nightmarish shift. The constant chiming of the bells attached to the front door of Lieu de Café had finally stopped. A steady stream of demanding customers had bombarded him over the last four hours.

Levi had no doubt he had a permanent frown etched on his tired face, and the headache he'd been fighting all evening spiked another notch. His short-lived relief at the quiet faded as he took in the state of the work station and dining area.

"What a mess," he groaned. Disgusting. He grabbed the spray bottle of cleaning solution and a clean hand towel before heading for the six small tables in the seating area. He hadn't had a moment free to clean all evening and the place showed it.

A few months ago, the owner had cut the staff to a bare minimum to save the struggling business. That left Levi on his own to handle all the customers, cleaning, and performing the closing responsibilities. Besides the staff cuts, the owner had also lowered his pay. Despite all that and an increase in the number of customers, nothing seemed to have changed for the business's bottom line. When several members of the owner's family stopped by on a regular basis to sneak money from the till—twenty dollars here, a hundred dollars there—it was no wonder the little coffee shop couldn't pay for itself. The place never stood a chance.

This job had taught him a lot about people. He'd learned he didn't care for the snooty, privileged class of people like his boss's family, with their boundless sense of entitlement.

The for-sale sign the owner had placed in the window earlier that evening wasn't a shock. They'd also handed Levi his final walking papers, officially laying him off. Well, he'd be without a job once he managed to single-handedly pack and move all the equipment and supplies to a storage unit. Apparently, the owner liked his work ethic, so they'd keep him until the bitter end. Yippee.

Stop all this negativity, he mentally chastised himself. It didn't help, and it damn sure wouldn't change anything. He just needed to find new evening part-time work. Truthfully, he hadn't ever liked this job anyway.

Levi tucked his lip between his teeth, gnawing on the sensitive skin as he sprayed several pumps of cleaning solution on a table. Maybe he should just give up on medical school and go find a real job—start becoming the man of the house. Perhaps even consider a trade. Construction was killing it right now.

All he had was a pre-med undergraduate degree, which didn't amount to much in the real world, and a physical therapy assistant certificate, which helped him find the day job that didn't quite keep them afloat financially. On top of that, he had a mountain of financial-aid debt, his dad's funeral to pay for, and bill collectors calling daily about his father's unpaid medical expenses. Factor in his brothers' needs, all their living expenses, and, boy, did their expenses weigh heavily on his shoulders. Maybe he should consider pharmaceutical sales. That was kind of medicine, wasn't it?

"What's a guy gotta do to get some coffee around here?"

Levi startled, caught off guard by the huskily asked question. Lost in thought, he hadn't even heard the annoying door chime, but he'd know that cocky voice anywhere. He abandoned the spray bottle and rag on the table before turning. He couldn't help the grin growing on his face as his eyes landed on Julian Cullen standing in front of the cash register. Except Julian didn't look like the broken patient he'd worked with at the PT clinic all those months ago. Instead, this Julian looked happy, strong, and professional.

Levi stepped toward him, wiping his right hand on his jeans before extending it to Julian. "You look great."

Julian waggled those perfectly plucked eyebrows and appraised him with that mischievous gleam in his eyes. "You know, I'm not in the business anymore, but for a compliment like that, I'd do you."

Levi busted out in genuine amusement at such a bold statement. That was just Julian; he said whatever he wanted and made no apologies. "Would you now? I think that's some of that bad-boy you were always talking about coming out in you. How's it going?"

"I remembered you had said you worked here in the evenings. I wondered if you still did," Julian answered with a complete dodge. For the months they'd worked out together at the physical therapy clinic, Levi had gotten used to Julian's non-answering ways. "How's it going with you?"

"Good. I guess." Levi gave a small chuckle or at least he hoped it sounded like one, not the hysterical laughter of a crazy man with too much worry under his belt. "Been working quite a bit."

"Well…" Julian drew the word out then paused for dramatic effect, making a show of looking back at the for-sale sign on the window. "I saw the place's closing."

Levi placed both hands on his hips and continued to stare at Julian. The guy looked like a million bucks. The clothes were expensive, and oddly conservative. His hair styled with an artful flip off the forehead. His pristinely pressed slacks hugged his long, muscular legs, and the crisp button-down underneath a lightweight sweater was perfectly paired with the shiny loafers on his feet. The transformation was quite remarkable, something he wondered if the counseling had anything to do with. Instead of asking that, Levi chose to keep the exchange light and only respond to the question asked.

"Yeah, I'll be looking for another side job soon."

"No doubt with as busy as you are…" Julian spread his arms wide. Levi barked out another laugh as he followed Julian's gaze around the bare coffee shop.

"I guess you're right. It still feels like a lot of work though." Another chuckle bubbled up again, and he went with it, feeling much lighter than minutes ago. Levi watched as Julian shamelessly stepped closer to him, the guy's hand smoothed over his bicep and gently squeezed before boldly reaching for his T-shirt, lifting from the hem.

"Huh. You were hiding all that and I never noticed?"

Levi swatted Julian's hand away, letting his T-shirt fall back in place. What the hell? Their gazes collided, and he couldn't help but notice the look of surprise in Julian's eyes.

"I must have been mentally ill. I would never have let a toned body like that slip past my radar."

Levi grinned at the outrageous appraisal and stepped behind the counter, heading toward the register. "It's good to see you."

"You too. How's your dad?"

The words draped him like a wet blanket weighing heavily on his shoulders. Levi's smile instantly faded.

"My dad didn't make it."

"I'm sorry. I was afraid of that. You have two brothers, correct?"

"I took guardianship of them." Levi nodded once and let his thoughts linger there a moment. Since his father died, Logan, his middle brother, rarely smiled, but Luke seemed the bigger problem. He rarely came out of his bedroom. He didn't engage with the family at all. Nothing Levi did seemed to get through to him, and honestly, he was at a loss. He didn't know how to fill the void his father's death had left.

"I thought that might be the case." Julian's face softened as they stared at one another. "Okay, forget I asked. What's the most popular drink you offer?"

Thankful for the change in subject, he let Julian take his mind off his family. "Café au lait followed closely by any iced coffee."

"Well then, let me try the café au lait, and I'll also get an iced cinnamon almond milk macchiato. Extra cinnamon," Julian said as he lifted his gaze to the menu board hanging behind the register.

"Sure thing." Levi went straight to work on the drinks. As he worked the espresso machine and waited for the big silver contraption to create its magic, he asked, "What are you doing now?"

"I'm heading up personnel at a new Dishology, Inc. restaurant and club in Coronado. It's called Reservations."

Levi started to dump the espresso shots in the glass, but paused, directing his focus toward Julian.

"You really got out of the business?" he asked, surprised only because of the way Julian had gone on and on about the money, trips, and gifts.

"I told you back then that that was the plan," Julian said, leaning a hip on the counter as he regarded Levi. Levi was impressed. Not too many people could just give up that kind of cash so easily.

"That's really good. The counseling went well?" he asked, going back to mixing the drinks. When Julian had started counseling, he'd switched to a different clinic, one with evening hours. Levi hadn't seen him since.

"Painful. I'm still going, but you were right, Dr. Silva. It's exactly what I needed."

"Good." Levi nodded. He hadn't had high hopes for Julian's counseling. The places they'd found within Julian's budget weren't the best quality, but clearly they seemed to have done wonders. Levi placed both drinks in front of Julian and punched in both orders before pushing total on the register. "Ten thirty-two."

Julian had his wallet out, thumbing through the bills. Levi noticed the large amount of cash as he pulled out a ten and a one and laid it on the counter. When Levi started to make change, Julian stopped him. "Keep that and here." Julian pulled out a hundred-dollar bill and held it out to him.

"What's that for?" Levi asked, accepting the money, but not immediately sliding the cash in his pocket. Instead, he held the single bill awkwardly extended to Julian.

"It's the real reason I stopped in tonight. I remembered you told me you worked here. I give you lots of credit for getting me back on my feet. I would have rewarded that at the time, but it wasn't my money. Now it is," he answered, tucking his wallet inside his back pocket. There was a moment of indecision on Levi's part, but he could use the money. Desperately. He drew his hand back, tucking the cash in his front pocket.

"Thank you. I'm glad you're doing great," Levi replied.

Julian gathered the coffees with what appeared to be a pleased grin on his face. He didn't turn into that outrageous larger-than-life guy like Levi had expected. Instead, Julian actually looked a little humbled as he took a couple of steps backward. Julian never broke eye contact and said nothing more as he turned toward the door.

"Take care, Julian."

Julian used his butt to push open the door, but stopped midway through, narrowing his eyes as he looked back at Levi. Whatever he was thinking about made a gleam grow in his gaze. A curious smile lit his features as he walked back to the counter and returned both cups to the granite top.

"I can do one better than that hundred-buck tip. I'll give you some evening work if you're interested," Julian said, and all Levi's instincts had him instantly on guard. If he wanted to prostitute himself, he'd have his own hookups right in his neighborhood. Lord knew he'd been approached enough.

"I don't know…" Levi said, trying not to offend his friend, but absolutely not interested in anything that had to do with that world.

"Not like that." Julian shook his head and chuckled. The laugh was definitely directed toward him, not laughing with him. "We need waiters. I manage a gentlemen's club. Reservations is more like a fine-dining establishment and dance club all under one roof. I manage the club's personnel, so it's all evening work with nothing during the day and less than fifteen minutes from here. It's in the back of Escape Coronado, right off 75. I promise, you'll make more in one night there than you do all month here, and I'll work with your hours at the clinic, give you time to get there—no problem." Julian dug out a business card from his wallet. When Levi didn't automatically reach for the card, Julian laughed again and tossed it on the counter in front of him.

He let his immediate resistance ease. He'd tried to get jobs waiting tables before, but the experience part had always killed him. "I haven't been a server before." He hesitantly picked up the card. "But I'd be interested in trying to wait tables. I'm good with handling money. I can make change like a champ."

"Does the rest of you look like that?" Julian asked, circling a finger in the general direction of his stomach. That had his positive thoughts turning instantly darker.

"I know you said fine dining and dancing, but what do you mean by gentleman's establishment?" Levi asked. The image he'd instantly created in his mind caused his brow to furrow.

"Not what you're thinking." Julian barked out a laugh at whatever disparaging emotion must have crossed his face. "Reservations is an exclusive high-end dinner and dance club that caters to gay men. Mostly single men, business men, not-out men. We have couples that come and enjoy themselves too." Julian lifted a hand, amusement sparkling in his eyes as he again genuinely laughed at Levi. He struggled for breath when he tried to speak. "Oh, man, you look all pinched up. It's hilarious. I wish I could snap that picture."

"Maybe it's not for me," Levi replied, placing the card back on the counter, but an inner needling had him questioning his unexplored refusal. If he could make money without having to do anything other than serve drinks, he'd totally be into that.

"No, it's legit. You'll fit there. No business transactions or money exchanging hands for sex are allowed on club property. We can't fully prevent all that from happening, but they'll lose their membership if we catch on. If you're an employee and get caught hooking up at the club, it's immediate termination. The reason for memberships is to help ensure our members and employees don't have to go through what I did. It's a place for men to make safe connections, nothing more. The worst you might get is a randy old man patting your ass. That's it. I swear." Julian pulled out his phone and started manipulating the screen with his finger. "Give me your contact information. This is something I could do to help pay you back for everything you gave me."

"I didn't do that much," Levi objected.

Julian's gaze lifted and held his. "Yeah, you did. You reminded me there were still good people in the world who had compassion and kind hearts. You helped me when I was scared and guilt-ridden over everything Thane was paying for. I needed to know that people just help others out of the goodness in their hearts. And now I want to do the same." Julian's sincerity came through loud and clear. "Tell me your number."

Levi rattled off his cell number as Julian requested, then asked, "What would I have to wear?"

"As little as possible makes for better tips, and you'll be wanting to shave that." Julian again pointed a finger, drawing an imaginary circle around his belly area. That good-natured laugh was back. When a chirp sounded on Levi's phone, Julian nodded. "That's my number. I think we're about the same age, Levi. Let me help you help your family. It's legit work. You'll be waiting tables. That's it."

Julian tucked his phone in his pocket and grabbed the coffee off the counter before turning toward the exit. Again, he used his ass to bump open the door. "If you don't call me, I'll call you, or better yet, you stop by. Text me, and I'll get you in. See for yourself."

Julian lifted a coffee cup as a goodbye and was gone.

Levi stood there, staring at the door even after the bells had stopped ringing. Could Julian be serious about making that much money in one night? Levi walked back to the tables to finish cleaning. He didn't make much. On a good week, he cleared a hundred and fifty bucks after taxes. If he made that in one night, his family would be so much better off.

Levi cringed slightly as he thought of Julian's flippant remark about guys' grabbing his butt. The butt-touch thing would be a problem. He didn't like to be touched or to parade around almost naked.

Normally, he wouldn't even consider the idea, but he could really use the money. That less-is-more theory hadn't been in any way true throughout his whole life. He wanted more for his brothers. They were his responsibility now.

Levi lifted his shirt and looked down at his stomach. He was cut and he'd been proud of that, but that was nothing new. When he'd gotten the job at the physical therapy clinic, he'd taken advantage of all that kickass workout equipment between patient appointments and during lunch.

Maybe he could wait tables one or two nights a week. Parading around in skimpy clothes wasn't prostitution. Julian had promised he'd be serving cocktails not cock. No different than serving coffee really. The bells chimed, drawing his attention to a group of teenagers coming through the door.

"Great," he whispered under his breath as he abandoned the partially cleaned table and walked toward the register.

~~~

Thane walked through the construction zone that had once been his corporate offices located on historic Main Street in Ellicott City, Maryland. The street ran downhill and was lined with store after store for as far as the eye could see. Last year, on a rainy July evening, his beloved adopted hometown had been swept away. Flood waters had rushed in unexpectedly, destroying every Main Street business in what had been referred to as an *"off the charts, thousand-year rainfall event."*

The flood should have been enough to have him moving to a more corporate-friendly environment. The historic district in Ellicott City was filled with small, diverse one-off restaurants and eclectic little stores. His growing office didn't fit well. The parking alone was a complete nightmare, but no matter how hard he tried, he couldn't bring himself to leave. His heart was here as well as most of his friends, and that wasn't always something he'd had a lot of.

As he looked over the remodel, Thane's phone began rattling like crazy. He palmed the device while starting out the front
~~~

doors. Instead of his gaze going down to the phone in his hand, it went up as a shadow covered from above. Ominous dark clouds began rolling in.

Shit, the cold front was early.

He didn't need to read his messages, the sky told the tale: his flight would be delayed. Instead of dwelling on the irritation of everything he'd have to reschedule, he took off out of the building, jogging toward the carved granite stairwell that led high up the side of the hill and ended directly at his rented townhome several stories above Main Street.

At the first droplet of water, Thane, only halfway up, started taking the steps two at a time, huffing as he pushed through his front door and ran for the open windows of his townhome. They'd had an unseasonably warm winter, the fresh air had been crisp and clean, but all that was about to change with the incoming cold front. By tomorrow, they'd be covered in snow.

As he locked the last window clasp in place, Thane took the moment, looking out as far as the eye could see at the sudden frenzy of treetops dancing in the strong wind. From this angle, at one of the highest points in the area, he could also look directly down over the historic beauty of the quaint town he'd just left. This view topped the reasons Ellicott City held such a special place in his heart.

He finally looked down at the cell phone still in his hand. Great. As suspected, his flight had been delayed, so far only by three hours. Thane pulled up his email application. He sent his assistant, Jenna, a quick email, asking her to reschedule his driver as well as take a close look at his itinerary, notifying anyone affected by this delay.

"Hey, you," Erin said, popping her head through his open patio door. "I've got the heater going, and I'm waiting for my storm-watching buddy to come outside."

"I'm on my way. They just delayed my flight." Thane didn't hesitate. He grabbed his lightweight jacket off the coatrack by the patio door and followed her outside. A brightly colored awning covered a large section of their shared garden patio, so they could watch the rain pour without getting wet. The wind added an extra thrill to the storm, whipping so hard at times that some of the water droplets landed within a foot of their chairs.

He and Erin had spent many hours under this covered patio, especially during storms. He loved sitting right there, looking out over the entire town, watching the thunderstorms rolling in from just about any direction. The storms somehow seemed symbolic of the constant internal struggles in his life and always calmed him in ways he couldn't explain.

"So how delayed are you this time?" she asked, already in her usual seat.

"Three hours," he said, shoving each arm through a sleeve then zipping up his jacket.

Lightning flashed across the sky, fanning out in a dramatic display, drawing Thane's attention at the same time a loud booming clap of thunder shook the ground underneath him.

"That was a good one," Thane said, taking his seat in the comfortable patio chair he'd bought especially for all the hours he'd spent right here. When Erin didn't speak, he glanced over, seeing he'd lost her to the enticing combination of thunderstorm and her long-time hobby, crocheting.

He didn't interrupt, instead letting her work, knowing he had benefited from her insanely good skill, and was always grateful for her gifts. The trendy scarves and warm throws came in especially handy during the cold winters. She even sold some of her crocheted soap holders to Sweet Suds, a bakery concept bath confectionery shop located close to his office on Main Street. The owners, Autumn and Jared, were neighbors as well as mutual friends. As far as he was concerned, the popular little shop sold the best cupcake bath bombs and all-natural bath products on the east coast. He might be biased, but he took great pride in that store, spending hours and hours talking with the owners about the business side of such a venture.

Besides Erin's knack for crocheting, she was a great conversationalist. They had shared more than one drunken philosophical conversation about the beauty and destruction of Mother Nature while splitting several bottles of wine. Her husband thought they were nuts. In that, he was probably right, but they had enjoyed themselves immensely.

"How long will you be away this time?" she asked, turning her full attention toward him, her fingers still manipulating the yarn with the hook in that repetitive, rhythmic pattern.

"Three-ish weeks," he answered, distracted, even if she wasn't, by the movement of her hands as she worked.

"That sucks even more. We're having our Valentine's Day yappy hour party next week if the weather holds." With her disappointment, her hands stopped moving and the yarn fell flat on her lap as her accusing stare landed on him. "You planned this trip on purpose."

"I keep telling you that I don't fit into yappy hour because I don't have a dog." That seemed so reasonable to him. How did she not get it?

"You have a love of wine and can go get a dog from the SPCA to walk. You fit in just fine. You're always trying to get out of it with your excuses," she countered, not even teasing a little bit. More times than not, Erin and Corey had dragged him down the hill for yappy hour. They met their little group there, which included Autumn and Jared as well as his single neighbor, Brock. They all had animals. Generally, he was one of a handful of people there without a dog, but she was right. It was always great fun, even with having to explain over and over why he chose to remain animal-less in his life.

The only true drawback to the night rested in having to navigate all those steps back up to his house while drunk off his ass and seeing double. He'd skinned his knees more than once trying to get up those damn things.

"I wanted to surprise you, but Brock's friend Noel's planning to come and stay for a few days. I thought it would give you two time to get to know each other."

"The same guy you tried to hook me up with before?"

Erin nodded eagerly.

"Absolutely not, Erin."

"Noel's fabulous and you should date him," she demanded.

Instead of being sucked into another debate about his love life, or as Erin referred to it, his lack of love in his life, Thane quickly changed the subject. "I'm going to St. Louis tonight, then renting a car and driving in three- or four-hour intervals across the country."

"No way. That sounds miserable."

"Made more miserable by the fact I'm hitting my under-performing restaurants in a surprise attack. I'll be laying down the law on them," he said dramatically, waggling his brows.

"Okay, you're right, that did get more miserable. They don't know you're coming?"

"Nope. After I finish up in Arizona, I'm heading to Coronado, taking a few days off there."

"I love Coronado. I bet it's warm there right now," she said dreamily, and her body gave a shiver. "Okay, listen. I'm getting cold, but did you hear the old colonial on the hill's going on the market?" Erin asked.

"No. Where did you hear that?"

"I just met with the old man's granddaughter. They're selling the place and moving him to a senior center."

The old home, built in the 1800s, sat at the top of the hill and was the focal point of the whole town. He'd always loved that place, had even wormed his way into an invitation inside. The house would require a complete overhaul, a total remodel, but would be worth every single dime. "I'd be interested in that house."

"I'm glad to hear you say that. I told her I knew someone who would be, and as a thank-you for my help, Corey and I would so rent the basement apartment," she informed him eagerly.

"You would?" Her well-thought out plan hadn't even been anywhere on his radar.

"Yep. She said the basement was divided into two units, and I know Brock would come too." Their little friendship circle hadn't been intact that long, but they had become fast friends. They were all his age, barely thirtyish, whether on the cusp or slightly over the hump, and all very down-to-earth people. He hadn't met very many people like his neighbors. Thane's parents were ivy-league, wound-up tight, scholarly type people. Very pretentious. Between them and his own time needed in coming out then starting his business at such a young age, he valued his neighbors' pure genuineness. He would absolutely consider letting them rent if he could get his hands on the house.

Erin pushed to her feet, gathering her stuff before starting for her house. "I'm going in. I'll get the information on the house and text you."

"Please do. If I don't respond in the next day or so, bother me until I do," he called out, knowing he should go inside too. The storm was letting up, and the airlines had no problem bumping the flight time up even if he wasn't there to board.

"Will do. Be safe."

CHAPTER 3

Underdressed and completely out of place, Levi sat in the principal's office of his old high school. The same one both his brothers currently attended. He stared down at his fifteen-year-old brother's file, looking at the gradual decline in Luke's grades over the last few months. His incredibly brilliant youngest brother, who had loved aviation his whole entire life, and had won the Junior High Science Fair by successfully challenging the physics of aviation, had an overall grade of thirty in his freshman AP Physics class. The rest of his classes weren't faring much better.

"Look at this." Mrs. Rustenhaven, who had been the principal even when he'd attended this same school almost eight years ago, sat in the chair next to him, and turned the page in the file he held. Levi, who had been leaning forward, resting his elbows on his knees took a swift intake of breath, pushing back against the seat.

"I didn't know. They didn't tell me," Levi said, staring at Luke's attendance records. From his father's funeral in early January until now, just around thirty days or so, the sliding scale attendance graph showed Luke regularly missing classes.

"We've been trying to give Luke room to grieve, but it's reached the point where I felt we needed to intervene," Mrs. Rustenhaven said, patting Levi's knee, and taking the file from his hands, before she moved to her chair behind the desk. "It's the only reason I called you out of work. Are you aware Luke's out again today?"

Dammit. Levi let out a frustrated sigh, crossed his arms over his chest, and shook his head no. In all the years he'd been inside this school, he'd never had a reason to visit the principal's office. He knew Logan, his seventeen-year-old brother, held his same views. The tickle of fear at even having to sit in this uncomfortable room made him nervous, his leg bouncing with the anxiety it caused. The principal's office was a place for punishment. He didn't like that Luke had broken the cycle of avoidance. He furrowed his brow and stared at Mrs. Rustenhaven.

Wait. At this point, he clearly shouldn't assume too much about either brother. "How's Logan doing?"

Mrs. Rustenhaven opened another folder, and Levi's gut twisted. Life was already hard enough without both his brothers losing their shit. There was no way they would make it if his brothers didn't pull their own weight.

"Logan's actually doing very well. I asked their teachers to give assessments. Logan's got his nose to the grindstone. He hasn't made below a ninety-seven on any assignment or test this semester. He's taking a heavy load; his grades are a lot like yours were, if I remember correctly. He's also got positive remarks on his social skills. He's on track to graduate a semester early, and if I'm reading this correctly, he's been accepted to the University of Virginia. They're working on a financial offer. Is that correct?"

Levi nodded when her gaze lifted to him. That was his understanding, but he hadn't gotten an update in a while. The tightness in his chest eased. Logan couldn't afford for anything to get in his way where his future was concerned.

"Now, Luke on the other hand has completely withdrawn. He's not engaging, he's sleeping a lot in class, and of course, not turning in his homework."

"So that would indicate depression?" Levi asked, his bouncing leg picked up a notch.

"Most likely. At least that's my initial thought. We have many resources at our disposal, Levi, but before I call someone in to help, I wanted to know what you're noticing at home," Mrs. Rustenhaven said.

"Ma'am, I'm not home a lot." Levi took a deep breath and centered himself, trying to remember the last time he'd spoken to

Luke more than just in passing. "I work two jobs. I have every Sunday off, and we get ready for the week that day. Luke does what he's supposed to, but he's always trying to get back in his room to his video games," Levi explained.

His heart grew heavy. He hoped he sounded more equipped to deal with the situation than he felt. He let out a sigh and reached up to scrub a hand over his face. He was so in over his head.

"Are Logan and Luke at home alone in the evenings?" the principal asked, leaning back in her seat.

"My neighbor's an older woman. She's lived next door to us my whole life. She helped take care of my dad before he died, and she comes over in the evening, gets everyone settled, makes sure they've had dinner. Logan's seventeen—you know that—and he keeps an eye on things. He quit his job because I make more, and we didn't think Luke should be home every night alone," Levi said, explaining the reasons behind their nightly routine. "Oh, and I get home about eleven thirty, so not super late."

"How're you doing financially?" Mrs. Rustenhaven asked.

Boy was that a seriously loaded question. He couldn't quite figure out how his dad had made it all those years. He had three boys and no help at all. His mom had taken off right after Luke was born. But where Mrs. Rustenhaven was concerned, Levi decided to stick with the theme of less-is-more in answering. "We're making it."

"I understand you were in medical school when you came home?" the principal probed, staring at Levi with speculation.

"Yes, ma'am. I just finished my first year at Johns Hopkins and started my summer internship when my dad's cancer reoccurred and I had to come home," Levi explained.

"Are you planning to go back?"

"I haven't given up on my goals. I deferred my enrollment to give us time. I guess, if there's any possible way, I'd like for us all to move to Maryland," Levi answered honestly.

"How's that looking?"

Levi's leg started double-timing its cadence against the floor. "More and more obstacles keep presenting themselves with each passing day, but I haven't given up hope. Social security's supposed to start coming soon. At least, I think it will, and that'll help."

Levi dropped his arms and his leg abruptly stopped bouncing as Mrs. Rustenhaven straightened in her seat, resting both elbows on her desk, lacing her fingers together.

"Okay, well, this is what I'd like to offer you guys. I'm trying to keep all this handled right here. Luke's attendance is a real issue. We have to straighten that out right away. I've called in some favors, and Mrs. Underwood, do you remember her? She's one of our counselors." She paused, and Levi nodded even though he wasn't at all certain he did. "She's agreed to work with you and your brothers three days a week. We're clearing out Luke's first period, giving him study hall the other two days a week with a real focused plan to help get him back on track. He's got a lot to do, but he can get where he needs to be if he pulls himself together. How does that sound to you?"

"I'll have to talk to my job," Levi started, but the principal lifted her hand, stopping him.

"That's the reason I asked about your finances. There're procedures to follow when a student has missed this much school, but I've decided to wait, see if we can work this out among ourselves. We need you here. First period ends at eight thirty. We need you to make accommodations and be here with your brother."

Levi nodded at the stern and maybe somewhat cryptic message the principal tried to relay. That would make him at least an hour and a half late to the physical therapy clinic—his main source of income. Shit.

"You Silva boys were hit with a hard blow. I remember you were about Logan's age when your father was first diagnosed with cancer. You're all good guys. We'll get this in order and make sure Luke has access to the help he needs." Mrs. Rustenhaven rose, and Levi watched as she came around the desk. He decided that probably meant they were done, and he pushed up out of the chair, reaching for her outstretched hand. She gave him a reassuring smile, and a pat on the back as she started walking toward the closed office door.

"I'll go home now and talk to Luke."

"And I'll call you by the end of the day. We'll get something worked out and begin this week."

Levi left the administration office and hit the front doors of the school, pushing through before he let himself expel the breath he'd been holding. He stopped in his tracks, scrubbed a hand over his face, and rolled his tense shoulders. He was so in over his head.

Why the hell wasn't Luke going to school, and what did he even say to the kid about that? More importantly, why hadn't Logan told him Luke was ditching class?

Levi started toward the car, praying for some insight, hoping something inventive and helpful would come to mind on the two miles it took for him to drive home.

Nothing. Not a single useful idea. And when he pulled into the driveway and glanced toward the windows, the place looked dark, as if no one were home. That would add a whole new layer of bullshit to this Luke deal. If the kid wasn't home, where did he go every day?

Levi pushed open the front door and looked around. The whole house was completely dark. The living room was stuffy and warm. His heart sank, and he prayed the neighborhood had had an electrical outage. Most likely not the case, and he let out a heavy sigh as he walked through the living room toward Luke and Logan's bedroom. He pushed open the door to see Luke sound asleep in bed.

"Get up, Luke," Levi said and reached down to shake his foot. His brother was out cold but woke with a start.

"What? What happened?" he asked groggily.

"Nothing happened except your school called me at work. I had a meeting with Mrs. Rustenhaven, so I need to talk to you. Get up."

Luke groaned and dropped his head back on the pillow.

"You had to know this was coming. A thirty in physics? Seriously? You're smarter than all of us."

Levi left the room, going toward the kitchen. Along the way, he picked up Logan's leftover plate from last night's dinner and a half-full glass of milk. He didn't dare take a whiff. He also grabbed Logan's stinky T-shirt and smelly socks off the sofa. Logan was the pig of the house. He deposited the dishes in the sink and tossed the clothes in the washroom before going to the refrigerator. He pulled the electric bill from underneath the magnet.

Shit, he'd missed the final cutoff date. Damn. As if to test the theory, he went for the kitchen light switch and flipped it on. The damn thing didn't work. His stomach sank and a feeling of hopelessness sat on his chest. How much would that cost to get turned back on?

Levi went for the cabinet, pulling out a glass and filling it with tap water before calling the electric company. With his phone on speaker mode, he listened to the automated voice message, pressing number one because he spoke English, then number two to pay his bill. He rested his ass against the counter, drinking the water, listening for any sign that Luke had actually gotten out of bed while continuing to follow the directions from the automated phone prompts.

Luke walked inside the kitchen and made his way over to the refrigerator, which was pretty damn bare. Between Luke and Logan, they ate a shit ton of food. Luke pulled out the gallon of milk, took several long gulps directly from the jug before pushing it back inside and shutting the door with his foot.

"You should keep that door closed. The electricity got turned off," Levi announced as if it weren't embarrassingly obvious.

"Yeah, they were doing it when I got home," Luke replied, taking a seat at the kitchen table.

"You shoulda called me," Levi said.

"I asked them if it would help and they said no. You had to call in and pay." Luke crossed his arms on the kitchen table and dropped his head there.

Levi watched his brother before he entered his credit card number into the phone, not even sure the charge would go through. It cost an extra hundred twenty-five bucks to get the electricity turned back on today. He had to get better about the bills. When he got the confirmation number, he breathed a sigh of relief. He still had that hundred-dollar bill from last night, but didn't have the time to stop by the bank. He'd already be docked two hours for the time he'd missed at work today.

He quickly jotted down the payment confirmation number and ended the call. He tossed the electric bill on the counter and turned back, resting his ass against the edge, staring at the top of Luke's head. He had no idea where to begin. Levi lowered his head, pressing his fingers into his eyes until weird spots and shifting patterns appeared from the pressure.

"Luke, do you have anything to say that'll help this situation?"

His brother never lifted his head as he mumbled, "I'm sad about Dad, and I can't shake it."

His brother could verbalize that right now, but not mention it a month or two ago, before everything had turned to shit in his life?

"The principal wants us all in counseling. She's arranged it. Apparently, you don't need your first period class, so we're doing it then, and I'm gonna be there with you," Levi explained.

"I'm sorry, Levi. I knew I was spinning. I can't help it. I'm tired all the time," Luke said, his head still down, resting on his folded arms.

"I thought you might be home playing video games," Levi said, trying to measure how many hours of games he was playing every day. That had Luke lifting his head to stare at Levi.

"I'm not playing anything right now. I just don't feel like it." The kid looked seriously exhausted. "I just miss him all the time. Sometimes I feel like it's just gonna suck me under."

Levi nodded and moved to the table to take a seat. "I miss him too, Luke. But you gotta get your grades up and you have to stay in school. That's what he would want. Plus, truancy court costs a lot of money, but worse than that, they're not gonna let us stay together if you don't do what you're supposed to." Levi didn't think it was possible, but Luke looked sadder in the moment. The look in his little brother's eyes almost made him lose his composure. "Do you need to talk to a psychiatrist? Do you need medication?"

"Isn't that what the school's doing?" Luke asked.

"No, I don't think so," Levi answered, but he honestly didn't know. "Well, maybe they are. I don't know, it sounded like just a counselor. Maybe they can refer us to someone. I'd never been sent to the principal's office before, so I was freaked out. I didn't even think to ask."

"Will Medi-Cal pay for it?"

"I don't know that either, but I'll pay for it. You gotta get better, Luke." Levi reached over and gripped his brother's forearm. "And starting right now, you gotta email each one of your teachers and apologize. Find out what you need to do to get your grades up. I'll help with that too. We can work on your schoolwork this weekend."

Luke nodded, his eyes becoming red-rimmed and filling with tears. Oh man, he looked like he was going to cry, and Levi just didn't know what to do with that.

"I'm sorry. You should probably ground me. I definitely need grounding. Dad would restrict my video games."

Levi fought the smile of such an honest reaction. Luke was such a good kid. "I don't know if that's a good idea with this. I kind of wish you'd play your games because then we'd be normal again." They stared at one another for several long seconds before Levi spoke again. "Luke, just come to me when you have a problem. I know I'm a poor substitute for Dad, but I'll help figure it out." Again, they stared at one another for a long moment, Luke not saying anything until he let out another long yawn and shoved away from the table, going for the coffee pot.

"You were in track in junior high, right?" Levi asked, turning in his chair to follow Luke's movements.

"Yeah. I missed signups this year," Luke said, pulling the coffee from a cabinet. "It was when Dad got sick again."

"Why don't we get up early and run in the mornings that you have counseling? I've been working out like crazy at the clinic. I swear it helps me with the depression," Levi suggested.

"You're already doing everything for us," Luke said while dumping water in the dispenser.

"I think it'll be good for all three of us. We can jog together at the track at school and go to the counseling deal afterward," Levi said, checking the time on his phone. Close to time for the city bus to arrive. If he could make it to the bus stop on time, he could leave the car for his brothers and catch a ride to the coffee shop, maybe he could makeup some of these hours he'd missed.

"Crap, I can't make this. We don't have electricity. I'm running over to Aunt Linda's," Luke said, heading for the back door.

"Make sure you lock the door when you leave her house. I'm going to work. Call me and check in," Levi said as he stood. His brother nodded as he stepped out the back door, leaving him standing there in the dark kitchen.

Levi left the house, stopping by their car to grab his duffel bag, silently wondering how the heck he could afford to get Luke professional care if he needed it. As he walked toward the bus stop, another worry landed on his shoulders. This neighborhood used to be filled with good people. Yes, they were poor, but still decent. As a kid, he used to play outside, but maybe as many as ten years ago, that all changed when the San Diego Housing Commission built an apartment complex at the end of the street near the bus stop. The closer he got to the already rundown set of buildings, the faster he walked. He passed by a drug deal in progress, then, only a few feet away from there, he walked past a couple of hookers who worked as a team with the dealer, creating a one-stop shop for the buyer. Levi kept his head down, ignoring their taunts—he thought he might have gone to junior high with one of those women.

He really needed to get his brothers away from there. He didn't want them out on the streets. He just didn't have a lot of options. The idea of quitting medical school made him want to cry. He had wanted to be a doctor his whole life. To give that up, no matter how out of reach it seemed, was more than his heart could take—the dream of becoming a doctor might be the only thing holding him together right now.

Levi arrived just as the bus pulled up. He stood to the side of the bus stop where everyone gathered and waited for his turn to board. He pulled out his phone and opened his contacts, calling Julian before this bad mood got the best of him.

"Hey. You called." Julian sounded surprised.

"You have a minute?" he asked, walking the length of the bus until he found an empty seat in the back. He tugged the strap of his duffle over his head, tossed the canvas bag in the seat before scooting in himself.

"Sure."

"I'm interested in that job you were talking about. Is the money really as good as you said?" Levi asked, situating himself closest to the aisle, hoping he could keep the entire seat to himself.

"Probably better," Julian answered immediately.

"And I wouldn't have to…" Levi lowered his voice, looking around the crowded bus, knowing there was no way for the other riders not to hear his whole conversation. "You know."

"Absolutely not. Now, if you get an offer and you decide you want to explore the territory, then go for it, but that's seriously on your time and away from the club. You should probably know that most of the guys eventually cross over to escorting. The money's too good."

No doubt, but just a glance out the window of the bus in this neighborhood was all anyone needed to see to understand why he'd pass on peddling sex for money. "Yeah, I don't think I will. That's not gonna be a problem, right?"

"No, no problem at all. Reservations is a safe meeting place that happens to have gorgeous guys and serves phenomenal food and drinks. Where are you? It sounds like a school bus," Julian asked

"Close. It's the city bus," he answered, looking around, spotting several familiar faces focused on him. Of course they were listening. Gossip spread fast in this neighborhood. They probably knew his dad. Levi would be the center of conversation later as they tried to figure out what he'd been talking about.

"You take the bus?" Julian asked incredulously. Levi rolled his eyes, and his shoulders drooped.

"My brothers take the bus to school, but I leave the car for them in case they need it at night," he explained quietly, covering the receiver with his hand, not wanting to alert the world that his younger brothers were home alone in the evening.

"Oh, Levi. You need me in your life so bad. When are you coming to the club?" Julian asked.

"I'm off on Friday night."

"Well, that's days away. Come out before then so we can get you started right away. You'll bank, but weekends are prime time. You gotta earn those shifts," Julian encouraged.

"I don't know if this is for me. I'd have to call in tonight. They don't have anyone at the coffee shop. If I get fired—"

Julian interrupted his flow of excuses, cutting him off in midsentence. "You're interested or you wouldn't have called me. Tell you what, come see me tonight. If you need a ride, I can get you one, but come out. You can talk to some of the guys and watch what goes on. It's Tuesday. A slow night. I'll show you all around. And if you decide to take me up on the offer, we can get you on the floor and training as soon as tomorrow."

There was silence as Levi thought through the offer. He wasn't sure he had the best personality. He wasn't flirty or charming like so many guys he knew. He absolutely didn't like to be touched without permission. He'd been told he was too serious all the time. Could he even pretend he was interesting and fun just to get more money out of lonely old men?

"Seriously, Levi, stop overthinking this. Call in to the coffee shop tonight and shag your ass to the club. Be there about seven. I'll show you around, then you can hang out and watch. Also, you can fill out your application. I promise you'll see it's not what you think," Julian assured him. "You'll pass a background check and drug test, right?"

"Of course," he said, furrowing his brow. Offended that he was even asked that question while wondering about the need for a background report.

"I knew you would. I'll see you tonight." Julian disconnected the call. Levi was slower to respond, lowering the phone to his lap but still staring at the screen. He couldn't believe he was actually considering going through with this. The sound of the air brakes pulled him from his thoughts. He glanced up just in time to see the familiar surroundings out his window. Damn it, he'd almost missed his stop with all the crazy bullshit running through his head.

CHAPTER 4

"I need the office," Thane said, abruptly pivoting on his heels, desperate to get out from underneath all the heavy attitude coming from the management staff he'd just severely disciplined.

Even his good friend and regional manager had stood there gaping, most likely at the severity Thane had used in pointing out all the failures in this on-site leadership team. But, dammit, customers waiting an hour for something as simple as a hamburger was just ridiculous. Even more ludicrous was the three-star average review rating on Yelp. This was St. Louis for God's sake. This restaurant served grill type foods, nothing complicated, but these managers had lost the respect of their employees, and Thane couldn't be certain they had it in them to gain that back.

Firmly shutting the office door, he effectively commandeered the only private space in the building, which had the added benefit of requiring those leaders to get out among their staff and actually lead rather than hiding and avoiding the issues they'd created.

Due to his own corporate personnel policy, he'd have to complete a formal write-up, which he'd get his assistant on right away. Thane opened his laptop, spent a few minutes documenting the changes he'd outlined in his rant before sending his assistant Jenna a message to have human resources draw up official written warnings for each of the on-site managers. He'd also have to bring his workforce development team into the grill to provide additional training. That would be costly and that just pissed him off too.

The rumble from his stomach reminded Thane he hadn't eaten since this morning. Out of all of the food he served, grill food was his least favorite and absolutely not worth the calories. If he had to spend time anywhere, why couldn't it be in his little Mexican food restaurant chain in Texas where they served those delicious shrimp ceviche towers?

His mouth watered thinking about that vinegar coleslaw, and his stomach growled a little louder. Damn, he was starving. He should go out there and fix himself a plate, but he wouldn't. That would only open a line of personal communication, and this restaurant had too much of that going on. Everyone was a friend, except the customers.

Instead of doing that, Thane buckled down and opened an email from Arik Layne. The email was to both him and Chef Ferico. The subject line read, *"Whole Foods and HSN, Bitches*!!!!" That instantly had Thane smiling. Home Shopping Network. Man, Arik had become a force in his life. The guy didn't seem to understand the value of hesitancy. Arik was a mover and shaker. Their joint venture of infused olive oils had taken off like lightning. Arik had secured sales on thousands of bottles before manufacturing had started. Now that they had production underway, they were blowing and going like wildfire. All Arik had to do was pick up the phone, and he secured another sale.

Thane scanned the message, reading how Whole Foods planned to add them in a test market now, with mass distribution the beginning of October. That was all great news. Arik had also secured a spot on the Home Shopping Network in November, about two weeks before Thanksgiving. Somehow he'd managed to squeeze them into an already set schedule on foods for the holidays. They'd also be given time on the sales floor. The anticipated sales were around twenty-five thousand bottles.

Wow. Okay.

The last lines on the email made Thane squelch the urge to laugh out loud, not wanting to undermine the stern tone he'd taken with his staff, but, man, Arik was hilarious. He listed ten reasons why he'd be a better choice than Thane to go on the HSN broadcast with Chef Ferico. Every single bullet point ended with "because I really want to sample all the foods made that day."

Literally, a man after his own heart.

Out of nothing more than the need to make Arik squirm, he decided to tease him. Thane quickly typed how glad he was for Arik's effort, along with a note that they should at least flip a coin for the TV slot. He chose tails. Grinning, he pushed send as his cell phone began to vibrate in his pocket. With a glance at the screen, he saw Julian's name and swiped to accept the call.

"Hey," he said, putting the call on speaker before fishing his Bluetooth out of the computer bag and hooking it around his ear.

"Hey, yourself. You still coming here?"

"I am. It'll be a few weeks though. Everything okay?"

"Of course, you know I run a tight ship, but I might have to break protocol."

Thane began shaking his head no as if Julian could see him.

"I can almost hear you shaking your head no."

"That's because that's what I'm doing. Absolutely no rule breakage, Julian. You do it one time and that opens the door…"

"Hang tight, *Papi Chulo*. Don't get all bent. I'm telling you before I do it. That should count."

The happy place he'd found after reading Arik's hilarious message was on the fast track to crashing and burning as Thane sat back in his chair and crossed his arms over his chest.

"Why?" he asked, instead of giving Julian the same dressing-down he'd just given this management team on the failures of flouting established protocol.

"Remember that kid I told you about months ago. My PT assistant, the one who got me into free counseling?"

Thane had to really think, which was kind of funny. Julian's care had been grossly expensive. He'd have thought he'd remember someone who'd saved him so much money in free counseling. He shrugged, lifting his brows, giving himself a break. He could vaguely recall the key components. "Maybe…"

"He needs a job."

"We don't hire our staff like that, Julian. Remember your training. Your guys…"

"Boss, slow your roll. He's a med student taking care of his family, and he's hot as hell. His body alone'll make the customers very happy. Happy customers equal more money."

"Is he in your previous line of work?" Thane asked, completely confused and trying to catch up.

"Hell no. I want him for waitstaff at the club. I saw him last night, and he's losing his job. He's coming to the club tonight to take a look around. I'll send his info off for a background check, but I'll probably put him on the floor as early as tomorrow," Julian stated matter-of-factly.

That was another huge issue he was having with Julian. The guy was a beast at work. He kept sticking his nose in every other manager's responsibilities, causing all sorts of ill will. Julian was a man on a mission. He governed that club with an iron fist, all to try and repay Thane for the expensive care. "Have you talked with Dave about whether he needs more waitstaff?"

"Dave-the-douchebag quit today. You didn't hear?" Julian said casually.

"What?" Thane pushed his fingers through his hair. Why was he just now hearing about this?

"Don't worry. I got this. I'll fill in until you figure out what to do. I, of course, think you just need to let me handle all personnel..."

"Stop, Julian. First, no one's hired without passing a background check. I'm not watching anyone go through what you did again. And second, you better stop pissing off all my people. Until I talk to Dave and see if I can get him back, you can handle the waitstaff scheduling, but you aren't..."

"Equipped to handle personnel issues," Julian said, finishing his sentence. "Are you getting laid regularly? Because I'm pretty sure you're not. You need to come on over here and bend me over this desk—"

"We have rules. I'm not having sex on that property, and I better not catch you having sex on that property!" Thane shot out, cutting Julian off.

"You're a very difficult man, Thane Walker," Julian replied, not missing a beat. "I'd say hard, but I have no way of truly knowing that."

He ignored Julian's baiting comments, absolutely refusing to go there with him again. "You need extensive leadership development before you jump in and take on some of these things, Julian. I'll get a team out there to work with you for a few days. If Dave's really gone, and my team assesses your ability and thinks you can handle yourself, I'll give you a shot, but only if they agree."

"Yeah, yeah, yeah. You're the best, yada yada yada. So, I'm gonna hire Levi. He needs the job and I owe him. Ciao." The phone went dead.

Thane just sat there staring at the laptop screen. On one hand, he had the slug management team from hell right there with him in St. Louis. On the other, he had Julian who was so overzealous in his need to prove himself that he couldn't be stopped.

Okay. Yeah, he'd take Julian, but damn, he wished his life didn't feel like his sole purpose on the planet was to babysit all these crazy personalities. Thane picked up his phone and texted Julian.

"Don't go outside of policy." Clear and to the point. He pushed send and waited. Julian texted right back.

"I understand."

Thane nodded, glad he'd made his point. He lowered his laptop lid, packed the computer in its case, and grabbed his phone before opening the office door. He was surprised to see his regional manager, Blaze, standing across the walkway, leaning against the built-in freezer door. He looked up, and Thane nodded toward the exit, getting him to follow.

"Thanks for bringing this site to my attention," Thane said quietly, walking side by side with the regional manager.

"You put the law down. That's what I needed," Blaze said, equally as quiet as they pushed through the back door.

"I'm scheduling workforce development to come here unannounced in the next seventy-two hours. Their expense will come out of this budget which will more than likely blow your bonus this year. It'll be costly, so put something in front of me as to why I should exempt you of this expense," Thane said, looking over at Blaze who had his head bent, studying the sidewalk as they slowly walked toward his car. The only response the guy gave was a slight nod before tucking his hands inside his slacks pockets. "There'll be interval training for all of the restaurant's staff. Front end first then kitchen staff. Management last. Whether that works or not doesn't matter. Things are gonna change. Also, disciplinary actions are being prepared. I'm leaving here first thing in the morning, so I'll video conference in, but you'll need to be the one to administer their disciplinary action," Thane added.

"Of course. They've been a thorn in my side since I took over this region," Blaze said.

When they made it to his rental, Thane stopped at the driver's side door. "I'll give them three months. Do you think they can pull it together by then?"

"I don't honestly know. I've spent more time here than any other location in my area."

"Okay, well, at least we'll have tried," Thane said, squinting in the bright sun. "Why don't you take me out and feed me. That would go a long way to saving that bonus. I'd love some good food with lots of rum."

"I have a date night planned, but I'm sure she's good with you tagging along," Blaze said with a grin. Thane saw that Blaze knew his end-of-year bonus money had never really been in jeopardy. No matter how hard Thane tried, being a hard-ass didn't come naturally to him. Blaze was a great employee, a true company man.

Just to insert himself into Blaze's date night, Thane asked, "Where to?"

"Eleven Eleven Mississippi at seven, but she thinks you're really good-looking. Ignore the drool," Blaze added, circling to the other side of a car parked right next to Thane's.

He barked out a laugh and opened his door. "I'll do that. If she wants alone time, text me. No problem."

"See you then."

CHAPTER 5

Levi pulled the old Toyota into a parking space in the lot farthest away from Reservations and let the vehicle idle as he stared at the backside of the massive resort. After a second of taking it all in, he realized he probably looked like an idiot just sitting in his car with his mouth gaping open. That thought managed to close his lips up tight. Gathering his nerve proved a little more difficult. He watched a valet open the door to a Ferrari, and two extremely well-dressed men emerged from the car.

What the hell had he gotten himself into?

He leaned back in his seat and looked down at his T-shirt, jeans, and sneakers. Julian had failed to mention a dress code. He couldn't go inside dressed like this.

Damn, and he'd called in for work tonight.

Feeling more defeated than ever, Levi's hope began to deflate. Coming here had been a mistake. He didn't fit inside this world. Where else could he get a job?

Levi closed his eyes, dropped his head back on the headrest while his brain shifted and started ticking off his contacts out in the professional world. His buddy from high school worked in a call center for Tropicana. Levi had a working knowledge of vitamins and some herbal remedies. Maybe he could use that to get a night job, answering customer service calls when Logan and Luke were home asleep. Surely that kind of job paid reasonably well.

Just as Levi lifted his hand to put the car in reverse, his phone vibrated, drawing his attention down to the screen. Julian's name popped up with three back-to-back text message notifications. He picked up the phone and opened the message.

"*I thought we agreed upon seven. Let me know when you're coming.*" That was immediately followed by, "*Don't be a puss and wimp out. Just come see what we're all about.*" Which was followed by, "*Why do I have this feeling you're freaking out?*"

Levi typed a quick message to a guy he didn't really know but who, for some reason, was dead set on helping him and his brothers. Even that kindness seemed suspicious now. "*I'm here, but this isn't going to work for me. I wore blue jeans. I didn't realize there was a dress code. I don't know why I didn't know. I should have.*" Levi lifted his thumbs from the keyboard. What else could he say? It wasn't like he was ungrateful, he was very thankful, but this was way out of his league. After pausing for a second, he pushed send then quickly followed with another message. "*I appreciate everything. I do, but I'm going to look for another job elsewhere.*"

Levi dropped the phone in the cubby and put the car in reverse. As he started to back out, he flipped on the headlights and caught a glimpse of Julian walking out the front doors with the phone stuck to his ear. Levi's cell started ringing. He stared at the phone then lifted it slowly to his ear, glancing in Julian's direction as he said, "Hello."

"Is that you way out there?" Julian lifted his hand and waved in his direction as he walked to the end of the sidewalk, flanked by the valet guys. "Come up here and come in. I've been waiting on you."

"I don't know," he hedged.

"There's nothing to know. Come on. You came this far, you might as well see."

Why did the guy sound so reasonable? Damn it! Levi let out a big sigh. It took a second more to make up his mind, but he finally put the car back in drive, rolled forward into the spot, and cut off the engine. As much as he didn't want to get out of the car, he forced himself to follow through.

Embarrassment was something he'd learned to live with a long time ago. "I'm in a T-shirt and jeans. I don't know why I didn't think to dress up."

"There's not a reason to." Julian disconnected the call and started walking toward him. They met in the closest parking lot to the front doors. Julian was dressed in a perfectly fitted suit, with no tie. He looked like a million bucks. Levi shoved his phone in his back pocket before shoving his fingers into his front jeans pocket. He hadn't even gone inside and already felt so out of place.

"I should go."

"Stop trying to leave and get in here." Julian placed a hand on his back then gave a little push to get Levi moving.

As they got closer, Julian clasped his arm, pulling him toward a side entrance. The sense of relief overwhelmed him. Luckily, he didn't have to go through those main doors.

"Generally, the restaurant side fills up about five thirtyish and stays packed until about nine. There's a firm dress code for the restaurant. This is the employee entrance to the lounge."

He followed Julian inside and down a long hall to a set of double oak doors. As soon as Julian pushed one open, the sound intensified.

"About this time of night, we begin a slow build with music and lights to help entice the diners over once they're finished with their meal."

Curiosity began to win out over nerves. The song playing was nowhere near the ear-splitting volume of the music in the nightclubs he'd gone to before. The ethereal glow and the erratic flashes of light were all the welcome he needed. They made him wonder what kind of show could be taking place just beyond the threshold.

Julian lifted his hand and motioned in the direction of another door, encouraging Levi to enter first. He stepped through and the beauty and tranquility of the room struck him immediately. His trepidation eased as all the negative images he'd imagined began releasing their hold.

"This is nothing like I imagined." Elegant wasn't a word he'd ever thought he'd use to describe a club, but this place was just that. Elegant. The lights danced hypnotically to the electronic beat, their beams bouncing off the dozen or so massive crystal chandeliers filling the space above him. They sent prisms of rainbows dancing throughout the room, bouncing off the chrome and glass bar.

The music and lights almost seemed out of place for the grandeur of the club. The sweeping black granite set of steps arched gracefully from the lower landing where he stood with Julian, his shoes planted firmly on the polished stone as he took it all in.

Julian shifted closer to him. "I don't know what you expected, but you should see it when it's full of paying customers." Julian gave him a wink. "Feels even better when there's more than just us and the DJ and lighting guys. They're working on getting the timing just right for when the doors open tonight."

The dance floor divided the large room in two equal spaces. The atmosphere, from what he could tell, had a laid-back vibe. Tables and chairs filled the floor space. Oversized booths lined the perimeter. They weren't the standard diner cubicles, but a more intimate seating arrangement. Zebra-striped chairs and purple rope lights ran along the floor, giving the marble a soft glow. A leather-cushioned bench provided comfortable seating along the long expanse of the back wall.

Two heavily stocked bars with chrome and mirrors anchored opposite sides of the massive space. Throughout the room were several large ornate cages draped in the same crystals decorating the chandeliers, but hanging in various heights. A long neon-lit runway led to a larger main stage with several smaller platforms shooting off the end in a starburst pattern with a single pole positioned vertically through the middle of each smaller stage.

"We don't officially open until eight. I should have told you that so you didn't needlessly worry about your clothes. Come this way."

Levi followed, trailing behind Julian as he nodded to several different men along the way. All looked about Levi's age, height, and build. They were super tanned, perfect hair, some tattoos and wore nothing but blue, silver, and black underwear and matching boots that reminded him of Doc Martens. All that flesh on display worried him on a couple of different levels. The most basic being that he didn't think he compared to any of those guys, and he really didn't want to be paraded around in skimpy underwear.

"Remington, come with me."

Remington eyed Levi up and down, grinned and nodded, before falling in step behind him as they went down a small hall to a set of stairs that led to a second-floor office. When shut inside the small office, the music faded away. Julian walked immediately to a closet as he spoke.

"Remington, this is Levi."

"Hey, sweetness," the guy said from directly behind him, so close that the guy's breath ghosted across his ear as he spoke, causing Levi to jerk around and take a step back. Clearly, he was hypersensitive to everything right now, and he needed to calm the fuck down. He finally nodded in greeting.

"Remington, tell Levi how much money in tips you earned last night."

"Just waiting tables?" Remington asked, standing a little taller. When Remington focused on Julian, Levi raked his eyes up and down the waiter's body, getting an eyeful in the groin area.

"Of course," Julian said, drawing Levi's gaze to him. He could feel the heat of embarrassment creeping up his cheeks. Remington looked half-aroused and the underwear did nothing to hide the half-hard dick he sported, yet no one seemed to care. "The rest is on your time."

"Three hundred and three dollars." Remington lifted a hand, giving a cocky little snap before settling on his cocked hip.

"On a Monday night?" Levi asked, not sure he'd heard that right.

"Yep. Weekends are better, but those are harder days to get. Everybody wants to work weekends," the guy replied, resting his other hand on his hip while openly staring at Levi. No question about it, Remington had sex appeal. Levi didn't have that kind of charm working for him, but if he could make even half that, it would seriously help his life.

"Thanks, Remington. We have a bachelor party tonight. Make sure we're good to go," Julian said, coming toward Levi, a suit jacket slung over his arm.

"I heard you're taking Jay's position," Remington said, his eyes lighting up as he came over and squeezed Levi's bicep. Julian just lifted his hand toward the door and cocked his head, urging Remington out. The guy had no problem with the rebuff; he just laughed and left, shutting the door behind him. When Levi looked back at Julian, he held out the suit coat to him.

"It's mine. Slide it on so I can give you a tour of downstairs, just in case the club opens before we're done. We have a firm dress code," Julian said.

"I'm sorry," Levi started, shrugging the jacket on.

"Totally my fault. I'll explain as we walk." Levi followed, fixing the collar as he trotted back down the stairs. "This whole concept came about because of my accident. Are you familiar with Thane Walker?"

"Only as the guy that you mentioned who helped you out." Levi remembered the name, because Julian had used it all the time.

"That's right. He owns this place. He also owns the chain restaurants the Iron Maya and Szechwan Dragon and a bunch of other places. I had planned to meet him the night he found me in the hospital. He stayed by my side until I could be discharged. He's something special and wanted to build a safer place for gay men to mingle." When Julian got to the bottom step, he faced Levi, placing a hand on his own chest. "The original concept was for guys like me, just the average escort, to have a safe place to meet men who were looking for that type of relationship."

"I'm not an escort, Julian," Levi immediately countered.

"That's painfully obvious," Julian teased, pointing a finger toward his wardrobe.

Still at the base of the stairs, Julian winked at him just like when they worked out together at the clinic, but that moment of honesty was gone as he gave a slight turn and extended both arms toward the club. "As it turned out, the concept evolved. It's a membership only club with every member and employee passing rigorous background checks." Julian strolled casually through the club, winding his way through the tables as he explained. "Reservations is a nightclub and fine-dining establishment where men can come and be themselves and meet other men who have gone through the same application process. We have both couples and singles coming to enjoy the company."

"With no sex?" Levi asked, having a hard time letting go of his misconceptions about 'Reservations' and 'fine dining' not being code-words for a fully operational fetish club with chains, whips, and a live sex show right there on the stage.

"Frowned upon in both the club and dining area. But let's say there's mutual attraction between two parties, the resort we're attached to has rooms always available."

"You're kidding?" Levi asked, surprised. He hadn't considered that option.

"Absolutely not. We have security stationed at all exits as well as posing as guests inside. The whole goal is safety for everyone involved."

"What if something still happens? Will you be sued?" he asked.

"It's doubtful," Julian explained. "Members sign paperwork that they won't sue, plus it's the same as any other restaurant or club out there. I'm sure Thane's got that part handled."

"Huh," Levi said, this time looking around the club as if seeing it for the first time. He couldn't imagine the overhead cost for such an undertaking. A shaft of light and movement caught Levi's eye. He glanced over to see the doors across the space close as two men stepped inside. "Are they coming from the restaurant?"

"Most do, but not all."

Levi let his gaze roam. Everyone from the bartenders, to the waitstaff, to a guy stepping into the DJ booth all wore about the same thing. Something skimpy.

"So what're you thinking?" Julian asked.

"I'd like to make three hundred dollars in a night, but I'm not sure I'm cut out for this." He let his gaze slide back to Julian as he contemplated his options. "What if the waiters get hit on?"

"My official response is that they don't engage. Since it's you, my unofficial response is that a lot of them will eventually take the men up on their offers. Sometimes it's just a quick hookup, sometimes there's money involved, but that's between them. We don't get involved," he explained as if he were talking about any other business matter.

"Really? You never truly get involved?" Levi asked, still on the fence about the whole thing.

"Nope. I don't want to know. Why are you asking? You thinking about making a little side money?" Julian said, waggling his brows.

"I'm not interested in that," Levi shot back immediately.

"You keep saying that, but if that changes, no one here's gonna judge you. We've all had a casual hookup, right? For a lot of the men, it's a one-time thing. You'll find some of these guys just want company, and then there are some that are looking for something more exclusive and long term. They find that too." Julian stopped at a nearby highboy table, resting an arm on the edge.

"New guy, Julian?" a waiter asked, dropping two cocktail napkins on the table in front of them.

"Possibly."

"Nice! I'm Quinn." The waiter stuck his hand over the table and Levi clasped it. "Can I get you guys something to drink?"

"Nah, not right now. Thanks anyway," Julian said, pushing away from the table. "Let's go back upstairs and finish."

Neither one spoke, and the silence was kind of nice as Levi followed Julian back up the stairs. It gave him some time to sort things out in his head. He had relaxed some. The bar was so fun, but also very classy. Seeing that it wasn't all whips and chains, and sexual debauchery, eased some of his stress about taking the job. After stepping through the door of the office, Levi shrugged off the coat and handed it to Julian.

"I've never seen anything like this before." Levi took in all the details of Julian's office that he'd missed when he'd first arrived. For some reason, this was exactly what he would have pictured for Julian. A shell-gray leather sectional with mismatched pillows of black, metallic pewter, and off-white fur commanded attention in the center of the room. The walls were painted a deep charcoal, which made the white trim and crown molding stand out against such a stark color. Two oversized wingback chairs with matching bold black and cream patterns sat to the left part of the room on either side of a mirrored end table. A plush rug anchored the pieces and colors together. Everything looked expensive, but not pretentious.

Fitting.

In the opposite corner of the room, a heavy black desk took up most of the angled wall. Levi's eyes were drawn to the unusual piece of art made of glass and mirrors that sat behind Julian's desk and made the wall shimmer. He figured that piece must have cost a fortune. Hell, the furniture in this office alone probably cost more than his house. It was the nicest he'd ever seen, like he'd stepped into a designer décor magazine shoot. But the most impressive detail in the office was the large glass panels stretched from floor to ceiling along the entire wall.

Out of curiosity, Levi walked across the highly-polished wood floor to the wall of windows and looked down over the club. The place looked glamorous and inviting, even from this view. The dancers in the cages reminded him of a flock of exotic birds captured in flight. They moved like one, each mirroring the other in a graceful dance. Their bodies glowed brightly from the neon paint; their hypnotic sways held his attention captive.

"Thane's a really good guy. I'm…blessed, for lack of a better word. It takes a lot to run a place like this, but he's not trying to turn a huge profit or at least I don't feel like that's the only reason he started Reservations."

Levi turned to look back at Julian, surprised at the sincerity and deep appreciation he heard in the words.

"So, tell me about your brothers?"

"My oldest brother's seventeen now. He's a junior, or I guess a senior, in high school. He's graduating early. My youngest brother's fifteen and struggling." Levi shook his head, thinking of Luke and the trip to the principal's office.

"I'm not sure you've ever mentioned your mother?" Julian asked as he poured himself a drink then lifted the bottle and offered it to Levi. He shook his head no and answered Julian's question.

"She took off about fifteen years ago. I found out a few months ago that she died of a drug overdose not too long after that. All I remember was a guy in a shiny red car parked out front waiting for her the day she left." Another tidbit of his life that he rarely shared with anyone.

"And you're from here?" Julian strolled to the large black desk across the room, drink in hand.

"Born and raised."

"Boyfriend? We don't need anyone in here causing problems. You seem the monogamous type." He looked up from the file cabinet he riffled through.

"I probably am. I haven't dated much. I generally just swipe right." Levi grinned. His relationships these days were more with the Tinder and Grindr apps than anyone he'd met in life. Even then, he hadn't had sex in more months than he could count.

"Yeah. Tinder. I'm into that now," Julian said and pulled out a manila envelope, tossing it on the clean desk before motioning for Levi to take a seat in one of the chairs facing the desk. "I'm sorry about your situation, Levi."

"It's okay. My brothers are good kids. We'll get it figured out," Levi said, not wanting to linger on the subject, he asked a question of his own. "How are you doing after everything you've been through?"

It was none of his business, but he asked anyway. Julian had this comfortable way in which he handled the world. He accepted himself and others in such a genuine way that Levi couldn't comprehend how Julian seemed perfectly at peace with himself. Levi had never felt comfortable with himself, or around the other people in his life. He appreciated the self-assured ease Julian projected. He wished he had the same confidence.

"As good as things have gotten for me, I'm still battling some trust issues." Julian took a long drink from his glass then tipped it back, draining the last of the liquid. "My Tinder experience is just talk. I haven't gone there yet. Weird, huh?"

"No, not at all. I don't have a lot of sex. I did more so on the east coast in school than here, but I figured you and this guy Thane would have rekindled your…you know."

If Julian noticed his hesitancy, he didn't say a word. "He's a really good guy, and now he's turned into an even better friend. I can't say I don't miss sharing a bed with him. He's got an amazing body that he definitely knows how to use, and he's a very attentive lover. You know what made him different? He took the time to make sure he knew what I liked. No one's ever done that before," Julian answered honestly, and Levi had no idea what to say. He wasn't sure he'd ever had sex where the other guy tried to please him. Most of the time they both just rushed to the getting off part. "So, what do you think?"

Still stuck on the amazing concept of a lover trying to please him sexually, Levi had to shift thoughts to even understand Julian's question. He blinked a couple of times as he sifted through the situation then remembered he was here for a job and answered truthfully. "About this job? I don't think I have the right personality to pull this off."

"But you're gonna give it a try, aren't you?" Julian's smirk spread into a grin.

"I don't wanna have sex for money. No offense, but it's not for me, and that's a hard line. If I was going to go that direction, I already would have. As soon as I can get back on my feet and get my brothers on the right track, I'm going back to medical school. If all that sounds good with you, and if you'll let me, I'll give waiting tables a try," he said nervously, stepping way outside his comfort zone.

Julian pointed to the legal-size envelope on the desk. "Fill those out and bring 'em back tomorrow. That's important."

Next, Julian riffled through the drawer then placed three hundred dollars in front of him. "I'll need receipts for petty cash. Go to Charade over on Kearny Mesa Road and get yourself several pair of briefs—purple, silver, blue, or black. Also get some black boots and a pair of white running shoes. Doesn't matter what brand as long as they're white. I'll get you the rest. That's the uniform. You'll get a calendar so you know what night you're expected to wear what. If we host an event or do something special, we provide the costume for you. Also, since you're waiting tables and dealing with food and drinks, you'll need to get your food handlers card. It's an online test. The information's in the packet. Pay for it with that cash—I need the receipt."

Julian paused, giving him a critical assessment before continuing. "It's probably better if you were waxed or shaved too, shows more definition. A tan can also make you look a little more cut, that is, if you're worried about the way you look. Just so you know, the men are gonna like what they see, so don't get too lost in your head about it."

Julian grew silent again and went back to searching through the drawer as Levi reached for the money. "We have a salon that works with us. A spa in San Diego. This first time, we'll cover that cost. Remember the receipts." Julian paused and smiled. "I always forget that part." He found a business card and wrote a name on the back. "Call her first thing in the morning; tell her I asked to get you in. Let's say day after tomorrow, be here for training and I'll get you on the schedule."

"Thank you," Levi said, lifting from the chair enough to tuck the money and the card in his front pocket. This had been tough on him for many different reasons. He knew he carried the poor-kid chip on his shoulders and had more hang-ups about that than most. Swallowing that lump of emotion that always came from situations where people tried to help him, Levi looked Julian straight in the eyes and said it again, "Truly, thank you for staying on me."

"No thanks needed. I'm not sure I'd be standing here today if you hadn't stepped in and pushed me in the right direction. If this works out, then I can call it even," Julian said as his cell phone started to ring. He looked down then over to him. "Levi, I need to take this. Do you remember your way out?"

"Yeah, I do." He lifted his hand as he rose, then grabbed the information packet before heading to the door. Julian answered, but held off speaking until he closed the door behind him. With a deep calming breath, Levi shoved down his nerves, trying to retain some of the peace he'd just held in taking such a job.

CHAPTER 6

Two days later, Levi balanced the tray on his palm as he carefully placed a martini then a cocktail glass on the high-top table. When he accomplished both without spilling, Julian, who stood a couple of feet away, started clapping his hands. The guy could be such a smartass at times. Levi resisted the urge to shoot the finger at his new boss and decided to take pride in his accomplishment, no matter how badly Julian teased him.

This was his first table as a trainee, and apparently the whole tray/drinks balancing thing didn't come naturally to Levi. He'd lost two separate orders to gravity combined with clumsiness. One round when he'd stumbled over his own feet trying to walk too carefully to the table, and the other when he lifted one glass off the off-center tray, sending the remaining drinks tumbling to the ground. He'd become the spectacle of the night.

But not anymore. He'd finally channeled his inner waiter, and amazingly, the swell of pride for such a feat just about rivaled his five-fifteen score on the MCAT. With a bit of attitude, Levi tucked the tray under his arm and asked the customers, "Anything else?"

"This is enough for now," one of the guys said.

When he started to turn away, he felt a firm pat on his ass and his happy turned to shock as he flipped around. The older gentlemen sat grinning from ear to ear as he winked Levi's way then hooked a thumb over his shoulder toward Julian. "He told me to."

Levi must have looked as outraged as he felt because both Julian and his trainer, Quinn, were doubled over laughing at him.

Regretfully, he didn't know either well enough to crack the tray over their heads like he wanted to.

"You did it!" Quinn started but couldn't get a hold of his laughter which sent Julian into another fit of giggles.

"Shut up." Levi pointed a finger at Julian. "I told you this wasn't gonna be easy for me."

"And who would have thought that meant more than just the come-ons," Julian teased. Quinn jumped off the barstool he'd been perched on, still grinning as he took hold of Levi's bicep and led him toward the bar. "You're gonna do just fine. You come off as charming as opposed to inept. Just keep that can-do attitude until you get some experience. It'll come together for you."

"Sure," Levi mumbled.

Quinn took him through a curtain to a small alcove. This area was for the waitstaff. The lighting was dim, but not dark enough that he couldn't see the stacks of handheld trays, and a row of slim pouches that he'd seen on the waiters.

"The way we operate is kind of like you're a subcontractor. Drink prices are set. You pay the bar for your order then the customer pays you. You also need to tip out the bar back at the end of your shift. You got it?" he asked, taking one of the pouches off the hook.

"What if they want to start a tab?" Levi tried to step back as Quinn leaned toward him.

"Stop being so skittish. Let me wrap this around you." Quinn moved toward him again. This time, he allowed the other man to tie the strap around his waist. He turned the material until the flap rested against his hip. "Most likely, they'll open a tab with cash, usually a hundred-dollar bill then when it's used up, you ask for more, but you need to keep track of the drink totals on a pad. I've seen some of the guys get royally screwed when they tried to keep it all in their heads. If a guest wants to use a credit card… Come on. I'll show you what to do. That's all in the software, but you'll be surprised at how little anyone wants to use a credit card around here."

"Why's that?" Levi asked, following Quinn back out to the floor. "They signed up for memberships. Surely, that has to be easy to track."

"You're so cute, but you have a lot to learn, my friend," Quinn said offhandedly, doing a quick sweep through his section of tables, checking everyone's drinks before heading back to one of the monitors on the far end of the bar. "The obvious reasons, of course. Many of these men don't want a trail that they were ever here. A lot of the older generation isn't as out in their lives as we are. You gotta always remember we're only here because of the hell they went through. Let me show you the software to process the credit card."

Quinn went through the steps of starting a tab. Levi watched, ticking off the bullet point instructions in his head until he was taken right out of the tutorial with another pat on his ass.

"What the hell?" he growled, looking all around.

"Man, you gotta lighten up," Quinn said, grabbing his arm, turning him back to the computer. "You stick out like a sore thumb. They're doing it because you're bowed up so tight. Well, that and because Julian promised them free drinks."

Of course, Julian would do that, and Quinn was right that he was uptight. Frustrated with himself, he nodded at the touchscreen. "Keep showing me."

"No, really," Quinn said, resting an arm on the edge of the bar, leaning in to Levi as he spoke more quietly, just loud enough to be heard over the music. "You're a smart guy. Your training's taken about an hour and most of that wasn't with the process, but learning to use the dang tray. But you gotta let go of whatever it is you think you know about the guys here. If you think you're better than this, you're probably right, but there's a reason you're here. Own it and get what you can out of this experience."

Everything faded under the weight of Quinn's blunt words. The music, the noise, just everything was gone as Levi stared at a pair of crystal blue eyes. Under all his internal self-loathing, he had missed what a nice-looking guy Quinn was.

"No one's here to judge. I've been here since we opened and already paid for my whole semester at Southern Cal. I graduate this year and this job's gonna pay for law school. And yes, I've absolutely hooked up here, but not for money. Look around. It's like a smorgasbord of men."

Levi didn't bother to look around because he was still hung up on Quinn's statement about paying for school. The guy looked like a male model straight off the pages of GQ. Honestly, Levi would have thought Quinn was an actor trying to break into the business; he was just that good-looking.

Quinn nudged him. "You're hot. You're ripped and your ass is absolutely delectable. It's gonna get touched. Work it to your advantage. Stay smart, but remove your judgment. No one here expects you to do anything other than wait a few tables. If you hook up, do it on your terms. If you don't, then do that on your terms. Stop getting hung up on the possibility of money changing hands somewhere. That's not your business, man."

Slowly Levi nodded. The guy was right. That was exactly what Levi had been doing. All day, from the grooming of his junk, to shaving his chest, getting a spray tan, to trying to figure out how to style this new haircut, he'd been feeling bad about himself. No one in this place knew anything about him. They didn't know his struggles or where he came from. His hang-up wasn't that he thought he was better than anyone—absolutely not. Quite the opposite, actually. He'd spent his whole life trying to do better than his meager beginning and the drug dealers and gangbangers that now populated his neighborhood.

"Finish showing me," he said, his voice softer now. He appreciated Quinn being so honest with him.

"One more thing. I wasn't joking earlier. Keep that quiet brooding thing going, just don't let it slip into condescension. Keep 'em guessing. Nobody else in here does that, and you'll stand out if you do. Got it?" Quinn said with a wink.

"Shouldn't be hard," Levi replied, raising his brows, fighting back the grin tugging at the corners of his mouth. Quinn nodded, turning back to the computer. Levi intently listened to a few more minutes of instruction before Quinn finished up.

"I think you can handle yourself tonight. I'll be here to answer any questions. Want to give it a try on your own?"

All that newfound confidence slipped a notched. "Sure. I guess."

"Then smile for me."

Levi did as asked, pleased he'd made Quinn's grin widen.

"There you go. You'll do well. Now get out there and figure out the persona you wanna portray. And for God's sake, ignore the ass pats. If they grab your dick, then you can be offended," Quinn teased. "But, Levi, you have the clean-cut, boy-next-door look. You have innocence written all over you. You're a challenge. You have to admit most men love that shit. Probably safe to say you'll be making an appearance in more than a few jackoff sessions."

Levi nodded again. He really didn't know what to think about someone picturing him while jacking off. It was definitely creepy but also a little flattering at the same time. He could deal with it as long as they kept the details to themselves.

"Okay, go. I'm pushing you out of the nest. You take tables forty-three and forty-four. Find me if you need me." Quinn gave him a light shove, then grabbed his own tray.

"All right." He gave Quinn a nod, trying to remember everything they'd talked about as he turned toward the tables. He didn't want anyone to think he was arrogant. He wasn't. He put a smile on his face and looked up as one of the guys at the table Quinn had given him lifted his martini glass. He'd get this down. He had to.

Two hours later, his feet hurt like crazy, he fought an exhausted yawn, and he was certain that flippy hair thing he'd tried hard to achieve had totally fallen flat. Levi had cleaned his area, performed all his end-of-shift responsibilities, and took a spot at the end of the bar, closing out his tickets. Tonight hadn't been as horrible as he'd built up in his mind. He'd stayed busy the whole shift which made the time go by quickly; he was thankful for that. A big yawn made his eyes water, causing his vision to blur momentarily as he looked over all his tickets. Quinn had been right. Not one single open credit card tab the whole night. Dealing with cash had its advantages, especially since the pocket dangling from his hip felt heavy, stuffed full of green dollar bills. Money that was all his.

"I'm impressed. You did good tonight," Julian said, leaning against the bar facing him. Levi didn't look up, just continued finishing out his tickets.

"I felt really stiff. It didn't come naturally," he said, focusing on the monitor in front of him, concentrating on touching the buttons correctly. The background music was slightly louder than the low murmur of the crowd, thankfully making it easier to think.

"You were, but it'll ease, and Quinn was right; you pulled off that innocent thing which is hard to do. After you get that sorted, I'll buy you a drink," Julian offered as the ticket on the attached printer started to run. He gave himself a mental high five watching the totals appear.

"Can't tonight. I gotta be up at six in the morning," Levi said, ripping the paper from the printer and handing it to Julian. His two tables had logged in a little over a thousand dollars. He had no idea if that was good or bad, just that he'd worked solidly the whole night. Julian gave him a nod and offered him an outstretched fist that he readily bumped.

"Go home. We can talk later," Julian said, tucking the tape in a bank bag as he turned to walk away.

His feet, more than anything else, needed relief. That was the reason he walked gingerly toward the back. He was the only one in the changing room, and the bright light of the fluorescent bulbs hurt his eyes as he went for his locker to pull out his clothes. He toed off his shoes, his feet singing hallelujah as he tugged on his jeans, pulling them over his hips, careful of the bag still hanging at his waist. Once completely dressed, he took the money out of his pouch. Since he was all alone, he decided to count his tips there. He'd have to get better at organizing his money. He could see mistakes happening if he didn't keep his bills in better order.

He counted out the money and was so shocked at the total that he counted a second time. Two hundred and seventy-three dollars for only two tables and two hours' worth of work. Oh my god. That was almost double what he made at the PT clinic today.

Hell, almost triple with his hours being cut in the mornings. He'd have to wait and see what he made next time, but if he could keep this up, there was a light at the end of the tunnel. This wad of cash in his hand was worth all the pats, accidental brushings, and sexual innuendos he'd had to put up with all night.

Levi stood, forgetting all about his feet as he stuffed the money in his front pocket while pulling his sandals out of the locker. He dropped them to the floor, slid his feet into the welcomed comfort, then tossed his new work shoes in the locker, before slamming the door shut. He was way past exhausted and needed sleep, but he couldn't take his mind off the money. If he kept the PT position and worked here four nights a week, he could get things paid off quickly. For the first time in a long time, he felt hopeful. Warning himself to slow down and keep it all in perspective didn't stop him from thinking about all the things he could do with the money as he walked through the parking lot toward his car.

CHAPTER 7

Two weeks later

Thane took the staircase up to the nightclub's office, using the handrail to pull himself forward. Man, he was dragging ass. The scowl on his face had guaranteed the club staff kept their distance. Whoever had the bright idea that he spend all that time driving from one low-performing restaurant to another was a fucking idiot, even if that someone was him.

He pushed through the office door, letting it slam shut behind him, thankfully blocking out most of the noise from the club below. What he liked most about this club was the fact the clientele had better taste in music. It wasn't thumping so loud he couldn't hear himself think.

"Hey, *papi.*" Julian snickered from behind the desk. The guy hadn't even bothered to look up, his fingers gliding swiftly over the keys of the calculator as he entered numbers from a spreadsheet.

Yes, Julian was a pain in his ass most of the time. His overeager attitude had him calling Thane at all hours of the day and night, but he was kicking ass with this venture. He'd taken Dave's position and was now working on ways to increase exposure through marketing and advertising campaigns. He was impossible to keep a thumb on, and the profits spoke volumes to the success of all Julian's efforts.

"I feel old enough to be your father."

Julian kept his eyes downcast until he got to the end of the row and penciled something in.

"You know they have computers for that type thing."

"Yeah, I'm just keeping a backup," Julian said as he finished working on whatever he was doing.

"Julian, you're working yourself too hard. Everyone here's too afraid to steal from you." That earned a straight up, loud bark of laughter.

"So you heard from your corporate trainers?" Julian asked, that handsome face now focused solely on him. He was such a nice-looking guy, and it was a shame that all Julian could see was the scar on the right side of his face, a reminder of the night he was attacked, but no one else even noticed, not even Thane, and he'd spent the most time with him, trying to get him back on his feet.

"Yeah, I did. They didn't have favorable reviews. They said you don't follow rules, you make split second decisions without looking at all the angles, and no one quite understands all the eye-candy sashaying around here." Thane easily ticked off the top three points of contention out of a list that was dozens long after his team returned from their training.

"That's because I'm doing my job." *And everyone else's,* Thane thought to himself. Instead of saying that, he changed the subject.

"How are the reservations in the dining room?"

"I'm happy to say we're booked about seventy percent full for the next six weeks." Technically, Julian shouldn't know that information. He had nothing to do with the restaurant side of things.

"And the diners are coming to the club afterward?" Thane asked, crossing his arms over his chest as he lifted a palm to cover the yawn he couldn't fight off.

"Very high transition rate. Maybe as much as sixty-five percent," Julian said.

"That's good."

"I think so too. We're having a theme night tonight. Mardi Gras. It seems to be going well." Julian pushed away from the desk and went to the floor-to-ceiling mirrored glass, looking down over the club. "Theme nights seem to please the older crowd."

"Do they?" Thane shoved to his feet and trailed after Julian, letting free another, louder yawn. He considered the clientele, deciding it might be the costumes, or maybe the different music playlists that were the draw. They may need to consider adding some of those changes into the day-to-day operation. "Have we done any research on what's the appeal to the older generations?"

"It's the body paint on the dancers. It's also the masks on the waiters. The regulars pretend they don't know who each of the servers are. We do an unveiling around ten. They get a rise out of playing the game."

Huh. He'd been way off base then. Thane decided to ignore the double meaning in Julian's comment and looked out over the bar instead. The club had been decorated festively in bright Mardi Gras colors and shades of purple lighting. Julian had a flair for setting the scene, and from the looks of the crowd, they loved what he'd done. He hadn't even glanced in that direction when he'd first arrived or he'd have praised Julian sooner.

"You're doing good," he said absently, tucking his hands in his slacks pockets. He had to give it to Julian, pain in the ass or not, he filled this club with paying customers and watched over all Thane's pennies as if they were his own.

"That's the guy I hired. The one I told you about."

Thane had no recollection and followed Julian's finger to a group of three servers waiting at the bar for their drinks to be poured. His eyes were immediately drawn to a very delectable ass in shimmery purple briefs standing away from the other two. Even though all the servers wore the same thing, there was just something about the one standing awkwardly on the end, something that caught his eye. Thane cocked a brow as he stirred a little down south, which was remarkable considering his exhaustion level. A different time or place and he might try to draw the group of sexy men back to his suite. Honestly, there wasn't a mediocre one in the mix.

"His background report came back clean, like I knew it would."

"What are you talking about?" Thane finally asked, not bothering to look at Julian. He was far more interested in what was going on down at the bar.

"Two weeks ago, early in the week, I called about hiring outside of policy." Julian's comment about breaking rules got his attention and drew Thane's gaze from the tempting men and that extraordinary rear he was admiring at the moment.

"And I told you not to hire him." That intense focus now landed on Julian who hadn't turned his way.

"And I told you I was going to anyway. He's doing great. A top earner. His sales are some of the highest on the floor." Julian used his well-manicured fingernail to tap the glass, like pointing from this far away would give him any clue as to which one of the guys he was.

"Does anyone else know you did that, Julian? I should fire your ass right now." Thane refused to be thwarted from this discipline. Julian couldn't just act on his own like this. His corporate trainers were right, Julian did things impulsively and he had to stop.

"But you won't. Now stop being such a meanie and pay attention. That's him right there." Julian tapped the glass again, drawing his focus back to the floor. Julian's reprimand was all but forgotten as one man in particular turned from the bar, the owner of the perfect ass he'd been admiring only a minute ago.

Thane's breath caught in his throat; the new guy was gorgeous. Even in the mask, Thane could see the boyish good looks. He seemed a little unsteady as he moved across the lounge floor with a tray full of drinks balanced on his palm, but his presence still commanded attention.

Besides, Thane didn't give a shit how the guy handled a tray, all he cared about was how well Mr. Perfect-ass knew his way around a cock. Thane's dick grew instantly hard. There was no use in trying to deny the immediate attraction. The new hire was every boy-next-door fantasy come to life. Thane took his time ogling the waiter, taking in every flex of muscle as he cut his way through the crowd. He let his gaze roam slowly up his body, from the stark white high-tops on his feet all the way up those muscular legs, thick thighs, cut abs, expansive chest and broad shoulders. His body was perfect, no doubt, but it was the face that had his heart hammering in his chest.

Dear God, his lips were full and pouty, perfectly fleshy and made for wrapping around his dick. He had that strong square jaw, high cheekbones, and wide almond-shaped eyes from what he could tell from behind the mask. He couldn't see the color, but he was betting they were green. His hair was short, and the way the lights hit, it looked like there were hints of auburn streaked throughout. No visible tattoos which was kind of unheard of in today's world.

"Who the fuck is that?" Thane asked. He seriously needed to meet the new hire.

"You're welcome." Julian's cocky purr caught him off guard. Thane looked over at his club manager, having no idea what Julian meant by that comment, but his gaze quickly darted back to the temptation in the shiny purple briefs.

"Answer the question," Thane said sternly, watching as the waiter acted almost shy to the point of brooding until the last drink was served, and then cracking a brilliant smile that once again stole Thane's breath. Oh, he was good. Thane looked at the men seated around the table who were all just as mesmerized as he. The oldest one, probably his own father's age, reached out and shoved money in the guy's waistband. His fingers lingered until the waiter moved away from the touch and headed toward his next table. Thane's gaze fixed on that firm bubble butt. So perfectly framed and highlighted by the fact that the underwear didn't quite cover each cheek, revealing a bit of tempting flesh. Damn, he bet those men down there were eating that shit up. "Are you gonna answer the question?"

"I did." When had Julian told him a name? Thane tore his gaze away from Mr. Perfect-ass and glanced back at his cocky club manager, standing there with that smug shit-eating grin plastered across his face.

Fuck this, he'd go figure out the waiter's name himself. It would be monumentally easier than dealing with Julian's smart ass. He cut his eyes back to the club, stealing one last glance at the waiter when he got to the office door. Julian's laughter echoed behind him until he made it about halfway down the stairs to the club foyer. Who could even know what was going on with his weirdo manager.

Thane stopped by the bar and scanned the room, looking for the nameless waiter. When he spotted him again, nothing had diminished, only intensified. The guy was even better-looking up close, hot as hell. All boy-next-door and that had Thane's dick standing up and taking notice, also had the wheels turning in his head.

Holy hell, how lucky could he get? He'd just found someone he really wanted to spend time with.

Thane scanned the club. Of course, he couldn't find any empty tables, but there were some unoccupied seats. He had no idea what tables belonged to what waiters, but that could quickly be remedied. Thane looked over to the bartender, Ricco, and cocked his head, drawing the guy over. The bartender stopped what he was doing to the frustration of the waiters and came straight over to Thane.

"What's up, boss man?"

Thane didn't look away from the nameless waiter. He just pointed. "What tables does he have?"

"He's new. I think he's got the four along the back wall and the booth in the corner."

"Does he have a name?" New and already earned four tables and a corner booth in the main section. Pretty impressive.

"Levi. Need a drink?" the bartender asked.

"Nah, I'll order one from him." Thane turned away from the vision he'd been watching and looked directly at the bartender. "Stay quiet about this conversation."

That earned him a confused look and perplexed nod. "You're the boss."

Thane was already scanning those four tables. Only one was full. The others had a couple of guys at each place, none looked ready to move. The booth was completely out of the question. There was a whole lot of heavy making out going on over there. When Levi passed by him on his way to the bar, Thane's gaze followed. His profile was rocking good, but it was the side-view of his ass that had Thane's mouth watering and his brain slipping into the gutter. He could worship that ass with the reverence it deserved. Thane reached down to adjust his overly enthusiastic dick. Suddenly, every bit of aggravation Julian gave him, all the exorbitant costs of this restaurant and bar, every single bit was worth the effort.

Levi.

He bet that name would sound even hotter forced from his lips as he came. He went to the first empty seat in Levi's section. "Can I use this chair?"

"Yeah, sure," the guy replied, before turning back to his friend. Thane dropped onto the seat and scooted up to the edge of the table before resting his forearms on the side. When he looked back up, the two men now stared back at him suspiciously.

"I'm Thane," he politely introduced himself before looking back over his shoulder to check Levi's position.

"Okay?" The guy that had given him the chair sounded a little testy.

Thane turned back to the annoyed customer. "I'll only be here a minute. I'm monitoring a new hire; you know, quality control and all…" His words trailed off as a napkin was placed in front of him. Thane looked over his shoulder, and his gaze collided with startled green eyes. Yeah, he'd nailed it. Green eyes. He bet those auburn streaks in the guy's hair were natural, and boy did that turn him on that much more.

Obviously, he'd gotten Levi's attention too. The unexpected shock of the moment lasted until one of the guys at the table laughed. Thane didn't look away from Levi. Instead, he turned his body in the waiter's direction, anchored his hand on a thigh, and grinned. The exhaustion and frustration of the last few weeks faded as anticipation and excitement took its place.

Damn, Levi even smelled good, all fresh and citrusy with a note of forbidden spice. Thane inhaled, discreetly filling his lungs with the intoxicating scent. He let his gaze travel, hitting the highlights he'd spotted before. Those lips, those shoulders, that firm stomach. He tilted his head to get a peek under the tray at the nicely encased package restrained by the shiny purple stretch of his underwear. Ah yeah, it was growing under his inspection. His grin broadened and his mouth watered.

"What can…" Levi's voice came out in a croak. The guy cleared his throat and started over. "What can I get you?" The deep rich timbre of Levi's voice coasted over his heart, easing his weary mind and setting his nerve endings on fire.

Thane smiled so big that he probably looked predatory. Fuck it. That was exactly what he was feeling, no need to try and hide it. He slowly lifted his gaze, taking time to enjoy the fleshy view before meeting Levi's eyes with his. A momentary flash of confusion crossed the waiter's face before those sexy brows snapped together. "I'll take a Grey Goose and tonic. Two limes."

Levi nodded and looked down at the small pad on his tray. It took several seconds before he started writing. "That'll be seven fifty. You can open a tab. I'll just need a retainer."

Thane's gaze never left Levi's handsome face, pleased he had the added benefit of being anonymous. Levi had no idea who he was, which meant the look of interest he spotted was genuine. Now for this retainer. He'd never heard it referred to quite like that, but he pulled out his wallet and looked over at his tablemates, clearly having a good time. He played it off like they were all together.

"You two need anything?" Of course both nodded even though their glasses were full. "Okay, a full round it is." He leaned closer to the waiter. "I missed your name."

~~~

What the hell? Levi had been instantly drawn in then struck dumb by those intense brown eyes staring back at him. The smoldering movie-star good looks completely caught him off guard too, but it was the scorching heat of the mirrored attraction climbing up his body and exploding through his veins that made his knees weak. Since day one of working there, nobody had asked his name. Levi started to say something, wanted to say
~~~

something, but what came out wasn't anything close to the English language.

His voice broke with that same mortifying croak as before, so he snapped his mouth shut and basically froze in place, feeling like an idiot. His muscles refused to move, even though all he wanted to do was escape his humiliation. He now had a complete understanding of the old saying, "like a deer in headlights." He stood there for God knew how long, lost in amused, whisky-colored eyes, unable to remember his own name. Finally, the burning in his lungs won out, and he sucked in a breath, his brain coming online in the process, and he quickly lowered his eyes to the floor.

"Levi," he all but whispered and didn't attempt another word. Instead, he turned away, but in his haste to escape the sexiest man in the room, he bumped into another table, knocking the tray out of his hand. So much for playing it cool.

"I'm s-sorry," he stuttered, managing to save the customer's drink before it tipped over. "I'm so sorry. I'm such a klutz." He bent to pick up the tray and pad that he'd dropped. His cheeks burned from the embarrassment and his body heated for an entirely different reason. He'd been blindsided by the new guy in his section, thrown off balance.

Stupidly, in his bent over position, he looked back and got an upside-down view of the hottest man he'd ever seen still watching him make a fool of himself. He grabbed the tray, straightened, and fought the urge to see if those eyes were still on him. He tucked the tray under his arm and took off, determined to fill the drink order. He would not turn around and take another look. He wouldn't. Absolutely not.

Morbid curiosity won out over anything rational, and he snuck that one last a glance over his shoulder. All the guy's attention remained on him, and damn it, if he didn't stumble over his own feet when he tried to walk off again. He was cursed, that was the only explanation he had for the crap that happened to him.

Tunnel vision and nervous energy were the only things that got him to the bar. He tried to take control of his breathing before his heart beat straight out of his chest. What just happened back there?

"You okay?" Quinn asked. Levi didn't even know how to respond to that question. No, he wasn't okay; his body was not cooperating. In fact, it was betraying him at the moment, reminding him of junior high all over again.

He looked over at Quinn and another server named Chase and shook his head at them before he looked down, embarrassed by what had drawn Chase's attention. Shit, Chase was staring at his rock-hard dick. He dropped his hand and adjusted himself in a vain attempt to hide the full-blown evidence of his interest in nothing but a tight pair of skimpy underwear.

"Damn! Who's the lucky guy?"

Quinn immediately looked toward his station; Levi unwisely turned back too. His gaze connected with the handsome customer, and the earth shifted under his feet. He quickly turned away, gripping the edge of the bar, squeezing his fingers tight, trying to get a hold of himself.

"Dude! Thane's sitting in your section. He tips like a boss! You're gonna bank tonight."

He heard the words, but they didn't register. Levi looked over at his friend, confused. "Who's Thane?"

"What'd you need, Levi?" the bartender asked. He dropped his head to his hand, and shoved his order pad in the bartender's direction. For almost two weeks, he'd dodged every advance, declined lucrative offers from men he found extremely attractive but hadn't been truly interested in. He honestly hadn't been into anyone. Until right now. He'd made a complete spectacle of himself because some hot guy wanted to know his name. How pathetic was that?

"Is that for Thane?"

"Who's Thane?" he asked, raising his head to look at Ricco.

"The owner of Reservations," the bartender answered and pointed to his section. As if in slow motion, Levi turned to see the man who had caused his body to betray him, was the very same man he'd heard mentioned so many times in the locker room, the one Julian had said such good things about, the same one that almost every waiter in this place wanted a chance to fuck. The sexy guy he'd made a fool of himself in front of was Thane…his boss's boss. The guy had somehow managed to find a seat in his section and was now staring directly at him. He almost swooned at the intensity of that gaze. Levi fully understood why his peers' eyes had gone out of focus when they'd talked about the sexy owner. Hell, his whole body went offline because the man smiled at him. He'd only half listened to their tall tales, but from where he stood, Levi knew their description hadn't done him justice.

"He's the one who owns the property?" Levi asked. He could hear the desperation in his voice. Desperate for someone, anyone, to take that table and give him a break before he came totally undone.

"Yep," Chase answered smugly.

"Well, of course he does." Levi sighed deeply and watched as Thane lifted a hundred-dollar bill in his direction. Shit, he'd forgotten the money for a tab. Levi turned back around, rolled his eyes, and sucked in a deep breath as the butterflies trapped in his stomach fought to break free. And... Oh. My. God. The realization hit him. He'd just sprung a boner in front of the owner of the club. Great. He scrubbed a hand over his face, dislodging the damn mask in the process, before reaching for his money to pay the bartender.

"He doesn't pay. Are all these his?"

Levi looked down at the three full glasses on his tray he hadn't even known was there.

"Yeah. He's buying the round."

"He's still staring at you," Quinn said to the small circle forming around him, bumping him in the shoulder like that was some sort of magical feat he'd achieved, effectively making everything a million times worse.

"He is," the bartender confirmed, lifting his head to look over his shoulder toward his section. Levi refused to look, all he saw was the teasing grin the guy gave. "He doesn't do things like this. He usually keeps his distance. He's got real clear ideas on who he does and when."

Levi lifted his eyes to the bartender and said the first thing that came to his mind. "He's gorgeous. I can't breathe."

As he dropped his head to his forearm, he just wanted to hide. The growing circle around him had an uproariously good laugh at his expense. Unfortunately, his humiliation had become their entertainment. It was all in good fun, but he hated being the center of attention. After a second more, Levi lifted his head and started to reach for his pad, knocking over a bowl of mints in the process. He dropped to his knees to pick up the scattered pieces. What else could possibly go wrong tonight? The owner was even more captivating than the guys had described. No one could compete with the locker-room talk he'd heard; yet, somehow the real Thane had. Surpassed it even. Seriously, no one could be that handsome.

"You okay?" A hand clamped on his shoulder and squeezed. Levi stayed in his squatted position, but turned his head, to look at Quinn who had bent to his level.

"I'm so clumsy, and I'm really embarrassed," Levi answered honestly.

"Of that peek of ass crack you're giving him now?" Quinn teased. The words took a second to sink in and as soon as the comment connected in his brain, he shot straight up, adjusting his waistband to the good-natured jabs of his co-workers.

"What's going on here?" Julian walked up on the scene, probably because none of the waitstaff was actually doing their job anymore.

"Levi's got Thane in his section, and he's got a chubby," Chase cheekily explained while staring at his package. Julian busted out a laugh, looking back at Thane then over at Levi.

"Yeah. He can do that to a guy. Everybody, get back to work. You can lose the masks. It's after ten," Julian said off-handedly, sliding right in next to Levi.

Levi did try to get a hold of himself as he pulled the mask over his head. He'd been at the bar too long. Slow service wasn't going to earn him any tips, especially where the owner was concerned, but damn, he couldn't stop the pounding of his heart or clear the fuzz from his brain so he could think a little straighter.

"You okay?" Julian asked, sounding concerned. Levi dropped his head, looking down at his own unruly dick; the heat of embarrassment crawled up his face once again. He couldn't hide the fact that his boss's boss had caused this reaction.

"I'm impressed. I didn't realize all that was going on down there. You should own it, he-man. Work it to your advantage. Just think about all the tips…" Julian's words trailed off.

Levi finally had the nerve to lift his eyes and meet Julian's amused stare. "I didn't…" He started then stumbled over those words. "He's really…" He stopped speaking and just blinked at Julian. "I can't. I'm embarrassed."

"You can and someday you'll figure all that out." Julian took the tray off the bar in an expert move, one Levi still hadn't gotten the hang of. "Take a break. Go take care of that." Julian nodded toward Levi's uncooperative dick. "And I'll take your tables until you've composed yourself, but hurry."

Levi couldn't even form enough coherent thought to utter a proper thank-you. He nodded at Julian, then turned and started for the breakroom. At the door, he couldn't help but glance over his shoulder toward his table. The owner of the club sat staring at him, some of the amusement gone as he lifted his brow in question. Fuck. The guy made him all flustered. Hell, he couldn't even control his own body around him it seemed. What a way to make a first impression, springing a boner in front of the owner. He so didn't need to have a hard-on for his new boss. He really needed this job. As he stepped behind the drape, he hoped he hadn't ruined everything.

~~~

Intrigued couldn't even begin to describe the way he felt. Thane sat alone at the table, his drink in hand and his gaze focused on the new hire, Levi. He'd been frozen in the same spot for the last three hours, watching, mesmerized as customer after customer made their move and was politely shot down. Damn, that boy was good-looking, and the brooding attitude only seemed to fascinate anyone in the vicinity, including Thane.
~~~

It was late and only the diehards were left behind. Thane decided on his plan of attack, and he'd implement that plan as soon as Levi came back with a refill. Levi hadn't made it easy. He was a reserved guy—hot as hell with those fuck-me green eyes, full lips, and all that smooth tempting skin, but he kept his distance. He didn't speak unless spoken to. Never furthering conversation, only answering questions asked directly to him. He was coy and had the playing hard to get down to an art. He knew how to garner the interest and keep the focus straight on him by turning down every single advance tossed his way, not only by Thane, but by everyone else too. No wonder Levi was a top earner of the group. Thane's interest had only skyrocketed with each passing minute, growing to an intense need to know everything about Levi in just a matter of a few hours.

Thane lifted the drink to his lips, draining the vodka before opening his mouth wider for an ice cube. He liked the idea of Levi turning everyone else down since he'd just decided the guy was the one he wanted to fill the paid companion spot Julian had vacated. Working at the club would complicate that though. He usually didn't have a problem sharing, but he didn't like to see it. He was selfish that way, shrewd enough to know he liked having his men focus their full attention on him, especially when he'd reserved their time. Those lines were going to be blurred if Levi kept this job.

"You're making him nervous, *papi*," Julian said, taking the seat closest to Thane.

"Good." Thane couldn't tear his eyes away from Levi who wiped a rag across the table he'd just cleaned.

"He's not like you and me," Julian stated. Thane didn't look over at his manager; he just kept staring at Levi and dropped another piece of ice in his mouth.

"Sure, he is. Everyone is," Thane answered confidently. Everyone had a price. Hell, he was honest enough with himself that he knew even he had a price. Thane just needed to figure out that price and nail Levi down.

"He's turned everyone down," Julian said like the Negative Nellie he'd become.

"Good," Thane countered. He wasn't going to be thwarted in his plan. "He should hold out for more money."

"Nah, that's not it. He could use the money. He sees himself in a different way. He's in medical school."

Thane lifted his brows, watching in fascination as all Levi's muscles flexed and shifted, working fluidly together even in something as mundane as cleaning the table. As if he had done something to gain attention, Levi glanced up, but only looking as far as Thane's glass before he dropped the rag on his tray and took off toward the bar with an unreadable expression on his face. Levi had never even asked if he wanted another drink. He was damn good at his job. Thane's drink didn't stay empty long.

"You know he was off thirty minutes ago," Julian said.

Thane continued tracking Levi's every move. "Then get lost so I can make my move."

Julian pushed away from the table, sliding off his chair. "I'm gonna love watching you crash and burn."

"Not likely," Thane said arrogantly. He was up for the challenge. Julian's statement just ensured Levi would make a mint off him tonight. He watched Levi talking to the bartender before he picked up the drink and the tray and headed his way.

"Here you go." Levi followed protocol every single time, laying a napkin on the table, followed by his drink, and then removing the empty glass and old napkin. "Ricco's gonna take care of you. I'm off for the night. My shift ended a while ago."

"Levi," he said before the handsome waiter could turn away. Levi used the old, soggy cocktail napkin to wipe at the already clean table, his brow lifted as if waiting to answer. "Levi, look at me." He grinned as he watched the subtle tightening of Levi's bare shoulders seconds before his gaze slid up, connecting to Thane's. Yeah, those eyes needed to stay right there. Thane sat up taller and shifted in his seat, aligning his body closer to the waiter's. "I'm interested in spending time with you. Are you interested? I'm willing to pay you handsomely for your companionship. Do you have a price or do I need to make you an offer?"

Levi's brows came together and uncertainty flashed briefly in those green eyes. His cheeks darkened just a bit, which made Thane's blood sizzle and his cock twitched with delight. Levi's innocent act pulled him right in, made him want to protect him, claim him, and keep him all to himself. The guy was totally playing the game, and he was damn good. He could only appear green under the collar once. He was more than likely calculating his next move, building his value by staying reserved and out of reach. You always wanted what you couldn't have, and Thane wanted Levi.

"I'll make you an offer," Thane growled, keeping his eyes locked with Levi's, which wasn't hard to do. So, the guy wanted something to brag about. He'd give it to him. Hell, he'd give him anything he asked for at this point, but he had to find a starting point. He was willing to start the offer at three times what some of the guys in here claimed to be the going rate. He was so confident he'd have his way, he even smiled as he said the amount. "Three thousand dollars, three hours starting in fifteen minutes, in my suite."

Levi stood to his full height, taking Thane's gaze with him. He was a tall guy, impressive in his size. "Did you say three thousand dollars?"

"I did indeed." Thane nodded, reaching for the new drink and taking a small sip. "I have a suite at Escape. I won't keep you all night. It's just been a little while for me and I want you in my bed."

A range of emotions crossed Levi's handsome face. He almost looked as if he were genuinely shocked. Again, all Thane could think was, if the guy played his part this well during negotiations, he couldn't wait to find out how well he played the part behind closed doors. He had to respect Levi for holding out for more. He was a businessman. He knew how it worked. The ball was in Levi's court now. So, Thane took a much longer drink this time, waiting for Levi to make the next move.

Levi opened his mouth, rocked back and forth on his heels. His gaze darted nervously around the club before he lowered the tray, placing it in front of his clearly willing cock. Thane grinned.

Hard to hide the body's natural response in so few clothes. Thane hadn't been mistaken—what he was feeling was definitely mutual. He couldn't wait to peel Levi out of that little swatch of material and taste him inch by glorious inch.

"I think Julian can help you find what you're looking for." As if Thane didn't already know that. Levi searched the club until he pointed at Julian who was having a giggling fit at the bar. Thane's brows snapped together at the implication Levi had just made. What the hell? His offer had been rejected, but he was willing to up the ante.

"But I want you. So I'm requesting you, not anyone else here," he explained, hoping they could come to an agreement quickly.

"Sir—"

Thane stopped him right there by holding up his hand. "Please don't call me sir." That one word put age on him that he didn't want Levi thinking about.

"I'm not interested in your money." Levi took a step backward, creating distance. "I appreciate the compliment, but check with Julian. He can help you out. Also, Ricco's got you covered. He'll be watching for your empty glass." Levi took another two or three steps backward before saying, "Goodnight."

He watched in confusion as Levi pivoted on his heels and walked away from him toward the employee locker room. He was at a loss, completely dumbfounded, as he watched the intriguing waiter disappear behind the thick, heavy curtain. Surely Levi was just making him sweat, guaranteeing himself a sweeter pot. Certainly, he would come back and take him up on his offer. But the curtain never moved; Levi didn't reappear. Laughter finally made him turn his head to see where the annoying noise was coming from. Julian, Ricco, and Quinn were clapping, applauding his very clearly predicted fail. Thane drained the glass, his beloved liquor tasting very much like the bitter pill he'd just been handed. Thane Walker, shot down in flames. He stayed seated for several minutes, going over the interaction that had just taken place.

Levi was interested, that was rigidly obvious. Maybe this was some sort of prank. After a good five minutes of him sitting there realizing that he was going to his suite alone and Julian and Ricco still smirking like his being turned down was the most hilarious thing they'd ever seen, Thane shoved off the stool.

He hadn't even tipped the guy for his service tonight.

He'd offered three thousand dollars for a few hours. He'd have gotten any of these guys for a third of that cost. Frustrated and horny, Thane looked around the club for someone to take the edge off. He stood there several minutes, scanning everyone, but none of them had auburn hair and startling green eyes.

Fuck.

CHAPTER 8

Days later, standing in the dead center of his grouping of tables, Levi fought the anxiety building in his chest. He could sense Thane Walker somewhere inside this club but couldn't quite locate exactly where he was. That thought thrilled him and unsettled him all at the same time. He scanned the entire area, trying in vain to spot the man before he popped up out of nowhere like he'd done several times before.

What the heck was wrong with him? Since the very first hour he'd started this job, he'd been hit on by men. He couldn't even take pride in the fact he had been hit on so much. Every waiter in the place got the same treatment. Julian sure had a knack for finding the hottest of the hot to work at the club. Sure, some of the guys made extra money giving blow jobs or letting some guy fuck them, but he certainly wasn't the only one who didn't go for that kind of thing. Half the guys there didn't give in to the advances. Yet, he'd wanted to give in to everything Thane had in mind.

Honestly, that three-thousand-dollar offer was what was wrong with him. Three thousand dollars would make a huge dent in their bills. Three thousand dollars for a few hours of sex with a man who made the guys in Levi's wet dreams look homely. Thane, who was so hot Levi should've been the one paying to have sex with him, certainly not the other way around. It had been a miserable two days to say the least. His dick hadn't let him forget he'd turned down one hell of a hookup. Levi couldn't jack himself enough to get any sort of relief. Thane Walker was a sexy, gorgeous man who had offered him three thousand dollars for sex.

One thing he hadn't considered until right that minute was how arrogant that made Thane sound. Levi had always thought the kinds of men who carelessly tossed money around were so full of themselves. After being on this job, he knew they were just proud of their accomplishments, and if anyone else benefited monetarily from their success, all the better. He looked down at his feet, then around him, and damn if he still wasn't standing right in the dead center of his section, trying to sort out the ramblings in his brain.

Having no idea how much time he'd wasted there, Levi looked toward his tables, caught some curious stares, and headed to the bar for refills.

"I got your request for time off. Mondays are hard nights to fill. Sure you don't want a different night off?" Julian asked. Levi hadn't even seen him sitting there. Papers were spread all over the bar, not that Levi had noticed them either. Man, he was off his game. All he could figure was that he needed some kind of break. He'd been working close to two full-time jobs, and trying to keep his family's lives together for months now.

Honestly, from the first moment he'd found out about his father's diagnosis, the worry he'd had for him consumed Levi's every action and all his thoughts. His father's memory still did even now. He had to be in mental overload; seriously, that was the only explanation he had for allowing Thane Walker to take up residence in his thoughts.

"Are you gonna answer or do I ask again?" Julian's abruptness got his attention.

Shit. "What was the question?" he asked, forcing himself to concentrate.

"Never mind. You need the time off." Julian dismissed him, leaning back over the documents on the bar. "We need to cut him first tonight," Julian said to Ricco who had grabbed Levi's pad. He hadn't even told the bartender the drinks. What was wrong with him? He was going to lose his job if he didn't pull himself together.

Levi didn't argue with being cut early. He needed it. Using two hands to hold his now-filled tray, he carefully weaved his way back to his tables, distributing the drinks before gathering the empty glasses and bottles. He paid no special attention to the customers, whether they were talking to him or each other. Instead, his mind focused on that set of deep brown, almost whisky-colored eyes he remembered so well. He wondered about Thane's ethnicity. Mediterranean? His dark smooth skin, black hair, and well-trimmed beard and mustache almost made him look devilish, but it was the eyes that kept coming back to haunt him. He'd been unsettled since the very moment he looked up to see that intense dark stare focused on him.

Three thousand dollars for one night… Hell, it would be worth *twenty* dollars for three hours. But what would he even have to do for three solid hours? That was a long time for sex. He'd never lasted anywhere close to that. That morning, while taking the bus into work, Thane's stamina became another burning question that had driven him to Google all the different ways to pleasure a man for hours. He'd gotten an eyeful in that search and had even expanded the query to find out about Viagra. He was relieved to discover the average sex act only lasted around five minutes. If that were the case, apparently, Levi wasn't so lacking after all.

"Hey, I need over there."

Levi looked up to see Chase waiting on him to move, and he didn't really remember walking to the bussing station to discard the dirty glasses.

"Sorry." He had to get Thane Walker out of his head.

"One of your tables wanted me to remind you he needed a refill," Chase said, moving in beside Levi as he took his tray and left the station.

Levi shook his head. He had to pull his shit together. He was panting around Thane like a teenage boy with a stupid crush. This had to stop.

~~~
~~~

Consumed was the only way to explain whatever the hell was happening to him. Thane's fascination bordered on obsession, which wasn't good. He stood in front of the glass in the office overlooking the man who seemed to have bewitched him, body and soul. Yes, that sounded dramatic, but that didn't make it any less true. He crossed his arms over his chest, keeping the background check they'd preformed on Levi Silva tightly in his grip.

Levi was younger than Thane had originally suspected, and that said a lot, because Thane's own age of twenty-nine seemed to take most people off guard too. But Levi was firmly on the younger side, having just turned twenty-six. The sixty-four-thousand-dollar question now was how a second-year medical student, from Thane's own alma mater, ended up on a completely opposite coast, waiting tables in a club designed to facilitate sexual companionship. What could have happened to cause such a contrasting change of scenery for this rousing guy?

The office door opened, and even if he hadn't got a whiff of Julian's cologne, he'd have known it was him. Julian had an air about him. His presence could be felt even before he was seen. Thane was glad the guy ran his club, couldn't ask for a better manager, even though said manager remained snide about his little defeat where Levi was concerned.

Julian had a quick mouth, the patience of Job, and wouldn't back down, not even with all the hostility Thane had been putting out into the world over the last forty-eight hours. Yeah, Thane was well aware how his constant barking out orders made most of the staff fearful of their jobs, but not Julian. Nope, not in the least. He always stood his ground, even laughing right in his face. The guy seriously had no trouble waving him off when he started picking apart the inadequacies he'd found over the last few days, and man, had those been plentiful, but Julian paid him no mind and straight out told him to get himself and his bad attitude out of the club.

Even when Thane went into a fiery explanation that he owned this club, Julian launched right back in a dramatic fashion, snapping his fingers, and reminding him he'd asked Julian to run this club not the other way around. Then he told him to go jack off or something because he was tired of all the testosterone-driven episodes.

"Are you done brooding?" Julian's smug tone was beginning to grate on Thane's nerves. He continued to stare down at the floor below, watching Levi Silva, refusing to speak to Julian. "Everybody gets shot down. He isn't like most of the guys who work here, Thane. He just reinforces the fact that not every person in the world can be bought. Build a fucking bridge; get the fuck over it. You're a damn buzz kill."

Thane heard Julian's message, but in the world he grew up in, someone on a full scholarship, who worked two jobs, could most definitely have enough money thrown their way to cave. He wondered why Levi was so different. There wasn't a boyfriend waiting in the wings, no committed relationship that he could find, and you'd better bet he'd asked around.

"He's smart, Thane. He's focused, and he knows what he wants."

"What's he doing here?" Thane turned to Julian who had pushed aside his laptop on the desk and laid his own paperwork on top of Thane's. Julian was bold. Too bold if you asked Thane. He could feel his scowl intensify as he stared at the disruption of his organized paperwork. He had no idea what he'd been working on but was certain it shouldn't be scattered around like that.

"Seriously?" Julian's disgruntled voice grabbed his attention. "Are you kidding me?"

"What?" he asked defensively.

"Didn't you hear me? The waiter you keep pretending not to watch down there is just as distracted and testy as you are. What else happened with you two that you're both so freaked out like this?" Julian asked.

That caught Thane's full attention. "What're you saying?"

"I just had this same thing happen. I speak, and you don't hear a damn word I say. Stop asking me questions if you're not listening to the answers." Julian yanked open his laptop and placed it on the desk.

"You know you work for me?" Thane stated in an attempt to clarify his position.

"Stop saying that. It's demeaning." Julian sighed dramatically then went back to what he'd been working on. Thane just blinked a couple of times. There were no words. And, by God, if Julian didn't have him by the balls. He wasn't going to fire him. If for no other reason than he'd spent too much money on training the guy. He was as much ingrained in this set-up as Thane himself. More so, even. Thane turned back to the window, and just like before, he zeroed in on Levi. He knew exactly where he was without having to look or search, zeroing straight in on him and watching everything he did.

He rested his palm on the glass as he leaned against it and shifted his weight from one foot to the other.

"Go talk to him. He's into you. Just don't offer him any money."

He slowly turned his head until he met Julian's stop-being-such-a-dumb-ass gaze. "I don't have sex without some sort of agreement. It's a lot less messy that way. No one gets hurt, and we both benefit, so I prefer money to exchange hands." Thane furrowed his brow and wondered why in the hell he'd phrased it like that to Julian. Julian knew the deal. Of course, he preferred a business relationship in all aspects of his life.

"Well then, you're gonna have to focus your attention elsewhere." Leave it to Julian to be so informative.

Thane was thankful Julian was done speaking. He'd been trying for two days to tell himself to focus his energies anywhere else—

"If you're gonna fuck him, then you'll have to stop your usual shit, and just put yourself out there. Save the money and buy him something nice if it makes you feel better."

Yeah, Mr. Bright-Ideas, he wasn't going to do that either. He risked the chance of Levi getting attached. To be honest, men like Levi—those seemingly honorable ones—were more prone to latch on like a stage-five clinger. Guys like Levi, if Julian's take on him was correct, usually harbored some unrealistic vision that a relationship meant security and trust. Hell, most guys their age seemed to have this idealistic view of love, marriage, and happily ever after. No. His parents' entire relationship proved a huge reminder of how fucked up two smart, reasonable people could truly be when they let emotions control a relationship.

Things would be so much easier if Levi would just take the damn money. Hell, three thousand dollars was more than fair. He was certain that no one else in the club made that kind of money for a few hours' worth of companionship.

"At the end of his shift, send him up here. I wanna talk to him alone," Thane said sternly.

"I'm not your assistant," Julian snapped. Thane looked over his shoulder. Julian hadn't budged, and his face remained buried in what he was working on.

"Just do it, Julian. Or better yet, get someone to cover his tables for a few minutes." Thane all but pleaded, before turning back to the mirrored glass, tightly crossing his arms over his chest when he located Levi.

"He's messing up tonight. He can't be making much money. I put him first on the cut list," Julian explained, giving Thane a small sliver of hope they might come to an understanding this evening after all.

"Then you better shag your sassy ass down there right now and tell him I want to see him."

"You don't pay me enough for this shit." Julian pushed back from the desk in a huff. Luckily for Thane, he went down without any further argument.

Thane watched Julian make his way across the crowded floor to Levi. They spoke for a few moments, then Julian pointed in his general direction. As if Levi knew the exact location where Thane stood, their gazes connected. Even if Levi couldn't see him, Thane felt the weight of his stare. Was there a hint of panic in his expression?

"Good. You need to look freaked."

Even then, it still took Levi some time. At least ten minutes passed before a knock landed on the door.

"Come in." Thane did little more than turn, keeping his arms crossed over his chest. He still held Levi's background report rolled in his hand. He waited until Levi was fully inside the office before he moved toward the desk. "Close the door, please."

There was a hesitation in Levi's steps and a strange expression crossed his face, but he did go back and shut the door. He remained close to the door, nervously shifting on his feet like he was about to bolt if Thane didn't start talking soon. Instead of rushing to speak, he placed the background check face down on his desk.

"I'm intrigued."

Damn if that wasn't the understatement of the year.

Levi's gaze didn't stray from his. Those penetrating green eyes disarmed him, erasing all the things he'd wanted to say. How was that even possible? The guy hadn't said a word, and Thane was thrown so far off his game he wrestled with his composure and struggled to push the unfamiliar feelings down.

"Julian explained that you helped him through his treatment. He says you picked up on things no one else did."

Levi remained silent. Thane instinctively knew that Levi was intuitive enough to know he was posturing. The silence spoke volumes. Thane took a closer look. Levi's expressive gaze held a seasoned maturity that he'd somehow missed before. Obviously, he'd lived life and learned lessons, perhaps a hard life to have mastered such a discerning stare.

"Are you mad or scared?" Thane asked.

Levi's broad shoulders rolled before his posture shifted to ramrod straight. "Neither."

"Then what are you?" Thane asked, moving to within a few feet.

"Wondering if I'm being fired." His gaze still didn't falter. *Very impressive.* Even Julian dropped his gaze on occasion.

"Why would you be fired?" Thane asked, although he probably knew that answer.

Levi didn't respond to the question. Instead, he remained silent, watching him.

"I'm attracted to you. I'd like to try things out, see if we can come to some sort of arrangement that would benefit us both. I can be very generous. What I'm offering isn't a traditional relationship in that sense, but it is a business relationship. Let's say an alternative arrangement between two consenting adults, nothing more. We can draw it up any way you like." Thane stopped speaking. He'd gotten ahead of himself. "I wanted you to know, unless we just don't mesh, I'm not talking about a one-time encounter." Thane moved closer. Levi's brow wrinkled. He must have started to panic, because he took a step back when Thane stepped forward.

Not willing to let the waiter slip away from him again, Thane reached forward, cupping the back of Levi's neck, feeling the slight tremor in his body as he pulled him forward and stepped firmly into the other man's personal space. Levi didn't struggle or push Thane away. Neither moved as everything around them faded away. He swore time stood still as he stared deeply into Levi's eyes. He'd never wanted anyone like he wanted Levi.

"I want to kiss you," Thane whispered.

Levi's intake of breath and the darkening of his eyes suggested Levi wanted the same. Thane gave in to the need coursing through his body and inched closer, waiting for an answer as the air around them sizzled with erotic tension. Levi's eyes darted to his lips, and he made a needy sound in the back of his throat as he closed the distance between them. The warm press of lips against his surprised him at first, but in the best of ways. One minute Levi was trying to escape out the door, and the next he was moving in for a kiss.

He'd expected some awkwardness. There was none. But what he hadn't been prepared for was the immediate current of electricity that spiked then surged through his veins and sent tingles racing up his spine. Nor had he anticipated the sweet taste of Levi's lips. They drove him to lick and nip greedily along the seam, needing and wanting more.

A quick exhale of breath caressed his face as Levi opened wider to allow Thane's tongue to slide forward and languidly stroke across Levi's. Fireworks exploded behind Thane's eyes as all thought and reason turned to uncontrollable desire. Levi deepened the kiss, tilting his head as his hands came to rest on

Thane's waist. Thane wrapped one then both arms around Levi, pulling him closer until their bodies were flush from head to toe.

He was instantly smitten.

Tenderly, the kiss continued. Their mouths fit perfectly together. Firm lips were warm, soft, and pliant under his. Thane gently urged Levi backward until his back hit the door. Something about that thump and Levi's hot skin under his palms had Thane's body beating a path straight to overdrive. He kissed Levi, hard and demanding, eating at his mouth while sliding his hands up Levi's sides. The waiter angled his body and ground his hips forward, matching his aching dick with one equally as rigid. And fuck it if this sensational guy didn't arch his hips, rolling them into Thane again, making it impossible for him to think.

Thane tore from the kiss, inching back to look at those beautiful kiss-swollen lips before he raised his gaze, watching as Levi's lust-filled gaze met his. "If it's not enough money, I'll up my offer to five thousand. I'll pay a monthly retainer for you to be available when I come to town. We could work it out where you don't have to work here any longer; you'll be taken care of. And just so you know, we both have the option of breaking it off if things don't work out. If you want out of this agreement at any time, I'll release you. I won't argue. If something changes, and I'm the one who wants out, I'll pay the agreed upon amount stated in our contract. It's better this way. We both know where we stand from the start. No messy breakup, no hurt feelings. Say yes."

Levi's breathing picked up, his eyelids closed, and the hands gripping Thane's shirt tugged him closer as that firm dick pressed firmly against his again. Thane allowed a small triumphant smile to curl his lips. They'd connected; that was obvious, and there was no denying Levi felt it too. They'd be explosive together.

Incendiary.

Something otherworldly.

Man, was he eager to get Levi upstairs to his suite to consummate their new business relationship. Yes, he wanted it all and was willing to do almost anything to get Levi to agree to the arrangement, even more so after the spontaneous combustion he'd experienced with one little taste. Thane rolled his hips, earning a small whimper as he cradled Levi's face in his palms. His eyes closed and he breathed Levi in as his mouth descended on those glorious lips once again.

The kiss lasted only a second before Levi's body tensed and the hands at his waist firmly shoved him back. He opened his eyes to see what might have caused the interruption, and his heart froze at the contempt staring back at him. He watched anger furrow Levi's brow as he pushed Thane firmly away, Levi's body heat stolen from him in a single shove. Unsure of what had caused the sudden change in the waiter, Thane stepped back to give Levi the room he was determined to have. His heart dropped to his stomach—it actually felt like a punch to the solar plexus. What the hell had happened? Levi had kissed him first. Surely, he hadn't been wrong about the connection. That kiss was what wet dreams were made of.

"I'm not for sale, and I won't be your whore."

Thane instantly went on the defensive. "Of course you're not a whore," he agreed, confused by Levi's sudden outburst and sharp tone. He jabbed his fingers through his hair in order to keep from reaching out and pulling the upset man against him and kissing this reaction away. "You were into the kiss."

"I got carried away. It was a hot kiss, but I'm not fucking you or anyone else for money. And I sure as hell won't be auditioning for a spot on your rent-boy roster. I have no interest in becoming one of the God knows how many guys on your payroll who wait for your summons to be fucked." Levi's anger seemed to spike, his eyes narrowing, and he grew more assertive with every word. But oh, holy hell! He was a glorious sight. His bare chest flushed, and the muscles in his arms flexed and tightened when Levi balled his hands into fists at his sides.

Thane couldn't think straight. Did Levi have a problem with exclusivity? Is that what this was about? That made no sense. How was Levi even thinking straight? *Shit*! This couldn't be happening. God damn, that kiss… They'd instinctively matched, touch for touch. That kind of connection didn't just happen every day. Thane should be on his knees, freeing that glorious cock right now. Not standing here hashing out every miniscule detail of their pending arrangement.

"I live across country, Levi. What're you wanting? A one-on-one exclusive agreement?" Shocking even himself, he'd consider the idea, if that was what Levi wanted. "You're gonna have to be damn good to keep me happy two thousand miles from here." His words hit the mark, but not like he'd intended. Levi reached for the door.

"Exactly why I'm not interested." Levi's shoulders straightened. "I don't do well with ultimatums, and I really don't like rich douche-bag assholes who use money to keep their consciences clear. Goodnight."

What? His brain had a hard time playing catch-up. "Wait," he called out franticly as Levi yanked the door open and stepped into the hallway. Thane couldn't go through another forty-eight hours like he'd just had. "If we test it out, and it works, you could fly…"

The door slammed shut before he could finish his sentence. Thane stood in disbelief. Well, that was a first. He threw open the door and trailed down the steps. He had to make this right. He wanted to explain. He needed to know why Levi had gone from hot and into him to cold and angry at him in the span of a few minutes.

Thane's heart beat quicker when he spotted Levi at the bar. Julian leaned in closer to Levi as Thane hit the last step. Whatever Levi said along with the look his manager must have seen on that expressive face had Julian intervening. Julian pointed Levi out of the bar while coming straight for him. Both of Julian's hands landed on his chest as Thane started toward the side of the bar Levi had just made a beeline too.

"Stop it, Thane. Not here," Julian said with authority in his voice.

"Move, Julian. I just want to talk to him. I need to know what I did," he growled, pushing his concerned friend's hands off his chest.

"Thane, just stop. Let him go. I sent him home for the night. He's not interested in the money. Stop being such a dense prick."

Julian stepped into Thane, blocking his path as Thane watched in regret as the exit door slammed shut.

Levi's kiss still burned on his lips, and all Thane wanted to do was run after him and convince him to give his way a try, but the look on Julian's face stopped him.

"Let him go, Thane. He's not ever gonna be one of your guys," Julian said, moving both hands to his shoulders and turning him back toward the office. "But there are plenty here willing to take his place."

Defeat rested heavy on his shoulders. Thane allowed himself to be redirected and led back to the office. He looked back over his shoulder toward the door Levi had escaped through, his intoxicating taste still lingering sweetly on Thane's lips. One single kiss and he'd been willing to give up everyone else. He didn't want to imagine what else he'd be willing to give up just to have those lips wrapped willingly around his dick.

"Thane, let it go," Julian repeated about halfway up the stairs.

"This is your fault. You hired him."

Julian had no response. All Julian did was shake his head, which was no help at all. Dragging his hands through his hair, Thane pivoted and rushed back down the stairs. This time he went in the opposite direction Levi had taken. He had to get away from this club. Thane let out a deep sigh as he crossed the walkway leading to the building which housed his suite. He needed a break…and a drink. This was all too much.

CHAPTER 9

Levi lay on his back in bed, staring up, watching the ceiling fan turn. His arms were crossed tightly over his chest, his ankles crossed, dressed for the day. He hadn't slept a wink all fucking night and now he just waited for six in the morning to hurry up and get there. To say he was wired was an understatement. He was stressed out. His scattered thoughts left him in an utter state of mental overload, and he absolutely refused to close his eyes. Any time he did, all he saw were the two most perfectly shaped lips descending to his and then the questioning stare and frantic state Thane had been in when he'd left.

Thane Walker had kissed him like he'd never been kissed before. From the way Thane's tongue had shamelessly slid across his, to the way he held Levi in his arms like he never wanted to let go, the moment was branded on his heart forever. The fact that he'd been so bold to kiss Thane first had taken him by surprise. That was so unlike him. Now that he'd had all night to think about his response, he could see how Thane could have misinterpreted his weakness as approval.

He'd wanted Thane so badly that he'd thrown all caution to the wind and decided to give in to his desire. Just being near him seemed to short circuit his brain. His cell phone rattled on the nightstand seconds before the alarm began to chirp. Thank God. Levi rolled off the bed, picking up his phone and turning off the alarm as he headed to his brothers' room. Levi pushed open the door with all the grace of a bull in a china shop and flipped on the overhead light. The groans started immediately.

"Up and at 'em."

Levi left his brothers whining about his insensitivity and made his way down the hall, going straight for the coffee maker in the kitchen.

By the time Logan reached the kitchen, Levi was guzzling his second cup of the strong, black brew. He saw lots of coffee in his future today.

"Why are you so on it?" Logan asked, dropping his tennis shoes on the table, heading to the cabinets with the coffee cups. Luke entered the room about twenty seconds later, pulling a T-shirt over his head, struggling with holding his shoes and putting his arms through the holes at the same time. Normally, Levi would have made fun of him, teasing the super-smart one of them about being seriously handicapped with his lack of common sense, but not this morning. He reached out, plucked the shoes from Luke's hand and dropped them on the floor. Luke looked at him like he'd solved the hardest mathematical equation on the planet and shoved the other arm through.

"You're already dressed?" Luke asked.

Just because he was in a testy mood, he threw out a "Nothing gets past you two." When they both looked up at him simultaneously, he let out a frustrated apology and grabbed the car keys off the hook. "Get your backpacks and clothes. Mrs. Rustenhaven said you could use the locker room to get dressed. I'm going to the car."

He was out the front door and waiting inside the driver's side of the car within minutes. Ten minutes later, they were parked alone in front of the dimly lit track. Levi climbed the fence to unlock the gate from the inside. As much as he could have used the rest, he and Luke were getting a lot out of this time. Logan was just taking one for the team, although he did seem to be smiling more these days. Levi appreciated that, but in this, Luke got to shine. The kid was Forest Gump. No kidding, he put his tennis shoes on and he could run for hours and never get tired.

They didn't have much to say this morning. Probably his fault, and after the first thirty or so minutes, Levi fell behind, Luke sped up, and Logan collapsed in the grass. Levi wasn't far behind Logan. He was a hot sweaty mess when he finally dropped to the ground, stretched out flat, and let the morning dew cool his skin as the sun began to rise. It had to be after seven by now.

"Luke, we got about ten minutes," Levi called out when he heard the rhythmic slap of shoes hitting the pavement as they drew closer.

"I think he's getting better," Logan said, tossing an arm over his eyes.

"We'll see today. They're including me," Levi said, half thinking about that, but dwelling more on this bad mood that had settled over him.

"We need to go to the Salvation Army after school. I gotta get new black slacks for my debate tonight. I tried mine on and they come up to my calves," Logan said.

"Did you see if I have any that fit?"

"Yeah, they're way too big in the waist, but they'll work with a belt if we can't swing the money."

"No, we can go. I'm off at the clinic at two today. I'll come by and pick you two up after school. We can go then."

"Whatever you want to do." Logan shoved up on his arm, looking at Levi. "Now that you're off on Friday and Saturday night, I should get a job and help."

Levi stared at Logan who busily pulled at the grass. "That's cool, if you want. Maybe I could take Luke out on Friday night, just me and him, but if I can get a weekend night, like I'm hoping, I'll have to take the shift. They tell me I'll make lots more money."

"I need to work. The debate team's going to Washington, DC, in May and we each have to come up with six hundred dollars. If I go to work at the print shop, they'll donate to my trip and pay me. I can make up the rest between now and then."

Another unexpected bill. Six hundred dollars was a lot of money to come up with over the next three months. Levi forced himself to stay chill, hide the anxiety from Logan. They'd figure it all out, hopefully. "I can help. And we should have the social security checks by then," Levi reasoned.

"I know, but it seems frivolous to me. I need to raise the money myself. They're gonna do some other fundraisers. If I can do them, I should be fine," Logan said and dropped back down on his back.

Luke came and flopped down on the ground beside them, barely huffing, but he did look happier. This had been a seriously good idea for the kid. "Will they let me help? I can do the fundraisers too."

Levi just lifted his brow and pushed up to sit next to Luke. "That would require social interaction," Levi said, raising a hand to ruffle his brother's hair. "Are you sure you can handle that? It might mean you have to talk to someone."

"Yeah. You've been babysitting me and losing work over it, so I have to try and pay that back."

Levi stared at his youngest brother as his grin spread. He didn't need that counseling update. Luke was doing better.

"You know what we haven't discussed? The way you two keep each other's secrets. Logan should have told me you weren't on the bus, that you were ditching school."

Both boys groaned and, suddenly, the grass they'd been so interested in earlier was forgotten as they scrambled to their feet. Seeing Luke engaged had settled some of Levi's bad mood. He sat there, watching his brothers start to walk toward the car.

"I think Dad would want me to ground you. Or give you more chores. Like Luke has to pick up Logan's dirty socks." Levi raised his voice so they'd hear him.

"Seriously, get over the socks," Logan called out, throwing his arms in the air, but not looking back.

"And how many bowls of cereal can one person eat in a day?" Levi mumbled, adding to the list of things he had to clean up.

Logan turned, walking backward. "Okay, I'll be truthful. Those are Luke's bowls."

"Dude. Why? He's already mad about the socks. Just take it all," Luke complained, shoving at Logan's arm. Levi laughed and pushed to his feet then jogged the small distance toward them. They were figuring it out.

~~~
~~~

Thane stood in the kitchen at Castelli's, arms crossed over his chest, legs spread wide in a dominant stance, as the entire kitchen staff worked feverishly on their knees, scrubbing the equipment to a pristine clean. He'd been at the restaurant all day, starting early that morning when he couldn't sleep and decided on doing a quality assurance check. It didn't matter that the Health Department had given them high marks on their last visit, Thane found them lacking and made his general manager call every person on his crew into work to rectify the problem. Minus Chef Ferico who was screaming at the top of his lungs at the GM behind the closed office door not ten feet away.

Apparently, the guy didn't like having his kitchen criticized. Too bad. Thane paid his salary.

"How's that?" One of the cooks who was on his knees asked, lowering the scrub brush he'd used. Thane bent at the knee and tilted his head, inspecting the work. He scanned the entire area, all the way around. Five other stations were being overhauled this same way. Thane finally nodded and motioned for the guy holding the hose to wash them down.

Thane went to the office and opened the door to an angry, red-faced chef in a full rant with the general manager trying to calm the guy down. He only paused when Thane spoke up. "I'm going next door. Tonight, let's say two in the morning, I want to meet you here to surprise the front-end cleaning company. We'll do this all over again."

"Thane, if you have a problem with how I'm—"

Thane shut the door in the man's face. He had no problem with anyone, except himself, and that tended to make those around him a little crazy. He couldn't help it. His mood was sour, his brain continued, over and over, to loop a set of emerald green eyes. Had the owner of those eyes not been so stubborn and stayed with him last night, none of this would be happening now. All his staff had Levi to thank for their midnight surprise inspection.

He left the restaurant, going to the front doors of the Chop House. They were locked and Thane wondered who might have warned them of his arrival. As he lifted his hand to bang on the door, his phone started to vibrate. He continued to bang as he answered the call.

"Hi, Thane, Julian called and suggested I make up some reason for you to come back here for an emergency," Jenna said happily.

"I'm sure he did," Thane said, staring in the small glass windows, looking for anyone who may be coming. He saw no one, which sent that spike of irritation soaring.

"How long are you there for?" she asked, unfazed by his answer or the tone he used. He needed more people like her working for him. These people were acting like babies.

"At least the next few days."

"All right. Well, Julian thinks you should come home now, but all I've got is a reminder that Saturday is the scheduled meeting here for the final blueprint inspection for the Reservations expansion. Outside of that, the Iron Maya's having their menu rollout. You're scheduled to fly to Texas a week from tomorrow…yes, next Tuesday. You've got a conference call scheduled with regionals Wednesday, I believe. It's all in your calendar."

"Right," Thane said, barely paying attention to a single word she said. He held the phone to his ear, anchored a hand against the door and dropped his head, wondering how the hell to get inside this restaurant without having to walk all the way around to the service entrance. When he closed his eyes, the images started again.

Levi's body so hard and yet so giving against his.

His muscular chest and stomach, ripped and toned. Perfect in every way. Except that damn flush that ran from his chest up his neck and colored his cheeks.

Fuck!

He was driving himself insane thinking about the all-American boy good looks. Clean-cut and innocent, but something in Levi's eyes said otherwise. The way he carried himself, proud of who he was but very afraid to let his guard down. Damn, this guy was a contradiction and one hell of a tempting distraction. His next thoughts were of that perfectly round ass and that hard as stone dick he'd felt grinding against him. Both were spectacular attributes—ones he desperately wanted to get his mouth on.

The frown tugged at his lips as dark thoughts started to fill his head. He'd offered more money than he'd ever paid anyone else. Hell, that amount would have made Julian giddy and Julian had been expensive to keep around.

"Maybe Julian's right. He's not for you," Thane whispered to himself, jolting upright when Jenna spoke.

"Thane! You aren't listening to me, are you?"

Hell no, he wasn't listening. "Email me, I gotta go." He ended the call, becoming more irritated by the second. He dialed the restaurant's telephone number. When the phone was answered, he barked, "Open the front doors. I've been out here knocking for ten minutes." He looked around when the Escape lobby grew silent, all eyes were on him.

He didn't care in the least, but he lifted a hand, hoping it showed as some sort of apology. When the doors opened, he came face-to-face with Steve. He'd been a long-time employee from the earliest days of his company, transferred out here when the restaurant opened.

"I've heard you're on a rampage which means something's not right in your personal life. That's fine, Thane, but we open in one hour. Whatever you're going to put us through can't stop prep."

Thane stepped past Steve, ignoring all his little revelations and declarations. "I want to check the grill gates. We keep getting hit for those."

Steve rolled his eyes and re-locked the doors. "Can't you go deal with Julian? He can handle you better than I can."

Thane left him standing there as he marched toward the kitchen. He scanned the dining room as he went and ticked off several possible concerns. No, they weren't terrible, but still outside his standards. "I already see three corporate violations. It's gonna be a long afternoon, Steve. You better call in extra staff."

CHAPTER 10

Three days later

How had the best possible paying job turned into the worst employment ever in a matter of a week? Levi grabbed a couple of empty beer mugs off a table, swiped another cocktail glass off the four-top while giving a nod at the raised finger refill request the guy at the booth gave him. He walked the long way around to the bar, still trying to sort his thoughts. He'd gone out of his way so many times tonight he had to have added an extra mile of walking, all to avoid a chance meeting with a man he couldn't get out of his head, a man who had the ability to wreck him with a single kiss. Thane Walker was a temptation he couldn't afford to tangle with, but unfortunately, all his thoughts centered on that man.

Earlier that evening, Levi had even been pleasantly surprised when he'd come home from his shift at the clinic to find Linda and Logan cooking dinner. Luke had been in the kitchen, not necessarily helping, but also not locked away in his bedroom. They'd eaten together like a normal family—they hadn't done that in so long. That had set a positive tone.

Yet, those few hopeful moments now paled with the tension Levi experienced. The rumor on the floor said Thane was in beast mode. He'd been finding fault with everybody and everything. The bar manager had quit before his shift had even started as well as the front-end manager in the fine-dining restaurant.

If the rumors were true, Thane had been working the dining manager's shift and ended up firing two of the restaurant's waiters after their shifts. Julian was in a tizzy, running around trying to put out all the little fires Thane started. Julian also helped tend bar, and Levi had just overheard an angry debate when Thane had entered the club tonight. Julian told Thane in no uncertain terms that he should never step foot inside this club again.

All the sexual tension from that shared mind-blowing kiss now seemed a distant memory, yet somehow, whatever was going on with Thane felt personal. Especially after the last half-hour. Thane had sat on the far side of the bar, perched on the edge of a barstool, sipping from a cocktail glass that never seemed to empty while staring at him. Tonight was hopping for the club, a drag show performance, the first for the bar, had the club packed. With the whole place virtually standing room only, Levi edged around the crowd to the small section of the bar designated for the waitstaff. The lights that had dimmed fifteen minutes ago, now shut off, throwing the club into darkness seconds before the stage lights turned on and the show's music began to play.

Levi ticked off a mental list of orders and called out three to the bartender. As he waited, a hand reached out from behind the curtain beside him and curled around his bicep. He was tugged behind the plush curtain. His body instinctively knew the identity of his assailant.

"Please, Levi. I'm sorry," Thane whispered, turning him, pulling them together, chest to chest. The drag show announcer's voice, along with the blood rushing through his pounding heart, completely faded away as Thane's breath tickled his ear. "You're driving me fucking crazy."

Firm lips crushed against his as Thane's persistent tongue pushed past his closed lips. Levi opened for Thane, welcoming the urgency of his kiss and letting the desperation of Thane's words drive him, and dear God, he wasn't disappointed. The man scrambled his brain. Like before, all thoughts of his problems fell away as Levi wrapped one of his arms around Thane's waist. How many times had he wished for this? For Thane to come to him, to want him. He couldn't pull the man close enough. Whatever this was between them felt too good.

Levi moved his fingers up Thane's back, one hand stopping to hold him firmly, the other slipping to the back of Thane's head, where he tangled his fingers in all that thick hair. Levi closed his eyes and just hung on. He surrendered to the frenzied domination Thane's kiss evoked.

Both Thane's palms slid to Levi's face, tilting his head. Levi's tongue prodded deeper, a growl of approval resonated from Thane's chest. Two strong arms wrapped like a vise around his body, pulling him snugly against Thane's hard chest.

The stolen moment ended as quickly as it had started. Levi whimpered when Thane withdrew from the kiss. Levi even followed, reaching out, searching for Thane's mouth, not ready to be done as Thane gasped, "Spend the night with me."

Desire coursed through him as Thane's palm smoothed over his cheek, his thumb tenderly caressing the skin as his forehead came to rest against Levi's.

"Tonight. Spend the night with me, tonight."

Levi wanted this to happen with Thane. He didn't care what that meant. He would deal with the consequences later. Right now, all he wanted was this man.

"Okay. I'll come up, but no talk of contracts." Levi moved, brushing his lips against Thane's, then Thane sealed the agreement with a simple press of their lips.

"I promise I won't push you. I have a suite. Come there right after you get cut."

Levi nodded, and Thane again placed a soft kiss on his lips, whispering right there.

"Promise me you'll be there."

"I will."

"Suite 602. Please at least come to talk to me. Six, zero, two."

Levi nodded. Thane's smile made Levi's knees weak as the arm locked around his waist loosened. He didn't want to leave the circle of Thane's arm, but he did, ducking back through the curtain, avoiding the curious stares of his team crowded there in line. His drinks were poured, sitting on his tray that had been pushed to the side. Julian stood in front of his tray, his keen stare boring into him. When Levi reached for the tray, Julian stopped him.

"You need me, I'm here." Julian's intensity turned to concern. Levi had no idea why, but his brain was still stuck in that devastatingly sexy kiss, his body still buzzing with all that pent-up energy and the anticipation of what the night held for him. He couldn't wait. The shift couldn't be over fast enough as far as he was concerned.

All he did was give Julian a nod as he took the tray and looked away, thinking over what he'd just committed himself to. His smile slid in place. Maybe now, he could think of something other than the possibility of being buried deep in that man or having that man moving inside him. He needed to call home, make sure his brothers were still good. Let them know he wouldn't be home until early in the morning.

~~~

Thane's heart raced as he took the elevator up to the sixth floor. The bad attitude he'd been throwing around for days had suddenly come to an abrupt end, transitioning to extreme anticipation. That second kiss had been as absolutely devastating as the first. Maybe even better, and when had that ever happened before? Thane closed his eyes, leaning back against the elevator wall, reliving that moment of startled green eyes turning seductive as they slid closed and Levi opened for him.

Dear Lord, the man could kiss. Even now, his dick wept in hope of what was to come. No question, he'd drop to his knees to pay homage to the bulge in Levi's underwear—maybe even the second he opened the door and pulled him inside. He wanted Levi there now. Thane opened his eyes and went for his cell phone. There were two middle-aged women in the elevator with him. His gaze skidded to the row of numbers above the doors. They were heading down.

Shit. Lost in his mental fantasy, he'd missed his floor. Hell, he hadn't even heard them enter.
~~~

Thane shook his head, ignored all that, and sent Julian a message. *"I'd probably cut him first if I were you."*

The excitement almost made him giddy. He was anxious about getting to his room and making everything perfect, which for anyone else in his shoes, would be par for the course, but he'd never been one to fret over details. How did Levi put him in such a state? He cursed the slow crawl of the elevator on his way back up to his missed floor. The ding sounded, and he was out of those doors and heading straight to his suite in seconds flat.

He'd only planned to be there a few days, and now, a week later, he had definitely outstayed his welcome. Thane ripped the *do not disturb* sign off the door and walked inside. The place was a mess, all the way to dirty dishes in the sink where he'd ordered room service and secluded himself in his suite while brooding about his situation with Levi.

He called out for Iris, the hotel's new AI interactive concierge, speaking to the hologram as it dropped down from the ceiling. "I need housekeeping in here, ASAP."

"Yes, sir, anything specific."

"I need a clean— Something substantial. I have a guest arriving in about an hour and a half."

"They're on their way up now, sir."

"Thanks, that's all," he said as her image began to fade.

Thane grabbed the dirty clothes off the sofa and lumped them under his arm while gathering the dishes and the newspaper as he reassured his irritatingly anxious analytical side. No, he hadn't forgotten the business arrangement he wanted with Levi. First, he just needed to see if they meshed well. He rolled his eyes at the absurdity of the thought; he'd bet everything he had that they would fit. As he passed by the front door on his way to the bedroom, he stopped abruptly and turned back to open the door. He knocked the kick stand in place to hold it open. Housecleaning would need immediate entry when they arrived. Nodding to himself that he had all in order, he continued to his bedroom.

~~~
~~~

In the short time he'd worked for Reservations, he'd never ventured far enough to even check out the inside lobby of Escape. To say he was impressed seemed such an understatement. He'd come inside through the back, assuming it was like any other large hotel, but not this one. There was an entire lobby, fully staffed, waiting to greet him. Nervous, he pulled out his phone for something to occupy his hands as he was greeted at the doors by a man in a suit.

"Can I help you, sir?"

Levi lifted a brow, looking down the length of his body at his new-to-him slim fit blue jeans and equally as new-to-him well-worn T-shirt all the way to his years-old fly-knit tennis shoes. He felt immediately underdressed. It seemed he always felt that way when coming to this side of town, especially when stepping onto the Escape property, even when he headed directly to the employee entrance. He adjusted the strap of his duffle bag that slung low from his shoulder and kept a tight grip on his phone.

"I'm going to room 602."

The guy nodded and started toward the elevators. "Come this way." It took the twenty-five or so steps for the guy to lift a hand to his ear, listen, then turned back to Levi. "You're Mr. Silva?"

Levi's brow furrowed, but he answered the man. "I am."

"Good. This is a private part of the resort. You have to be listed. You are." There was a brilliant smile as the greeter touched a box and an automated voice said *"Elevator D."* His guide walked the few feet to the automatically opening doors. "It'll take you straight there."

That was new. He'd never seen anything like this before. Within a minute, the doors were opening to the sixth floor. Wonderment more than anything else had Levi getting off the elevator, looking around at the grandeur of the foyer. He stopped at the guide panel. There were four rooms on this hall. Thane's was the only door in the direction the arrow pointed. He walked the length of that hall with his heart pounding in his chest until he got to the door marked 602. He stood there, staring. This wasn't the first time he'd hooked up with somebody, but he was still nervous.

"It's just sex," he whispered out loud. Yeah right. *Just sex with the man I've been fantasizing about for the last several days. The same man who owns the company I work for.* Shit! He was probably in over his head. National sexual harassment laws were made for boss/employee relationships for a reason.

What if he fires me?

Levi doubted that possibility, because the owner was the willing partner involved in *just sex.* Levi lifted his hand to knock but stopped mid-motion. Crap, he was going to text home and see how Linda, who'd volunteered to stay the night, and his brothers were holding up before he'd ever gotten this far. How had he forgotten that? Probably explained why he was still gripping his cell phone like a life-saving device. Damn, his nerves. Levi quickly typed a text to Logan.

The door opened in front of him. Levi kept his head down, but lifted his eyes from his phone as he pushed send. Thane stood in the doorway, looking like smoldering temptation and forbidden desire. *Fuck!* He smelled so good too.

Levi's dick was already trying to get the party started, agreeing excitedly that, yes, indeed Thane was sex-on-a-stick.

He tried to hold his nerves in check, not so sure he could pull this off. Thane had changed out of his suit, put on something more casual. Except Levi wasn't certain anything with Thane could ever be casual. Those brown eyes flickered with carnal promise. Levi was way out of his league with this guy. The choice of dark clothes did little more than accent the devilishly good looks, and Lord, did it feel like he was being invited into the devil's lair when Thane stepped back and extended a hand to welcome him in.

"Come in."

Levi's phone vibrated, drawing his attention down to the thumbs-up emoji. Steeling his spine, Levi took a breath, dropped his phone in his back jeans pocket, and entered the suite. Nervous and excited all at the same time.

"I'm glad you came."

Levi walked inside and just stared. He'd lived in the San Diego area his whole life. He knew people lived like this on the beach, but he had no idea how lavish the hotels were. His gaze swept the room, taking it all in. It was large and had a beautifully decorated living room, kitchen, and dining area with the whole back wall open to the patio. The dramatic blue seascape in the distance completely overshadowed the gray, black, and silver color scheme running throughout the plush room. The alluring ocean view beckoned him straight toward the patio until Thane lifted his duffle bag off his shoulder drawing his attention there.

"I'd like to think I'm the reason you're so distracted." Thane chuckled as Levi shrugged off the bag. The guy smelled so damn good. Levi turned and watched as Thane took his bag to the coat hanger and placed it on the hook. Levi needed to get himself under control, so he continued his path to the balcony, stepping through the open door into the unseasonably warm air outside, loving the feel of the breeze against his skin. He walked slowly all the way to the rail, breathing in the salty scent of ocean air. It was so welcoming and freeing.

"You don't say much." Thane's smooth voice sent a shiver up his spine as the sexy club owner slid in beside him. Levi split his attention between the churn of the water and the man leaning against the rail, staring at him. He could feel the weight of Thane's stare and the excited tingle starting to sizzle just under his skin from being watched.

"I'm in awe," Levi said, glancing over at Thane, grinning. He turned back to the ocean, not really understanding how much the water soothed him until right that minute.

"Again, not about me. It's the ocean that wins out this time."

Levi gave him a sideways glance, grinning broadly at the man who just made him feel like he was on cloud nine.

"I love when you smile, but I don't see you do it nearly enough."

Levi didn't know what to say to that. All he wanted was to feel Thane's lips against his. He wasn't good at small talk, and he was shit at accepting compliments. His brain was short circuiting, and having Thane so near had him wishing they'd skip the chitchat.

Thankfully, Thane's warm palm landed against the back of his neck. No other words were spoken as he was slowly drawn to Thane's lips. Chills broke out along his skin at the other man's touch. He angled his body, moving chest to chest with Thane as firm lips slanted over his. Thane's tongue licked across the seam of his lips, and he opened, their tongues meeting halfway. Levi groaned and sucked Thane's tongue between his lips. He didn't care if he seemed needy. Fuck it—he *was* needy. He slid his hands up Thane's back and deepened the kiss as his dick ardently pushed against his zipper.

Their tongues tangled, Thane's sweet taste branding itself straight into his memory. Thane had just upped the game in the kiss department. Damn, the man could kiss. He wasn't sure he'd ever been kissed so thoroughly in his life. He'd never thought that much about kissing, simply because he'd always raced to the finish—meaning most guys his age were all about the payoff—but there was something to be said for the slow build and the promises Thane's kisses held.

As his T-shirt was lifted, Levi moved his arms, holding them above his head, only breaking from the unforgettable kiss when the cotton was pulled over his head. The evening breeze cooled his heated skin as he dove straight back to Thane's eager lips, sliding his hands to the hem of Thane's polo and lifting his shirt. Thane wasn't near as helpful in removing the unwanted garment, his hands staying locked on Levi's ass, gripping him roughly and drawing him closer.

Levi wouldn't be thwarted. "Let me see you," he pleaded and lifted one of Thane's arms, nervously laughing as he tugged the shirt up. It got caught halfway, and he couldn't get it the rest of the way off until Thane agreed to participate in the removal. As Thane removed his shirt, Levi took the opportunity to see what those clothes were hiding. Thane's chest was broad, muscular, and when those brawny arms wrapped back around him, Thane's scent engulfed him, making him reach down to adjust his aching dick. He leaned backward to take in the tempting sight, because the first look hadn't been nearly long enough. Levi wanted to explore that expansive chest and tease those flat brown nipples with his tongue. Thane was everything he'd fantasized about.

Levi couldn't help his reaction as he leaned forward and ran his tongue across one of those dark disks, earning a surprised hiss from Thane. Yeah, they were outside, but from what he could tell, no one could see them, and to be honest, the thrill of doing something so forbidden while on this balcony made his dick even harder. He couldn't explain it, because he sure as hell wasn't an exhibitionist, but something about doing it with Thane had him throwing caution to the wind.

Thane's hand slipped into his waistband. "You're such a contradiction, Levi. You didn't wear underwear. Naughty boy." That husky growl had his dick twitching and his eyes rolling back in his head at the feel of Thane's fingers teasing across his length. Thane's other arm snaked up Levi's back, drawing him forward, back to Thane's waiting lips.

Thane was all over him, stroking him through his pants. So many sensations all at once had him melting against the other man. Levi tried to catch up, keep his body under control, but it was impossible. Thane made him feel wanted and wanton at the same time. Thane had rid him of his clothing, yet Levi had only managed to shove Thane's pants down before Thane broke from the kiss and nipped at his collarbone, trailing kisses down his stomach as he dropped to his knees.

Levi almost lost it when Thane's thick hand wrapped around his dick and started to stroke.

~~~

Best laid plans and all that, but Thane couldn't contain himself. Everything he'd planned to ease Levi into, all the well-thought-out scenarios, faded when he'd pressed his lips against Levi's. Even the need to have Levi's pouty lips wrapped around his dick first hadn't panned out. All his intentions were pushed to the side as Levi threw him off balance, made him want more from a lover than he ever had before. He hadn't expected Levi to be so
~~~

forward. And oh, how he now craved the small sounds Levi made when he touched him, stroked him.

Thane teased the beautiful dick in his hand while leaning forward, opening his mouth, licking slowly up the veiny underside, and lapping at the salty bead gathering at the tip. Levi's taste excited him, and he sucked the thick head into his mouth, teasing the slit with his tongue, drawing a mumbled curse from Levi as fingers tightened against his head. He'd thought the kiss had been perfect, but this moment topped anything before.

He swallowed Levi's cock greedily and was rewarded with the most delicious sounding moan. Thane lifted his gaze and connected with Levi's at the same moment one of Levi's hands left his hair and slid to his cheek, moving lower until the handsome man's fingers rested lightly on his jaw, and Levi began rocking his hips, sliding out then pushing back in.

Thane shut his eyes and opened his throat, imagining Levi pinning him down and pushing his way into his body. Levi moving inside him, making him burn—pounding into his body till he came. He took all of Levi, going down on him until his lips met the short perfectly groomed pubes. Levi's hands cradled his head, holding him in place as he began to fuck his mouth.

"I'm gonna come, Thane. Your mouth feels too good." Levi's thrusts didn't stop, but they became more controlled and measured. Oh no, that was in no plan Thane had. He lifted his eyes to Levi's and pushed his head back, releasing Levi's dick with a raunchy pop.

"So, what if you do? We have all night, and I sure as hell plan on coming more than once," he said, steadily stroking Levi as he spoke. He tilted his head to the side, his eyes still on Levi's as he lowered himself and leaned forward, mouthing Levi's sack. That got him a deep, swift intake of breath, which delighted him. He used the hand resting on Levi's thigh to help manipulate Levi's balls, alternating between licking them and rolling them in his palm.

"Damn! I wanna shoot down your throat."

Mission accomplished. Those words made Thane grin. That was exactly what he wanted too. Thane didn't have to be told twice. He licked up the side of Levi's dick then pressed his lips over the bulging vein before curling his tongue around the waiter's leaking tip. He swallowed him until Levi hit the back of his throat a little rougher than originally expected, making him gag.

Levi immediately pulled back. "I'm sorry. I didn't mean to be so…"

"I won't break, and honestly, I prefer for my lovers to be rough." He gave Levi a wink. "Fuck my mouth, Levi, and then I want you to fuck my ass." Yeah, he was being crass, but by the way Levi's eyes darkened and the way his breathing ramped up, the guy was completely on board. He had wondered if Levi would shy away from his requests, and he was pleasantly surprised when Levi took the initiative and shoved a thumb in Thane's mouth, holding his jaw open as he pushed his cock inside, never taking his eyes off Thane as he began to fuck into his mouth with complete abandon.

Thane had always tried to be a giving lover, but it was true he loved to be manhandled, and lost his shit when it strayed to the rougher side. He always wanted his partner's pleasure as well as his own, but this was different. He wanted everything Levi could give him. The carnal sounds Levi made took Thane's level of turned on into the stratosphere. He bobbed back and forth, working Levi with his mouth as well as he could. Levi's grip grew tighter and his thrusts more demanding. He held Thane's head in place as that hard dick filled his throat, and Thane swallowed around him.

Levi was doing as he'd requested, using him so deliciously. Thane barely had time to catch his breath as Levi's hips snapped forward, cutting off Thane's air again. Thane's own dick leaked like secrets from the Oval Office against his naked thigh. He couldn't let go of Levi's leg to stroke himself, which would probably have been a bad thing anyway. No doubt he'd come the second he touched his cock. He craved the feeling of being helpless and kept on the edge of madness. He wanted to come with Levi pounding into him like a madman. He shuddered at the delectable thought.

"Ah, fuck… I'm gonna…" Levi tried to shove him away, but Thane locked his hands around Levi's thighs and swallowed, hoping to send him fully over the ledge. Levi's dick swelled against his tongue seconds before Thane was rewarded with the salty taste of Levi's come as it coated his tongue and throat. Thane swallowed again, greedily this time, taking everything Levi gave.

That was all it took. Levi's essence completely intoxicated him.

~~~

Levi's head spun and his lungs screamed for air as he recovered from the intensity of his orgasm. Thane had completely blown his mind, not to mention his dick. All the talk about fucking Thane's ass had been enough to make him lose his shit.

Levi had come there expecting something completely different, but when Thane had confessed his intentions, that deep sexy voice clarifying his desires, Levi'd been so turned on that was all it took. He lost his load. Levi liked to bottom as much as he liked to top. He was honestly up for anything, so he would gladly take Thane's offer. Besides, more than once this week, he'd rocked that fantasy about burying himself in Thane and fucking him till he came screaming his name.

He didn't understand the need for labels, he liked sex any way he could get it, with or without anal penetration. In college, he had experimented every chance he got, but he hadn't ever experienced anything that had affected him like Thane Walker. He'd never forget having sex with Thane. He logically understood Thane wasn't going to magically fall for someone like him, but he kind of hoped Thane would remember their time together. Now, Levi had the ability to make sure he did.

Thane kissed his way up his body and took Levi's mouth in a demanding kiss. He could feel the hardness of Thane's erection sliding against his groin. That rigid, hot cock rubbed against him as Thane's zealous tongue ravished his mouth. Levi finally came to his senses enough to reach down and take Thane in hand.
~~~

Thane groaned when Levi slipped his hand around the thick length of Thane's dick and started to stroke him. It all seemed so surreal, the soft sound of the water meeting the shore, the cool breeze dancing across his skin, and Thane's hot body plastered to his. Somewhere on the way up Levi's body, Thane had lost his jeans.

"Let's go inside," Thane whispered against his lips.

All Levi could do was nod. He didn't want to lose the heat of Thane's body warming his, but he released Thane from his grip and allowed the man to lead him back inside, where they would have more privacy for all the things he wanted to do to this sexy man.

Levi stood in the bedroom doorway, watching Thane gather the supplies from the nightstand and toss them to the bed. Levi appreciated the display—Thane's perfect ass, his amazing body, his dick still hard as stone because he hadn't come. Thane had pushed his own needs aside and had selflessly taken care of Levi, and, man, he'd wanted him so badly it'd hurt.

Thane glanced over as if he'd just read Levi's thoughts and gave that sexy smile. Levi didn't say a word as he stalked across the room, tugged Thane back to him and caught Thane's mouth with his. Thane moaned into the kiss and Levi ran his hands over every inch of heated flesh he could reach.

Everything about Thane set him on fire, the way his body fit so perfectly against his, the way Thane made those sexy noises every time he traced the tip of Thane's dick with his thumb.

Thane broke from the kiss. "Are you gonna stand there teasing me, or are you going to fuck me?" He reached down and gripped Levi's cock. Thankfully, it rarely took him long to recover, and even with the mind-shattering blow job on the balcony, he was already plumped and eager for round two. Thane's touch sent his nerve endings into overdrive once again.

"Yes," he gasped as Thane gripped him tighter and squeezed the head of his cock. His mind was still reeling from Thane's words.

"Yes to the teasing or the fucking?" Thane laughed, releasing Levi's dick to pinch a nipple. That tweak ran through his body, making his dick twitch. His brain was scrambled enough as it was, and Thane's hands on him left him no time to catch up. Thane stepped away, taking all that wonderful heat with him as he crawled to the middle of the bed, rolled to his back, and spread his legs. "I guess since you can't make up your mind, I'm gonna have to start without you."

The snick of the plastic lid ripped Levi's attention from that tantalizing flesh laid out so provocatively to zero in on Thane's hands. The gorgeous guy had the lube open and was spreading it on his fingers. He tossed the bottle to the side and reached down to jack his dick a couple of times. Levi stood there, frozen in anticipation like a voyeur in a peep show, waiting for Thane to make his next move.

And move he did. Thane held him mesmerized, propping his feet on the bed, bending his knees so that Levi could see everything. Levi's dick leaked as Thane slid a finger across the puckered opening several times before it disappeared inside.

His knees went weak, and he took the opportunity to move to the end of the bed, watching as Thane fucked himself with his own fingers. He glanced up to Thane's face, the look in those whisky eyes as his pink tongue slid across his parted lips, made Levi move again. He crawled between Thane's parted legs and slid his hands up Thane's stomach and chest before slowly lowering himself on top of Thane's body.

"I'm glad you decided to join the party," Thane said in a deep, husky rumble as his hands slid around Levi's back.

Levi leaned in and pressed his lips to Thane's. The soft hair on Thane's legs brushed against his, driving him mad as their legs tangled on the cool sheets.

Thane moved under him, and he ground his hard dick against Thane's, both moaning at the pleasure the friction caused. He buried his face in Thane's neck, nipping at the soft skin. He was careful not to leave marks even though that was exactly what he wanted to do. He shook off the sudden swell of unwanted emotion and possessiveness swamping him and moved down to lick and tease Thane's nipple with his tongue, lightly biting and sucking the hardened bud into his mouth before moving to the other. Just as he started to trail wet kisses down Thane's stomach, strong hands gripped his head.

"No, I'll come if you put your mouth anywhere near my dick."

"Isn't that the plan?" he asked, confused. Levi pushed up on his knees, watching Thane's devilish smile grow. His heart skipped a beat at the sight. Damn those lips and those eyes.

"Yes, but I want you to fuck me till I come." Thane let his leg fall to the side, opening himself up in what Levi took as a blatant invitation.

Levi almost lost it for the second time since they'd been in that bedroom. Thane was quickly becoming his dream guy and truly seemed to want to be fucked. Levi didn't waste any time grabbing for the bottle of lube. He drizzled a good amount of the slick on his fingers and pushed Thane's leg back, opening him wider. Thane was so beautiful like this. The look in his eyes wrapped around both Levi's heart and balls and tightened, fanning the fire deep in his body. His only concern was pleasing this man. Levi took his time and circled the puckered skin with his index finger before pushing the digit inside the welcoming heat, letting the lube ease the way.

"More." Thane hissed and wiggled his ass. "I like the burn. It's okay. Give me more," Thane begged. So, Levi did as asked and pushed three fingers into Thane, and that decision earned him a satisfied throaty moan. He pumped his fingers in and out of Thane's body a few times, just to make sure he was ready.

"I thought you were going to fuck me, Levi."

"You didn't tell me you were as bossy in bed as you are at work," Levi replied lightheartedly as he rolled the condom on his aching length and lined up perfectly with Thane's entrance. The heat of Thane's body warming the tip of his cock as he pushed in had him struggling to go slow. He closed his eyes and fought the need to slam forward. The hard intake of Thane's breath as Levi sank into all that tight heat was erotic as hell.

"Fuck!" Thane's voice drew his attention as Levi froze in place and opened his eyes to judge the look on Thane's face. He stayed completely still, giving Thane a second to adjust; well, that wasn't true, but at least that reason sounded better than he was going to lose his load if he moved a muscle. All that intense heat gripping him, pulling him in, and holding him there threatened his stamina. He took a deep breath and pulled out, then immediately sank back in, doing it over and over till they both began to sweat. It felt so good to be in Thane, surrounded by this man.

No question, Levi had understood the deal before agreeing to meet Thane in his room. To Thane this was nothing more than a hookup, but from the very second he entered this suite, to right now, Levi couldn't help wanting more. They were good together. It felt right. They clicked from the very first touch. Levi sat up higher and gripped Thane's knee, pushing it back to his chest as he snapped his hips, fucking him for all he was worth.

"Right there!" Thane panted. Their eyes locked, stealing any perspective Levi had managed to hang on to. His hips faltered as he held the stare. His breath heaved and his heart pounded, not from exertion—no, something far, far different. It was too much for Levi to handle. He couldn't do it. He couldn't look into Thane's eyes, afraid he'd get lost in those amber orbs. How had he ever thought this could just be a casual hookup?

Self-preservation had Levi slowing his hips as he reached down and gripped the edge of the condom with his fingers. Carefully, he pulled out of Thane's body, avoiding eye-contact while he did. Facing Thane like this made everything all too real. Even as he told himself this was nothing more than a means to get off, he should be happy he had the chance, for him, at least, that had become a lie. He craved more.

"Why're you stopping? It felt so good. Come back," Thane protested, reaching out, trying to pull him down. He resisted Thane's pleas and sat up. None of this was as easy as he thought it would be.

"On all fours," he demanded.

"You're full of surprises, aren't you, Levi?" Thane quickly rolled to his stomach and pushed up on his knees, sticking his ass in the air.

"You have no idea." Levi crawled in behind him and slapped that perfect ass. He slid his hands over the smooth skin of Thane's ass. He had to push his emotions down and never let Thane know how much he truly affected him. Levi quickly gripped his dick and pushed back into Thane's amazing heat and held his hips in place as he started to fuck him in small measured thrusts.

"So good. Harder." Thane hissed, using his weight to speed up Levi's thrusts.

Yes, it was so good, too good. His nerve endings were firing with forbidden energy that ran up and down his spine in an unbreakable current. He needed to move inside Thane hard and fast, with complete abandon. Levi planted one foot on the bed and flexed his hips faster, giving in to Thane's demands. Thane tried to push himself up on his arms, but Levi wanted him right where he had him. He slid one palm up Thane's spine to the base of his neck. His fingers tangled roughly in Thane's thick hair as he forced the man's upper body back down onto the mattress, holding him there as he fucked him relentlessly. The sound of their bodies coming together was dirty and carnal and pushing him closer to the edge with every thrust.

"You're squeezing me so tight. I don't think I can last." Levi's other fingers tightened on Thane's hips as he drove mindlessly into the man over and over.

"I'm close. Don't stop," Thane panted, the muscles in his ass tightening and squeezing around Levi's dick like a vise.

Sweat rolled down his temple, and his lungs and thighs burned from his exertions. Levi continued the pounding rhythm, biting his lip hard to keep from giving in to his body's natural reaction, hoping beyond hope the pain would keep his mind focused and his hips moving. Nobody he'd ever been with felt as good as the man he was losing himself to. He squeezed his eyes shut and slid a hand around to grip Thane's hard cock.

The moan Thane gave when Levi's fingers wrapped around the hot, fleshy length went straight to Levi's balls, causing them to draw up tightly against his body. He stroked Thane in time with his thrusts and fought the need to come deep in Thane's ass. He released his grip on Thane's hair and moved that hand to his muscular shoulder, gripping there so he could pull Thane's body against him with even more force with every thrust. Thane's moans and clenching body urged him on with every snap of his hips.

"*Aggh, gadh…* Levi…" Thane groaned. His body stiffened, and his dick jerked, coating Levi's fingers in hot come.

It was all too much. The pressure that had been on a steady build shattered into a million points of pleasure. Spasms racked his body as his release hit him hard. The pounding of his heart thundered in his ears as his blood rushed from his brain as he emptied himself in the condom deep in Thane's ass, moments before collapsing on Thane's back. His weight pushed Thane down into the mattress. They both just lay there, breathing heavily, neither trying to move.

After a second or two, he turned his head and instinctively pressed a kiss to the side of Thane's neck. This had been too good. He was already so messed up for this man, and he didn't have the strength to fight it. His cheek caressed upward until his nose slid across Thane's sweat-soaked scalp, breathing him in. Maybe he could pull off the rest of the night without revealing how much he really liked Thane. Live in the moment. Take good memories away from this night. Maybe.

CHAPTER 11

Lazily Thane turned his head and reached back to run his fingers through Levi's damp hair and pull him in for a kiss, smiling even in the haze of the mind-blowing sex and his utter exhaustion. No, that wasn't the right word. Maybe…exertion better described it. Exhausted implied too tired to continue, and he planned at least two repeat performances before daylight arrived.

Levi might have the innocent boy-next-door look down, but he was assertive in bed. Thane had been more than surprised and fully delighted to discover the shy, hot waiter had a totally different side when it came to sex, and glory hallelujah, Thane couldn't have been happier with the possibility of his newfound arrangement. Now, he had something to look forward to and would thoroughly enjoy his visits to Coronado every chance he got.

Levi gave a grunt and pushed off him. The loss of Levi's hot body made Thane want to pout. It took a couple of solid tries before he managed to roll to his back where he ventured a peek, cracking his eyelids to see the same goofy satisfied grin spreading across Levi's handsome face that he felt on his.

"That was amaz—" Levi started.

"Fucking amazing. We're good together," Thane blurted out, not letting Levi finish his sentence.

"We are." Minutes passed before Levi spoke again. "Hey, was that a nude beach below?"

Huh? Of all the things Levi could have said after their time together, that wasn't even on the long list.

"Yeah. But why are you thinking about *them*. I want you to focus on me." Thane draped an arm over his eyes as he reached down to hold Levi's hand. Never one to cuddle, suddenly, he needed the intimacy and craved Levi's attention and touch. He didn't know if that was because Levi had just fucked him like a beast or he was becoming a tad bit possessive when it came to this handsome guy.

Levi chuckled. "Like anyone down there could compare to you on any level…"

Thane liked the nicely, and hopefully genuinely, uttered compliment. Levi's repeated rejections had seriously made him begin to question his confidence.

"You think I'm incomparable?" Thane asked, teasing a bit.

Levi's body tensed, and since Thane seemed tuned to everything Levi Silva, he looked over to see horror spreading across that beautiful face before Levi started to rise, pulling free of Thane's hold, even when he tightened his grip.

Wait. What just happened?

"Where are you going?" Thane asked, moving faster than he thought possible as he hooked an arm around Levi's waist, keeping Levi there where he belonged, against his chest. He wanted more serious cuddle time, and since Levi was an instrumental player in his plan, the sweet guy couldn't leave. Not yet.

"We need to clean up."

"Not yet. Please. Stay here." Thane locked his arms around Levi's waist, holding him there when he started to rise once again. "Tell me more about me being incomparable. I need reassurance."

Those words were meant to tease, but suddenly it seemed hard for Levi to lighten up. The guy was too young to be so serious all the time. When Levi finally turned back, Thane used both arms and drew him back to a lying position. He angled his body along Levi's, wrapping his arms and a leg over the guy's. He couldn't help himself; he buried his nose in Levi's hair and inhaled. The fresh clean scent of citrus shampoo was there under the smell of their combined exertions.

"Tell me what just happened that freaked you out," Thane said quietly, close to Levi's ear.

"You know you're gorgeous. No way you don't know that."

Thane propped his head on his elbow and looked down at Levi. That soothed his heart, but he didn't understand how that answered the question.

Thane leaned in, brushed his lips across Levi's cheek and whispered, "I'm really glad you think I am." The words were the truth and maybe more telling than he wanted to admit or convey. "I called down to the bar before you got here. They're open until four and serve their full menu."

Levi remained silent, lying there looking so beautiful and sated, gazing inquisitively back at him.

"What do you think about going down and having dinner with me?"

That brilliant smile flashed across Levi's handsome face. "I was trying to decide if that meant you were inviting me or kicking me out."

"What? No. You said the night. I'm not anywhere close to being finished with you," Thane said and, this time, leaned all the way in to kiss Levi's lips.

"So, you're feeding me to keep my energy up?" Levi asked, lifting a hand to push a stray piece of hair off Thane's forehead. Levi's mood was lighter again, very charming, maybe even enchanting with the way Thane's heart connected to that addicting smile. Right then, he knew, whatever caused Levi Silva to be so serious and remain at a distance, needed to change, and Thane wanted to be the one who changed it.

"Sounds good to me," Thane teased back, unprepared for the sudden move as Levi pushed up, dislodging him in the process.

"Then let's go. I'm starving." Levi was off the bed and heading for the bathroom in seconds flat, and Thane got the unexpected treat of watching Levi strut his naked, sexy ass through the bedroom. He tracked him all the way to the bathroom where unfortunately he disappeared behind the door. Next time, he would insist they have dinner in the room. Maybe he could talk Levi into naked sushi night and he could enjoy sampling fresh sushi off Levi's perfect body. Yeah, he was so going to suggest it.

~~~

Levi tried his best to be casual, roll with whatever came his way, but damn, it was hard to do. He was enjoying himself too much. Thane Walker was everything he had always wanted. All of his dreams coming true in a sexy, sweet package, which made the man dangerous. Levi had to find a way to keep perspective.

This elevator opened to the front of the resort and the nicest lobby Levi had ever seen anywhere, at any time. Thane insisted on letting him go first, although he had zero clue where he was heading. That didn't seem to matter to either one of them. Thane seemed happy to indulge Levi's curiosity, following as Levi went toward the magnificent indoor fountain. From there, he went immediately back across the lobby to the series of floor to ceiling paintings that caught his eye. He'd never seen anything like them before.

"The paintings or sculptures, or whatever they are, are incredible," Levi said, coming to a stop within two feet of the three individual panels, maybe fifteen feet high, mounted to the wall. They were so intricately put together that no space stood alone; the entire design seemed woven together with purpose, and Levi got lost in the colors. "They're like the ones you have in the club's office."

"You have a good eye. They're Kellus Hardin designs. He's the resort owner's husband. They're newly married," Thane said from behind him, wrapping both arms around his waist, drawing him back as Thane pressed the full length of his body against Levi's. Levi's body quivered, hyper-sensitive to Thane's touch. So when Thane's half-aroused dick aligned perfectly with his jean-covered crease, Levi grew hard himself, wanting that erection to be just for him. He resisted the sudden, slutty urge to grind himself against Thane.
~~~

"Gay?" Levi asked, looking over his shoulder. Thane was slow to answer as he laid a simple kiss on his temple. Levi's heart almost beat out of his chest at the sweet gesture.

"Very. Out and proud," Thane answered in a bit of a whisper.

"Mmm," Levi muttered, looking back at the painting.

"Come on. Let's eat so we can go back upstairs." Thane's breath burned his skin as he whispered the words in his ear; Levi's eyelids slid closed of their own accord. Man, Thane had smoldering down. In direct contrast to his words, Thane didn't let go. Instead, he placed another kiss on the skin just below Levi's ear then slid his hand underneath the front of Levi's T-shirt, his fingertips lightly tracing the valley between each muscle. Levi leaned in to the touch, resting his back against Thane's chest. "Have I told you I have a thing for auburn-headed guys?"

Levi tucked his chin to his chest, smiling at the sweetly uttered words. "No, and I'm not sure I should believe you."

Thane turned Levi while keeping him in the circle of his arms. "I don't lie. I might omit, but I don't lie. I've wondered if your hair color's real."

Levi slid both his arms around Thane, holding him tightly against his waist, hoping Thane could feel his desire. "I added some lowlights. Most of the time I do it on my own, but Julian made me clean myself up, so I went to his salon," Levi added, uncharacteristically unconcerned that they were standing in the middle of the lobby, chest to chest, and could be drawing anyone's eye.

"You cover the natural color?" he asked, his brow furrowing as if it were a crazy thought, making Levi laugh.

"I'm a weird contrast. My mom's mixed Hispanic and Dutch, so that's where I get my eyes, my height, and ability to tan. My dad was Brazilian, and I get my hair from him. I rarely freckle. My brothers both tend to freckle," he explained. "I started adding darker to my hair because otherwise people ask about my heritage a lot. I'm not good at talking to people, if you haven't noticed, so when I enrolled at Johns Hopkins, I added chestnut to my hair. With my skin tone and lighter hair color, I didn't make sense to them."

"I've heard you or Julian mention your dad and brothers. Where's your mom?" Thane asked.

Levi had no way of knowing how much Thane knew about his situation, and he decided not to expand. Talking about his life turned people weird, so he decided less-is-more might be the best approach.

"She died when I was younger. Wrong place at the wrong time kind of deal."

"I'm sorry. If it helps, I used to wish my father was dead…"

Levi's brow lifted in surprise at such a confession. Thane's face changed into something unreadable, and he immediately retracted those words.

"I didn't actually wish he was dead. That was horrible. I'm sorry. I wished he was gone from my life. I'm sorry to have said it that way." Thane grimaced and shook his head slightly.

"Have I not provided a very nice room where you two could get to?"

Levi turned to see a handsome man, grinning ear to ear, less than a foot from them. He hadn't even heard him walk up.

Thane loosened his hold, keeping one arm wrapped firmly around Levi as he turned. "We were actually heading to the grill." He noticed the arm at his back tightened, drawing him closer to Thane's side. Just another in a long line of moments that made him feel special. "Levi, meet Arik Layne."

Levi nodded, taking Arik's outstretched hand.

"Kellus is coming. He got sidetracked in the bar."

"I heard my name."

Levi recognized the name from the art and looked back to see a dark-haired man a few inches taller than he, strolling casually toward them.

Kellus moved in beside Arik and quietly whispered, "You've got to stop telling people I do the art. They feel obliged to tell me how good they think it is."

"I will, right after I introduce you to Thane Walker. He's the one we're doing the oils and vinegars with."

Kellus's face lit up as he looked over at Thane, taking his hand in one of those genuine thrilled-to-meet-you handshakes that lasted several seconds. "It's a pleasure to meet you. You've made me a happy man. Just so you know, our first few months of getting to know each other, A here pretended to eat somewhat healthy." Kellus gave Arik a critical look then started up again. "Anyway, he changed into a total foodie and his cravings were crazy and unhealthy, that is until he brought home your olive oils. Now he's eating all sorts of vegetables and fruits just to use all your blends. Thank you," Kellus said, grinning broadly.

"I'm not sure how much I had to do with it, but I'm glad he's eating better. Meet Levi. He's my date." All sets of eyes turned his way. These men were a force in all their focus, and out of nothing but practiced manners, Levi reached out, accepting Kellus's handshake. When silence lingered and he felt like he should say something, he turned to the art that Kellus may or may not like to talk about. "I was drawn to your art. It's a pleasure to meet you."

"I'm not sure he's telling you the truth, Kel. His back was to the art when I walked up," Arik teased, and Kellus knocked his husband in the arm.

"No, I just turned away. I was standing here for several minutes. It's beautiful…" Levi tried to explain even when Thane and Arik both started laughing.

"Ignore him. He's giving me a hard time at your expense," Kellus offered, nodding his head in Levi's direction. "Thank you for the compliment."

"We're late for dinner," Thane said, pulling him away, much to Levi's relief. He turned back, switching the arm that held Levi as he walked backward toward the bar. "We'll talk tomorrow about the holidays?"

"Only if we've agreed I'm going," Arik called back.

Levi watched Arik wave, saying goodbye before taking Kellus's hand in his as Thane turned around and started to explain. "He thinks I'm letting him have my spot on the HSN Thanksgiving special."

"Are you?" Levi asked, raising his brow. HSN sounded impressive.

"I might if you consider going out with me again that night," Thane cheekily answered with a complete non-answer. "You're very consuming. You'd definitely take my mind off my missed opportunity," Thane said again, coming in right next to him, wrapping an arm around his waist, bumping his hip as they came to a stop at the host stand.

Yep, he'd done it again. Levi was so off balance with Thane. The man oozed confidence. He knew how to chitchat, which drew people to him. He was so uninhibited with his attention, then saying things like wanting a date with him in nine months' time… Levi could feel the heartstrings pulling in his chest at the attention. Levi had never had this reaction before—to anyone. No one had been able to break down all the protective boundaries he'd placed around himself.

"I'm confused by that lack of answer. Is that possibly a yes or a solid maybe and I have my work cut out for me?" Thane winked at him before turning to the host. "I reserved a table in the grill."

"Yes, Thane. We have a table reserved, but we aren't too busy. You can really pick wherever you want to sit."

Thane took Levi's hand, guiding him inside the bar. From the hands lifted in greeting as they passed by, Thane knew several people there. But Thane didn't stop walking until he got to a back table in the corner. It was a highball table, and Thane extended a hand, letting him go first then following, moving his stool close to Levi.

"Do you need menus?" the host asked as they settled at that table.

"I think Levi may," Thane responded, resting his elbows on the table, leaning in closer to him.

"What do you normally get?" Levi asked, nervously wringing his hands under the table until one of Thane's palms slid between both of his.

"I go lean because of all the taste-testing I do. Grilled chicken and whatever the steamed vegetable is," Thane said as those whisky-colored eyes locked onto his.

"It's broccoli," the waitress added, relieving the host. Thane never turned away from him.

"Then broccoli it is."

"That sounds great to me," Levi said.

Thane finally looked the waitress's way. "I'll take a vodka tonic."

"Grey Goose with two limes?" the waitress questioned. Thane gave his grin, and Levi completely understood the waitress's dazed and confused stare as she had to force her eyes down after a pause. He wanted to commiserate with her; he totally got the Thane-effect. It was hard to concentrate on anything when Thane focused solely on him.

"I'll have the same," Levi said when she didn't look up. He had to throw her a bone. She just nodded, scribbling on the pad, without looking back at either of them as she headed off.

"You do that a lot," Levi said, bumping Thane in the shoulder, drawing his attention back to him.

"What?"

"You're really handsome. People get mesmerized," Levi answered honestly.

"That's how I feel about you," Thane said, resting an arm on the table, propping his head on his hand, just staring at Levi. Levi burst out in nervous laughter, embarrassed his laugh may have sounded a little hysterical. That was all right because he felt frantic, especially when Thane rubbed a hand up his thigh, moving his palm all the way to his dick. He lightly massaged there, Levi growing even harder at the touch. Damn, Thane's hand on him felt good. Thane made an appreciative noise in the back of his throat as he rubbed the heel of his palm along Levi's aching length.

Levi quickly covered Thane's hand, trying to stop him. The pressure was too much and felt too good. He had to put a halt to that. "People'll see."

"They'll be envious," Thane said and continued to stroke him. "Besides, the table drape hides you. It's why I chose this spot."

Levi pushed at Thane's hand until Thane performed another unexpected move and teased his fingers over Levi's nipples.

"You're gonna get us in trouble," Levi whispered, certain that everyone had to be watching them. Thane made him feel so good he almost didn't care. Almost.

Thane just laughed and tucked his fingers under Levi's thigh as the drinks came. He picked his glass up, extending it in a toast. "Drink up, lover boy. We're dancing. I bet you can bounce that ass, something I'm looking forward to watching, then I'm taking you back upstairs and plan to fuck you nice and slow."

Levi fought to hold back his groan as he lifted his glass. He'd lost his train of thought halfway into the toast. Thane laughed at him, then reached the rest of the way over to clink their glasses together. Levi took a long drink, downing the whole thing as his body heated at Thane's implication. God, he hoped Thane kept that promise.

~~~

"I think you got me drunk on purpose." Levi sighed as he swayed to the music, his warm breath tickling Thane's neck as his head rested on Thane's shoulder. Thane loved that move more than he wanted to admit—his arms wrapped around Levi, holding him close. He lowered his head to Levi's shoulder and tightened his arms. His hands had already found their way underneath the T-shirt, skimming the entirety of the skin on Levi's broad back. After watching Levi endlessly the last several days, waiting tables in that arousing uniform he wore, Thane had plenty of opportunity to see Levi's muscles in action, even before their hedonistic evening so far. Now, his fingers traced each and every one of those dents and curves as Levi moved in a languid rhythm to the sounds in the bar.

"I don't think you're drunk," Thane said and lifted Levi's face by the chin, kissing his lips. "You can twerk, and you're so damn sexy doing it."

Levi broke out in a brilliant smile, causing Thane's heart to stutter. "I've never done anything like that before."
~~~

"That's hard to believe. Your ass is made to bounce. I could watch you all day long. When you're working, your uniform doesn't fully cover the curve of your ass, either on the top or bottom. I don't think you realize that, do you?" Thane slid his fingers along the waistband of Levi's jeans until he slipped his fingers inside. He pushed them a little lower to feel the indentation leading to his crack. Thank God they'd gotten past Levi's initial reservations to touching, because he was pretty sure he'd never get tired of exploring this man's body.

Levi looked confused as he started to lower his head back to Thane's shoulder. "You fidget, and when you pull them up, your ass cheeks hang out, or when you draw them down over your ass cheeks, I see a little hint of crack. You're very tantalizing to watch," Thane confessed, pressing Levi's head back down to his shoulder.

"I'm having a good time. I needed a good time," Levi said quietly. It was late, the music not much louder than his speaking voice, making the sweet man in his arms easy to hear.

"Me too. It's been a while since I enjoyed myself this much." Shocked at his statement, Thane decided he might be a little tipsy too. Those kinds of words didn't slip out. But he didn't remember ever feeling this content. Certainly, never with one man before.

Thane decided to get bolder, wondering just how far Levi would let them go. He wouldn't have thought his shy, reserved guy would have allowed himself to be fondled under the table or touched on every inch of skin Thane could get to. Now, Thane slid his full hand inside the waistband of Levi's jeans. He turned the two of them, slowly angling Levi toward the back wall before shoving his hand lower and running his fingers lightly over the top of Levi's crack, earning an encouraging little groan.

Levi didn't lift his head, but he moved his arm to remove Thane's hand from his jeans. "Not here," he whispered.

Thane grinned. Levi would get used to his depravity. Thane preferred things a little naughty; being sneaky and doing things in public turned him on even more. His hand went back underneath Levi's T-shirt, slowly sliding up and around, his fingers teasing Levi's pebbled nipples. Levi's body concaved to get away from his touch, and this time he lifted his head, staring at Thane as he moved his hand again.

"Not here. It's not fair."

"Why not?" Thane grinned, tugging Levi against his chest. "It's foreplay."

"It's maddening."

"It's almost three o'clock in the morning. We're alone," Thane challenged. Levi looked over his shoulder and moved away.

"There're still people here. I can't get off in front of them."

"They don't count," Thane countered and Levi chuckled. Thane pushed Levi's head back to his shoulder. "Oh, listen. It's our song. Act like you care." After another second, Levi let out a long sigh, his breath coating Thane's skin, drawing Thane in as if he wasn't already there, flat against his body.

"It's Adele's 'Rolling in the Deep'," Levi replied, his head popping up. A look of amusement in his eyes. "You seriously want a depressing song to be our song?"

Thane hadn't even paid attention to what was playing. He listened for a second and chuckled himself. He guessed it wasn't quite right no matter how great her voice. Instead of saying that, he decided to tease Levi.

"You don't like the song I picked for us?" Thane asked, feigning hurt.

"Turn my sorrow into treasured gold?" Levi asked, echoing the words of the song.

Thane took that as an offer and reached down, gently grabbing Levi's package. The shock in his guy's eyes didn't quite match the needy arch his body gave, grinding his hard cock deeper into his palm. Levi definitely had a naughty side just waiting to be explored. Thane got two full rolls of Levi's balls in his hand before Levi managed to push his hand out of the way.

"Stop, you're gonna make me come."

The genuine banter and fun that was in no way formulated to entice had turned Thane's desire up a notch, and he stepped into Levi. "Then come. I won't tell." He crowded the handsome guy, snaking an arm around Levi's back, drawing him close as he traced the outline of Levi's hard cock, before giving him a gentle squeeze. "No one can see. They won't know unless you tell them."

Levi's eyes went wide. He stared at Thane as he continued to massage the hard length of flesh beneath his hand. Levi tore his gaze away, looking over Thane's shoulder with a huff of breath escaping. He could tell Levi was hesitant, but he also saw true desire smoldering beneath the surface, so Thane picked up the tempo.

"Relax. You look like a deer in headlights."

Levi's gaze landed back on him. This time desire was reflected in those glorious green eyes.

"Your eyes become vibrant when you're turned on." Thane removed his hand to slip his fingers under Levi's T-shirt, sliding his hand down the front of his jeans. If anyone got a good look their way, they'd know what he was doing, so he stepped forward, pushing Levi into a darker corner as his fingers grazed the hot flesh while his palm slid lower. He took Levi in his hand and stroked, caressed the tip with his thumb, then stroked again. "It feels good, doesn't it?"

"Thane…" Levi managed in a sensual, husky tone.

"Shh. I can feel you leaking for me, handsome."

Levi's eyes closed, and his forehead dropped to Thane's shoulder. Thane could feel Levi's heart pound against his chest where they were pressed together, the beat picking up with every stroke of his thumb across Levi's thick, broad head as he smeared the moisture gathered there. He worked him harder, causing Levi's unsteady breaths to come in shallow pants against his neck.

"You could touch me, too," Thane said breathily against Levi's ear. Surprisingly, Levi did. Levi's hand felt so good on his cock. Thane ground his hips forward, seeking more of Levi's touch. He could probably come right there on the dance floor if Levi kept it up.

Minutes later, Levi pulled his hand back and gently pushed him away, forcing Thane to remove his hand from inside Levi's pants.

"Can't… I need you, Thane. Take me back to the room. I want to feel you inside me." Levi was a sight to behold. That thick chest heaving, those spectacular eyes as vibrant as Thane had ever seen them. Thane didn't think it would take much to continue. He could get Levi to come in his arms, right there on the dance floor. As much as he'd like to do just that, ultimately, Thane wanted inside Levi's tight ass too.

This side of Levi was an unexpected treat. Instead of saying that, he chuckled and made a show of licking Levi's wetness from his fingers before cupping Levi's neck and drawing him forward. Levi's lips were pliant against his. God, Levi could kiss. Slow and demanding, a prelude of what was to come. He took his time and explored Levi's mouth with his tongue, chasing the intoxicating taste that was all Levi right there on the dance floor before taking his hand and guiding him out of the bar.

CHAPTER 12

The dinner had been fabulous, and the dancing had been a complete surprise. Levi had had a blast, more fun than he'd allowed himself to have in such a long time. Spending time with Thane was dangerous; he recognized that, but he couldn't bring himself to worry about that right now. Yes, he'd drunk a little more than usual, hence the make-out session in the elevator and all the way down the empty hallway. Thane had him so worked up by the time they made it back to the room he was nothing more than a quivering mess.

When the door to the suite closed, Thane again caught his mouth in a possessive kiss. All teeth, tongue, and passion as their mouths moved together in a frenzied give and take. Not even ten seconds inside the room, they were all over each other, seeking pleasure in the other's touch.

God, what this man did to him. When Levi had agreed to come upstairs, he hadn't expected it to mean anything, but it did. This whole night had weirdly begun to matter.

If Thane had any idea how much just being with him had affected Levi, would it make a difference? Levi tried to shut the unwanted allure down right there, stay in the moment. Their worlds were too different. No matter how good this night was, they didn't make sense together. He needed to focus on the time he did have with Thane. He would make the best of it and enjoy what he could get.

"I want you, Levi." Thane's lips moved along his jaw, and Levi tilted his head back to let Thane's teeth scrape against his neck. His dick throbbed and jerked behind the tight confines of his pants. Levi ground his dick hard against Thane's groin, moaning at the small amount of relief the pressure on his aching cock gave him.

"Yes." He slid his hands down Thane's side, stopping to lift the hem of his shirt over his head. He wanted Thane in him. He'd been thinking about that all through dinner. Every time they touched, it was like spontaneous combustion, their chemistry was off the charts. Thane helped with the shirt, then roughly stripped Levi of his. Levi took the moment to gaze at the expansive chest, the perfect, pebbled nipples. He lifted his gaze to Thane's amber eyes staring back at him, and what Levi saw made him take notice.

"Is something wrong?" he asked, trying to decipher the strange look.

"Just thinking about all the things I want to do to you." Thane reached out and palmed Levi's dick through his pants, squeezing just enough to make his hips flex and his body push into the touch. Damn, it felt good to have Thane's hands on him.

Thane licked his lips, drawing Levi's attention to the full pout that had looked so amazing wrapped around his dick earlier, but begged to be kissed now. This time, he took control and slanted his mouth over Thane's and used his body to push Thane against the nearest wall, pinning him there as they ravished each other's mouths. Thane's hands worked frantically to free him of his pants. God, how he wanted that too.

Levi broke free from the kiss, desperate to feel Thane's heated skin on his. Levi rushed to strip off his clothing, Thane doing the same, neither caring where their clothing ended up, just as long as they had bare skin to touch. No sooner had Thane stepped out of his pants and kicked them to the side than Levi was back on him, forcing him against the wall again. His mouth on Thane, drinking in the sweetness from his lips, tasting the salty skin along his jaw. Thane grabbed his ass cheeks, squeezing him roughly as he buried his face against Levi's neck, biting and teasing his earlobe.

"You make me crave things, Levi. I want your ass so bad." Thane pulled him in roughly and thrust against his thigh. "Can you feel how hard you make me?"

"Yes, I want to feel all that moving inside me." Heat coursed through him as he rutted against the man he had pinned to the wall. They were blissfully naked. The heat of Thane's skin and the feeling of Thane's hard cock brushing against his sent him into overdrive. He nipped and sucked at Thane's lips, before licking his way into Thane's mouth. He could still taste the alcohol and a hint of the sweet strawberries and chocolate they'd shared for dessert. Kissing this man was something he could become addicted to. Hell, he was already addicted.

He took Thane's hands and moved them above his head, trapping Thane's wrists in his palm while they kissed. He wanted to dominate him, possess him. Thane struggled in his grip, and damn if that didn't make him grind his dick harder against Thane. He liked these kissing sessions with Thane. No, *liked* only implied a little, he loved them. Kissing wasn't something he did a lot of. Most of the guys he'd been with, himself included, didn't take the time to draw it out like Thane did. Liquid fire coursed through his veins because of this man. He'd come twice tonight already, and he was hard as a rock and so ready to come again. Levi relaxed his grip, and Thane's hands slid free. In a surprise move, Thane swiveled his hips, turning Levi's back to the wall. Thane dropped to his knees and began to stroke him. *Oh, fuck, and yes, please!*

Levi sank against the wall to keep his balance and widened his stance.

"I simply can't get enough of your taste, Levi." Thane's hot breath swirled against his thigh as he nosed his balls and teased his dick, circling the tip, then rubbing a callused thumb across the slit. To have Thane paying so much attention to him was a heady feeling, something he'd never experienced before. Thane wasn't a selfish lover; that was for sure. This was the second time the man had dropped to his knees since he'd shown up at Thane's suite tonight.

All his thoughts vanished as the warm moist heat of Thane's mouth engulfed him. Damn! Thane could suck a dick. He'd never had anyone take care of him like this, see to his pleasure before their own. Levi's eyes slid shut as he slipped his fingers into Thane's hair. Holding Thane's head, he tipped his hips forward, taking advantage of the wet heat of Thane's throat.

"So good." He let himself go and just fucked into that welcoming mouth.

Thane pulled back, the cold air a stark contrast from the heat of Thane's throat. Levi heard Thane spit before wet fingers slid firmly behind his sac, pressing along the strip of flesh between his balls and ass. Thane mouthed him and rubbed him, applying the perfect amount of pressure as he sucked him deeper. Holy hell, the intensity of that sensation sent jolts of electricity racing straight to his balls. That mouth and those deft, wet fingers moved, teasing and massaging his most intimate spot, causing the muscles in his stomach to tighten with anticipation.

He pushed back against the delicious intrusion in his ass, loving the initial burn of Thane's finger breaching him. Thane sucked him deeper as he fucked back against that thick finger moving in his ass, opening him. When Thane's finger brushed over that spot deep inside him, he saw stars, his knees almost giving out from the surge of pleasure.

As much as he enjoyed Thane's mouth on him, he needed something more intense: he wanted Thane in him. He'd even fantasized a time or two about Thane bending him over the desk in the office and shoving into him. His hips sped up of their own accord; he was getting so close. Thane's mouth and the mental image of him being pounded over the desk bounced around his brain and threatened to send him over. He needed to get control of himself, because he wanted to come apart with Thane moving in him. Levi tightened his fingers in Thane's hair and pulled his head up. When Thane's gaze lifted to his, he all but begged. "Take me to the bedroom."

~~~
~~~

Levi Silva looked sexy as hell propped up on the thick pillows on his bed. That strong muscular body stretched out against the gray sheets still rumpled from their earlier exertions. His thick cock, hard and straining against his flat stomach, begged to be tasted yet again. Thane should have known that once he'd gotten a taste of the sexy waiter, he'd crave more. Once would never be enough. Levi was quickly becoming an addiction.

Levi regarded him intently, those searing green eyes hooded with lust and full of desire held a look that went straight to his balls. Yeah, that sexy look did it to him every time.

"Touch yourself for me." Thane noticed the hesitation in Levi's eyes. Maybe reassuring him would be a better approach, because he really wanted to see Levi stroking himself and giving over to the pleasure. "I wanna watch you. Show me, Levi," he said a little more assertively this time.

Levi lowered his eyes as he slowly took hold of that beautiful cock and dragged his fist up the thick shaft. Then that green gaze lifted to him again. The passion he saw there stole his breath. He couldn't help but wrap his fingers around his own aching length and stroke. The sexual tension in the room amped up as Levi's gaze dropped to where Thane slowly fucked into his own fist.

"That's it. Watch me, because I sure as hell like watching you." Thane stalked to the end of the bed and smoothed his free hand up Levi's naked thigh as he slowly crawled in next to that long, tempting body. "You're beautiful, Levi. Gorgeous like that." Thane praised him while continuing to stroke himself.

"Kiss me," Levi whispered breathlessly.

Thane bent down and took control of Levi's mouth, pushing his tongue in deep as he abandoned the hold he had on his own cock, shifted his position, and lowered himself between Levi's spread legs. His body fit perfectly in the cradle of those muscular thighs and effectively trapped both of their cocks between their bodies.

Levi threw a leg over him and arched his body up against him, the friction of their cocks sliding together made them both moan loudly. Levi's fingers skimmed over Thane's shoulders and slid into his hair as the kiss went from heated to sweltering.

Their tongues danced and swirled together in a frenzy of sizzling exploration. He didn't try to dominate the kiss; he was more than content to let Levi take what he wanted. The handsome man wasn't holding back. He demanded attention, and Thane was happy to oblige. Levi's mouth moved hungrily against his as their hips rocked together. The fingers in his hair tightened.

"I want to feel you in me." Levi panted into his mouth.

Thane didn't pull away from Levi's sweet lips as he pushed up on his knees and reached across to the nightstand to feel for the bottle of lube. Bingo. He hit the jackpot, finding both the condoms and lube. He wrapped his fingers around the strip of condoms and the small plastic bottle. Dropping condoms on the bed, he reluctantly pulled away from Levi's mouth to drizzle a fair amount of the lube on his fingers before getting himself in position.

Thane hiked up Levi's leg and pressed it toward his chest, then took his time and circled Levi's opening to spread the lube and tease it into his hole. He slowly and carefully pushed two fingers deep inside Levi then withdrew them almost completely before sliding them in again. He bent in and kissed the inside of Levi's knee as he pumped his fingers in and out of Levi's clenching hole a few times, enjoying the view as his digits disappeared into Levi's body. He curled his fingers and pressed against the spongy bundle of nerves, earning a loud whimper. When Levi's body tensed again, he glanced up to see Levi watching him intently, a strange look etched on his face this time. Concern flooded Thane, and he immediately stopped what he was doing.

"Are you okay?" he asked.

"More than. It feels really good. I'm ready." Levi held his gaze as he moved his hand over the mattress and picked up the strip of condoms that Thane had dropped there earlier.

"C'mere," Levi said huskily and reached for him. Damn if that deep timbre in Levi's voice didn't have him doing exactly as commanded. Levi's fingers wrapped around Thane's cock and began stroking. Thane groaned in pleasure, Levi's touch was like heaven on his aching length, but just as soon as he started to thrust into Levi's fist, the heat of his touch vanished.

"So not fair, Mr. Silva," he protested.

Levi's eyes bore into him as a smug grin spread across those full lips made even fuller from their kissing. Levi ripped the condom packet open with his teeth and, with undeniable skill, quickly rolled it down Thane's angry dick. "Then fuck me, Mr. Walker."

Oh, hell. He could get used to that dirty mouth. Those words coming from the innocent boy next door flipped every damn switch he had, and his dick jerked in complete agreement. Thane scooted in closer, grabbing a pillow in the process, and helped Levi lift his hips so he could put the pillow under them. Levi settled into place with his thighs spread over the top of Thane's and his ass tilted up just where Thane wanted. Thane sat up a little more, reaching for the lube again. He opened the top and dripped it on his length. After tossing the bottle to the side, he gripped his dick and stroked himself to spread the lube evenly along his shaft. He pushed Levi's legs back, opening him up even more as he slid his cock along Levi's crack to tease that enticing opening. Thane lined up right where he wanted and held his breath as he pushed in ever so slowly.

Warmth swamped the head of his cock as he pushed against the initial resistance of Levi's body. "Fuck, you're tight." He hissed through gritted teeth when Levi's body gave and those muscles grabbed him, tightened around him, and threatened to undo him. Thane's body trembled as he sank into all of that breath-stealing heat. He froze above Levi, stopping only long enough to let Levi relax beneath him before withdrawing and pushing back in again. He bit his lip as thrills of heat trailed up and down his spine.

Sweet Jesus, no one had ever felt as good, so hot and so perfect all at the same time. He thrust slow and steady with determination.

"Not complaining about fairness now, are you, Mr. Walker?"

Thane's dick twitched in response to the tone in Levi's smartass words. Smart and funny… God, this guy was wiggling his way into Thane's heart.

"Fuck no," he retorted. Gripping Levi's hips hard, he pulled him onto his cock, pushing Levi's legs back toward his chest as he did.

"Aahhh! God, you feel so good in me. I knew you would." Levi's words blanketed his heart and made him feel all warm and tingly inside.

"See, I'm so sma… Fuck! You're so smart. Damn, I can't think straight when I'm in you," he admitted and rolled his hips again, placing his hands on the back of Levi's thighs for leverage as he thrust in and out of all that tight heat. He wasn't moving too fast, but he was working diligently to stroke Levi's prostate. He wanted Levi begging, and he wanted to be the only one in control of Levi's pleasure.

Thane loved sex, loved it most any way he could get it. He especially loved the build-up of it all, got off on the games and doing it in public. He usually preferred it on the rougher side, but tonight, for some reason, he wanted to take Levi nice and slow. Just like this.

No doubt Levi's body was made for pleasure—for Thane to enjoy—and he planned on drawing it out for as long as possible.

Yeah, he could stay buried balls deep in Levi all night, and that was exactly what he planned on. He pushed in deep and circled his hips. Damn, he was losing himself in this man. Thane picked up the tempo, making his thrusts just hard enough to keep Levi whimpering softly as he took his mouth in a sweet and tender sampling of lips.

Levi hung on to him, fingers digging into his thighs, making breathless sounds that Thane greedily swallowed with his kisses.

Thane shifted his position, curled his arms under Levi's shoulders, and buried his face in Levi's neck, filling his lungs with the intoxicating scent that was all Levi Silva. He nibbled the soft skin below Levi's ear, before drawing the flesh between his lips, intent on leaving a mark. His hips sped up on their own as he thought about marking Levi and claiming him.

This infatuation he was developing for Levi was something new and completely unexpected and the thought lodged his heart in his throat.

He pushed up on his forearms and perched over the beautiful male, staring down at him as he pumped into his body.

Levi opened his eyes. Their gazes collided, and Thane swore the earth shook in that moment. Something passed between them, but before he could sort through the feeling, uncertainty flashed in Levi's eyes and he broke eye contact, looking anywhere but at Thane.

The awkward moment only lasted a fraction of a second. It was something he couldn't help but notice. He never wanted Levi to shy away from him. Maybe he needed reassurance.

"You're so beautiful, Levi." Thane lowered his head and took Levi's mouth like he took his ass, deliberate and oh so sweet, wet and so deep. Levi rocked his hips, meeting Thane thrust for thrust. Thane nipped at Levi's jaw as he fought to get closer to the man beneath him. Levi's strong thighs squeezed his sides then locked firmly around his body, forcing Thane deeper.

"Yes. There. Don't stop. I'm close." Levi's words tightened Thane's balls. His need to push Levi over the edge drove him, spurred him on. He wanted to feel Levi come undone all around him. Needed that shit like he needed air. Thane slid his hand between their sweat-slicked bodies, wrapped his fingers around Levi's leaking cock, and stroked him firmly.

Thane was so close too, eager for his own release, but he refused to come before Levi. He canted his hips, working to hit Levi's prostate with each snap of his hips.

"Let me feel you come," he pleaded desperately against the hot, damp skin of Levi's neck, gliding his fist over the hard flesh of Levi's erection.

"Gahhd... Thane...yes," Levi gasped ruggedly. The thick cock in Thane's hand jerked then coated his fingers in warmth, and Levi's ass clamped down on his dick, squeezing him so damn tight he thought he might have died and gone to heaven. He fucked Levi through his release. Levi's fingers dug into his back, the pain from his nails tipping the scale and speeding up Thane's thrusts. Pleasure built quickly along his spine then erupted in every nerve ending before shooting straight to his balls.

"Fuck, Levi… So damn hot." Thane screwed his eyes shut, pulled out then shoved back into Levi's quivering body one last time, a strangled cry escaping his lips as he wedged himself deeper in Levi's clenching ass. His muscles seized; his orgasm hit him so hard he saw stars. Adrenaline rushed like molten lava through every vein, the sound of his heart trying to beat out of his chest echoed in his ears. Oxygen was suddenly hard to find as those bright bursts continued flashing behind his eyes as he came completely undone buried deep in Levi's perfect ass. Levi's legs loosened from around his waist as Thane collapsed completely on top of Levi from the intensity of his release.

Both men lay motionless, their bodies still locked together as the sound of their heavy breathing filled the room. He was in no rush to pull away from Levi. He enjoyed the feel of the man beneath him, plus he didn't have the strength just yet.

~~~

"It's four forty-five in the morning," Thane whispered. He couldn't remember the last time he'd had such an enchanting evening. Honestly, he didn't want their time together to end. Levi was so different than any of the others before. Thane's fingers trailed lazily up then down the length of Levi's arm. Levi had most of his whole body wrapped tightly around Thane's. He'd have to remember to compliment Arik on his mattresses. He hadn't realized until tonight how comfortable they were. He'd been lying just like this for thirty solid minutes and had zero desire to move.

Levi's hand drifted toward his face, his fingers lightly brushing across his trimmed beard before sliding to his neck, tangling in the short hairs there. "This has been a much-needed mental break. I forgot myself tonight. I needed that."

"Hmm, I could say the same thing. You're really good company." Thane turned his head slightly to the left, kissing Levi's temple.
~~~

"We're good together," Levi said, emphasizing what Thane already knew. Levi let out a jaw-cracking yawn. "If I don't get up and leave, I'll probably end up falling asleep."

"Don't leave yet. Sleep. I like you here in my arms."

Levi seemed on board as he snuggled close enough his head lay partially on Thane's pillow, but mostly in the crook of his neck. The whole left side of his body was covered in Levi Silva, and Thane found himself drawing the covers up, tucking Levi in, making sure he was warm. Levi's soft snores had warm breath caressing Thane's chest. He liked that a lot. He felt renewed. Thane tightened his hold on Levi's body and let himself revel in the feeling.

There was no question in Thane's mind—he could lie just like this forever. Cuddling wasn't something he normally did. He closed his eyes, breathing Levi in, even as warning bells rang in the farthest recesses of his mind. He refused to pay them any attention. He'd never had a situation in his life where he fit so well with another person.

Thane's eyelids slid open. He stared at the darkness of the room while his heart ached. This was exactly what he'd done before. He was all-in then reality came crashing back.

But his emotions had never been as strong as this. His heart had connected tonight. He wanted more of these moments with this man. Nevertheless, the infatuation he was feeling was the getting-to-know-each-other, the butterflies, the learning-each-other part of any new relationship. Everything was fresh and new to both of them right now and didn't count in the overall big picture of what happened after. The main reason he'd created safeguards was to avoid ever being caught off guard again. Newness didn't replace reason, no matter how good it felt.

He'd never in his life experienced the raw, organic sense of peace and needing he had with Levi. His arms tightened around the body resting on his. He never wanted to let him go. He ran his hand up Levi's back, and Levi shifted, arms and legs wrapping all around him, Levi's lips moving over his skin, placing a kiss along his jaw.

"You make me feel wanted," Levi whispered, running his nose along the length of Thane's skin. As suddenly as he woke, the silent snores were back, and Levi was completely asleep again.

Thane couldn't push Levi's words out of his head as he lay there thinking about the evening and how much he loved the feel of this man in his arms. Admittedly, a little more than he should. Their night together had been a fairytale—an enchanting, magical dream with no basis in reality. Levi had somehow wedged his way into Thane's heart in just a matter of a few hours. But Thane couldn't risk starting a relationship, not with this man. He'd ruin everything, like always. He'd break Levi, make him jaded, and it would ultimately crush Thane's heart to hurt Levi.

Even though Thane knew what he needed to do, he still couldn't release Levi from his arms. What if Levi was the one? What if they were meant to be? The thought caused him to lean over and place a kiss against the exposed skin of Levi's shoulder. Levi could certainly be his prince charming, not completely out of the question.

What the hell was wrong with him? He had to stop this line of thinking. He couldn't entertain the thought of forever with anyone, especially someone like Levi, because forever wasn't real. He knew this; his parents were prime examples. There wasn't a happily ever after; he learned that a long time ago.

So, why did his heart say differently? The weird emotional tingles he'd felt could be blamed on the newness of the whole situation; plus, he hadn't had sex in a while. Yeah, that was where all the crazy thoughts were coming from, had to be.

He'd met this beautiful man on the club floor wearing nothing but a tiny scrap of shiny material. He'd been so shy and somewhat standoffish, but Thane had been instantly taken with Levi, almost to the point of obsession. Not only by his boy-next-door good looks, but he'd quickly found out Levi was kind, smart, and wise beyond his twenty-six years. Levi flipped every switch he had.

Was he confusing lust with love? Yes, and he couldn't go there again. That was the bottom line. Never again.

Unfortunately, Thane had just discovered his weakness: sexy, sweet, smart but vulnerable men with auburn hair and green eyes. No. He chastised himself; he wouldn't do this again. He hadn't dug in and found out what made Levi such a guarded man, because the less he knew, the less involved he was in Levi's life, the better off they both were.

Thane allowed himself one hour to hold Levi in his arms before he carefully pulled free. Leaving Levi sleeping alone in that bed might have been the hardest thing he'd ever done, especially when everything inside him wanted to wake his sleeping beauty and make love to him right there. But he couldn't, not with all this vulnerability coursing through him. Maybe once he had himself under control and an agreement in place that could protect them both from the emotional fallout.

Luckily, the ache in his heart ebbed as he pushed away those feelings, growing void of emotion as if his heart ceased to do anything more than beat to keep him alive. This was how it had to be. He pulled the blanket over Levi and turned away. With each step he took, the place where his heart had rested turned colder. Now that he wasn't letting his emotions guide him, logic could reign supreme. With his plan in place, Thane quietly dressed then went for his safe in the living room. He would make it quick and as painless as possible. It was best for both of them this way.

After gathering what he needed, he quickly scrawled out a note. At this point, part of him hoped Levi didn't take him up on his offer. Thane had a feeling that every time with Levi would be more special than the last. And that was something he was afraid his heart couldn't handle. He would be fighting an internal struggle with his emotions every time he came to Coronado.

CHAPTER 13

Levi's eyelids fluttered opened as he looked around and lifted himself enough to stare at the clock on the nightstand. Ten fifteen in the morning. He never slept this late. Thankfully, the PT clinic was doing some restructuring, reworking everyone's schedule, and they had given him the afternoon shift. He didn't have to rush.

Levi searched the room. No sign of Thane. One of his first thoughts was how pretty the room was; his second was wondering if those windows opened to the outside. He hadn't noticed that last night, and his next thought was that it was quiet, not a sound inside the suite. Thane was either super silent or gone.

Levi whipped the blankets off his body, yawning as he got to his feet and went immediately to the bathroom. His clothes were folded together with his tennis shoes lying right underneath. A toothbrush and toothpaste, along with a brush were close by. That must mean Thane was gone. Damn. His hard dick could've gone for another round this morning. He wished he would have woken before Thane left.

Levi quickly relieved himself then got hold of his dick—literally—before dressing as he tried to remember if he had clothes in the car to change into for work. He hoped he did, but if not, he'd have time to swing by the house. He'd just like to get in a workout before his shift. In the bedroom, he flipped on the light switch, hoping Thane had left a note. If not, he'd have to.

It wasn't the best time in his life to start something up, but their connection was too strong. He couldn't just let something like this slip through his fingers. He'd enjoyed everything they'd done last night. His gaze slid across the dresser then the nightstand on his side of the bed.

What the…?

Oh, God no. It couldn't be. Pain shot through him seconds before his heart shattered into a million tiny pieces and dropped into his stomach making him physically ill. He sucked in a deep breath as he hesitantly stepped closer to the stack of money taunting him. He stood there, staring down at what felt like a slap in the face. His hands trembled, and the heaviness of the implications weighed down on him.

Everything he'd felt last night, everything Thane had whispered to him had been a lie. To Thane, he was nothing more than a whore. The pain was almost too much, the humiliation unbearable. He was mortified. He couldn't touch the cash. It represented his total stupidity. How had he not known better? He just stared at the small stack with a simple printed band that said one thousand dollars. There were five of them.

His shoulders slumped as he broke on the inside. The weight of it all too much to bear. He reached behind him for the side of the bed. His brain froze, having a much harder time processing what was happening. No, he knew what was happening. His heart just didn't want to recognize it for what it was. His heart pounded so loud now that he heard nothing but the frantic drumming as he picked up the handwritten note.

Levi,

We can do things your way if you're willing to fly to me a couple of times a month. I've been spending significant time here in Coronado. I'm sure I can continue these trips. There's more in the dresser's right-side drawer to help get you set up. I have dinner parties which require formal clothing. I have a shopper who helped Julian. I'll give her your telephone number. We can discuss a monthly stipend and the logistics. I'd prefer you not continue to work at the bar. I seem to get a little possessive where you're concerned. Don't worry. I'm sure that will work out. I'll get you all my contact information.

I'm looking forward to continuing our relationship. I thoroughly enjoyed myself last night. Knew you'd be worth the chase.

I like the natural color of your hair. We'll talk soon.
Thane

He sank lower on the bed. How had he gone from floating on such a high because he thought he was wanted and life was evening out again to waking this morning and being back to nothing more than a paid fuck in less than a minute? He stared down at the carpet, the note still dangling in his hand. Man, he'd loved last night. He'd needed last night. How could he have been so stupid?

Levi crumpled the note in his hand, angrily tossing the wadded paper to the floor, and dropped his head to his hands. Through the whole deal with his father, he'd tried to be strong, tried to do right by his brothers. He had refused to do anything more than keep hope alive, not allow the past-due bills, all the stress of suddenly becoming the caretaker to two teenage boys, delaying his dream of becoming a doctor get to him…until right this moment.

Every single minute of their night together had been etched in both his heart and head. Permanently cemented there. Thane had built him up, made him feel special, and cut him to the quick in less than twenty-four hours. Now the only thing he felt was tawdry and sordid.

Levi pushed off the side of the bed. His legs felt like rubber. His stomach threatened to revolt. How could he have been so blind? He reached down, picking up the bundles still taunting him.

Money ran the world. He should be thankful for the amount. Hell, he should be thankful for the offer. All he had to do was let some guy fuck him for more money than he made in a month and a half of daily work. But he wasn't thankful; he felt used and lost. He let the money slip through his fingers too, dropping it all to the floor. He felt around his pockets, found his keys in the front, and went for his cell phone on the bar counter. He swiped his finger across the screen to find a text from his brother.

"We have a half day. We're out at 11:30 and we're out of food. We think El Pollo Loco's a good idea. I'd go, but you still have the car."

Levi took a deep breath and fought the tears forming behind his closed eyes. He didn't even know why he wanted to cry, but he swore to hell he wouldn't. One thing was certain: he never wanted to feel like this ever again.

He needed to quit his job.

No, he couldn't.

He had the boys to worry about. His little brother wanted to go to DC. How could he deny him that chance? God, he was screwed! He wanted to rage. He wasn't a whore. But he sure as hell felt like one. He needed the job, needed the money.

He could find another job waiting tables somewhere else. But nowhere would pay as much as he made at Reservations.

Levi shook his head and walked in a daze to the suite door, refusing to look at any of the opulence surrounding him. He grabbed his duffle bag and decided to put the job decision off. It was Friday, and he didn't have to be at work at the club until Sunday evening. He'd decide what to do tomorrow. Tucking his phone in his back pocket, Levi left the hotel room. The loud click of the lock as the door closed behind him echoed in the empty corridor. Humiliation was a normal part of life. He just wished his heart didn't hurt so bad.

~~~

Thane sat in his fine-dining restaurant alone, his computer and paperwork spread across a table strategically placed closest to the window facing the parking lot outside. The same lot where Levi's car still sat parked in the back. Thane had spent the last couple of hours peeking out the window, watching for Levi. Most of that time holding himself at a distance, wanting nothing more than to crawl back inside that bed and make love to Levi as he woke then spend the remainder of the day, and quite possibly the
~~~

night, burying himself over and over in that sweet sexy ass until Levi agreed to everything. What that everything meant was a complete mystery, but he was certain he'd learn the answers the more time he spent with that brilliant, sexy man.

He stared out at Levi's car. Only two were left in the employee parking lot and one was a sporty little car. He didn't see Levi driving that, so he decided the old Toyota was probably his.

As if on some sort of cosmic cue, Levi pushed through the exit doors. Interestingly enough, Thane's heart gave a little excited flutter at the sight of the auburn-haired temptation. His eyes stayed riveted on the man taking long, quick strides with his fingers stuffed into his jeans as he ate up the distance to the car. Thane had to rub his palms along his jeans to ease the tingle for how badly they wanted to take Levi's hand in his own.

Thane never stopped staring as Levi got behind the wheel, stayed there a second then got out, opening the hood. He messed with something under the hood while Thane stared at his backside. Levi went back and forth from the hood to the driver's side seat until he shut the hood and crawled back into the driver's seat, shut the door, and backed out of the parking space.

Thane added that to the list of things Levi needed. A new car. He would buy him one. Levi was going to be expensive. He didn't really care about the cost; he'd be worth it. He thought about how the handsome Levi enticed all the men at the club, and suddenly, possessiveness flared on an ugly level, making him slam his laptop lid shut and shove away from the seat. The idea of anyone else touching Levi made him want to punch something. Thane's brow furrowed. He hadn't felt that way with Julian or any of the others. No. That would have to be brought up in their agreement. He would ask that Levi remain exclusive to him.

Thane gathered his stuff and went straight upstairs. The boundaries and control he'd enacted when leaving his room earlier left a sour taste in his mouth. Had he thought he'd hold some sort of upper hand by writing a note and leaving cash? Yeah. He sighed. That nailed it. Maybe he should come clean and just admit to himself and Levi that he'd run scared when he left. He should have been in that bed making love to Levi right now.

Stop saying it like that, he scolded himself.

That was the exact reason he'd left the bed. Clarity and purpose. He and Levi needed those two components in their relationship. Levi was a smart, intuitive guy. Surely, he could see through all Thane's head issues and just let him do things this way until he could work his mind around another solution. He wasn't asking for the world. He just needed to define all the damn emotion beating him the hell up. He wanted to protect them both from the heartache that was destined to come.

Thane entered the suite and placed the laptop on the dining table as he went for his bedroom. The light was on, the bed still rumpled, and his gaze landed on the bundles of money lying on the floor. His eyes narrowed. Levi hadn't taken the money.

Thane picked up the stacks and found his note crumpled in a ball by the foot of the bed. Okay. Levi hadn't agreed to his offer. Thane sat on the edge of the bed, absorbing that blow. Levi had been there last night; he'd been a willing participant and knew full well what a relationship with Thane involved. Levi had even admitted in a moment of sleepy confession that they were good together. It shouldn't matter that he wanted to compensate Levi.

Wasn't it better than a traditional relationship? Both parties knew exactly where they stood. Levi would be compensated nicely for his time. Thane would get to enjoy his time with Levi. Neither would have to worry where the other's headspace would be. He'd even agreed to exclusivity. They should have been set. Win-win, right?

Without even a fuck you, Levi had just left the money there? Thane went for his cell phone. He needed to know why Levi hadn't taken the money.

He didn't have Levi's number. He stared down at the bed where Levi had slept not more than an hour ago. He reached for a pillow and breathed in Levi's clean, fresh scent that still lingered heavily in the soft down. It was actually their combined scent. The uniqueness of Levi's scent blended with his. The combination reached out and wrapped around his soul.

No way was Levi getting out of this that easily. He'd made Thane crave things he didn't want to crave. Levi had to be convinced to do this Thane's way, the only way to protect them both and allow them to continue having great sex.

With no other choice, Thane went through the corporate personnel files and got Levi's home address off his application. He found an envelope to place the money inside, and then he was off.

Twenty-five minutes later, he drove through one of the roughest neighborhoods he'd ever actually been to. He turned and passed by an old, rundown apartment complex. They couldn't be more than one or two bedrooms. The complex gave way to an older neighborhood. Most of the houses were dilapidated and uncared for by both the residents and the city. Kids who should be in school were on street corners, running up to cars. Women lingered around the one street corner closest to the main road.

He kept driving until he spotted Levi's car. As he came to a stop in front of the house, he looked for an address marker. It wasn't there. Thane took a closer look around. These little houses were better maintained than the ones closer to the main road. The houses on either side of Levi had fences in the front yard, but Levi's yard was open. Thane pulled the car into the driveway behind Levi's. The street didn't feel so safe.

As he got out, he felt the curious stares of the people hanging out on the street. He looked around, making eye contact with some, wondering why it seemed like no one was at work or school, before ducking his head and walking toward the front door. This neighborhood in no way matched the man he'd been watching for well over a week. The fact that Levi didn't wear a white tank top or a hoodie and bagged out jeans was vastly different than ninety percent of the guys on this street. Thane took the stairs, dodged the broken step, and forced himself to follow through when all he wanted was a moment to fully comprehend this newest piece to the complex puzzle that was Levi Silva.

He knocked. The door opened to a younger version of Levi standing before him. He was scragglier than Levi, his clothes most definitely hand-me-downs, his hair sticking out every which way. Thane registered the slight sprinkling of freckles along the bridge of his nose then the fierce, frowning woman standing behind him. She was a little bitty thing. Looked nothing like Levi or the boy in front of her, so much so, he wasn't sure she was part of the family.

"We belong to the St. Rita's Catholic Church," she said sternly.

That was the comic relief he needed as he looked down at his zipped jacket and pressed jeans. "I'm actually here because…" He stopped midsentence. Okay, no he couldn't say that. "No. I'm here for…" Thane just stopped again and pulled the folded envelope from his pocket. Whether Levi planned to take his offer or not didn't matter. This family clearly needed this money more than he did.

"I'm Levi's boss. This is his house, correct?" The boy's face turned as serious as the woman's, and he gave a single nod. "He left his bonus at work. I wanted to bring it to him personally."

He extended his hand, and the boy took the offering.

"Are you with the coffee shop or PT clinic?" the woman asked, her smile growing as the kid began unfolding the envelope. Thane almost missed the only two employment references she gave him. Did they not know about the club?

"Logan's got to stop throwing his dirty socks under the sofa. He's at that age where he smells like a burrito…"

From the front door, Thane could see the small, odd-shaped living room that was barely big enough to hold a sofa and a TV. Levi came through one of the openings, carrying a bowl and a pair of socks. His hair was wet. He had on a pair of cut-off sweatpants and a T-shirt that molded to his perfect frame. He looked like an ad from a workout magazine. His presence in the room dwarfed everything. He looked so out of place. Yet all Thane could manage to do was to rake his gaze up and down that irresistible body, cursing his dick when it plumped up at the tempting sight. It didn't go unnoticed by him that he hadn't wanted to shower ever again in fear of losing Levi's irresistible scent. Apparently, Levi didn't share the sentiment.

When Levi's gaze lifted to the door, he stopped dead in his tracks. Panic and something he couldn't quite make out crossed his handsome face. Levi lowered his gaze to his hand that held the socks before lifting again and colliding with Thane's.

"He brought your bonus," the boy announced happily, as if it were a surprise on Christmas morning. The kid stuck his hand inside, pulling out the bundles. "It's five thousand dollars! You made a five-thousand-dollar bonus?" he asked excitedly.

Everything changed on Levi's already anxious face. Heat flooded his features, and his brow cocked as his now angry gaze fixed on Thane. "No, I didn't, Luke."

"He says you did. Come in…" the woman said, stepping back and grabbing Luke's arm to pull him out of the doorway. Levi's family dynamic grew more intriguing, and Thane started to take a step inside. The bowl and socks were carelessly discarded as Levi rushed to block his way.

"He can't stay." Levi glared at him, the abruptness in his voice caused him to take a step backward.

"Levi!" the woman chastised. Thane saw the respect Levi had for her. The care he took as he rolled his shoulders and schooled his features before turning back to the woman Thane assumed was Levi's mother.

"Give me a minute, Aunt Linda. Please." Levi stared at her. She stared at him, and for a minute, he thought she was going to argue, but in the end, she nodded and shut the door behind Levi, showing the respect was mutual. "What the fuck are you doing here?"

"You left without a word," Thane started in immediately, because he honestly had no idea where to begin. Since he'd driven into this neighborhood, hell, since he'd first met Levi, he'd been so off balance and now completely unsure of everything he thought he knew about the man staring angrily at him.

Apparently, he should have given more thought in explaining his sudden appearance, because Levi obviously hadn't taken those words very well and stepped forward aggressively.

"I made my position more than clear. Now, leave."

"Don't I have a say?" Thane asked, taking a small step back in hopes of defusing the situation. He needed to calm Levi down. More than ever, they needed to talk. "Levi, listen to me. I enjoyed last night more than I want to admit. I know you did too, or at least, I thought you did. I don't understand why you're so mad." His attempt at a peaceful resolution resulted in Levi's chest expanding and both large fists clenching into balls at his side. The more Thane tried to fix this, the angrier Levi got. Thane readied himself for a punch in the face. Maybe coming here wasn't as brilliant an idea as he'd thought earlier. Thane took another step back, remembering the broken step when his foot caught in the wood. He lost his balance, pitching backward, landing embarrassingly on his ass in the front yard.

~~~

When Thane Walker tripped on his broken step porch, Levi's brain might have actually exploded. Everything wrong with this picture came together in this one defining moment.

"You had your say, and I declined the offer," Levi yelled, watching as Thane did this fluid move, easily getting back to his feet. He saw red as the reality of this situation landed squarely on his shoulders. This man. This cultured, gorgeous, accomplished man had come to his barely standing house to ease his conscience. People like Thane didn't lower themselves to enter this side of town, and they certainly didn't come calling for a friendly visit. Levi's humiliation levels peaked into uncharted territory, and the heat flooding his face turned to volcanic proportions. Shame and regret swelled in his chest. He hadn't signed up for any of this.

Thane stood feet away from him, still trying to defuse Levi's anger. He held out his hands, trying to calm Levi down. How could Thane even begin to understand how degraded he felt? Even more so since Thane's ideas were absolutely correct. If he would become Thane's whore, it would help his family.

His fists clenched tighter as his stomach churned at the sudden need to beat something up, starting with himself. Thane
~~~

had very effectively showed him exactly how selfish his moral code was to the family around him. Five thousand dollars a month would be life changing for the people he loved.

Levi kept his gaze locked on Thane as he slowly took each step down, knowing without any question that Thane's view of him was no better than the dirt under Thane's expensive loafer-covered feet.

Thane assessed each of his moves and remained remarkably calm, taking a step backward as he came forward.

"I told you no money."

Thane nodded at him. Fuck yeah, he needed to nod.

"So you think I fucked you last night because I had a change of heart?"

"Of course not," Thane said, but he could see in every action since Levi woke this morning that he absolutely assumed everything they did last night was Levi auditioning for Julian's open spot. Fuck, if his brain hadn't exploded, it did right then. He was so damn stupid. He rolled his eyes, remembering how he had hoped to enjoy Thane's company in the future. The heat when they came together was undeniable, but so was the humiliation and embarrassment now laced together with his degradation.

Levi had been worried his heart was involved, hoping Thane might be willing to date him. While Thane had been testing his ability to whore.

Another huge blow. There was no way to take that money from his brother's hand without some sort of explanation, and there was no plausible one in sight.

"I'm not one of your fucking rent boys, Thane."

~~~

Thane watched as Levi animatedly threw out his hands in both directions as he was forced to take one step back, then another.

"You think if I wanted to hook, I couldn't have done that way before now? Every single time I've walked down that street since I was fifteen years old, I've been harassed about screwing people
~~~

for money. I swore I would be different. I've worked hard since grade school at making myself better than the trash that runs this street, and then you show up in your pretentious car and designer clothing and condescending attitude, throwing money at the poor boy. You're so full of yourself that you think your money will somehow entice me to change my mind." Levi finally stopped moving forward, but his flow of words kept coming, hitting their mark, causing Thane to take another step backward. "In exchange for fucking you, I could somehow change my status in life. By coming here and handing my brother that money... You so arrogantly shoved my character and all my hard work aside. Everything I've worked for, all my accomplishments, the fact that I made it into one of the top medical schools in this country on my own, you made me and everything I believe in irrelevant. You put me right back here where those people always told me I'd be. For what? To ease your fragile conscience?"

The feelings Thane thought he had control over now hurt him on a level he'd never thought possible. The picture was placed in front of him, and he didn't like any part of it. Levi was so angry. The accusations Levi flung out stung. No matter what the guy thought, he hadn't intended to make him feel less than—quite the opposite. Thane was just at a complete loss for how to make this better. He'd fucked up royally, and his heart begged him to salvage whatever he could.

"Levi..."

"Thane, stop." Levi started backward, putting distance between them. "It's been made crystal clear what you truly think of me. I might not look or act like I fit in your world, and that's fine, because I'm pretty sure I never asked to be in your world. Not if it means selling my soul. Fuck you, Thane Walker. I have value outside of being your play toy no matter what you think. Now, get out of my life."

Levi pivoted on his heels, turning away, leaving him standing there. He was still reeling from the harsh words Levi had slung at him. He deserved it. He deserved every one of those words, but Levi didn't deserve to feel the way Thane had made him feel. He was so sorry. He just wanted a chance to explain his side.

"Levi, give me a minute," he said and started toward Levi. Thane was stricken with contempt for himself as he witnessed the defeated slump he'd put in Levi's broad shoulders. He had no idea how to make this right, but he couldn't leave with Levi feeling so low. Thane's head issues drove him to this point.

"Oh God, of course." Levi had made it back on the porch, but suddenly swung around, his eyes wide. He quickly trotted down the steps, storming his way. "You don't have to worry. I'd hate for you to lose sleep on my account. My life's more than full. I never wanted anything more with you. No matter how you may have interpreted anything I said last night, I didn't really expect anything from you. You were just a fuck and that's it. As good as it was, it's done. I needed the release, mission accomplished, now it's fucking over."

He couldn't accept this as the end. Thane's voice broke as he said, "It's not over, Levi. We can work this out. We could…"

"Stop saying it like that!" Levi roared, advancing on him again. "It's never gonna happen again, and if you don't leave me alone, I'll be forced to quit the only job I've found to help me pay for all of our expenses. I wouldn't expect someone like you to even understand the compassion required to do what I ask." Levi scrubbed his hands down his face. "Never mind. I'm quitting."

"No," Thane almost yelled, his tone frantic as he grabbed Levi's arm, but Levi immediately yanked out of his hold like he was repulsed by Thane's touch. "Look, I'm leaving today. I won't be back for quite some time. Don't quit because of my stupidity. I'll do as you ask. I'll leave you alone."

Levi didn't look back as he turned, trotted up the steps, and marched toward the door. Levi's brother stood in the open doorway, confusion on his face. There was no question that boy idolized his brother. Levi carefully moved him backward and slammed the door. Thane stood there a minute, staring at the closed door.

He hated the feeling gnawing in the pit of his stomach. He finally decided Levi wasn't coming back out, and there was no hope of salvaging this moment. He turned, the street littered with people looking his direction, and he felt terrible they'd witnessed his and Levi's fight.

Somehow knowing that made it all worse, but he couldn't take that back either. When he got closer to his car, a woman called out something about taking Levi's place. He hadn't thought he could feel lower until right that minute. He was wrong…again. Thane didn't respond to the invitation. Instead, he got inside the car and pulled away from the house, ignoring everything but the intense ache in his chest that wouldn't ease.

His need to control everything in his world had just made everything worse. How was that even possible?

CHAPTER 14

Seven hours later, Thane stared out the small window in the coach seat he'd been cramped in for far too long. His tired, sleep-deprived eyes burned as he watched the lights of the runway rise up to greet him as the airplane landed at BWI airport. He hadn't slept a wink the entire flight although he was past the point of exhaustion. Over and over, he continually rehashed the argument he'd had with Levi. Dwelling on every word and the hurt and angry expression he'd seen on Levi's face. The images haunted him. He'd royally messed things up, and he couldn't let it go.

Luckily, he'd been able to sit in the front of the plane, close to the exit. He hadn't notified anyone of his arrival, and having left the suite with only his laptop and carry-on, he quickly pulled both from the overhead bin and made his exit from the airport terminal in record-breaking time. The crisp, freezing Maryland air barely registered, though the temperature was probably a fifty-degree decline compared to California's sunny skies. He wasn't quite to the curb when his Bluetooth alerted him of a call. He tapped the side of his earpiece, answering without checking caller ID.

"Yes," he said sharply.

"Why's Levi trying to quit?" Julian asked just as harshly, foregoing any greeting on his end.

"Don't let him." Thane's jaw tightened, his teeth clamped together as he lifted a hand and waved for a taxi. The driver pulled forward a couple of seconds later and popped open the trunk before the vehicle even came to a stop.

"Yeah." Julian gave a disingenuous bark of laughter. "Wish I had thought of that. Seriously, that's your answer?" Julian gave another irritatingly long pause that grated on Thane's last nerve. "That didn't work, *papi*. He's up in the office now, insisting he's done."

"Tell him I'll stay away." The words were like bile in his mouth. Knowing he'd caused Levi so much pain was a sobering and bitter pill to swallow. He looked down, shaking his head, knowing that staying away from the handsome man would be a monumental task, one he wasn't sure he could accomplish. Thane let out a pent-up breath and tossed his carry-on inside the trunk followed by the laptop case. "Levi doesn't have to worry about me. I know I screwed up and I'm willing to admit it. I just hate how I left things."

"If that's true, then you need to find a way to make it right. Where are you? It sounds like a raceway."

"I'm back home. I just got off the plane." Thane slammed the trunk closed, rounded the back of the taxi, and climbed in the backseat, calling out to the driver before the door shut, "1030 Court Avenue, Ellicott City."

"That's a bit of a ways," the driver answered in a hard New England accent. The guy never looked back or moved a single muscle to get the car started, and that seemed to piss Thane off more than Julian's irritating attitude.

"Goddammit. Julian, don't let him quit and call me back in thirty minutes." Thane ended the call and reached for his wallet to pull out a fifty-dollar bill. "Here, I didn't have time to call a ride. It can't be more than that."

"Not enough time to get a coat?" The driver's eyes raked over him as he took the cash, laid it in the cubby.

"Commentary's not necessary. Just drive."

The guy did. He took off as if he were trying to outrun a fire. Thane fell back against the vinyl backrest, scrambling to brace an arm on the passenger side seat to help keep him in place. It took an arm locked on the door and one gripping the seat to keep him upright. He tried to stare out the window, to keep the nausea from roiling in his gut, but that didn't work. The driver drove like an eighteen-year-old boy in a tricked-out Corvette. As his body shifted from side to side and he concentrated on keeping the contents of his stomach down, he closed his eyes, thankful that fearing for his life was probably the only thing that kept Levi off his mind.

And there Levi was again.

Thane held on tight as the images of their time together played out in his head. No matter how he tried, he couldn't get out of his mind the pain etched on Levi's handsome face. It physically hurt, knowing he'd caused Levi so much anguish.

"We're here. I need six more dollars." Thane's eyes popped open, and he scanned his neighborhood. He'd again gotten lost in his thoughts. With a quick glance at the digital display on the dash, he tugged his wallet free, thumbed through the bills and pulled out a twenty before handing the money over. Without a word, he exited the car, and went around to the trunk to retrieve his things. All he needed at the moment was a bottle of the good stuff and the comfort of his bed.

Based on the sounds coming from the patio, there was a gathering going on. He heard music—some 1940's jazz Erin loved—and laughter. Normally that sound would ease his troubled thoughts. He'd be all in to crash whatever party they were having. Instead, Thane let himself into his townhome and tossed his suitcase on the sofa, immediately unzipping the flap. The only thing inside was the pillow he and Levi had shared. He grabbed it, bringing the soft cotton to his nose, breathing Levi in. Lord, it still smelled like the guy, stirring both Thane's heart and his dick.

As he started for the patio door, his phone rang again. He paused at the door and contemplated not answering. In the end, the idea of knowing whether Levi kept the job became more compelling than the dressing-down Julian was sure to give him. Tapping the side of his earpiece, Thane answered, "Did he stay?"

"Just barely. You went to his house? Really?" Julian asked incredulously. "You'd know this better than me, but doesn't that break just about every single employment law on the planet?"

Thane let out a humorless laugh. Funny that Julian lectured him on corporate personnel procedures.

Instead of rehashing any of Thane's clearly not so bright events of the morning, he concentrated on the key points. Thane needed time to think, and Levi needed to stay put until he figured out how to handle all his missteps. "You make sure Levi has everything he needs. Don't let him quit."

"You offered him more money and exclusivity, seriously? Were you paying attention to the part where he said he doesn't fuck for money? Because, I'm pretty sure every man that comes inside this club figures that out about Levi in less than five minutes."

The disapproval in Julian's voice hit its mark. Thane's brows snapped together. "You're pissing me off."

"And you're pissing me off, Thane. He's my friend—"

"That right there." He stopped Julian's argumentative flow. This wasn't entirely his fault. Julian had been Levi's champion since day one and not that Thane hadn't gone along with everything Julian had ever suggested, but Julian was just about as bad as they came and naughty as fuck. The entirety of Julian's adult life had been spent having lots of sex for money. The guy was neither cheap nor anything close to prudish. "Don't you see how I could have made the assumptions I did? He's your friend, Julian. I thought he might be holding out for more money."

A disgusted moan sounded on the other end of the line before Julian said, "He needs this job. You guys in that top income tier up there don't get what we go through."

Thane scrubbed a hand over his face and resisted the urge to remind Julian that he wasn't anywhere close to the top of anything financially.

"I'm hanging up now. Just make sure he has what he needs. Give him the best shifts and the best tables. He needs it." Thane hung up the phone, took the Bluetooth off his ear, and tossed the device on the kitchen counter. No more phone calls tonight. He was too strung-out to hear any more about all his missteps tonight.

Thane pulled open the side door to see four or five of his neighbors hanging out on the shared patio. They were having a good time. Normally, he'd be right there, ready to enjoy the company, but not tonight. He scanned the small crowd until he found Erin and headed straight toward her with the pillow he'd taken still in hand.

"Thane! You're back!" Erin's delighted squeal had all the attention landing in his direction. Her broad grin faded when she got a good look at his face. The happy mood changed as her husband Corey came from behind and clasped a hand on his shoulder.

"What's wrong?" Corey asked, coming around to stand at Thane's side. Someone turned the music down and a silence descended. He hated being such a buzz kill. Honestly, he had no idea what they were seeing that had them rushing to his side, but he tried hard to school his features and shook his head.

"Just tired," he muttered, patting the large comforting hand still resting on his shoulder.

"Have a drink. I just got this." Jared held out his bottle of beer, proving Thane must seriously look wrecked. The guy never willingly parted with his beer.

"Not tonight. I was just hoping Erin would know this cologne." She stood directly in front of him, confusion clouding her eyes. Yeah, the request was an odd one, he got it, but she didn't waver as she took the pillow from him, brought it to her nose, and inhaled.

"It's your cologne," she said, before slightly lowering the pillow.

"There's another scent mixed in there. It's lighter, sweeter," Thane said. Erin smelled around then lifted her head, her grin growing as she looked at him.

"You two smell great together. I think it's Armani Code. Corey has some. Hang on." Erin spun around and went through her townhome back door, pillow in her hands. He knew she'd know. She was good about those kinds of things. His relief was short-lived as he looked around and the rest of the people at the gathering just stared at him. He'd seen that look quite a bit today—as he walked through both airports and then again on the plane. Probably the same reason the flight attendant made sure his glass was never empty. Out of nothing more than the fact he did not want to talk about anything meaningful, he forced a smile and looked around.

"I'm exhausted. Ignore me. It's been a hellacious trip."

Corey nodded and again patted his back before going to his cooler and drawing out a Two Hearted Ale, Thane's beer of choice, and his smile turned sincere as he nodded. Corey handed it over while the group of his other friends continued to stare at him with genuine concern.

"I don't know business on your level, but I know whatever's goin' on will pass." It was a nice attempt at easing the tension Thane had created. He nodded before turning up the bottle, taking a couple of hearty swallows. Somehow, Corey's encouragement had managed to freak him out even more. Thane wasn't certain he wanted anything with Levi to pass or end. The exact opposite actually.

"Here!" Erin held out a bottle of cologne and the pillow. She lifted his wrist and sprayed. He brought it to his nose, closed his eyes, and took a whiff. *Bingo.* He nodded and continued to smell his wrist. It was like breathing in Levi. He could almost envision Levi standing there.

Opening his eyes, he smiled dreamily at Erin, then took the pillow, and shoved it under his arm before starting to turn away.

"Here take this. Corey doesn't wear it. I hope we meet him soon." Erin seemed oblivious to his pain. Instead, she waggled her brows as she handed over the cologne.

He gave a noncommittal laugh and took the offering. Yeah, in no scenario could he see any of them spending time with Levi anytime soon. "I'm going to sleep. I'll see you guys later."

"We'll keep it down."

"No need. I'm so tired nothing'll wake me." Thane downed the beer as he entered the house, tossing the bottle across the kitchen into the trash bin before taking the stairs down to his bedroom. He didn't bother charging his phone, plugging in his laptop, or checking email. He tossed the pillow toward the headboard and undressed at the foot of the bed. He'd been awake a good thirty-six hours. When he crawled under the covers, he snuggled into the softness of the bed with the pillow tucked into his side. Levi's scent was strong, and the weight of the pillow was comforting in his arms. When he closed his eyes, he could visualize Levi's face. Thane barely got that thought out before sleep took him under.

~~~

Levi's eyes popped open. Pancakes. The delicious smells and the memories of the happier times of his childhood had him pushing off the mattress. Luckily, he'd worn his athletic shorts to bed so nothing got in the way of heading straight for his brothers' room. He reached for Logan's foot, giving a good shake before moving toward Luke, doing the same thing there.

"I think Aunt Linda's making pancakes," he said, rubbing his palm against one eye as a big yawn tore free.

"What?" Logan asked groggily, lifting his head. Levi didn't need to answer, he saw immediate recognition on Logan's face as he quickly sat up, all sleepy-eyed, automatically rolling from his bed. Luke followed his lead, looking around the floor for his shorts.

"I love that smell," Luke said, the tiredness leaving his voice as his stomach began to rumble loudly.

"I love that smell, too." Levi went back to his bedroom and grabbed a T-shirt hanging off the end of the bed. He shrugged it on while walking through the house toward the kitchen. He could hear Linda talking, and when he came around the corner, he was a little surprised. Linda was busily cooking at the stove while Luke's high school counselor, Mrs. Underwood, sat at the table.

This was not what he'd expected to find.

"It smells good in here," Logan said, brushing past him into the room. His brother was like a bull in a china shop, bumping into the counter, before skidding to a stop right in front of the stove. Luke also shrugged past him while Linda swatted Logan's hand as he tried to swipe one of the pancakes.
~~~

"Go sit down," Linda said, waving the spatula as Logan dodged her first move and managed to grab one of the pancakes off the stack. "We wanted to have a good breakfast together this morning."

"Hi, guys," Mrs. Underwood said, standing up. For the first time, both Luke and Logan spotted her at the table. "Linda and I were talking yesterday, and she invited me over for breakfast."

Levi's brow furrowed, but his brothers were the exact opposite. They seemingly found nothing out of the ordinary as they went for their seats at the already set table. When Levi still hadn't moved, Mrs. Underwood's head shifted his direction, their gazes met and held until she gave a slight shake of her head at him.

That confused him more. What did that even mean?

"I love bacon and maple syrup," Logan said.

"You love all food," Luke shot back, laughing at Logan.

"You're both so skinny," Linda said from where she stood at the stove. Levi was slower to take his seat, skeptical of everything going on around him. His gut churned as dread began to build. Something wasn't right.

"I don't know how I'm so skinny. Dad always called me a human garbage disposal," Logan said, spearing another pancake before Linda set the full plate in the middle of the table. Logan seemed oblivious to the tension building in the room, but Luke started looking between Levi, Linda, and Mrs. Underwood. The look on his face showed he was beginning to clue in that this wasn't just a family breakfast. His dark gaze finally landed and stuck on Levi as Luke sat straighter in his seat and placed his fork on the table.

Linda put a pancake on Luke's plate. "It seems the more you eat, the skinnier you get."

Luke didn't move, his concerned gaze fixed on Levi.

"What's going on?" Levi finally asked and mimicked his brother's posture, sitting back in his seat with his hands in his lap.

"Let's eat before we talk," Linda said, turning to him, looking very serious.

Finally, Logan felt the tension in the room and lifted his head. He'd already managed to finish one whole pancake and continued dipping a piece of bacon in the syrup on his plate. He added the bite to his mouth as his eyes narrowed, and he reached for a napkin. With his mouth full, he asked, "What's going on?"

Linda looked more dejected than she had a minute ago. "I wanted us to have a good breakfast before we all talked."

"Talked about what?" Levi asked, becoming a little frantic inside. His gaze went from Linda to the counselor, his appetite completely lost as anxiety swam in his gut. "What's going on?"

"Levi." Linda reached out her hand, gripping Levi's forearm. He had to force himself to remember Linda was on their side. She had been since the beginning when he first took over guardianship, even before that. She'd cared for their family when his father couldn't. As if she were a lifeline, Levi adjusted the hold, taking her hand in his. "You know how much I love you three, right?"

"Oh no," Logan said and put his fork down. Levi completely agreed with Logan's well-stated sentiment. He looked from brother to brother, Luke's face turning pale as he just stared at Linda.

"No, now listen to me, Logan. I need the support of all three of you right now. Now more than ever."

"You're not gonna let us live together anymore, are you?" Luke asked.

The better mood around the house the last few weeks instantly began to fade. Tears sprang to Luke's eyes so fast they brimmed and spilled down his cheeks within a second. Levi sat there, helplessly watching the defeat happen.

Damn, he wished he'd sat closer to Luke.

"It's not that," Linda said, shaking her head no at Luke. "I just think it's time we look closer at this arrangement. We made all these decisions in the emotion of the moment. I believe this might be getting to be too much for you guys."

"It's not too much. We're doing okay. Better, now that Luke's in counseling," Logan shot back. Luke had been Levi's main concern since he'd walked into the kitchen and sensed the heavy tone to this breakfast. He let his gaze travel to Logan who seemed exactly on his page; his middle brother's eyes darted back and forth with uncertainty from Linda to Luke.

Levi stayed absolutely quiet as his own fears rose to the surface and threatened to overwhelm him. The little bit he'd had left of his heart after yesterday morning actually broke in two at the thought he might lose his brothers. So, Linda didn't think they had managed as well as they should. Levi looked down at his lap, closing his eyes, willing himself to be reasonable.

Truly, he had thought they were managing pretty well. Sure, things had been rocky in the beginning, but the three of them were bonding, becoming a functioning unit, or at least he thought they were.

The weight on his shoulders grew heavier. He was failing at his final promise to his dad.

"Logan, your brother's working night and day. You two are unsupervised much of the time. If we switched things up, you and Luke move in with me, then Levi could get back on his career path and finish medical school. That would help everyone," Linda explained.

"Is it too much for you to keep an eye on them at night?" Levi asked, staring at Linda as he tried to understand the problem. His work schedule had lightened since he'd started at the club. He now had both Friday and Saturday nights off and all day Sunday.

"I'm seventeen years old," Logan said defensively. "I'm an adult by most standards. I can take care of things around here just fine."

"Of course, it's not too much for me, but, guys, listen. It's got to be too much for Levi." Linda turned directly to Levi. "When do you sleep? You're up with Luke at the crack of dawn. You work all day then all night."

"Then I'll quit my day job. I earn enough at my new night job for us to get by," he said, absolutely not wanting to give up the second source of income. He'd finally gotten to a point where he could stash some money away. If everything kept going like it was, he might be able to make enough to get them moved.

Luke reached across the table for the napkins. He grabbed a handful, drawing everyone's gaze his direction.

"This is my fault," Luke said, staring directly at Levi as he rubbed the bundle in his hand across his cheeks. His little brother dropped his head to his hands and buried his face in the napkins. Levi huffed out a harsh breath; his shoulders slumped as the devastating sense of defeat washed over him. In a matter of a few minutes, all the progress Luke had made in counseling slipped away.

"Boys, now listen to me. It's not this complicated. This plan gives everyone a couple of years to get Logan in college and Luke older. Maybe when Levi finishes school, Luke could move up there with him. It's a good reasonable solution that I think needs to be considered." Clearly set in her decision, Linda's voice grew stern as she spoke.

"Have you talked this over with Child Protective Services?" Levi asked, to find out if this decision had already been made or if he still had a chance to keep them together.

"Of course not, but I have talked the idea over with Mrs. Underwood. She sees the value in what I'm proposing."

Levi nodded, looking over at the counselor who had remained absolutely stone-faced and silent. More concerning to him was the fact that Linda had done all this planning without any of them knowing.

Luke looked up over the napkin, the tears still filling his eyes. "Levi, please don't let them do this. I'm doing better. I'll do better," Luke begged. "Dad wanted us to be together. He knew it would be hard, but he had faith in us."

"Guys, I believe your dad would agree with me now. This is hard to watch. You three are giving up everything when nothing's going to change how this ends. You're living in your father's shadow here. You need to live your lives," Linda explained, trying her best to make all three of them see the reason behind her suggestion. Not from the angle that Levi was failing his brothers, but from how stagnant they'd all become. Their father and his illness had been reflected in every step they took for months now. In that, Linda was right.

Levi swallowed that bitter bit of news and furrowed his brow, staring at his overly distraught little brother. In their defense, Dad had only been gone less than six months. They'd had adversity, yes, but they were dealing and overcoming. If they were separated now, they'd risk the very foundation that made them a family. They had to stay together and rebuild what family meant to them, and to Levi, that meant the three of them stuck together no matter how hard things got.

"They stay with me." He meant every word.

Levi swallowed the worry that bubbled at his declaration and prayed Linda and Mrs. Underwood wouldn't fight him on this. He and his brothers were all still grieving. Of course, they lived in their father's shadow. He was right there with them in everything they did and always would be. That wasn't a bad thing. He was their ultimate foundation. Levi reached across the table toward Luke, extending a hand. At first, he thought Luke planned to shrug him off, but he didn't. He finally clasped Levi's hand, clinging to him like a life preserver tossed to a drowning man in a stormy ocean, where one misstep could seal their fate. That did it for Levi; the tears he fought slid free, trailing down his cheeks as Logan's palm landed on theirs.

"You have to go on to medical school, Levi. You must finish. Luke and Logan need you to finish. That's what I wanted to say to you. I'm willing to have you all move in if that helps that goal happen." Linda reached across the table, putting her hands on top of Logan's. Her words broke as they all held on to one another. Linda's concerned gaze moved to Levi's. "You're so smart. You have the power to change their lives. I can't see how you can add medical school into everything you're currently doing."

She was right, but he wasn't leaving his brothers behind. "I'll figure it out. These are my brothers, and they practically take care of themselves. They're with me."

Luke crumpled, the sob drew every bit of attention his way as he shoved away from the table, pulling his hand free from theirs. Luke's chair banged loudly against the kitchen floor as he darted from the room.

Levi sat there a minute and closed his eyes, absorbing this latest blow. Logan was next to go. His heart caved in his chest as Logan went after Luke. Yes, this was an impossible situation. He wasn't making the best decisions, but it was just too much to bear. Levi pushed to his feet and reached for Linda, giving her a quick side hug. He couldn't quite look her in the eyes when he added, "You might be right, but I won't leave them."

Levi left the kitchen in search of his brothers. It wouldn't be easy, and they were in for a fight, but with his brothers by his side, he would make sure they got through this.

~~~

Thane stirred awake, listening to the sounds coming from above. He heard a clank then a series of cabinets slamming shut. His eyes popped fully open. He glanced out the window. He rarely closed the blinds—the sight from his bedroom was too amazing, and besides, no one could see in. It was early, at least it felt that way to him. The time difference between Maryland and California always took a little getting used to. He rolled to his side, determined to get another thirty minutes or so just as another noise came from above. What the hell? Daytime robbers made no sense.

Annoyed, Thane flipped the covers back and begrudgingly got out of bed. He grabbed his pants from yesterday and started for the stairs, working quickly to shove one foot then the other in each pant leg as he headed up the steps. The smell hit at the same time as an "oh, shit" was muttered from above.

Thane grinned, shoving his fingers through his bedhead hair as he trotted the rest of the way up. He came to a stop at the entrance of his kitchen and watched Erin flip a pancake in the air. She did a little cheer for herself, even throwing a fist in the air when the cake landed just right on the skillet.

"What are you doing?"

Erin jumped a foot, jerking around as the pancake dropped to the floor. "Shoot! Five second rule. This one goes to the hubby." She scurried, picking the pancake up off the floor, then tossed it
~~~

back in the pan. "We'll let it cook a bit longer to burn off the germs."

He must have slept through a lot. She had a pile of cakes waiting on him. Thane had no idea what he'd done to earn breakfast, but he'd take it. "What are you doing?" he asked again as he headed to the Keurig to start a cup of coffee. "I figured you'd be nursing a hangover this morning."

"I am, but I wrote myself a note about the cologne, and it jarred my memory." She flipped the pancake, and when it landed perfectly, Erin set the skillet down and threw both arms in the air. "Yes! She shoots, she scores."

Thane chuckled at her antics before making his coffee and taking a seat at the small, two-seater table already set with all his mismatched plates and silverware. He smiled at the place settings. He hadn't even realized he had these color plates. "I'm surprised you found all this in my cabinets."

"Are you kidding? I brought these over," she said, bringing the stack of hot pancakes to the table. "Honestly, from your choice of dishes, I'd never know you were in the food business." Erin took her seat and placed several pancakes on his plate then grabbed for her open can of soda before settling back in her chair.

"You aren't eating?" he asked as he reached for the syrup, surprised she hadn't filled her plate. There had to be fifteen hot and ready to serve pancakes sitting there, waiting.

"I'll pass. Hangover, remember?" She held her stomach and winced. "Not feeling all that hungry right now."

"You cooked all this for me?" Thane asked and didn't even try to school his enthusiasm. He hadn't eaten at all yesterday. With Levi still on his lips, nothing would have tasted as satisfying. This morning seemed a different story altogether. A self-proclaimed foodie could only be deprived of food for so long, and his time was up. With renewed gusto, he dove in, cutting a big bite, not even trying for manners as he shoved the whole thing in his mouth.

"I'm a giver, what can I say," she teased, drawing one of her long legs up against her chest, resting her heel on the edge of the chair. "Eat and spill. Tell me what happened that had you so messed up last night."

Just the thought of the last week turned Thane's mood darker. He lifted a finger, asking for a second as he shoveled another too large bite inside his mouth. "Mmmm…" He chewed and reached for his coffee. He loved pancakes in the morning. "You did really good. Thank you. First, tell me what you've heard about the house, then I'll tell you what you wanna know."

"Okay, she said you contacted her." Erin paused, lifting a perfectly arched brow until he nodded. "And she said you lowballed her." He nodded again. It never hurt to ask, or at least that was the way he saw it. "Why'd you lowball her? We're all moving in together. We all can't fit inside this townhome. It's a one bedroom."

He managed his laugh while keeping his mouth closed. That right there…that was what he loved about Erin. He never really knew if she was joking or if she was serious and that made her teasing so much more fun. She always lightened his mood.

"She came in too high. She asked almost three quarters of a million dollars. Did you tell her I was the one who was interested?" he asked and looked over at Erin who looked sheepish. "That's what I thought. I offered her what the houses in this neighborhood go for. I haven't heard back."

"I think she thinks she's holding out. Gonna make you up your offer," Erin confessed, biting her lip.

"I've played the game longer than she has," Thane said, taking another big bite before leaning back in his seat with his coffee mug in hand.

"Okay, I'll wait somewhat patiently. Now tell me why I'm randomly sniffing colognes in the middle of the night." She lifted her other leg so that both feet were now on the chair, and she hugged her legs against her chest, resting her chin against her knee, waiting for his answer.

"It was like nine o'clock, definitely not middle of the night, and I was having a bit of a breakdown. I don't ever have those, but I suspect there'll be more over the next couple of weeks, so be prepared." Thane took a long drink of his coffee, watching as

Erin's face turned serious. When she started to speak, he cut her off, knowing they'd play twenty questions until he rehashed every detail of the whole ordeal. This tentative internal calm he had achieved this morning needed to stay intact or he was certain he'd crawl back into that bed again and stay there the rest of the day or even the week. "Let's see, I met a guy. I chased the guy. I did the guy, and it was better than great." Erin's smile was immediate. "Then I ruined it by trying to fit him inside my box of rules for relationships and he didn't want to be there. Apparently, he has his own box that's vastly different than mine."

"So change your box," she said, as if that were the easiest thing in the world to do.

Thane just shook his head. "I can't do that."

Both her feet landed on the floor with a thud as she leaned forward, her fist dropping to the table as she started to speak. "Thane! I'm gonna be brutally honest, and I'm truly not trying to add to your heartsick, in love thing—"

"I'm not in love." He interrupted immediately. He was not in love. He'd never been in love. He had no idea what gave her the idea he was in love.

She laughed, staring him in the eyes as she continued, "But you seriously have a warped way of dealing with a relationship. It's okay to date one man. People do it every day, and it works out fine."

She didn't understand the half of it, and that wasn't her fault. She was a good friend to him, a confidante. Probably more so than anyone before her. He just felt so weirdly vulnerable about Levi. He couldn't explain this weird depth of emotion that one really great night with Levi had brought on. He'd connected with everything Levi Silva.

Everything.

They liked the same foods, the same music, the same books. Levi laughed at his silliness and didn't completely freak out at his naughtiness. Images of shoving his hand down Levi's pants at the bar came to mind. Of course, they could be seen by anyone who turned their direction, but Levi had grown hard in his palm as if he were excited about the prospect while playfully scolding him.

The whole scenario had turned Thane on that much more. He'd been so horny when they'd returned to the bedroom. All he wanted to do was to bury himself in Levi over and over, and he did. God, the way Levi's body responded to him. And the way Levi took the reins…

"You might not realize it because you haven't been in this position before, but you're falling in love," Erin said dreamily, jarring Thane from his thoughts. He'd been staring at her unfocused, not giving her his full attention until he heard that love word again. "You know that, right? Infatuation's the first step of love."

Thane shook his head no. He reasonably understood that theory and didn't like what he heard. He'd never lost any sleep over pining for a man, but the bottom line was that he didn't want to deal with what his parents had gone through. He wouldn't risk a relationship, because he'd seen how horribly they ended. He liked his life. He knew his limitations, and always, no matter the circumstance, set himself up for success. These feelings inside him were anything but positive; they were mangled and skewed. A relationship would add chaos to his life, a lack of control he just flat didn't want any part of.

"Does this guy feel the same about you?"

Well, that was a loaded question. Thane took another long drink while he thought about the answer. Levi might have been into him the night before, but clearly not enough to play the game the way Thane wanted to play. But Levi had to know that kind of connection didn't just happen. They were so in sync. Fantasies were written about the kind of night they had shared. That was all before he factored in Levi's unguarded, sleepy time words, *"You make me feel wanted."* Yeah, Levi had connected. Thane had no doubt in his mind.

"He felt it until I ruined it."

"What did you do?" Erin immediately asked.

Again, he never went there with Erin. Not ever. Happily married, Erin would never understand the benefit of an escort over a mate. Thane carefully chose his words. "I proposed something he wasn't interested in, then I made it worse by going to his house to try to talk to him."

"Was he married? I read that gay men often marry women while hiding," she said with a note of authority. Her face grew serious at the prospect, perhaps worrying how Levi's wife might have taken Thane appearing on their doorstep. Thane just wrinkled his brow at the idea, chuckling a little, and shook his head no.

"Nothing quite so simple. I'm not sure what's going on, but something's not quite right in Levi's life." He held eye contact with Erin to drive the severity of the condition home. "Even outside of that, I made him feel shallow."

"Not quite right, how?" Her expressive face turned sad. Maybe he should pay more attention to her when she spoke; he had no idea she could switch her range of emotions so easily. A very compassionate and impressive feat.

"I'm not certain. I'm gonna get those details today, but there's a sadness there that I didn't immediately recognize," he answered honestly.

"Oh, no."

"I suspect he's keeping his family afloat." Thane gave a humorless laugh at his obvious assumption. "He told me he was keeping them together, so I'm not suspecting."

"He lives with his mother?"

Thane nodded then stopped. He honestly didn't know that answer, and he again furrowed his brow, realizing how little he knew about Levi. "I guess his mother. He's been in med school. Here at Hopkins, so I'm guessing he's gone home to take care of something. They don't have a lot, but he's proud." He let out a deep sigh, feeling even more like a heel. This had all been about him. His wants, his desires. He'd never really considered Levi's point of view.

Again, the obviousness of his thought hit him. Clearly, he hadn't respected Levi when he'd driven to his house with money in hand. That had been a real asshole thing to do, but he'd been so damn desperate and full of himself and his ideas. Thane cringed while remembering that he'd tried to use Levi's lack of money in his favor. Lord, that was such a bastard thing to do.

"Well, that's sweet and responsible and sad all at the same time. How old is he?"

Funny, he'd not wanted to play twenty questions, but talking about Levi gave him a sense of completion. As if he still had a chance, and he found he'd gladly answer all her questions.

"He's an older twenty-six-ish. At first, I thought he was a baby. Now I know his maturity levels are probably higher than my own. He doesn't expect anything to be given to him. He works two jobs. It can't be easy to stay afloat with the cost of living so high in California," Thane mused. Levi had met Julian at the physical therapy clinic. He wondered if he still worked at the physical therapy clinic and how that income compared to what he made at the club. Thane also wondered how that proud man had ever reconciled taking a job in that kind of nightclub.

"Oh man, his life, Thane. That's terrible."

Thane only nodded. Verbalizing everything he'd learned about Levi was really a bitter pill to swallow and made his own actions that much more deplorable.

"I didn't handle things right. My feelings were so strong after our time together… They made me nervous. I freaked." Thane again thought about his own behavior. He'd put himself first and refused to see what was really happening there. Maybe that was what had him so messed up—images of Levi raging at him in that front yard. Thane struggled with knowing the pain and degradation he'd caused that independent, caring man. "I can't see him giving me another chance. I really fucked up."

"Then if you're truly interested, go at it a different way. Do you have any connection with him through the school? You're an alumnus there, right?" she asked.

Thane looked up at her, not completely following her train of thought. His father had tenure at JHU. Thane himself graduated from there then donated money every year. Maybe he did have some pull there. "Keep going."

"Well, I don't know, really. At my school, we have a social media deal on the school's website. All the current students have automatic accounts, and if we graduate, we keep them forever to help mentor new students. Does your school have that?" she asked.

Thane had no real idea. "Keep going…"

"I don't know, Thane. If you could find a way to talk to him… At my school, Secret Networks powers our community. It's an easier interface, designed like personal chat rooms. It's kind of a sleeker, older version of social media." Erin got up and went for her phone on the cabinet in the kitchen. "It's like different components of social media. It's not designed to just chat with anyone. Instead, it's more of a one-on-one mechanism that facilitates easier communication. Kind of like Wilder Hangouts. Are you familiar with that?"

"I don't do social media at all, but I do teleconferencing all the time," Thane reminded Erin as she grabbed her seat and dragged the chair around the table closer to him. She worked her phone until she found what she was looking for then turned the screen so he could see.

"This is a smaller, very basic profile that I can link to my real social media pages or just have this one like it is. Most of the younger generations have pictures, the older ones not so much," Erin explained, crossing one leg over the other as she positioned the phone for him to see as she showed him the workings of her profile. "Think of it like this: it's just alumni, staff, and students working together for a better school experience. If you don't have a college email address, you can't get in. Secret Networks created the concept a couple of years ago, and it's really taken off as a source of networking for students and new graduates."

Thane took her phone and swiped around a bit, familiarizing himself with the site. His eyes narrowed as he contemplated the possibility of how this application could help him with Levi. Maybe he could get Levi talking to him over something like this. Build a friendship with Levi… His heart immediately rejected that idea. He wanted more than that, but dammit, Thane just wasn't anywhere close to giving up his requirements.

"I don't know," he said, handing her the phone.

"Let me search Johns Hopkins."

He waited, taking another bite of the neglected pancakes then drinking his cooling coffee while she worked her phone.

"I found it."

Thane tilted his head enough to watch everything she did. "What's his name?"

"Levi Silva. With an *i*. L-e-v-i."

"Oh, Thane, he's hot," she stated, turning the phone his way.

He was unprepared for the jolt of desire sweeping through his body as he took the phone and isolated the photo, making the picture larger. Nice-looking didn't begin to describe Levi, at least not to him. Even in what looked like a standard, run-of-the-mill enrollment picture, Levi's extraordinary handsomeness came shining through. His look just did it for Thane. He was exotic, yet all-American, and those perfect suck-me lips… Shit.

Thane forced himself to hand the phone back.

"Okay, well, he's in here. Your school's in here. It might be a way to talk to him without being aggressive, but you have to be the one to do it. I can't access anything inside there," Erin said.

"Send me that link?" he asked, completely unsure if this were a good or bad idea.

"Sure. I also can't see the alumni accounts, but I'm certain you have a profile. I'll help if you want me to," she offered eagerly.

"Will he think it's stalkerish?" Thane asked.

That was his biggest concern. He had vowed to leave Levi alone, and exactly twenty-four hours later, he now wanted to make contact. Probably not the best idea.

"Not if you handle it right. Besides, what's it hurt?" she said with a casual shrug.

"You're right. It can't possibly get any worse." Which sounded dramatic and understated all at the same time.

"Good, then give it a try," she said, unfolding her long body from the chair. "I'm taking these to Corey. You start on your profile, and I'll be back to check on you." She pushed the chair back to the other side of the table and lifted the pancakes and syrup. "I'm leaving the mess for you to clean up. Also, I found the SPCA does let you walk the dogs, so no more excuse about yappie hour, mister. Thursday night." She kissed the top of his head and exited through the patio door.

Thane sat there, thinking. Maybe the alumni thing could work. His heart sure saw the benefits. His head, not so much. Maybe he should wait. A sudden slice of pain over that irritating organ in his chest nearly crippled him. Apparently, his heart was determined to make anything but doing the right thing impossible. If for nothing more than to apologize, the sooner he reached out to Levi, the better. Thane got to his feet and went to warm his coffee. He needed to shower, call the resort to have someone store the belongings he'd left behind, and then he'd take a look at that alumni software. It surely couldn't hurt to build an account.

~~~

Levi stepped out, quietly shutting the screen door behind him. His brothers were sitting on the steps of the back porch. Luke sat about mid-step down in one corner; Logan sat a little lower on the other side. Neither spoke. The cool temperature had Levi wrapping his arms around his chest and heading to the step closest to Luke, taking a seat right beside him. Luke was sniffling, bent over, holding his legs, studying the broken concrete, probably still crying. His head was angled away, and he wouldn't look at Levi. Logan looked over his shoulder and up at him. His eyes were red-rimmed, but dry. Thank God for that.

"I have a story," Levi started and paused, seeing if it would draw Luke's attention. It didn't, but Logan turned, shifting to where he could easily look up at Levi. "Luke, when I found out mom was pregnant with you, I seriously couldn't wait for you to get here. I was so excited." Still Luke didn't do or say anything.

Levi let out a slow calming breath, pausing as he stared out into the small backyard, remembering that time in his life.

"I'm gonna tell you guys a secret. Something I haven't told anyone. That was about the time I realized that I wasn't like the other boys in my class. I remember just kind of being aware that I didn't buy into the boy-girl thing. I remember praying that Luke
~~~

came as a little girl, because I assumed any children that came from my parents would come liking boys, and I didn't want Luke to have to deal with the things I had started going through. I'd also read somewhere girls were supposedly made of sugar and spice and everything nice and boys were made of snips of snails and puppy dog tails. That was just too much for me to sort out in my head. Everything nice sounded so much better to me than chopped up snails."

That had Luke tilting his head in Levi's direction with a genuine grin as Levi continued.

"It's kind of shocking that someone so dumb made it to medical school, isn't it?" Levi chuckled at his own ridiculousness and clapped Logan, who had also started laughing, on the shoulder. "And with you, I just knew we were gonna have all sorts of bigger problems because of how much you liked to eat dirt."

That had Logan sincerely laughing, because there was no lie in his words. When he was little, Logan did prefer eating dirt over just about anything.

Levi lifted his arm, wrapping it tightly around Luke's back, drawing him closer. He'd thought he might have pulled Luke out of the funk until his brother dropped his head to his hands and stared down at the cracked concrete.

Concerned, Levi looked at Logan whose smile instantly faded as he watched Luke retreat again. Luke's mental health was the only thing that would get in the way of his resolve for them to stay together. If it were better for Luke to be with Linda, he'd let him go. He didn't want to, but he would.

The way Luke's body shook left no doubt he was crying. At least Levi thought his little brother was crying until Luke lifted his face and the look touched his heart. His brother's tear-stained face had genuine amusement crinkling the corners of his eyes. With a huge broad smile, he beamed. "Logan ate dirt? How is this the first time I'm hearing this?"

"I know, right?" Levi added and wanted to add to Luke's amusement, even if it was at Logan's expense. "I remember Dad and I saw a toddler with a helmet on. Dad told me it was designed to protect the baby, and I immediately asked him to get one for Logan even though he wasn't a baby anymore." All three of them laughed at that. "That's not information I really let out. It was pretty dumb. But when you were born, Luke, I remember praying to God that if he made you regular, I'd take care of you always. I even told him I'd take care of you if you weren't regular but I'd prefer regular."

"What'd you think regular was?" Logan asked, looking genuinely confused.

He seriously had the best brothers in the world. Before he had a chance to say those very words, Luke looked at him, held his gaze, and said, "I don't think your prayers helped much."

Everything faded as Levi focused in on his brother who again ducked his head to stare down at his bare feet. Instinctively Levi tightened his hold. After a second, Luke turned his head slightly, staring back up at Levi. The look said everything the words hadn't.

"What'd I miss?" Logan asked.

Levi's gut had told him there was more to Luke's depression than just his father's death. He wondered if his dad had known. Probably so. He was always so good about those things. Oh, man, reality slapped him firmly in the face. That was why his dad insisted he be the one to take care of Luke and Logan. He'd give the love and support to Luke that his father had given him. Levi ignored Logan and spoke directly to Luke. "You know we're gonna be okay. If we stick together, I can make it all work. No one says I have to finish medical school right now."

"I don't want you to give it up. You have a chance," Logan said, spouting his father's words as he inserted himself in their conversation.

"Then we can all go to Maryland together. Maybe that should be our goal. It's a million times better than here," Levi said, adding an affirmative nod to that fact because no one in Maryland had any idea they came from the slums of San Diego. "What'd you guys say? Let's start working in that direction. I haven't let myself think about it too much, but maybe before the start of next school year, let's go there."

"I'd be okay with that," Luke said and looked at Logan. Levi kept his gaze on his littlest brother. It was the way Luke's face morphed into years younger as he sucked his lip between his teeth that had Levi's determination setting in.

"Me too," Logan said. "I have to be careful of my classes, but I'm graduating early anyway, and I can email University of Virginia to make sure it doesn't mess with anything, but I'll go."

The hinges squeaked as the door opened. Linda came through, taking a seat behind them on the top step. "Guys, I probably shouldn't have had Mrs. Underwood here. I just thought she could handle any crisis that came up," Linda said, apologetically. "I envisioned that turning out differently in my head."

"We've been talking," Levi said, not looking back at her. He wrapped his arm tighter around Luke and again lifted his hand to Logan's shoulder. Here lately, happy moments were rare, and he wasn't ready to let go of the one they had just shared.

"That's good," Linda said. "I only want to help."

"We know, but we want to try and make this work." Levi didn't finish with the rest of their plan, not sure if anyone should know before Logan had a chance to talk to his college and the high school. It could seriously be a pipe dream that they might not be able to pull off.

"We're going to Maryland together," Luke, his usually quiet brother, blurted out. "We have that bonus Levi got, and we're gonna start working together to make our lives better."

Levi rolled his eyes. Not only was silence about the plan no longer an option, but Luke had managed to remind him of Thane. His entire body tightened, betraying the sense of fury he should feel toward the man. Instead, his emotions ran the full gamut. Ricocheting passion, desire, and need mixed with unbelievable frustration and anger. That had been his problem for the last twenty-four hours. His emotions were so all over the place where Thane was concerned that he had to use a herculean effort to shut all those thoughts down. Levi refused to let himself think about Thane. Yes, technically, he'd barely stopped, but Linda's announcement this morning had helped change that course. Levi was determined to only focus on his brothers and their future from this point forward.

"And when are you going to try to make this move?" Linda asked.

"We're gonna have to figure that out," Levi answered, tightening his grip on his brothers, hoping to quiet them until they found out all the details. "Definitely finish out the school year."

"Luke, is that a smile?" Linda asked.

"Yes, ma'am. We talked." Luke moved his thumb between him and Levi. It wasn't much of a talk, absolutely minimal words spoken in his brother's apparent coming out, but he guessed it was enough. Linda brought a hand to her heart, tears filling her voice.

"This is all I wanted in the world." She dropped down a step, drawing all of them into a tight, if awkward, hug. "Okay, I'm in for your new goal too. You're all three always welcome wherever I am. You're my boys, but if we can get you outta here, that's far better."

"Thank you. It helps to have a backup plan," Luke said, pulling from the hold. "I'm starving." Luke was up, climbing over Levi then Linda to go back inside. In a sudden shift of moods, it seemed his brother was suddenly on the right track. Levi looked back to see the door swing shut as Linda began to chuckle.

"I'm going too," Logan said and started to stand. He looked back at Linda, grinning. Levi swore he needed to learn how to roll with all these changing moods a little better.

CHAPTER 15

That night, Thane sat burrowed beneath a throw on his sofa in front of a roaring fire with a glass of Passeggiata, his current favorite wine from a local vineyard, in his hand and his laptop in his lap. A winter storm had blanketed the area and the snow continued to fall. Thank goodness this hadn't happened twenty-four hours ago, or he'd have gotten stuck trying to travel home.

Thane had left his blinds open so he could watch the pristine white flakes dance in the wind right outside his window. The extreme differences in weather were hard to digest. Two nights ago, he could have worn shorts out on the beach. Tonight, the temperatures barely hit twenty-five degrees. He wasn't sure which he preferred, except Coronado had Levi and that pretty much said it all.

Where Levi was concerned, he still felt like an ass. That was his single motivating reason in moving forward with Erin's idea. At the very least, Thane planned to make up his bad behavior to the man. On the flip side, he desperately wanted a repeat of their night together. A lot of repeats. He couldn't explain what made Levi so different, but there was no denying Thane wanted Levi right there beside him, wrapped inside this blanket, watching the snow fall.

That never-before-experienced need for another person resulted in uncertainty that turned into anxiety as his chest constricted and his heart ached. Instead of letting his mind run wild and ultimately freak him out, he opened his JHU social media site on both his laptop and his phone and spent some time familiarizing himself with the website. It seemed to have a Reddit feel—public message boards where anyone could ask a question and get a plethora of answers. There was also a private messaging option.

He completed his brief profile and made all the information about himself private. He absolutely didn't want to talk to anyone but Levi. He then sought out Levi's profile. Levi had the one picture he'd seen this morning, probably a school ID photo. Levi was extraordinarily handsome; his look just did it for Thane, and he saved that photo to both his laptop and his phone.

Now, with the messages option open on Levi's page, Thane sat ready to fire off his message, yet he hesitated. It was vital to get this first interaction right. The stakes grew higher by the second because he couldn't stop thinking about the man. Levi never left his head. He lingered there no matter what Thane did, even when he purposefully tried to push the guy out.

Maybe that was what caused this most recent bout of desperation. Levi had been so angry. Thane closed his eyes, his memory drifting to the old, run-down house. Seeing Levi's disheveled, skinny brother. Remembering the minute Levi came around the corner, carrying his brother's bowl and the instant exasperated look that appeared on his face.

Levi had taken his impromptu visit as an insinuation that Levi was in fact nothing more than a rent boy. That was where everything blurred for Thane. He'd caused Levi embarrassment and pain. He'd never meant to do either of those things.

Instead of lingering on those thoughts, Thane reached for his cell phone and called Julian who answered with a quickly stated, "I'll call you back."

Julian never did that. If he couldn't talk, he didn't answer. Thane looked at the phone, confused, then stuck it back to his ear. That was when he picked up the faint sounds of a voice. Thane increased the volume and stuck a finger in his other ear, trying to listen to the conversation on the other end.

"I think it's better that I quit. I can put in a two-week notice. Whatever you need."

Thane's heart lurched as he heard Levi's deep tenor. Thane's eyelids drifted closed, and he bent his head, concentrating on listening to every single word.

"Levi, stay. We'll work with you. If something comes up and you can't make it, the guys are always looking for shifts. Quit the PT clinic, but stay here. You'll make more money with us."

Good boy, Julian. Thane had no idea the circumstance, but Julian had done real good with that answer.

"My brothers need me at home more," Levi said, his tone of voice changing, becoming sadder maybe, and Thane's brow furrowed. "The clinic has sites all over the United States, and I can move with them."

"We're part of a much larger company. We have an employee assistance program that'll help with expenses and offer all those same benefits as the clinic. You've got a lot going on, I understand, but your sales are crazy good. Your tips have to be great," Julian countered.

"They are. It's not just that." He heard nothing but silence, and Thane strained to hear, hoping he wasn't missing anything. "I can't take a bunch of bullshit right now. My brother's freaked out, but we hit a turning point this morning. I've gotta stay balanced, and I can't deal with all that crap Thane put me through last week. I just can't do it again. I find myself thinking about him and not my family. They don't deserve it."

Thane's heart sank at the turmoil he heard in Levi's voice. The man that had brought so much emotion out in him, emotion he didn't even know he could have, now suffered because of his stupid actions. How had he let things get so out of control for the both of them?

"I've gotten his word that he won't bother you." Julian's voice became clearer in the receiver. "He's seen the error of his ways, and he's gone. We only see him every few months, and that's usually just a brief stop in. Now that we're up and running, I expect to see him even less."

There was silence, then Julian's voice turned softer.

"Levi, just stay. I'll fill out the employee assistance paperwork myself. I promise to be flexible with you. The guys on the floor won't mind divvying up your tables if we can't get someone to fill in. These are extraordinary circumstances and I want to help." Hearing those words made Thane smile. Julian was doing so well. All the expense of training Julian was paying off. He had turned into a true leader.

There was silence again and Thane continued to listen intently. When Levi spoke, the uncertainty Thane heard in his voice broke his heart. "I just think I need to quit this and go find a real job. Julian, I feel so stupid. I'm really into him. Even after everything, I can't stop thinking…" Levi's words became distorted. Thane looked at the screen and stuck it back to his ear. The line went dead.

No! No. Thane immediately called Julian again, frustrated when the call went to voicemail. Had Julian cut him off on purpose? Was Levi talking about him when he said "into him?" His heart sped up at the thought he might still have a chance to set things right, but then dropped just as suddenly. Levi had been more than clear with what he thought of him.

Thane pushed call again and the phone again went to voicemail. Frustrated, Thane reached for his wineglass, downing the contents while getting to his feet. His mind raced with all the scenarios playing out at warp speed then settling on the most likely answer. Julian had cut him off on purpose. Who the hell was Levi into? It had to be him. Why else would he talk to Julian about it? Why would he quit Reservations? But…could it be another guy?

This time Thane lifted the bottle, drinking straight from the opening, trying to drown out the possibility that Levi might have a boyfriend. They'd gotten along so well that night that it had never occurred to him to even ask the boyfriend question.

He was seriously such a selfish ass. Thane looked around the room as if he were seeing it for the first time. How had he not thought to ask about a boyfriend? His cell phone started to ring in his hand, stopping his overactive imagination before it exploded into an ugly, terrible tirade. He glanced down to see Julian's name and swiped across the screen with his thumb.

"Why the fuck did you hang up?" he asked before he ever got the phone to his ear.

"Because that was giving you way too much insider information and would give you all the power. He doesn't need anyone coming in and bulldozing over his life right now," Julian said, defensively as hell.

"I'm not bulldozing," he countered with just as much attitude.

"Yeah. Right. Keep telling yourself that," Julian shot back.

What the hell was happening? He wanted to rip Julian's head off for being so damned defiant. Thane saw red and forced himself to calm down before he had a heart attack over this shit.

"Julian. Tell me what he said." His voice was as sharp as his words were clipped.

"You know, Thane. I've been with you long enough to know your tastes, what makes you stop and take a good long look at a man. So, when I walked into that coffee shop and saw Levi again, my first thought was that I knew you'd be into him. He fits you. I know you like guys that look like him. Who are smart, reasonable, and sexy, all at the same time. I put a nice glittery bow on his ass and pointed him out to you. All you had to do was get to know him. He doesn't want your money, Thane. He doesn't care what baggage you have. You just had to be anything but a dick, and since I've never known you to be one before, that shouldn't have been a problem. How could you have fucked this up so royally?" Julian asked, the cocky, sassy guy Thane had known for years was back in every syllable uttered.

Thane stayed silent and sat down on the sofa, dropping his head back on to the headrest behind him, and closed his eyes. The phone never left his ear. So, Julian's criticism made it clear Levi was in fact into him. Instead of dwelling on Julian's lecture, Thane's mind immediately drifted to his and Levi's night together and a tiny ray of hope sprang forward from the dark recesses of his hurting heart.

"Was he trying to quit again?" Thane asked.

"His life is shit. His father died of cancer a few months back. He's responsible for raising his younger brothers, and they're struggling." Julian paused.

As his words sank in, they hit Thane like a Mack truck. His actions were even more deplorable in light of that revelation. Why hadn't anyone told him about Levi's father? His heart broke a little more as he imagined the pain Levi must be going through.

"And, we're paying his rent and easing some of that guy's burdens. I don't care if you like that or not," Julian declared.

Thane instinctively wanted to try to make this hard-headed man understand he didn't have the authority to make such sweeping decisions, but he held his tongue. Julian had made the right decision; Thane just wished he'd initiated it instead of his outspoken manager.

"Okay. What about the woman who answered the door?"

"I don't know a lot. I believe his mother died years ago. He doesn't ever talk about his shit. I only know with certainty that his dad died recently, he came home from med school, and that his brothers are teenagers, but not old enough to support themselves."

"I saw one. He was early high school age," Thane said, the kid's image coming to mind. Losing their father to such a devastating disease... What a horrific experience for all of them. He couldn't imagine.

"Nice deduction, Sherlock." That tone had Thane cocking a brow. Julian seriously didn't know how to read a room.

"Why are you being mean to me? I've been good to you," Thane asked.

"Because you're being such a prick. What the hell happened to you? I told that guy the best things about you, all in hopes of giving you a shot at normal, Thane. You're seriously not as fucked up as you think you are." Julian paused a second, probably for some sort of dramatic effect, then continued. "And you've been such a motherfucker for days. You need to get over yourself."

"I don't do relationships," Thane said, sticking to the main problem between him and Levi. "It's not that I'm dysfunctional. I just don't like the inevitable end that always comes."

"You *do* do relationships. I was in one with you. You took care of me at the worst time in my life. You put me back on my feet. No, we weren't in love romantically, but you love and care about me, and I love and care for you. And here's another light bulb moment: get over your parents' divorce. Man, build a damn bridge and get over your self-made hang-ups."

A deep exhale escaped Thane's lips as he absorbed all those well-executed blows.

"You pay for just about everyone in your life, so we're obligated not to point these truths out. Then your other friends, like those I hear about who live next door, you don't tell them the finer details of your life. You gotta work on you before you ever try to work things out with Levi."

Silence ensued for several long moments. Thane could barely wrap his head around all that Julian had just dumped at his feet. He had no idea Julian felt this way. They'd always had a nice time together. Thane stared at the window, watching the snow fall as his mood took a further nose dive. Julian's words stung; he'd hurt Thane when he was already so low.

"Was any of that designed to hit below the belt? Because you sure seemed to know your mark."

"Well, I tried for your heart. You know I try to be like freakin' Mother Teresa, but in a diva kinda way."

Thane gave a small smile at the America's Next Top Model reference, a show he and Julian had watched together on occasion. It was just like Julian to slam him, then try to lighten the mood with a joke.

"For the record, I'm not sure I love you," Thane replied, letting the conversation turn away from his very clear faults. And seriously, backing up the conversation further, how had Julian known he liked guys who looked like Levi? He'd thought he was attentive to his men. He couldn't ever remember letting something like that out. "Most of the time I want to fire you."

"Stop sexy-talking me, I'm not sleeping with you," Julian said then released an audible, heavy sigh before he continued. "I'm sorry if what I said was overly harsh. I knew if you two could get together it was gonna be a struggle, but damn if you two aren't hardheaded as shit."

"So, he's into me?" Thane asked the question he'd wanted an answer to for their entire conversation.

"Yes. He likes you. I knew he would. You're a good guy and a very attentive lover. Well, at least you used to be. I don't know this crazy man you've become. Are you really sure you have the money to be going around acting like you can buy everyone? And if you do have that kind of money, why the hell didn't you buy all my time? That measly thousand dollar monthly stipend you gave me didn't pay for jack," Julian quipped, back to all sass and attitude.

Thane barked out a laugh at the money crack. Julian didn't get out of bed in the morning for a mere thousand dollars. "Talking to you's like playing verbal volleyball. My God, focus, Julian," Thane said. Every time he got to a subject where his heart needed some sort of validation, Julian segued in a different direction.

"Let me be very clear about this, it's not a good time for Levi. His plate's all filled up with a whole lot of crap. He needs friends, not the chaos known as Thane Walker."

"All right," Thane said, acknowledging he'd paid attention to Julian.

"And for full disclosure, I'm pretty sure he's planning on raising his brothers. I wasn't fully aware of that before, so he has complicated responsibilities. Not as complicated as your head-game baggage, but you should know that while you're trying to figure out your next move," Julian advised.

The thought of kids did take his comfort zone to the next level of crazy, but for some reason, they didn't really matter to his heart. Weird. "How old is the other one?"

"I don't know for sure, both in high school. They're old enough that he works nights here with no known problems."

Thane found himself nodding to no one. "Okay, I'll authorize the funds for the house on Monday. I'll do six months with a revisit then," Thane said and stared unseeingly at the embers glowing in the fireplace. "And it freaks me out to say, but I'll admit to you and only you…I'm into him too."

"Then stop being a douchebag and be yourself. But first, give him some space. He wasn't happy that you went to his house. I'm guessing you showing up embarrassed him," Julian replied, finally staying on topic.

"Yeah, I regret that decision, but it helped me see things more clearly. You filled in all the missing pieces. I'll also admit I was an ass," Thane confessed.

"I know. I've been dealing with the aftermath for the last couple of days," Julian said dryly. "All right. I'm hanging up my relationship specialist hat; I have a club to run."

"Thanks, Julian," Thane said and lowered the phone, not paying attention to whatever sassy reply the guy made to end the call.

Thane rose enough to pour himself another glass of wine. He agreed whole-heartedly with Julian's sentiment: this was all too much. The last week and a half had been an out-of-body experience for him. He didn't like the obsessive ogre he'd become.

And Levi had brothers, as in more than one, to take care of… Mmm.

Julian had nailed his core problem. Thane did have a hang-up over his parents' divorce, but dammit, he had lived with his father's selfishness his whole damn life. When he was a young boy, he never really understood what was happening, but now that he was older, he got it. His mother was in love and weak. His father was a cheat and a user.

His old man would come like clockwork to pick him up for visitation. Thane would have to wait by the door for a solid hour while his mother and father went to the bedroom to "talk." From a young age, he learned not to move from his spot by the front door because his father didn't want to be made to wait. Thane had gotten more than one spanking when he'd ventured off from his perch on the stairs before it was time to leave. As he'd gotten older, he'd made sure his old man would have to search for him. Defiance was all he had to show his disgust for the situation. Thane had willingly taken those licks, praying the whole time that his father would stop coming around altogether.

His parents' talks would leave his mother depressed and in bed for days to follow. She'd barely have herself back together before his father was there again to pick him up. The cycle never stopped through his father's three other wives. Hell, it could still be going on today for all he knew. Until he'd started this company, Thane's only goals in life were to never hurt anyone like his father had hurt all the women in his life. Yet inevitably, Thane had seemed to do that very thing to the few men he'd chosen to date.

"Damn," he growled to the empty room and reached for the remote control to drown out all the bullshit in his head. After he turned the volume up on whatever show was on, he picked up his laptop and decided to start making this right with Levi. Even if they went no further, he'd have the peace of mind that he'd tried to help the man of his dreams in his time of need. He chose five simple words in the form of a message.

"Do you need any help?"

He pushed send, still thinking about those words. They were nonintrusive and straightforward. That was good, right? He rolled his eyes at all this second-guessing and moved the laptop to the sofa while reaching for the wineglass.

He felt a decent drunk coming on.

~~~

Twisting the lock in place, Levi barely got inside the house before his phone began to vibrate in his pocket. He reached for the cell as he took in the scene in his living room. Luke was asleep, stretched out along the length of the couch, his head resting on a pillow. Logan was on the floor, his back against the armrest of the couch, watching television.
~~~

Logan looked up, raising a single finger to his lips, motioning for him to be quiet. Levi nodded and looked over at the television. He'd missed the significance of the show at first glance. They were watching *Iron Man*. Their absolute favorite movie as children.

The sadness in the house didn't seem quite as prevalent as it had before. He paid little to no attention to the TV, instead going to the edge of the sofa and staring at his youngest brother who still looked even younger while sleeping. He prayed his father would help guide him in making good decisions where his brothers were concerned. His dad had been such a good father to all three of them. He'd tried so hard to get them out of this life and he'd almost done it too. If that disease hadn't come back, Levi was certain everything about their lives would be far different today.

With a lump forming in his throat, Levi forced his thoughts away from his father. Maybe not the best idea, because Thane was right there ready to take his place. Levi didn't want to think about him either. That was fresh pain and humiliation, but also deep, desperate desire. He couldn't let Thane in right now; Levi would crave things he couldn't have. Levi had to stay focused on the here and now. So he went for the side chair and sat, hoping his presence in the house helped Logan not feel so alone all the time.

Levi palmed his phone and saw a text from Julian. With a swipe of his finger, he opened the message. *"I filed the paperwork with HR and got an immediate reply. It's being processed, but I feel sure we've got your house rent covered for the next six months. I hope that helps."*

Levi had no real idea how that miracle had happened, but that would save them almost two thousand dollars a month. If he socked that money away, it would grow their nest egg to help make their move a reality. That lifted such a burden off his shoulders, and he quickly typed back, thanking Julian for everything. The man had been an absolute lifesaver when his life had needed the most saving.

Fiddling with his phone, Levi saw a new notification from his school. He'd never used this particular application before, but the timing seemed destined. He had so much to find out about on-campus family housing. Would financial aid pay for something like that for all of them? Another thought sprang forward. Did Baltimore have a good school district for Luke?

Making a mental checklist of everything he needed to find out, Levi clicked the school's mascot icon and began familiarizing himself with the application. If he remembered correctly… Okay, he didn't remember, so he started to click whatever he could find until the mail symbol in the corner popped open and he saw a new direct message waiting. It took less than a second for the words to fill his screen.

"Do you need any help?"

Weird. But he'd just randomly gotten his rent covered for six months, so weirder things had happened today. Levi quickly scanned all the details of the message. Someone named Nathaniel was offering help. Huh. Okay. He couldn't remember a Nathaniel. Levi clicked the non-photo of Nathaniel's university hosted email address and went to his page. Not a lot of information there. He was an alum, attended JHU eight years ago, and his page was locked to private. Confused, Levi went back to the message and read the single question again. *"Do you need any help?"*

Maybe this was some sort of counseling program since he'd left school so abruptly. Or maybe the sender reached out to the wrong person. Both equally possible. Instead of guessing any further, Levi typed back, *"Do we know each other?"*

Levi looked up at his sleeping brother then Logan who was doing something on his phone. This had all the makings of being a long drawn-out time in their lives. He saw a lot of these moments in his future. He figured they were probably more healing than boring, and they needed this time together to bond as a family unit without their dad at the helm. Levi tilted his head, listening to Luke's slightly labored breath; it sounded like he might have a sinus problem, and Levi mentally added that to the list of things to have checked out. His phone vibrated in his hand, drawing his eyes down to the bright screen. He had a text message from Logan.

"Luke said for you to check email. They cancelled the counseling appointment for Monday morning. Someone's sick."

Levi nodded, lifting his eyes to his brother, then his phone vibrated again. So few people ever messaged him, he looked down, half expecting Logan to have sent another text message. Instead, there was a new direct message from Nathaniel.

"I'm not trying to start any problems. I just wanted to reach out to you."

Levi's brows slid together as he tried to understand the message. He was even more confused now. What problem would Nathaniel start? He stared at the cell phone, willing himself to remember a Nathaniel connected to Johns Hopkins. In the furthest recesses of his mind, he might have known a Nate. Maybe he worked with him for a few weeks as Dr. Hofstede's teacher's aide. The guy wouldn't be alum though. He'd be classified as a student.

Unsure what to do, Levi decided just to go with it. Professors didn't always have the best social skills. They also tended to like themselves a lot. Well, some of them did… Wait, if Nathaniel worked at the school, he'd then be classified as faculty, not alumni. This got more confusing by the second. Levi started typing, hoping he could give enough information to satisfy the question then get Nathaniel talking to help fill in the blanks.

"We're as good as can be expected. I'm not sure I remember a Nathaniel, that's all I was implying. I appreciate the offer."

He pushed send, and on instinct, he immediately typed another message.

"I look forward to being back at school. I hope leaving like I did hasn't messed with my scholarship. I'll be back as soon as I settle things here. Thank you again."

With that, Levi placed his phone on the coffee table and went to wake his brother.

"Luke, let's get you to bed," Levi said loudly. Luke blinked, looked up, and gave a small smile before closing his eyelids again. "Come on. You'll be more comfortable in bed," he coaxed, standing over his sleeping brother.

"Hmmm," Luke muttered.

His brother was always hard to wake unless there was food in the mix. Levi reached for his arm, lifting a wobbly Luke to his feet.

"Let's get up and go jogging in the morning," Levi said as Luke finally woke enough to head toward his room.

"Okay." That was all he got before Luke disappeared behind the bedroom door.

"I'm going to bed," Levi said to Logan, who'd taken Luke's space on the sofa.

"Hey, I need to tell you something." Logan seemed to always have more energy than anyone. He bounded up to his feet, trailing after Levi who stopped at the hall entrance and anchored an arm against the wall as he stifled his yawn. He hadn't slept well since waking up in Thane's bed, and then, he'd only gotten in a few hours' sleep. He was exhausted and needed some serious rest.

"I can be home every night."

Levi had to think about that one. Logan was already home every night anyway. Levi took a closer look at his brother, trying to figure out what that statement was code for. Logan stood there, crossing his arms over his chest, giving nothing away. Levi had no idea what he tried to convey in that moment, so he waited for more.

"I don't know how much you know, but I did early registration, and University of Virginia accepted me for the winter semester next year with full scholarship money. Did dad tell you?"

"I knew they accepted you, and I'm real proud of you. Can we talk about that tomorrow? My goal this week is to sit down with everything and see where we are. We can call the university and see what they think about you switching districts to finish your last semester," Levi said and changed his position, crossing his arms over his chest as he stifled another longer yawn. "Maybe we could do that during the canceled appointment if you want. I bet someone at your school could help us figure it all out."

Levi reached out to pat his brother on the shoulder and started to turn away, feeling like they'd set their plan. Logan trailed a few feet behind him until Levi stopped just inside his bedroom, turning back to Logan as his brother rested a shoulder on the doorframe. He was so tired; why was Logan choosing then to talk? Levi turned on the lamp then sat on the edge of the bed before reaching down to untie his tennis shoes.

"Yeah, that's good idea, because I was thinking that I've already got all my credits I need to graduate. Well, except for half an English and a history, and I could take those in summer school, or maybe a night class at SDC. Then I could graduate another semester early—like at the end of summer. Then maybe I could get a full-time job in Maryland until I go to school in January. That would help pay for all of us," Logan offered, showing he'd been really thinking about solutions for their family. Levi tossed the shoes toward his closet, nodding his approval.

"It sounds like a good idea. Let's go talk to your guidance counselor first thing Monday morning. Then we'll call the college. I gotta call social security too and find out where those checks are," Levi said. Normally the list of things he needed to do became daunting, but not this time. Instead, they were finally getting on the same page, looking toward the future. When Levi started to remove his T-shirt, he saw Logan still standing there, staring at him. He squashed the sigh and the new yawn forming and finally said, "I gotta sleep. This has been the longest day of my life in a string of really long days."

Logan left him sitting there, freeing Levi. Maybe as much as a minute later, he was undressed, climbing into bed as Logan reappeared in the doorway. The bed felt so good. He grabbed a stack of pillows, pushing them behind his head, and prayed he didn't fall asleep before Logan got the nerve to say whatever he'd planned to say. Again, as much as a minute passed with Logan still just standing there.

Levi flat out said, "Just tell me. I'm tired."

"You said to tell you things, so I have a girlfriend I haven't talked about." Logan's shoulder hit the doorframe under the weight of his confession, making Levi's grin grow.

"You do?" Levi asked, surprised. For some reason, that eased his heart where this brother was concerned. If Logan had someone by his side, someone looking out for him, it had to make this whole thing easier on him. "Do I know her?"

"I don't think so. I've been sticking close to home. She comes over and hangs out with me and Luke," Logan said, studying the carpet on the floor. "It's all straight-up fine. We stay in the living room. She's not like that."

He supposed that "not like that" meant sex. He should make sure Logan had condoms and the always cringe-worthy talk about using them, but that felt weird. He'd think about that talk tomorrow. "Good. That's good, Logan. You need to take her out. I'll give you the money or maybe we can all go somewhere this Friday night. Get Luke out of the house too," Levi suggested.

"That sounds good." Logan's gaze lifted to his, turning serious. "Dad knew her."

"Did he like her?" Levi asked.

"Yeah. We weren't dating back then. She's going to Virginia too, but she'll start next fall," Logan added. His nervousness seemed to fade, and he was back to staring Levi in the eyes.

"Thanks for telling me," he said, hoping his brothers were both done keeping secrets. "I feel like knowing things is better than not knowing."

Logan nodded his agreement, taking his phone out of his pocket as he pushed away from the doorframe.

"Does this mean you'll finally start picking up your nasty socks?"

"Probably not," Logan said, dropping his jeans right where he stood, kicking them up with his foot. "She's already seen them lying around and didn't say anything. I took that to mean she's okay with it." He left the doorway.

Levi could hear him chuckling all the way down the small hall. Levi shook his head as the hall light turned off, and he pulled some of the pillows from under his head before reaching for the lamp. That bit of news had cheered him up. All of it had, and maybe, when he closed his eyes, he'd be too tired to think about Thane. He wasn't, but luckily, he did fall asleep quickly.

~~~

Thane reread Levi's message and then went back to his own profile, staring at all his information on the page. His full name was clearly stated at the top. Nathaniel "Thane" Walker. How did Levi not know who he was? Was the guy messing with him? Levi's message hadn't sounded like a sarcastic joke. Levi seemed genuinely unsure of Thane's identity, and Thane had no idea what was going on. Yes, Nathaniel was his full first name, but his nickname and last names were clearly displayed at the top of his profile. How had Levi not put two and two together?

Knowing he was borderline inappropriate, Thane still decided to call Tristan Wilder. Downing an entire bottle of wine in the last couple of hours played a part in his bold move, but resources were resources, and surely the owner of the site would know the answer to his question.

"Hello," Tristan answered on the fourth ring.

"Hey, are you busy?" he asked, bouncing his leg as he stared at the laptop on the coffee table that still displayed Levi's messages.

"I'm trying to be. What's up?" Tristan asked, somewhat harried. And yes, technically he got Tristan's meaning, but the guy had still asked *"what's up,"* so Thane went that direction instead of hanging up the phone like a good friend might have.

"I'm having a problem with your social media site—"

"Are you seriously calling me to answer a question about Secret?" Tristan asked, and Thane got the impression he better ask fast because Tristan would be hanging up soon.

"And the guy on the other end called me Nathaniel..." Thane continued.

"Who's Nathaniel?"

Thane ignored Tristan's question and persevered. "Is he seeing my whole name or just part of it?" Thane finally got to the reason for the call.

Tristan didn't respond to him. Instead, he started talking to someone else. It was muffled, and Thane stuck a finger in his ear
~~~

to better hear. He heard a rustling then Dylan's voice almost took out his eardrum when he spoke directly into the phone.

"Now, what are you asking?"

Thane quickly moved the phone back an inch or two, ignored the instant headache, and sat on the edge of his sofa, still staring at the screen. "I'm on my alumni messaging app—I think that's what it's called. It's a community in Secret. Did I say that right?"

"Sort of," Dylan said, sounding somewhat confused. "Keep going."

"Okay, so I'm catching up with a student and he keeps calling me Nathaniel—"

"Who's Nathaniel?" Dylan asked, cutting him off.

Thane never strayed off course. "Is there a chance he can't see my whole name? Or is he just being annoying?"

"I don't know. Hang on. I'll call in for you." He heard Tristan begin to whine in the background and that made Thane smile as he used the mouse pad to click back to Levi's profile picture. How had he missed the opportunity to take a few shots of Levi before he'd messed things up so badly? If he ever got the chance again, he'd absolutely get as many photos as he could.

"Babe, tell him to use Secret's live chat option to find his answers," Tristan said from a distance.

"I can get the answer for him faster. Hang on, Thane," Dylan yelled from even farther away.

He heard Tristan's irritation too clearly for the guy not to have picked up the phone, "You know I was working my way to gettin' lucky tonight."

"Well, don't stop on my account," Thane encouraged. For the first time in days, a genuine grin spread across his face as he got to his feet and began pacing across his small living room floor.

"I only stopped on your account," Tristan shot back defensively. "You know, he lives a five-hour plane ride from me—"

"No. You told me he moved to California." Thane cut off that lie before Tristan could even fully get it out of his mouth.

"He did, but he lived away from me for so long, we have a lot to make up for."

Thane laughed straight out loud. Tristan had effectively justified his lie in good form. Very well done. He'd have to give that a point in Tristan's favor.

"Hey, tell me, how's Julian? I haven't heard from him in a while."

Tristan had all the answers tonight. The thought of the irritating Julian was the buzz-kill that abruptly ended his good time. With a deep sigh, Thane stopped in front of his window, looking down, absently watching snow cover the town he loved.

"Tristan, I'm straight up telling you Julian's a pain in my ass."

Now it was Tristan's turn to bark out a laugh. "I bet. He's unstoppable."

"You have no idea. He runs off every manager I have, then he takes that job and incorporates it into his. He's got his nose in everyone's business, and dammit, he never misses a beat. He's a workhorse. It's all he does," Thane said, his brow slowly furrowed as he thought about his words. Work was truly all Julian did, and why did that feel off all of a sudden?

"Makes it hard to fire him," Tristan added, drawing Thane's attention back to the conversation.

"Damn straight."

"Tell Thane," Dylan said, his voice close to the receiver, "if his profile's set to private, all anyone can see is his first name from the school record and his school status of three options: student, faculty, or alum. The application's designed to be a helpful communication tool, not a full social media site."

Ah. Okay, that explained it. Levi didn't know who Nathaniel was. "Tell him thank you," Thane finally said.

"Next time do live chat," Tristan teased, yet sounded completely sincere at the same time.

"Why would I ever do that? This was so much simpler. Goodnight." Thane disconnected the call before Tristan got the chance to hang up on him and went back to the sofa. Levi's picture was still taking up the entire screen.

He wasn't sure how he felt about this now. The little high he'd gotten when Levi had responded so quickly began to fade.

They hadn't had a coming together. They were technically still at deep odds with one another. Shutting the laptop lid, Thane decided he needed time to think. Like Julian had said several times, Levi didn't need him creating more chaos in his life. Not right now. On that thought, Thane picked up his wine bottle and glass, taking them to the kitchen. He needed to really consider his actions, each and every one of them, before moving forward.

He trotted down the stairs, dropping his robe over a chair, and his pajama pants on the floor beside his bed. He crawled on top of the mattress, pulling the blanket over his body as he reached for his Levi-scented pillow. Several minutes passed as he stared out the window at the heavy snowfall. Thane guessed the decision was made.

On one level, it did make him a bit of an asshole. His past relationships revealed his patterns. He'd lose interest in Levi rather quickly, ultimately hurting him more in the end, but unfortunately, that didn't seem to matter. His heart wanted Levi like it had never wanted anything before. And he did see differences in this situation compared to previous relationships with men he'd dated before. For the first time ever, his attraction wasn't just sexual desire that pushed him to pursue. He wanted Levi to be a part of his day-to-day life, and he also found he wanted to help Levi. He wanted Levi's warm body to be what he snuggled up with at night, and he wanted Levi to have someone there with him so he didn't have to bear all those burdens alone.

It seemed crazy and spoke volumes about his sanity, pining for a man he barely knew. Maybe Erin was on to something. That just freaked him out, though. Thane closed his eyes, refusing to entertain the thought of saying the L-word out loud. It was way too soon for that, but he was headed there nonetheless. He just needed to be careful. From this point forward, he had to take the right steps and keep from freaking himself out too much.

He wasn't his father. Nowhere near close. He could do the right thing by people.

Hopefully.

CHAPTER 16

This staring out the window he'd been doing for most of the last couple of days needed come to an end. Thane eased out of his reclining office chair and walked the length of his temporary office to close the blinds of both windows before he went to the door, pulling it open, hoping that some of the noise from the masses out front might help interrupt his Levi-focused thoughts.

The temporary corporate office space beyond the door looked very much like the contents of a sardine can. So much so, it shocked him that none of his staff had quit. Glancing out over the large room filled with row after row of desks pushed together with employees sitting side by side while trying to complete their jobs filled him with claustrophobia.

He'd never be able to work in that environment. How had he not really noticed this before?

What the hell was happening to him? Thane took an involuntary step backward at the revelation. He'd always tried to be a decent person; he tried hard to be giving and caring, to help the people in his life, but now it seemed an awakening of sorts had taken place inside him. Since the moment he had driven into Levi's neighborhood, from that very minute, the world had opened his tunnel-vision perceptions to everything going on around him.

All his failures smacked him in the face.

He'd have to find a way to reward his people for all the inconvenience they'd endured and also begin to dog the hell out of Layne Construction, his construction team doing the remodel back on Main Street. Better yet, Thane stepped back to his desk and sent an email directly to the senior Mr. Layne, personally asking for his involvement on the jobsite. He needed that rebuild completed as soon as possible, and they had fallen way behind schedule.

Sally, his HR Manager, stuck her head inside the doorway as he pushed send on the message. "Thane, I got your expedited EAP on Levi Silva. Julian sent over everything but the payee's address. I was told this was to be handled sensitively. Can I call Mr. Silva directly or should I have Julian call? If I call, we can have a check mailed by end of tomorrow."

"I think it's okay for you to call," Thane said, leaning back in his office chair. "Let Julian know it's been taken care of for me." Sally nodded as David, one of his regional managers stuck his head inside the open doorway, reminding him the exact reason why he always kept his door closed.

"We're implementing the new menu rollout for the Iron Maya tomorrow. Is there anything we need to know before we head to Dallas for the kick off?"

Thane just stared blankly at him. How the hell was he supposed to know? He hadn't been in one single planning meeting since the new menu had been created months ago. With the expectant stare still focused straight on him, Thane finally said, "Talk it over with Jenna. She's better prepared, and shut my door for me."

He got a thumbs up from David, and Thane scrubbed a hand over his face when the door clicked closed behind the guy. He was frustrated as hell. All he could think about in every situation was an auburn-headed hottie with green eyes and a great smile. He'd even spent the first hour of his Monday morning talking to the student affairs staff at Johns Hopkins.

This had to stop.

Even with that self-lecture, when his cell phone vibrated on his desk, Thane picked it up to clear the alarm he had set while at the JHU meeting that morning. At the time, he didn't want to come off too overeager so he'd decided to wait what he deemed an appropriate amount of time to message Levi the details. Instead of using his cell phone and its frustratingly tiny keyboard,

Thane put that aside and reached for his laptop, typing on the message he already had open.

"I hope I didn't overstep, but I reached out to student affairs who sent me to financial services to check on your scholarship. Everything's intact. If I understood correctly, your deferment is good until the fall semester. I took the liberty of issuing an extenuating circumstance report that would allow you to extend the deferment past that point, but only one time.

"I hope this helps."

Thane read the words and read them again, deciding not to sign the message. How could he justify signing Nathaniel when Thane was the name he went by? He pushed send and minimized the program on his screen, forcing himself to focus. No more dilly-dallying. He had work to do.

~~~

Levi sat at the kitchen table, going over the household bills. Another much smaller stack was from the financial aid he'd taken out over the last five or six years. The last pile held the bill collectors; for bills he hadn't been able to talk the companies into giving him more time to pay. No matter how he organized the stacks, nothing ever changed. No magical wand had been waved, wiping out the debt, and his shoulders began to slump.

Instead of letting the heavy financial load mess with his head, Levi flipped through the household utility bills, making sure nothing was scheduled for disconnect this week. Thankfully, he had time on those. Grabbing all the bills, Levi put them together and placed them on the cabinet, the same location where they'd always belonged.

Grabbing a screwdriver from the cabinet drawer, Levi went to his bedroom and pushed the dresser aside. Carefully, he popped a board out of the flooring. No one in the world knew about this hiding place. He couldn't see into the dark recesses, but he reached down and pulled out a slim lockbox. He rose, grabbing his wallet off the dresser, and moved to his bed. He'd managed to save four hundred dollars from last week. He took
~~~

the money from his wallet and opened the lockbox. Like he always did, he counted out all the bills.

Twenty-six hundred dollars. He didn't know how far that would take them, but if he could keep saving like this, they might actually stand a chance of getting to Maryland and making a go of things.

Levi purposefully ignored the envelope holding five thousand dollars; that was going back to Thane Walker the first chance he got. The reminder had him recalling the simple things about the night he'd shared with Thane. He remembered laughing a lot, even Thane seemed uproariously happy when he'd somehow managed to talk Levi into giving twerking a try. How Thane had even gotten him out on the dance floor in the first place was a mystery. Except it really wasn't. From the very beginning, Thane had pushed him past his restrictive boundaries in everything they did. Even before he knew the guy, Thane's nightclub had Levi shucking his clothes, stripping down to just his underwear, serving drinks to horny older men. Not in a million years would he have ever considered a job like that; yet, he had, and he'd done well there. All thanks to Thane's vision.

Since that initial anger over Thane coming to the house had begun to fade, Levi seemed to be committing every moment of their time together to memory. He'd even somehow gotten to where he excused all of Thane's assumptions about what kind of man he was. After all, Levi was working in the nightclub, hanging out in that environment. Men throwing money around like nothing he'd ever seen before. And hell, Julian was his friend as well as his boss. Of course, Thane would come to those conclusions—it wasn't rocket science. Anyone would have thought those things; it's the exact reason he hadn't been forthcoming to the people in his life about where he worked.

In the future, he just had to keep his distance from Thane. That wouldn't be a problem, since he hadn't heard a word from the man and didn't expect to. No matter how good they were together, their life philosophies were too far off. Levi had a simplistic view to life. He believed in love and marriage and family. He craved monogamy and normalcy. Thane oozed sophistication and ran in the fast lane. He preferred the Julians of the world—quick, gratifying moments of intimacy with no strings attached. Levi liked all those strings. He hadn't really known that before, but he did now.

Instead of dwelling on what could have been, Levi took a deep cleansing breath and placed the money back inside the box. He carefully put the lockbox back in its hiding place, sealed the panel in the floor, and moved the dresser back in place.

He looked around the bedroom before heading out into the hall and stopping abruptly. He was in uncharted territory—alone in the house with time to kill before work. The clinic had closed after lunch today. A regional inspection or something like that had sent all the aides home early. He and his brothers had done all the household chores yesterday. He just didn't know what to do with himself. At a loss, Levi tugged his phone out of his back pocket, found the remote-control app, and went for the sofa before turning on the television.

Minutes later, he had flipped through the small list of channels and couldn't find anything interesting to watch. What was wrong with him? He didn't even know how to have free time. Levi clicked off the television and stared at the time on his phone. He had wasted less than ten minutes.

Luckily, his phone vibrated in his hand, and he eagerly clicked open the notification to Nathaniel's email. He still had no memory of the man, but his message added to this newfound sense of ease coming over his heart. Whoever Nathaniel was didn't truly matter. It seemed he had an advocate inside the university. If the guy could help this transition, Levi would gladly add Nathaniel's name to his lengthy pay it forward list and give back the first chance he got.

"I hope I didn't overstep, but I reached out to student affairs who sent me to financial services to check on your scholarship. Everything's intact. If I understood correctly, your deferment is good until the fall semester. I took the liberty of issuing an extenuating circumstance report that would allow you to extend the deferment past that point, but only one time.

"I hope this helps."

After reading the message, he began to type.

"That's a load off my mind, thank you. The way things are going here, I'm hoping I'll be back in Maryland by the fall. I'll have my teenage brothers with me. Do you have any idea how to apply for on-campus family housing?"

He pushed send and shoved off the sofa, barely starting for his room when the phone vibrated in his palm. Nathaniel had immediately responded.

"I can check into that tomorrow for you. How many brothers?"

Levi stopped in the hall, and instead of answering Nathaniel's question, he quickly typed back, *"I don't want to put you out."*

He stood there the few seconds, waiting, and got an almost instant reply. *"No, I'd like to do this for you. I get the impression you've been saddled with a heavy load. I want to help you with that. The alumni mentoring program is a community of networking and camaraderie (as per written in the brochure). I'm here for you."*

Levi grinned at the brochure remark and typed back. *"I have two brothers. One has been accepted to University of Virginia; he's graduating from high school early and plans to start Virginia in January. The other is younger—fifteen. He'll be with me for a while."*

After a second more, he typed, *"Thank you for all this."*

Levi left the phone on the nightstand as he crawled in bed. Minutes later, thankfully, he was sound asleep.

~~~

Thane paced the small office, berating himself, wearing a hole in the carpet. He was dressed in his tuxedo and painful new dress shoes that needed a good stretching, waiting for cocktail hour at whatever gala he'd been scheduled to speak at this evening.

Guilt ate at him. He knew the right thing to do. He should bow out right this minute. End this farce with Levi and be done with the whole thing. If he wanted to win Levi, then he should
~~~

get his ass to Coronado and make that shit happen, stop being deceptive inside the university's application.

That sounded like an easy, reasonable solution.

Work-wise, with everything he'd missed over the last few days, he couldn't deny how off-center Levi made him. For well over a week, he'd been acting like an ass for no other reason than he wanted that one particular man to do what he wanted him to do. Levi didn't need his selfish, bullheaded issues right now, and honestly, neither did his staff.

Besides, if he were as good a man as he liked to think, he'd cool his jets and wait this out.

He'd just gotten the confirmation Levi planned to come to Maryland in the fall. That would give Thane more than enough time to decide what emotions he had going on inside him. He could deal with all this internal chaos, and more than likely, bury all the unwanted emotion. If his past was anything to go by, then history would prove he'd be long over Levi by then.

Thane barked out a harsh laugh. He had a feeling he'd remember every vivid detail of the man that got away until the day he died. He dropped his phone in his breast pocket, forcing himself not to type one single word to Levi.

Lifting his hands to his hair, he stopped seconds before pushing his fingers through the styled strands. Dammit, he was like a loose thread, slowly unraveling, bit by bit. He couldn't make himself focus on anything more than Levi Silva, and after four long, painful days, he should be well past the point of caring. They'd had one night together. Yes, it was spectacular, but still, it was only one night.

Thane reached for his cell phone. Maybe if he could continue to do something as small as secure Levi's place in school, then he could justify hiding behind the Nathaniel name for a little longer. As crappy a person as his father was, his tenure and position in JHU could certainly make family housing happen for Levi.

Thane went back to the desktop and took the time he'd been refusing himself for the last couple of hours, and sent his father's secretary, Doris, an email asking about the possibility of securing family housing for a fall term medical student. Maybe less than a minute later, a message from Doris came back; she'd included Associate Vice Provost Lehman in her reply. Thane barely had time to read her message before Lehman responded, asking for Levi's name and student ID number. For something as cumbersome as higher education, that had all happened way too easily. He sent Levi's profile; that was all he had, and Lehman replied with a quick, *"I'll get them slated and confirm to you when complete. Should I contact the student directly?"*

Thane immediately shook his head at the monitor. Oh no. No contact. He panicked, letting his fingers fly over the keyboard, maybe faster than he had ever typed before. *"No. Please send me the information. I'll forward."*

Seconds felt like hours as he waited until he got the simple *"will do"* email in return. His heart hadn't settled when Jenna stuck her head through his open doorway.

"Your car's here," she said. "You only have to stay at the gala through cocktails—no later than seven. The car will wait for you."

"Okay. I'll be down in a minute," he replied and sat back in his seat, scrubbing a hand down his face. If the school contacted Levi, would they inadvertently out him? Most likely. He had to remember that in all this finagling he was doing. Reaching for the power button on his computer, his inbox flashed again as a new message appeared. He stared at the screen, the defeat at seeing the name of the sender was debilitating. Man, how he wished he'd gotten up and left when Jenna first came to the door. Doris hadn't included his father in her forward, but still must have shared the information. Damn. Thane reached for his mouse and clicked open the email.

"Let's catch up this Friday. I have time between one and three. My office hasn't changed."

Fuck. Sending a few emails for Levi was one thing, meeting with his father was a whole different matter. This weird internal battle he'd been facing just spiked to an all-time high of anxiety. His stomach churned in automatic defiance, and he scolded himself for ever emailing Doris in the first place.

Karma was already paying his ass back for this.

"Calm down," Thane demanded of himself and manned-up to type a quick message in return.

"*I'm tied up Friday.*" Clear and to the point.

The response was immediate, and clearly, his old man didn't want to be put off. "*Saturday or Sunday then. Lunch or dinner at the Iron Maya. I'm looking forward to the new menu.*"

Thane sat back in his chair. In the sixish years he'd had this company, he and his father had never shared a meal together in one of his restaurants. Up until right this minute, he'd have assumed his father didn't even know what he did for a living.

The cynical side of Thane had him wondering what this meeting actually meant, what game his father was playing.

On the flip side, by going, maybe he could secure the housing Levi needed. Levi, a man who made him laugh. A man who, when he danced with Thane, fit so perfectly against him that it felt like Levi was made to be in his arms. A man he couldn't stop thinking about. A man he'd considered the L-word with.

Could Thane tolerate his father's presence to help Levi? The honest truth was he'd walk through fire to help Levi. His eyes closed as dread coiled in his gut. A single meeting didn't mean he owed his father anything. He typed a quick message, tentatively accepting an invitation for Sunday brunch before shutting off his computer.

Numbness took over. He refused to consider what he'd just done or the level of distrust he had toward his old man. Thane went for the door, patting his pockets. His phone and wallet were where they should be. Maybe that was a sign he was finally pulling his shit back together.

~~~

Levi tugged on his jeans while stepping into his sandals. The yawn he'd been stifling turned into a jaw-cracker that he felt all over his tired body. He'd never worked this late, those last few hours in the club were coveted time slots, and he could certainly see why. Even with half the regular clientele, Levi had solidly
~~~

banked. After the midnight hour, the men who had come there with purpose began to find their companions. Something about the prospect of getting lucky made them big spenders. To impress, they dropped fifty-dollar tips instead of twenties, and that was all right by Levi.

The only negative was that it was close to three o'clock in the morning. He had to be at the clinic in six hours, work all day there, then be back at the club by seven that evening. Levi tugged on his T-shirt, reached for his jacket, and slammed the locker closed. Maybe he could squeeze in a nap during his lunch break.

When he pushed open the exit door, a gust of wind hit, sending a shiver through his body. The weather forecast had called for storms, but he hadn't anticipated the large drop in temperature. Slightly unusual for March. The smell of rain floated in the air as he hightailed it toward his car, his scattered thoughts shifting all around as he jogged across the quiet parking lot.

Interestingly enough, his half-aroused dick, the one he'd sported all night long had finally relented. Levi adjusted himself as he got behind the wheel of his car and started the engine. He definitely didn't have the mind over matter concept down with his body. It was like his dick was on the lookout tonight, ready and waiting for Thane to pop up and surprise him. No matter how much he tried to explain to his overly excited friend that Thane was gone, more than likely never to be heard from again, his cock wouldn't listen.

He figured that would eventually work itself out. Before he pulled out of his parking space, Levi grabbed a pair of earbuds his brother left behind. He opened his phone to play some music and noticed a waiting message from Nathaniel. As the car sat idling, he hurriedly opened and read the message.

"I managed to speak with the associate over housing. I wasn't prepared for how easy that process was, but I've got verbal confirmation that you've been slotted for a two-bedroom on-campus apartment for the fall. When it gets closer, they'll reach out to you for specific details, but for now, you're set."

No way! That little piece of news perked Levi right up. He sat there, closed his eyes, and let the happiness flood his heart. Their goals were seriously within reach. After a second of allowing himself to absorb the unexpected good news, he replied to Nathaniel, typing the words from his heart.

"I can't thank you enough. Medical school has always been my dream. Since my father died, I've been playing with the idea of quitting school and getting a real job to better help my brothers, but you've stepped in to help me achieve my dreams. I can't thank you enough. Should I contact them now?"

Levi pushed send as big water droplets began to hit his windshield. He flipped on the windshield wipers then lowered the gearshift, pulling out of the parking space as his phone vibrated in the cubby. He glanced over to see a new return message. Once he got to the red street light, Levi picked up the phone and read Nathaniel's messages.

"I'm glad to hear back from you. Levi, I'm very sorry for your circumstance. I'm absolutely certain the school offers more programs to help you. There's no need to give up your dreams, not ever. I'll relay all this to the associate of student affairs. If you think of anything else, please message me.

"Also, it seems I'm not too much older than you. Probably not the best mentor I know, but I'd like to be a friend and confidant. If you need a sounding board, I'm here. Actually, I'd really like to be here for you."

The light turned green. Levi looked all around, saw no other cars in sight, and sat there, letting the car idle at the intersection as he typed back.

"I'm sorry if I woke you. I didn't factor in the time before texting. I'm in San Diego, and I have a couple of jobs. This one is waiting tables at a bar. I just got off. I'm driving right now. I'm about ten minutes from home, but I could honestly use a friend. My life's spinning right now. I'm in situations I wouldn't normally put myself in. I appreciate the offer."

He pushed send and started driving, ignoring the chirp until he pulled into his driveway. He hurriedly grabbed his phone and jumped out of the car, running as fast as he could toward the covered porch. The driving rain made it impossible to be anything but soaked through even in such a short distance. It took a second to unlock all the locks and deadbolts on the front door. He entered to a silent house; the kitchen light had been left on. There was a covered plate on the table he assumed Linda had left for him. As quietly as possible, he warmed the meal while checking his messages.

"No apology necessary. Drive. If you can't go to sleep when you get home, message me. I'm up. It's almost morning here. To get the friendship ball rolling, how'd you wind up in Maryland from California?"

Levi leaned against the counter, letting out a long yawn. He was tired. It wouldn't take much to fall asleep. He started typing, even ignoring the ding of the microwave as he drafted his message.

"Johns Hopkins offered me the most scholarship money. I had to take some time off before starting my undergrad when my dad first got sick. He was in remission for a few years before I decided it was okay to go that far away from home. Maryland's like a different world from California. It has seasons. I wasn't there long, but I like that part of the world. California's great, but can be very pretentious. I didn't experience that same attitude in Maryland. Are you from around there? How'd you wind up at Johns Hopkins?"

Levi pushed send and took the plate from the microwave to the table. He got down two solid bites of panko chicken and broccoli florets before Nathaniel responded.

"Born and raised. My father worked at the school so I got a free education. It wasn't quite the fun time others had with my every move being monitored by my pop. I worked hard and graduated early. I've stuck around the area because I'm much like you. I love it here. I love the seasons, and I like the political culture. It has its share of pretense, but for the most part, I think we're good people. My business started here and has thrived."

With his mouth full of food, Levi typed as he concentrated on not choking to death on the huge bite he tried to swallow.

"What do you do? I assumed something medical."

He took a long drink of water before sitting back in his seat, the food completely forgotten as he waited.

"No, not medical. I actually think the medical field ardently resists my product, but I'd rather keep that private for now. I hope you understand. It's more protective than personal."

Levi pushed away from the table, adding the foil to his half-eaten plate before taking it to the refrigerator. One of the boys would finish it off tomorrow. He flipped off the lights in the kitchen and walked through the darkness to his bedroom. He knew he should sleep, and he would, but he kicked his shoes off in the closet and dropped his pants, pushing them close to his shoes. He threw his dirty socks to the laundry basket in the corner of his room.

He flopped down on the bed, reaching for the blanket at the end. He kept the phone in his hand, his head reeling with the possibility of what Nathaniel's text might mean. Protective... Chuckling a little, he let his tired brain go as it thought of all the secret service, military type jobs in that part of the country. Thinking James Bond, Levi typed back.

"I've conjured every possible 007 secret spy scenario my head could come up with in the last two minutes. Don't spoil the image if it's not true."

~~~

Thane squinted at the bright light from the small screen then pressed his fingers against his eyes, rubbing them before a loud yawn ripped free. It hadn't taken Levi more than a couple of minutes to reply, but Thane must have fallen back asleep with how disoriented he was. Man, he was tired. He'd only been asleep a few hours before Levi's message came through. He should have left it for morning, but damn, talking to Levi like this was better than his dreams, and he'd had some damn good dreams about the guy.

When the small words came into better focus, Thane busted out with a laugh and started typing.
~~~

"No, I like the idea of you thinking of me as James Bond or maybe Max Steel. I used to watch Max as a child. I was going to be him when I grew up. Either Max Steele or Will from Will & Grace. Funny that my parents didn't catch on to my sexuality until I told them a few years ago. Clearly not very observant."

Thane looked at the alarm clock seconds before it went off. That was Jenna's handiwork, along with the packed bag by his front door, ready for his flight to Texas this morning. Knowing Jenna had his time artfully planned to the very last minute, Thane still lay there waiting for Levi's response. It didn't take long.

"Do you know I'm gay?"

Thane rolled his eyes. Dodging direct questions was hard. He so much liked the easy, getting to know one another dialogue better. Deciding to be honest about everything except who he was, Thane responded, *"I do. And if I tell you how, I'll have to off you."*

He sent an immediate second message hoping to be vague and lead Levi a different direction. *"I also believe we're close in age. I'm 29, and 30 is fast approaching. I love food, all food. Every type of food. I haven't met a food I don't like. My favorite day out is a trip to Williams-Sonoma then Whole Foods then a night spent in the kitchen hopefully creating delicious goodness. For me, life doesn't get much better than that."*

Unless, of course, that time was spent with Levi. Funny, he desperately hoped Levi enjoyed cooking or, at the very least, eating. He'd love to cook and have Levi eating what he'd made. Naked sushi night came to mind... His phone vibrated in his hand, destroying the mental image he had just began to conjure.

"I've never been much of a chef, but I'm a great eater. There's been plenty of times in my life, especially in college, that I lived off ramen noodles. I bet that makes you cringe."

Thane lifted his brow at Levi's response and gave a slight nod. It kind of did make him cringe until a second message came.

"I've never had hobbies like cooking. I've always worked and focused on school. I started working out in my free time, so I guess that's my hobby."

His grin grew, remembering how he'd appreciated all that time Levi spent in the gym.

"No significant other? Either in California or Maryland." Thane asked hesitantly. He wasn't sure about that question. Maybe he should have waited. It was a very clear fact-finding question, potentially showing interest, and that was the last thing he needed—Levi having those kinds of feelings for Nathaniel.

"No, never. I definitely haven't had time for that. What about you?" Levi asked.

Thane nodded. Good answer.

"No, no real dating. It hasn't worked well for me in the past, but I've met someone recently. I'm extremely interested in him. I don't know if he feels the same. Well, I'm almost certain he doesn't. I'm not sure if I should pursue him. I'm beginning to think he might be a bit too good for me."

Thane pushed send and shifted his position, sitting back against the headboard, touching the base of the lamp, waiting for the light to slowly turn on. He loved that feature. Not too blinding, but his eyes were well past the glare, thanks to the cell phone. Levi's message took a little longer this time. He scanned the length of the response before he started reading. This was working. They were talking as friends. Levi was opening up to him. Erin had nailed it when she'd suggested this idea.

"That's funny, I've met someone recently too. We had a good time together, but he's not interested in anything I'm interested in. I had such a great time. It's been a struggle letting go. Probably because between meeting him and you reaching out, you've both given me hope for the future. Something I lacked. Things were dismal at best. Seriously, thank you for everything."

Thane stared at the words, hopeful that perhaps Levi was talking about him. Had Levi let go of some of the anger from their last meeting? He started to type and paused with his thumbs hanging in the air in mid-motion. What did he say? He knew what he wanted to say: give the guy a second chance, things aren't what they seem.

No, he absolutely couldn't say that, because what if Levi was talking about someone else? After a minute more, he slowly started to form words, backing out more than he typed until he settled on a message.

"I'm glad to hear you have hope. That's a terrible thing to lose. As long as he's a quality guy, perhaps you should give him a second chance. I don't know how you feel about second chances, but he might pull himself together enough to surprise you."

Thane pushed send and closed his eyes. He honestly had no idea what Levi wanted out of a relationship or if the guy even wanted one at all, but Thane found it suddenly hard to breathe, and his heart pounded as anxiety raced through his body at the thought of Levi possibly giving him another chance.

Again, Erin had been so right—a clear relationship mastermind. Thane was so into Levi Silva he couldn't even think properly.

The phone vibrated in his hand, and he still couldn't look down. A revelation he'd come to last night, and the true bottom line, was that Levi *was* too good for him. Levi had worried that Thane saw him as nothing more than a whore. Hell, Levi wasn't the whore…Thane was. He had his work cut out for him to even be able to stand on the same level as someone like Levi.

On a deep sigh, Thane slowly lowered his gaze and slid a finger over the power saver that had popped into place.

"He's quality, no question there. Honestly, I'm not even sure how I feel. I know he pulled me out of my shell, let me be a me I didn't even know was me. He's most definitely quality. I guess I would have enjoyed doing what we were doing. I wouldn't even have wanted exclusivity. IDK. He's stuck in my head. It was that good.

"What about you? He can't be better than you. You seem like a really good guy."

Thane barked out a laugh at the last line. Not that good a guy. Look what he was doing right now. And just sentences like "he's stuck in my head" and "he's quality, no question there" eased him on a level that made no sense. All his anxiety vanished with those two telling sentences.

"Thank you for the compliment. I'm finding I'm not as good as I thought. I'm assessing my next steps; you should too. I bet this guy appreciates you more than you realize. How could he not? No one's stupid enough to let the keepers get away. You just need to make sure to protect yourself. Men can be assholes."

Levi immediately replied. *"Yeah, I know. But everyone can be an asshole at times. I'll admit I'm guilty of it too. I've got to go to bed. I've got a few hours to sleep before I work the next fourteen. Thanks for talking to me. I really feel comfortable talking to you."*

Thane smiled at Levi's admission and typed back. *"I've got a flight to catch. I've got to go too. Sleep well. We'll talk more later. I'll message once I've gotten more from the school."*

Thane waited several minutes to see if Levi would respond. He didn't.

He was a little late to start the day; that knowledge sped him up. He felt good, and whipped the covers off. He needed to harness this positivity and be functioning today. Maybe the melancholy was fading. Who knew.

CHAPTER 17

48 hours later

With a broad grin, Thane stared down at the cell phone that seemed stuck to his hand as he walked the length of the first-floor remodel of his corporate office. He'd been the one to insist upon this walk-through with the Layne Construction superintendents. A catch up of sorts on where they were on the project and how much longer until completion, but Thane honestly wasn't paying any attention. The Hopkins housing department had sent a written confirmation of a reserved space for the fall semester, and he had forwarded that message to Levi, initiating this latest round of conversation between the two of them and his reason for being distracted.

Thane had learned over the last few days that he'd never had a friend like Levi. Someone he just got along with for the sake of getting along. Their personalities seemed to have similarities. Sometimes bold, sometimes timid, yet always striving to do better in life. Levi was also funny. Thane had sensed that in the time they'd shared together, but he completely got it now. Levi fiercely loved his family. His brothers were his world, and Levi would do anything to protect what he deemed worthy.

Interestingly enough, Julian seemed to fall into Levi's loyalty category. Levi even mentioned him by name when he spoke of what a quality man his boss and friend had turned out to be. Without any question, Thane wanted to be on that list of important things in Levi's life. He had a feeling if he ever managed to make the list, his name would be added with permanent ink and that didn't even make him a little bit nervous.

Thane absently trailed behind the two Layne men, but paused at the bottom step leading up to the second floor in order to type a message on his phone. *"I've got to go. I'm on a construction site, doing a walk through that I requested, and I'm not paying any attention, which is technically more your fault than mine."*

Thane looked up at the stairs, both the foreman and the general manager were staring down at him, exasperation clear on their weather-roughened faces.

"I'm sorry," Thane said and started trotting up the steps. "I'll pay attention now."

Almost to the top, his phone again vibrated in his hand, and he couldn't help himself, he stopped and looked down at Levi's message. *"Enjoy your day. I have a patient coming in anyway. I just want to thank you again for securing that housing. You're a miracle worker. I'm certain now that we can make it in Maryland. I owe you."*

Thane sucked his lip between his teeth and thought about that. He didn't want Levi's debt; he wanted his friendship. And if he were being honest, he really just wanted Levi. He wanted those green eyes focused only on him as they teased one another face-to-face.

Thane quickly typed back. *"You owe me nothing. I'm certain you would have had the same results had you contacted housing yourself. I'm just glad to help relieve some of your burden."*

He waited the second, but he'd spoken with Levi enough over the last few days to know he wouldn't respond. He'd said his goodbyes in the previous message and the patient would take precedence over everything. Thane enjoyed finding the subtlety in Levi's messages, getting to know how he'd respond, and boy, did his guy have integrity down to an art form. Levi was so damn impressive.

Thane's grin grew as he tucked the phone in his back pocket. Shit. He'd done it again, forgotten where he was. He couldn't seem to replace the smile plastered on his face, but he did lift both hands in an "I give" motion and started up the final steps. "I'm done. I promise."

"The youth of today," the foreman muttered. Thane supposed the guy tried for teasing, but the implication was sincere.

"Can't keep the phones out of their hands," the general manager finished the foreman's thought. Since Thane had already heard every single derogatory millennial reference that knocked the way he did everything, he felt more than comfortable giving a careful whack to the older man's shoulder.

"Come on, grandpa, explain to me why your ways are so much better while you keep making excuses as to why this project fell so far behind." He passed by the men, feeling the weight of their stare landing heavily on his back. After he'd walked a few feet away, he turned back to the two. "Don't mistake this smile as humor. I need this remodel finished. You got thirty days or I'm exercising my option to begin deducting percentages from the final totals. Will that affect your bonus?" He paused for dramatic effect, then added, "Damn, millennials." Thane even chuckled after he dropped that little bomb. He was seriously happy.

Midmorning Friday, Thane idly drummed his fingers along the conference room table while reading over the latest set of proposals to begin the expansion of the Reservations concept. This was a critical do or die meeting. He'd called in his own attorney, Reed Kensington, for the gathering. Arik Layne was also conferenced in through video link as they listened to various representatives from the Layne construction team talk about the logistics of building five additional clubs within the next year.

For Thane, this seemed a very cut-and-dry decision. He'd already committed to spend the money, and Reed rivaled Arik's legal team in combing over the contracts, making sure everything was in place to represent his best interests. Yes, it was a risk, more so than any other venture he'd thrown his hat into, but Reservations Coronado was doing well. Better than expected. Even bringing members in from all across the world. His target clientele seemed happy with their offering.

Thane's gut said they could easily repeat that progress nationally, perhaps even expanding internationally, and open the membership to any and all clubs they own. It could work, and he felt good about his effort. Absently, he fought a mischievous grin while wondering what role Julian might expect to play in this expansion. The guy would absolutely have to learn to delegate if he wanted to move higher in the company. No way could he hold such tight reins on all the restaurants, but he had a feeling Julian would try.

His gaze shifted as his cell phone began to rattle. Instinctively, he reached for the phone, leaning back in the seat. He tuned out of the Layne Construction contractor intent on painstakingly covering each of the finer points, probably because of all the ruckus he had caused with his corporate remodel.

When he opened the screen to Levi's message, like normal, everything but the phone and Levi faded away as he read. *"We're friends, right? I just got notice from my landlord that my company's paying our rent. It's a kind, helpful gesture. We get six months of paid rent under our employee assistance program. How involved in this decision would the owner of the company be?"*

Thane's brows slid together as he tried to decipher the meaning behind this message. Where was Levi going with this question? Would he equate the EAP program to Thane paying him for their night together? Thane leaned farther back in his seat and let out a deep sigh. He hadn't considered that possibility. Unsure how to proceed, he decided to ask directly. *"Is this a negative or positive thing to you? Are you happy about the rent being paid?"*

Thane waited maybe as much as two minutes. Just when he was afraid Levi wouldn't answer, a new message arrived. *"It's positive. Very positive. I'm sitting my brothers down today and mapping out the steps to our move. I've got to see if Logan got approval to graduate earlier than planned, but I can sock all this money away now. We should be set. I haven't even worked for the company that long. It's really nice."*

Thane gave a genuine grin at the text. Levi had gotten very personal in that message. He'd mentioned Logan's school, and the family's financial state, all new things in their discussions. It made Thane unreasonably happy that Levi thought well enough of him to ask these questions. Not ever before had he shared such personal day to day thoughts with anyone. It seemed they got along outside the bedroom as well as they did between the sheets.

Before he got a chance to respond, another message came from Levi. *"I just wonder if I should reach out and thank the owner or leave it to Julian. I'm not sure what's appropriate with our not so great history. It's why I asked. You seem to have all the best answers."*

Thane grabbed the opportunity and quickly replied. *"Is this also the man you told me about? The one you spent time with recently that you enjoyed?"* He pushed send, knowing it was a cheap attempt to get validation, but he took the chance to know once and for all if Levi had truly been talking about him.

Thane held his breath until Levi answered.

"Oh yeah, you don't know everything that went down. Yes. The guy I've referenced owns the company I work for. We spent time together. I left that part out. It seems like we've been friends for a long time and you should just know that bit of intel."

Thane closed his eyes and let those words help heal his fragile heart. Another altogether different problem came by way of his aching balls. His dick had given him hell since he'd made that dumbass move and left Levi alone in his bed. The damn thing hadn't forgiven him since. He got a full-on hard-on about twenty times a day, which ironically was also the average number of messages they were now exchanging each day.

This time Thane chose to answer Levi's question with sincere honesty. *"Sounds like he's into you, Levi. No way around it. If you're still interested, I'd thank him in person."* Thane stopped himself from typing '*by taking his ass*' and continued on with, *"In person is always better."*

Several minutes passed with Levi not responding, and his dick had grown so fucking hard it hurt. Frustrated, Thane tossed the phone on the table, letting out a dramatic, somewhat disgusted groan. Maybe he'd messed up with that response, but damn, thinking about Levi taking his ass just did it for him.

"What's happened?" Arik's voice penetrated his haze. Thane looked around the room; all eyes except Arik's were looking straight at him. "What'd I miss?"

"Something's happened," Reed answered Arik, that intense legal-eagle stare focused straight on Thane. The phone began rattling relentlessly on the table. Thane grabbed it, ignoring everyone else around him as he read Levi's message.

"I don't know. I worry he'd think he was buying me. He's got money, and I think he prefers his relationships like that. I know that's getting very personal, and I'm sorry if it crosses any line with you. He's way more sophisticated than I am. He has money. I don't, so I feel like I'm at a disadvantage."

They had gone full circle, back to the root of the problem. It was do or die time for Thane. He stared at the screen, typing each word slowly, making sure he could truly handle what he was suggesting.

"You're articulate, full of integrity, and genuinely a good person. Levi, your value is high. I feel certain he understands your position. Do something unexpected. Show him how you feel. Don't overthink things. Just act on your instinct."

Thane waited with bated breath; thank God Levi replied instantly. *"You really think so?"*

He barked out a humor-filled laugh as he typed. *"Absolutely. What could it hurt? If you really like him, then take a chance."*

"Then I will. The next time I see him." Levi's declaration had Thane standing straight up from his chair. He didn't say another word to Levi. Instead, he pulled up Jenna's contact information and dialed her immediately. With the phone to his ear, he looked around the room at all the confused faces staring at him.

"I've got to run. I can finish this by phone…" He looked up at the overhead projector and got even more hopeful. "Unless we're done?"

"We still have the final section," the speaker announced.

"Dammit! I'm missing too much. Turn the monitor around so I can see Thane," Arik called out. "What's he doing?"

"He's risen and I'm not entirely sure why," Reed answered, turning the monitor so Arik could see.

"Give me five minutes to book this flight and call me. I'll take the proposal with me," Thane said, ignoring Arik who, for whatever reason, thought this moment was hilarious. His laughter could be heard from across the room. Thane grabbed his folder and pivoted on his heels, stalking from the room as he spoke to Jenna, requesting the next available flight to San Diego.

He was in his car, speeding toward the airport when she found one leaving in fifty-five minutes. Perfect! Thane stepped on the gas, forgetting about the meeting. He weaved in and out of traffic, taking the airport entrance and speeding to the parking terminal. He parked the car, then dodged his way through the crowded airport. Thane was the last one to board, so he gladly took the only seat left in the very back of the plane. Buckling himself in, he finally let himself consider his plan. A five-hour flight to spend time with Levi. This had to take desperation to a whole new level.

~~~

The oppressive fear that Levi had lived under for months was beginning to lift. Losing his father had been unbearable, but worrying he couldn't live up to his dad's final wishes was the heaviest weight he'd ever carried.

Finally, all the pieces of his life had begun to fall back in place. The earth and the stars had magically aligned at the same time. Logan had gotten permission to move up graduation if he could complete his final classes by the end of summer, and Luke's grades were all back to a minimum of passing. The three of them had also met at the bank after school today, opening a joint account in all three of their names. He'd deposited his saved three thousand dollars plus the lump sum social security check that had arrived today in the mail.

On top of all that news, Levi had even managed to get a Friday night shift. The club was having a show tonight, one of the first ever of its kind, and it turned out that all hands were
~~~

needed. Even the drive to the club hadn't seemed as hurried. He made it in record time, and by being scheduled to open, he got a primo parking spot right up front. Levi grabbed his bag and walked across the lot, waving at one of the valets as he used the side door entrance to the club.

The sound check going on in the main club could be heard from out in the hall. This was the first of a two-night traveling drag show, which technically made today even better. He didn't have to work at being personable on show nights. He only had to keep the drinks filled and do everything in his power to stay out of the way. Both were very easy tasks for someone who preferred to fade into the background.

"Hey," Levi said as he met Chase pushing through the locker room door.

"Hey. They need us out on the floor. The show's behind in getting set up. They're sectioning off a lot of the back wall with curtains, and they didn't make that clear in the contracts. Jules is fit to be tied. We gotta move the tables out of the way," Chase explained, never breaking stride as he walked backward toward the main room.

"Let me put my bag up." Levi hooked a thumb over his shoulder toward the locker room. "I'll meet you out front."

~~~

Pointing a finger for the driver, Thane instructed the taxi to pull to the side entrance of the restaurant, hoping to go unrecognized. He tossed a tip to the driver before pushing open his door. He slid out, quietly sneaking into the building through the club's employee entrance. The flight had made good time, and with the time difference, he'd managed to fly across country and still make it to the club before opening. Once inside, he heard what sounded like a construction zone in progress.

Lights flickered off, plunging the area into total darkness seconds before bright flashes of light in different colors came from every direction and lit his way. A deep voice came from the overhead speaker, testing the microphone for a sound check.
~~~

Thane smiled. They were having a special performance tonight, which meant there would be lots of darkened corners available. The perfect setting to make up with Levi.

Right before Thane turned the corner leading into the main room of the club, he forced a finger into the knot of his tie, loosening its tight grip, then flipped open the top button on his shirt. He was nervous. Everything had him claustrophobic. Damn, the anxiety increased, trying to get the best of him.

The desperations of his actions finally sank in. He'd dropped everything to fly across country based on an emailed conversation. His confidence waned; he wasn't at all certain how the evening would go. He hoped Levi would give him a chance to make everything right.

Thane stepped into the club's main room and instantly homed in on Levi who had just placed a table in a new location. As if he and Levi had some cosmic connection, Levi's head swept around and his curious gaze landed right on Thane. The air around them electrified and thickened. Levi didn't look away. Instead, he straightened his shoulders and held his ground, continuing to stare straight at him from across the room.

Oh yeah, his guy had lost the timid air about him. Levi seemed bolder, more confident.

Thane didn't break eye contact. He couldn't even if he'd wanted to. Damn, Levi was gorgeous even in all those clothes. There was no question in his mind he wanted that man like he'd never wanted anything in his life. His traitorous heart had won the battle. It was doing a happy dance in his chest as his entire being centered on everything Levi Silva.

Based on the intense scowl now marring Levi's handsome face, Thane supposed Levi hadn't felt that same draw, or if he had, he wasn't happy about it. Did Levi know he held the ability to smash Thane's heart into a million pieces? Thane absently lifted a hand to his chest, placing a palm over the erratic thumping there. He had to do whatever it took to make sure that didn't happen.

"You said you weren't going to bother him."

Thane didn't turn away even when Levi purposefully dismissed him by spinning on his heels and turning from him, continuing his work as if Thane weren't standing a few feet away, completely lost in his stunning glow.

"I'm not."

Julian's hand gripped his arm, tugging on him till his persistent manager finally broke the spell Levi had him under.

"I'm leaving in the early morning hours."

"What's going on?" Julian asked with all of his normal attitude, and right when Thane started to speak, Julian lifted a single finger to Thane's face, stopping him. "Don't you say I work for you. I'm past tired of hearing that."

He'd prepared for this conversation with Julian, came up with the perfect excuse for showing up unannounced when he'd promised to stay away. So, Thane cocked a critical brow, paused for dramatic effect that seemed wasted on Julian, and continued speaking. "The expansion's been approved. We're moving forward. You're going to play a bigger role in the company. We need you to keep all the sites running at this level."

"And you could have told me that on the phone," Julian replied.

Thane gave an exasperated sigh, throwing his hands in the air as he started to turn away. He'd just told Julian how important he was to the company, something the man kept trying to get Thane to see for almost a year now, and Julian didn't seem the least bit interested in the praise, or the possible promotion, or even the raise he'd be getting. What a frustrating, bull-headed man Julian had turned out to be. Thane turned back, squaring off with Julian, propping his hands on his hips as he just glared at Julian who mockingly shook his head in a so-what attitude and stared right back at him.

A full minute passed before Thane rolled his eyes. "Okay, you win. I'm into him and I needed to see him," Thane confessed quietly, folding his arms over his chest. The lights flashed, turning the room several colors as he stared at Julian's face, waiting for whatever snarky answer was to come.

"I'm glad you finally decided to quit being an ass and open yourself up." Julian patted his chest before again lifting a finger and pointing it in his face. "Don't fuck this chance up, and for God's sake, don't be a dick."

All Thane could do was grin and shake his head. Julian was something else. Thane pulled the silk tie completely free of his collar, and hung the length of material over Julian's shoulder. "I'm leaving in about ten hours, but I gotta start somewhere."

Julian nodded and turned his head. Thane followed the direction his manager's attention had drifted to. His heart dropped to his stomach when he spotted Levi frowning, ignoring him as he carried chairs across the room. "He's ignoring you on purpose. He was happy when he got here. He and Chase were joking around, but he's shut down again. I've learned that means he's nervous, unsure of himself."

"Hmmm…" Thane considered that revelation for a moment. He felt exactly the same way, and he gave a prayer, hoping Levi had meant his words and intended to at least speak to him tonight. Thane began rolling up each shirtsleeve as he rounded behind Julian and headed toward the bar for a drink. He needed liquid courage.

"Hey, let's talk about the raise I'm gonna get," Julian said, trailing behind him.

Thane barked out a laugh, looking back over his shoulder. Levi caught his eye, standing as still as a statue while staring intently at him. Thane's gaze hung on every detail of the other man's face as Levi boldly assessed him in return. God, he hoped that meant he planned to make some sort of move soon. Without taking his eyes off Levi, Thane finally said to Julian, "It's a pay decrease, but one hell of a title."

"Yeah, that's not gonna cut it for me." Julian's hands came to rest on Thane's shoulders guiding him to the left seconds before he would have collided with a barstool.

"Ricco," Julian called out then pointed a finger at Thane. He got the nod, and the guy started fixing his drink. "I've got to run over to the restaurant. The front end—"

"Just stop," Thane said, turning his full attention back to Julian. "Don't tell me until tomorrow. Give me one peaceful night, Julian. Please."

The laugh he got from Julian didn't help settle his soul on whatever Julian had done this time. Instead of dwelling on that, he grabbed a stool and took his drink. "Keep 'em coming."

~~~

Levi stood with his arms crossed over his chest, his tray in one fist, staring at his two tables or what should be his tables because the club was packed tight—standing room only. He'd stayed crazy busy all night, too busy, but now they were loaded full of waiters. It eased some of the burden, probably because the customers were all drunk and the show had finally started. The place was hopping, even his regulars were up dancing and singing with the musical acts.

Usually, Levi would be content to stand back and keep an eye on things. Not tonight. Like he'd done a million times already, he cut his gaze sideways in Thane's direction and was immediately hit with the need to be near the man. Like every other time tonight, the guy was watching him. Always watching. Even in the darkly lit club, he felt those whisky-colored eyes boring into him.

No one else seemed to notice the current flowing between them or the draw that Thane had over him. Everyone in the whole place seemed mesmerized by the show, while Levi remained spellbound by the owner. Levi finally broke the hold and slid his gaze back over the crowd.

Uncertainty nagged at him and anxiety had his foot tapping with impatient energy. He just needed to man up and go after Thane; he'd told himself he would. Nathaniel was a smart guy. He wouldn't steer him wrong, and to this point, the only thing Levi had done was glare Thane down. So not the thank-you he'd intended to give.

After a second more, Levi placed his tray on the side of the bar and motioned for Chase. "Can you watch my section?"

"Yeah. You taking a break?" Chase yelled over the music.
~~~

"I won't be gone long."

Chase nodded, and Levi started toward Thane who was no longer there. He panicked, immediately scanning the bar. Had he missed his opportunity? The guy had been at the other end of the bar all night long.

Suddenly, a strong arm locked around his waist, and Levi twisted in alarm, coming chest to chest with Thane. Before he could say anything, he was drawn behind the dark curtain.

"Here," Thane said. A warm breath ghosted across Levi's cheek. Two small packages were placed in his palm. Thane used his fingers to close Levi's fist over the small foil squares. The spike of adrenaline coursing through his veins had his heart racing excitedly. Although it was dark behind the curtain, it wasn't rocket science. Thane had handed him a condom and lube packet, and his dick twitched with eagerness. Just being near Thane made him instantly hard; something that was difficult as hell to hide with the uniform he wore.

Thane's scent surrounded him, made him crazy with unbridled need. He couldn't think, not with all of his blood rushing from his brain. He should be angry, mad at the audacity of the man holding him in his arms. But he wasn't, none of that mattered at the moment. Especially not when the firmness of Thane's arousal pressed readily against his own. Suddenly he was up for anything Thane had in mind, but he also remembered the club rules.

"Not here," Levi hissed, pulling back from the kiss he was certain Thane was seconds from planting on his lips. "I'll get fired."

Thane's immediate laugh sent a sweet puff of cinnamon breath dancing across Levi's face. "I know the owner. You aren't going anywhere."

Even with that declaration, Levi still tried to pull away, which was a hard thing to do. He'd spent the last several hours planning to catch Thane alone and thank him, but in none of his strategizing had he considered sex inside the nightclub. He'd envisioned doing Thane in the parking lot when he got off work or maybe even in the bathroom of the closed restaurant. He couldn't afford to lose his job; he had to be stronger than this.

"There's no sex in the club, Thane. Your rule."

Another laugh floated between them, barely audible over the song now playing in the club. "You think anyone follows that rule?" Thane's fingers slid deeply inside Levi's underwear, fondling his erection. He grew painfully harder, his hips involuntary rolling into Thane's skillful touch. God, yes, he craved Thane's attention and loved it when that focus centered only on him. He closed his eyes and let Thane do as he pleased, not even bothering to open his eyes as Thane shoved the thin strip of material down and freed him from his tight briefs, then firmly but gently cupped his balls, rolling them in the palm of his hand before fisting his cock again.

"I want this in me," Thane growled huskily against his ear.

Levi's eyes opened when the condom was plucked from his hand. Thane fumbled with the package, stealing his breath when he expertly rolled the condom down Levi's aching cock. Thane's hands felt so good squeezing him, playing with him. One of Thane's hands slid up his side, his arm locking firmly around his back, holding him in place when he started to take a step back.

"Fuck me, Levi. I can't think of anything else but you taking me hard and fast like before."

When Thane unbuckled his slacks and let them fall to the floor, Levi's hesitation vanished. Thane reached out and once again wrapped those long sure fingers around Levi's leaking cock and started stroking him. Overwhelming desire swamped his body. God, he wanted Thane, wanted him so badly that nothing else mattered. Without a second thought, he shoved Thane roughly against the wall, capturing the surprised sound that escaped Thane's mouth with his own as he used his body to pin Thane in place and dominate him.

Memories of their first night together flooded his thoughts; it was a heady feeling to have Thane submit so quickly. He loved the control Thane turned over to him so willingly. There were so many things he craved with Thane, but nothing sent a rush coursing through his veins faster than when Thane squirmed against him, taunting him with each calculated movement of his body. His hands drifted to the bottom of Thane's shirt, and he worked quickly to push the buttons through their holes.

The taste of cinnamon and liquor burst across his tongue as the kiss deepened. Thane let out another needy moan when Levi licked at the fleshy part of Thane's perfect lips. This man was made for kissing. Levi gripped the sexy man's wrists and forced them above his head, holding him captive as he took his time leisurely sampling Thane's mouth. Their cocks were caught between their bodies, and he could feel Thane's enthusiasm slicking his stomach as their erections rubbed together. Thane pulled back from the kiss.

"Fuck me." No sooner had the words left Thane's mouth than Levi spun Thane around so that he faced the wall. He pressed his chest against Thane's shirt-covered back and leaned in close to his ear.

"Don't know what it is about you, Thane. You make me crazy." He ground his erection against Thane's naked ass, trying to relieve just a fraction of the growing pressure building in his balls as he tore the lube packet open.

"Show me how crazy I make you." Thane pushed back against him impatiently.

Levi couldn't squeeze the lube on his fingers fast enough. Just knowing Thane wanted him like this had him almost blowing it when he gripped his condom-covered cock to spread the slick. When he finished coating himself, he pushed Thane's shirt up and out of the way, then made sure Thane was lubed before pressing two fingers against Thane's entrance. He massaged Thane's opening then slowly pushed more lube and his middle digit deep inside, adding a second finger. Levi ignored the resistance as his fingers slipped past the tight ring of muscle.

He didn't waste time as he pumped his fingers in and out of Thane's tight ass, opening him, and deliberately brushing his fingers across the bundle of nerves to make Thane whimper. His adrenaline spiked and his need to be inside Thane grew even stronger with every little noise Thane made.

Levi pulled his fingers free only when he was certain Thane was ready for him. He gripped his dick and teased it up and down the crevice of Thane's ass, drawing even more desperate sounds from the gorgeous club owner. Levi closed his eyes and guarded his heart as he pushed into the welcoming body of the man he could never truly have.

Instantly Thane's constricting heat enveloped him, surrounding him completely, and it took every bit of restraint he possessed to hold himself back and not pound selfishly into Thane's warmth. There was something about being in this man that brought out an animalistic side of him, stirred feelings he hadn't had to deal with before. He wanted to claim Thane, make him his, fuck him so hard Thane forgot anyone but Levi.

~~~

Thane blew out a relaxing breath and rested his cheek against the cool wall as his body accepted the delicious invasion. The initial burn of Levi entering him made his knees buckle. If Levi hadn't wrapped an arm around him to hold him up, he would have crumpled to the floor from the pleasure of it all.

Levi tensed up behind him. He didn't want that, not with Levi.

"Please, don't hold back. I want to remember this," he said, on the verge of desperation. He needed Levi so deep and so hard that he would feel him for days. Levi pulled out then forcefully pushed back in, the move stealing Thane's breath and setting his nerve endings on fire. Thane groaned loudly, in complete rapture, when Levi's hands moved to his hips as Levi rocked into him.

The music drifting in from the other side of the curtains set up a perfect tempo for the thrust of Levi's hips. Being with Levi in such a public place, where anyone could stumble on them, only heightened the excitement.

Levi's thrusts sped up, his fingertips digging firmly into Thane's hips as he held him in place. Thane thought he might die of ecstasy from the hard pounding Levi gave him. He gripped
~~~

himself and started to stroke with each of Levi's thrusts, giving in to the frenzy of the moment.

The familiar heat started in the base of his spine, growing uncontrollably, enflaming him, burning him from the inside. He hung on the edge, fighting to draw out the pleasure and keep Levi in him for as long as he could. He didn't want this amazing connection to ever end.

Levi mouthed the side of his neck, heightening his pleasure, sending goose pimples springing up all over his body as that sexy mouth licked and nipped the sensitive skin there. The urge to have Levi mark him so everyone in the club could see he'd been claimed, hit him hard, which was so out of character for him, but he couldn't deny the feeling. He was consumed by Levi.

Levi shoved into him one last time as his teeth sank into the material of Thane's shirt that covered the strip of flesh between his neck and shoulder blade, and he lost it. "Yes, fuck! Levi…" He couldn't hold back any longer, didn't want to. The intensity was too much. Hard spasms racked his body, leaving him helpless to do anything but ride out the intense pleasure as his dick pulsed wildly in his grip.

~~~

Levi's breathing came in gasps, and his heart stuttered in his chest as he fought off the sated after-sex haze. He had no idea if Thane had gotten off. He'd kind of lost his mind buried inside that tight ass. He kissed Thane's shoulder and reached between their joined bodies to hold the condom's rim as he pulled free of the warm confines. The loss of such a mind-blowing connection left an immediate emptiness in his soul. God, he loved being inside Thane. He had never experienced anything like that with anyone.

"Are you good?" His voice sounded husky and deep even to him.

"More than," Thane said in a harsh whisper Levi could barely hear. The thick sound of the other man's voice proved he'd gotten to Thane just as much as Thane had gotten to him. Levi closed
~~~

his eyes, squinting as he tried everything in his power to pull himself together. He could barely remember where he was or what he had been doing before he'd lost himself in Thane Walker.

"I need to get a rag to clean up." Levi was still a little unsteady on his feet, his knees weak and his legs like rubber as he stepped back and pulled the condom off before tying it in a knot.

"I got it," Thane said, his voice a little stronger. He had evidently recovered faster than Levi. Thane straightened, stretching to reach something on a shelf near the back wall. With his slacks still pooling at his feet, Thane turned toward him while running the towel over his hand. "Let's get a room for a few hours when you get off. I think we need to talk. There's something I need to tell you."

Of course, Levi loved their sex. The first time hadn't been a fluke after all. He and Thane fit well together, more so than anyone he'd been with before. The offer to spend time together was tempting, very alluring, but talking seemed more a code word for Thane trying to persuade him to take money, and he wasn't ever putting himself in that position again.

Levi shook his head, not trusting his voice as he looked around for a place to discard the condom while taking the towel from Thane's hand, swiping it over his sensitive dick.

Thane leaned into him as Levi started to turn away, then reached out, grabbing Levi's arm, stopping his retreat. "Please. I was wrong. I'm sorry for hurting you. That was never my intention. Let me make up for how I made you feel."

"No." Levi prayed his voice sounded stronger than he felt. He wasn't open to discussing what had happened between them. He couldn't, not without revealing the inner turmoil inside his heart. This was the way it had to be with a man like Thane—he had to keep the boundaries in place. He tugged from Thane's hold, severing the contact as he walked the few steps toward a trashcan to discard the condom.

Levi tossed the rag in the trashcan and pulled his briefs in place as he started for the curtain. From the corner of his eye, he saw Thane pull his pants up and start to follow, but Levi had to stop him. They couldn't take this out to the floor.

"Don't follow me. And please don't bring it up again. It'll ruin this."

The club, the music, the low chatter of the guests just feet away slowly sank in. Levi was back to himself as Thane tucked in his shirt, fastened his pants, and buckled his belt. He should go. His break had to be long over by now, but for some reason, he stalled. His attention remained focused on the stunning Thane Walker standing in complete submission less than a foot away from him. Melancholy slowly blanketed his heart as he watched Thane straighten his clothing. No question, he was into this man. Really into him. Thane just did it for him, checked every single box of what he wanted in a man.

The loneliness he'd always fought grew stronger, almost suffocating him, knowing his heart's desire was emotionally out of reach.

"I hadn't planned on this happening like this. I just wanted to thank you for the employee assistance and show you there were no hard feelings."

Thane's face fell, and he started to speak, but Levi immediately lifted a hand, stopping him from interrupting.

"If you're planning to be around tomorrow, I'll bring that money back to you. Maybe during my lunch break at the clinic."

"I'm leaving in a few hours, and I don't want the money back, Levi. I want you to keep it, please. Look, we really need to talk," Thane said, stepping into his space.

Levi fought the urge to pull Thane against him and kiss that sad expression off his face. What he wouldn't give to be able to confess to Thane all this passion building inside him. Sex with Thane seemed to make him a little emotional. Levi's resolve wavered. No, he didn't want that. Thane was too sophisticated, too worldly. He'd sense weakness then manipulate Levi if for nothing more than the knowledge that he could.

"Talking's the last thing we need to do." Levi took a couple of steps backward. "It's when we talk that everything gets messed up." Levi quickly turned away and ducked back through the curtain. He had to get away from Thane before he caved. He grabbed his tray off the edge of the bar and left the area, going straight for his tables, losing himself in the crowd in case Thane tried to follow.

CHAPTER 18

There was no doubt about it, Thane loved Levi. He did. He was in love with Levi Silva. His heart began to pound as the thought gripped him, taking hold, not letting him go. Thane banged his forehead on the mirrored glass of the office window overlooking the club. He'd fallen in love with a medical student raising two teenage brothers.

Oh Lord, how had this happened? He'd been so firm, so set that relationships sucked and always ended horribly. Yet all he could do was imagine building a life with the smart, stubborn man who had stolen his heart.

Out of every man Thane had ever known, Levi would probably be the least likely one he'd see himself aligning with. Levi had boundaries. He lived by a ton of rules that all had a moral foundation. His integrity reached heights Thane couldn't even actually understand. Levi's conduct code rivaled even the Pope's… Well, if the Pope could fuck like a porn star. The crass thought had Thane smiling to himself.

He dropped his head against the cool glass, leaving his forehead pressed there. Thane's heart wanted him to tie himself down to a man with domestic responsibilities. Those obligations would have to be considered in everything they did. Levi couldn't just jet off to whatever restaurant opening Thane had scheduled or mandatory event he had to attend. Thane sighed, a deep heavy exhale of breath, and closed his eyes, forcing himself to take a step backward. He was putting the cart before the horse. Levi wasn't interested in getting serious with someone as fucked up as he was. He'd even said as much.

This whole situation drove him absolutely crazy. His emotions ran wild, his thoughts were all over the place, now taking him back to the mind-blowing sex they'd just shared. Levi instinctively knew exactly how to please him from the very first roll of his hips, making Thane have to work hard to fight off his release. Levi made him crave more.

And dammit, Thane had misled Levi again. This lying shit—he was on serious foreign ground there. He didn't lie, but when Levi resisted for fear of losing his job, Thane had easily uttered those misleading words. *People have sex in the club all the time.*

No, they didn't. At least not that he was aware of. He'd had to fire and pull memberships on some of the men in the first few months they'd been open. Even more alarming was that now he'd given the idea to Levi. The possibility of Levi fucking someone other than him inside this club seized his heart. The thought of Levi with anyone…period…

Unexpected jealousy spiked and a sneer formed on his face as he balled up his fist tightly. Where the hell had that come from? It wasn't like him to be so possessive. He was losing it, and if he wasn't careful, he would mess up again.

What the hell was he doing? Standing in an empty office, thinking about raising Levi's brothers and wanting to promise exclusivity to a man who wouldn't even consider the idea of spending real time alone with him. Yeah, he was crazy.

Frustrated with the whole situation, Thane stalked across the office for the silk tie folded neatly on the desk. He was out of there. He shouldn't have even come. Flying five hours for nothing more than a hookup… That was ridiculous. Still more proof that Levi had him all mixed up.

Thane trotted down the steps, deciding the airport would be a better place to wait. He refused to allow himself one last look at Levi. He fought the need all the way out the front door before he pivoted around. He couldn't resist that final brief glance, then he was gone. He had his work cut out for him. He just had to get a hold of himself.

~~~
~~~

The end of his shift couldn't have come fast enough. All these freaking emotions ricocheting around in his brain were absolute ball busters, dragging him through all the highs and lows. How could he have possibly gone from happily looking forward to life with his brothers in Maryland to ready to rip out someone's throat in a matter of a few hours?

No matter how hard he tried, he couldn't shut out the connection being with Thane stirred. He and Thane were never going to be a one-and-done kind of deal. Sex with Thane mattered, at least for Levi, and that had to be considered in any future hookups. He'd always have to hide his true feelings, and that was getting harder and harder to do.

Levi lifted his phone from the locker, slamming the door shut while thinking over his missed opportunity of being alone with Thane in his hotel room this very minute. His dick actually hurt with the need that mental image created. If he weren't so dumb, so self-righteous, he could have had Thane on his knees sucking him off right now. Hell, they didn't even have to have sex; just being near Thane would be enough. He'd love to discuss nothing important while lying in that comfortable bed, holding Thane, their bodies aligned as he ran his fingertips along the light fur covering Thane's chest.

Levi closed his eyes and dropped his head forward, banging against the cold metal while remembering the sense of loss he'd experienced when he slipped free of Thane's body earlier.

Levi pushed away from the locker. He didn't need any more mental bullshit. Not now. He was too vulnerable, and his focus had to be on the future. His brothers were doing well right now. He couldn't lose himself to a man who ran as fast and loose as Thane Walker.

"Goodnight." Chase's voice came out of nowhere.

Levi turned back to him. He hadn't even noticed he wasn't alone. "I'll see you tomorrow," Levi said, lifting a hand to wave goodbye.

"Some of the guys are hanging out after they get off. You should come."

Levi looked back over his shoulder. Chase had dropped his underwear, standing completely nude as he shoved a foot through one pant leg while facing his way. The guy was very nice-looking and had a great body, but Levi sensed a possible come-on, and he just wasn't interested.

Levi's shoulders drooped. Why couldn't he be interested in that? Chase seemed willing. From what he'd heard, the waiters regularly hooked up with each other. Why couldn't he just make things easier on himself and be into one of them? No, he had to pick the owner of the company to be interested in. What a dumbass move.

He had to make a change. He'd heard the chatter on the floor. Chase's parties sounded like a legit good time. Maybe something to take his mind off Thane. But in the end, Logan and Luke were home alone and not in the best neighborhood.

"I can't. I gotta get home."

"I figured that'd be your answer, but I thought I'd ask," Chase said, pulling the jeans over his ass.

Levi went for the door, stopping before pushing through. He had to get his mind off Thane. This moody thing that had taken over his personality needed to end. Maybe he could get Linda to stay over one night. He'd never had too many buddies. Not really. Maybe the guys he worked with could help alleviate all this loneliness he experienced. Looking back over his shoulder, he asked, "Do you guys get together every night?"

"Nah, but I'll give you the heads up earlier next week," Chase answered, pulling his T-shirt out of his locker.

"Thanks. I'll see if I can find someone to stay with my brothers. It sounds like a good time." Levi pushed through the door and immediately started working his phone, opening his messages. The desperation of this melancholy that settled over him had him seeking out the safest of all his friends. Levi walked slowly toward his car, typing Nathaniel a message.

"I saw him unexpectedly. I did what you suggested. I thanked him and walked away. Even when he asked for more."

Levi had expected an immediate reply. It seemed Nathaniel was always there, but he didn't receive a return message until he was pulling into the driveway of his home.

"I'm not sure I said to walk away."

The street was more active tonight. The scene that usually played out farther down the block, outside the apartments, was closer to his house. Levi didn't like that at all. He checked over Linda's house and everything seemed in order, then he looked at his house. It appeared quiet, too. He grabbed his phone, locked the doors to his car, and went for the front door. He was locked inside before he replied.

"I had to walk away. He likes escorts. He'd throw money at me if I stayed. I think he's got a head issue about that." Levi bypassed the kitchen, left the light on, hoping to show that people were awake inside the house, and went for his bedroom. He sent a second message. *"Or he just likes it that way. I don't."*

Having no idea if this unsettled feeling had anything to do with the neighborhood or not, Levi didn't shut his bedroom door. Instead, he sat in the dark on the edge of the bed and waited for Nathaniel to reply.

"I honestly doubt he thinks of you like that." Nathaniel clearly didn't run in these circles. Levi got it. He used to think differently too, until he started working at the club.

"He does. He's put me in that box several times." Levi pushed send and dropped back on the bed, sprawling out across the mattress. He tried hard to center himself back into the sex he and Thane had shared, let those moments of completion tide his heart over. In those few minutes of being so intimately connected to Thane, his world had opened and peace settled over him. Not one single burden caused him worry or grief. It was just him and Thane. Levi's eyelids slid closed, reliving their time together, the connection so intense he had to fight the ache as his hands fisted to keep from reaching out to the vivid image he'd created in his mind.

Levi bolted up. Holy hell, he hadn't ever experienced anything like this before. He had over-the-top feelings for Thane. His heart stuttered at the realization and panic set in. Shit. He had to stay away from Thane at all cost. Thane held too much power over him.

With his phone completely forgotten, Levi looked at the alarm clock. One fifteen in the morning. A twinge of jealousy rippled across his already erratic heart. Visions of the different waiters he worked with came to mind. Levi wondered who Thane had managed to get to spend the night with him tonight. Anger flared, then quickly fizzled as he was hit with the sudden overwhelming feeling of loss. How had he never considered any of this before? How could he possibly face any of those men tomorrow night, wondering which one had taken his place?

He wrinkled his brow, shaking free all the unwanted thoughts. No more of this. He ignored the notification alert on his phone. He had to be done with all this uncertainty. He had to hang on for six months, then he could quit the job and they'd be gone.

Levi pushed out of his shorts and crawled under the covers. He huddled under the blankets, tucking his arm under his pillow, staring into the darkness. "Please give me the strength to be done. Please."

CHAPTER 19

Sunday morning

Any bit of the lingering positivity Thane had managed to hang on to came to a crashing halt when he spotted his father, Walt Walker, strolling through the front doors of the Baltimore Iron Maya, a grin growing as he stepped up to the hostess stand. Thane hadn't seen his father in so long, and he wasn't prepared for the gray streaking his dark hair or that he'd grown out a bit of a beard. As he continued to stare, he saw a reflection of himself in twenty years.

Always the charmer, his father had the young hostess immediately smiling as she extended a hand, pointing as they both turned Thane's direction. He'd chosen a corner of the closed bar, away from all the customers, and decided to be his own waiter. Honestly, he hadn't anticipated anything good coming from this meeting and didn't need any of his staff intimately witnessing their inevitable dark exchange.

Like normal, his father's manufactured easygoing nature grated on his nerves. His dad strolled across the restaurant like he didn't have a care in the world, when Thane knew firsthand that the man was wound tighter than a clock. His casual gait as he took the steps up to the bar had Thane's own anxiety spiking.

Standing at the head of the table, Thane paused when his dad extended a hand his direction. His fist balled with how badly he didn't want to shake his old man's outstretched hand. Ingrained manners were the only thing that had him giving a deep sigh while reaching out to shake the other man's hand. "I have us up here."

His father looked down at the booth and his gaze lifted back to Thane. "Your mom's joining us, son. I told her to come in about thirty minutes to give me some time to explain."

Every word had the effect of little warning bombs thrown his way, proving his theory on his dad's leisurely stroll through his restaurant. Part of his youthful protective measures rushed forward, walls dropping in place, shielding him as he tried to understand how in the world his mother and his father planned to sit in the same restaurant together, let alone at the same table with him. He could feel his brows sliding together as he fought the urge to take a step backward, needing space to contemplate his next actions.

"Why's she coming? What's going on?"

"Can we sit first? Maybe get a glass of water?" his father asked, extending a hand toward the table. Thane saw the move as intended to redefine the real boss between the two of them. "I've been giving lectures. My throat's dry. I don't seem to bounce back like I once did."

More than anything, Thane wanted to refuse the request and demand his father lay it all out, say what he needed to say so Thane could throw his ass out, but instead, he nodded like any good little boy might do. He left his father standing beside the booth and walked behind the mahogany bar not more than a few feet away, frustrated because he always felt like that same small, insignificant burden of a child when his father was around.

Thane poured them both a glass of water, glancing over at the shelves that held the liquor bottles. He sure could use something stronger right about now. "Would you like something else?"

His father gave a single nod, still standing by the table, facing Thane's direction. "Liquid courage."

The words made the anxiety swell deeper inside his gut. He smelled a trap; he didn't yet know the extent of how badly he'd been set up.

Thane used a tray to bring the water glasses and two scotch and waters, heavy on the scotch—his father's drink of choice. He slid inside the booth first, his father finally taking the seat across from him as Thane put each drink on the table, placing the tray at the table behind him.

"Just tell me whatever it is you have to say." Thane stared straight at his father while taking two hearty gulps of the scotch, forcing his facial features to remain neutral as the drink's trademark bite dragged across his tongue and down his throat. Scotch was an acquired taste, one he'd never taken the time to develop.

His father didn't take a drink of either his water or his cocktail. Instead, he crossed his arms over one another, resting them on the table. The casual demeanor was back, and his dad leaned in, staring him straight in the eyes. "Nathaniel, I've been trying to tell you this for a while. I thought you needed to hear it face-to-face. You've always held so much contempt where I'm concerned."

Thane nodded, confirming that last sentence. All their baggage had been well established, made very clear years ago after a particularly harsh scolding about Thane's grades in college. Thane had snapped that afternoon and left his father's office upset. He was certain no student or faculty member on that particular hall could have gone without hearing him raging at his old man. Not one of his prouder moments.

"I'm fine not knowing whatever it is you think I need to know."

Interestingly, his father's face dropped in a show of defeat and that seemed odd to Thane. His father had never cared one way or another about how Thane felt about anything. "Son, any request you make to the university is reflection upon me…"

Thane cut his father off right there. For days, Thane had assumed this meeting was about his requests. He'd almost tripped Thane up with the diversion of his mother meeting them, but he'd prepared for this battle and stopped his father's flow of words with a slice of the hand as he spoke. "I only made some inquiries to point a friend in the right direction. I didn't ask anything of the school and never used your name."

His father lifted a hand, stopping him from continuing. "I didn't say you did, Nathaniel. Please, let me get through this."

Thane shut his mouth and sat back in his seat, taking the drink with him.

"Whether you like it or not, I became included in your inquiries. Since this was a first, I took the liberty of looking into the person you wanted to help, and I had hoped he might be important to you. I wanted to encourage you to find love in your life."

Thane kept his poker face in place, trying to figure out what hand his father was playing. Certainly, Walt Walker didn't feel qualified to give Thane advice about his love life when his old man had made such a mockery of his own. More than anything, his father needed to stay out of his love life and totally away from Levi.

"You've never known what happened between your mother and me. She never wanted you to know. I loved your mother, Nathaniel. I loved her as if my last breath depended on her, and in many ways, it did."

Thane couldn't help the scornful laugh that spontaneously erupted from his throat. His dad didn't think he'd believe that, did he? He'd had front row seats to his father's treatment of his mother.

"I deserve that. You were the collateral damage to the intensity of my love. I'm sorry for that, Thane, but it also resulted in the man you've become..." His father lifted his hands, spreading them to include the restaurant, showing what Thane had built.

"You had no involvement with any of this..." Thane's contempt resonated in every harshly uttered word.

"No, you're right. I didn't." The smile his father had started to form fell from his face, and for the first time since taking a seat, Walt picked up the scotch and downed the liquid in two long gulps before looking down at his watch. "Son, we've got less than fifteen minutes before your mom arrives. If you're still angry, I'd like to keep her from all the fallout. She carries guilt where you're concerned."

Shockingly, his father's need to protect her from being hurt seemed genuine. He couldn't even imagine such an about-face from the man who seemed to live his life to hurt his mother.

"You remember your uncle Ed? He was my best childhood friend." His father's voice grew quieter, his eyes drifting down to the tablecloth like he was remembering something from the past. "As teenagers, we met your mom on the lake and I fell in love that day. She was my world. I loved her on a level I can't possibly convey. I was so taken with her. We married shortly after—less than a year later—and we were very young but very happy. We had you within a couple of years and planned for a huge family." His father stopped speaking as wonderment filled his thoughtful expression. He lifted his gaze, staring at the wall behind Thane. Seconds passed before Thane looked over his shoulder to see what had caught his father's attention just as his father snapped out of it and his face turned hard as he started speaking again. "And I thought we'd be together forever. Less than three years later, I found your mother and Ed together."

Oh hell no! Thane shook his head and said disgustedly, "I don't want to know this. I don't."

"I couldn't stay away," Thane's mother, Clara, said, surprising them both.

She shimmied into the booth without waiting for an invitation, sitting next to his father who scooted over to include her. What he'd missed on his father's hand was now blinding under the dim light above their table. His mom was wearing a giant diamond wedding ring. Thane's gaze slid to his father's left hand. He also wore a shiny gold band. He'd never remembered seeing his father wearing a wedding band before. Not through any of his marriages.

Caught completely off guard, Thane lost some of his venom as confusion and uncertainty took its place. He stared between the two of them as the complete picture slowly emerged. His mother's mouth was moving, but he hadn't heard a single word she'd said. Those moments of being a little boy so worried and concerned for her care had Thane resting his back against the seat as his hands dropped to his lap in utter disbelief.

"You're married again?"

His father took his mother's hand, holding her close for the world to see. He saw her mashed to his side. They were sitting as close as two people could. "Clara, he's not listening."

"Of course, I'm not listening. You're married? To each other?" Thane's brow wrinkled. The words made no sense. Had they married other people and were here together to explain why they hadn't told him? That seemed more feasible than the idea that these two bitter people had remarried one another.

"She's the only woman I've ever loved. She hurt me deeply then I lashed out, hurting her in return. We were hardheaded, but we've worked all that out. We've been together again for the last couple or so years," his father confirmed.

Years? *Seriously?* The shock and confusion had to be written across his face. "And you're just now telling me?"

"You've declined every invitation..." His father started, sounding somewhat defensive, but whatever—fuck that excuse. Had they not heard of email? He had voicemail on every one of his phones.

His mom lifted her hand, interrupting his father. "Nathaniel, we know we hurt you. The one person who proved our love..."

"Okay, wait. Let's stop the bullshit," Thane said, the immediate spike of anger at her words faded as soon as he'd spoken. He moved forward, putting both elbows on the edge of the table and just stared at his parents. In the back of his mind, he registered his father saying not to speak to his mother that way. What was more important, he also focused on the way his father held on to his mother's hand. Like she was his life preserver, which in his mind was the way two people who committed to a life together should behave.

They'd been together for a couple of years.

"Are you happy?" he asked, looking pointedly at his mother.

A calm reassurance sounded in her voice. "Very much so, Nathaniel."

He nodded. This changed everything.

The years of self-imposed isolation and fear began to slowly strip away. Thane closed his eyes, digging his forefinger and thumb into his eyeballs, deliberating over what he'd been told. He hadn't known his mother had cheated. That was a big betrayal. Just the thought that Levi might be sexing it up with other waiters made him physically ill, and he had quite a ways to go before Levi would ever owe him loyalty.

"We can't make up for the past. Not really. We were young and dumb. You paid that price," his father said quietly. He hadn't gotten an apology from his old man, but still very close, and for the first time in Thane's life, his father shouldered some of the responsibility of the problems in their lives.

"When Walt told me about your inquiries, I knew it was time to try and reach out again. I looked up that young man on the internet, I saw he was your type—"

"How does everyone know I have a type?" Thane asked incredulously, stopping her flow of words only momentarily.

"I was afraid you might be resistant to a relationship because of us and how we acted. I know we weren't the best example." His mother managed to finish her thought before answering his question. "And I'm your mother. Even if you didn't think I was watching out for you, I always was. You aren't that difficult to read."

"We're Walkers, son. We're headstrong, but confident when we find the one," his father said.

"And it's okay to love him, Nathaniel," his mother added. "Love him as completely as you can. I hurt your father, and in turn, hurt you." His mother looked over at his father. They stared at one another, exchanging thoughts in their silent stare. There was just no denying how these two people that looked so much like his parents were acting nothing like the people he'd known his whole life.

"And forgive him his mistakes. Don't hold them over his head. No one's perfect," his father added, finally breaking the trance with his mother and looking back at him.

Thane scrubbed a hand down his face. This was like some weird Lifetime TV movie. What the hell just happened? The two people he would have bet his cold hard cash on not knowing anything about him had figured out the depth of his emotions for

Levi so easily? This made no sense at all. As if his mother read his mind, she gave him a gentle growing smile.

"We might not have been good parents, but we are a family, Nathaniel. Now tell us about this guy. What's his name, Walt?"

"Levi Silva?" his dad asked, looking over at him for verification.

This was all too much.

"Yes." He started to say more, then paused. He was protective of Levi, and old habits were hard to overcome. His feelings were far too new. They made him vulnerable. "He's not open for discussion."

"At some point you're going to have to knock that chip off your shoulder..." his dad started, his voice changing to something hard, and full of discipline, a tone Thane was more familiar with.

"Walt..." his mother scolded.

"No, he needs to listen to me," his father said, looking straight at his mother before turning a hard, penetrating gaze back to Thane. "You've done well, but your entire focus is building this company. You're avoiding anything meaningful. You need more to your life than just a company. You can't continue the way you are. You just can't."

Thane watched his mother nudge his father with her elbow. "Tell him, Walt." His father's face softened, but he didn't say another word as he continued to stare at Thane. "You two are so hardheaded." Her brows lifted as she spoke. "Your father's done some digging. Tell him, Walt."

"I told you I looked into this Levi. I've read his file and had a couple of conversations. He's been through a lot. We can ensure his full scholarship, have housing covered from my budget which means he won't have to take any additional loans, and I can give him a job in my department. He was a professor's aide in the English department. My department can pay him more, give him more hours. Of course, that depends on what's going on between you two. Why you've taken an interest in him and where you are in your relationship by then."

The surprises kept coming. Thane stared at his father, blinking several times, really getting a good look at him, and ultimately decided no one could have such a role reversal and change this much. It just wasn't possible for his father to be a total prick his whole life yet graciously and selflessly offer to help him. "What do you want from me?"

"Two things," his father said, holding up two fingers. Thane gave a bitter laugh and sat back against the seat again. Of course, the deal came with a price. "First, you tell me the truth. Is he important to you?"

"Yes," Thane said as if he were playing a game of chess, considering his next move.

"Are you in love with him?" his mother asked excitedly.

"I am," Thane answered, nodding once, letting his most private secret out and her smile grew brighter.

"Second, you lose the attitude toward us. You have to stop going through life as that hurt little boy. You must open yourself up, even if it means getting hurt in the end. Why are you living here and him there? If you want him, go get him," his father stated firmly.

When Thane hedged, his mother reached across the table, motioning for his hand. He reluctantly gave it to her, entwining their fingers. "Babe, you're a wonderful man, but you have the makings of a great man who has a good fulfilling life. Go get your guy and be smart enough to see that, when love happens, it's a gift. Cherish, protect, and hold your love close. Don't make the same mistakes we did."

Any residual resentment toward his mother began to fall away, leaving behind an emotion he didn't fully understand. Thane felt vulnerable, yet eager, all at the same time.

"And he has kids?" his father blurted out, tarnishing the unexpectedly sweet moment with his mother. His father couldn't help the chuckle as he added, "Will they call you Dad?"

"Not good timing, Walt," his mother scolded, playfully slapping his arm. They seemed truly happy together. Thane stopped second-guessing them and just let himself be in the moment, seeing them together like this was every childhood dream come true.

"I was trying for humor. I've never been very good at it," his father said, though clearly genuinely proud of his attempt with the laughter he tried to hide. "I agree with everything she said and will add…we want to meet him." His mother nodded her agreement with enthusiasm.

So much had been coming at him over the last thirty minutes that he'd need time to process it all. No one spoke as he stared at his parents, lost in the happiness staring back at him. Thane gave a single confirming nod before he began to slide out of his seat. Again, he'd been wrong in how he'd handled things with Levi, skirting around the inevitable, and he had been since the beginning.

All that was done. Like his mother said, now he had to go after his man. Figure out how to make this right. All these hard-to-process feelings had him scared to death and made him completely unsure of himself. That was all right too. First thing he had to do was come clean about Nathaniel. No more lies between them. Levi deserved better than that.

Thane placed his hand on his mother's shoulder and looked down at her. "Thank you for being honest with me. I'll get someone over to take your order. Lunch's on me."

"Let us know how it goes," his mom said. Thane nodded, still not entirely sure of his plan, but the urgency of going to Levi had him stalking through the restaurant toward the front doors. Thane passed the manager on duty and pointing to his parents' table.

"Take care of them. They're my parents. Their meal's on me." Thane pulled twenty dollars from his wallet. "Give this to the waiter."

He left the restaurant and minutes later sped down I-95 while calling Jenna. The only plan he'd managed to come up with was to get to Coronado as soon as humanly possible. He could office in California while he tried everything in his power to win Levi over. Doubt edged around his goals, but he couldn't let that stop him. He had to do whatever it took to make things right. His happiness depended on it.

~~~

Inside the club, Levi sat at a grouping of tables that had been pushed together and worked his fingers over his phone. Julian had scheduled a mandatory staff meeting, something to do with their employee benefits changing, and as Levi had come to learn, Julian usually served a pretty good meal when he held these gatherings. Julian said amazing food was the only thing he'd ever done that tempted the entire staff to show up on a Sunday afternoon.

A pack of men and a buffet-style meal had the serving line filling fast. Instead of waiting in line, Levi sat back and checked messages. He hadn't talked to Nathaniel since the other night, and it seemed both of them were keeping their distance. He wasn't entirely sure why Nathaniel did, but Levi's reasons were solid. His heart and his head were at odds. His heart wanted his boss, and his head said he needed to cut that cord and find a guy like Nathaniel.

His head seemed to win today which he took as a good sign. Thane had been so solidly stuck in his head that a melancholy had taken up permanent residence in his heart. He couldn't shake it no matter how hard he tried, and it had him completely out of sorts. So much so that everyone from his brothers to his manager at the clinic had asked about the changes they'd noticed in his personality. He'd been surly to everyone, and no one deserved his bad attitude.

Levi opened the application to see messages waiting. The same one that had come through night before last that he had ignored.

"You're sure on that thing quite a bit," Julian said, placing his Styrofoam plate on the table and taking the seat next to him.

"A friend in Maryland," he said, absently typing out a sentence of apology before he even read the waiting message. Levi just didn't understand why he couldn't be attracted to someone like Nathaniel, someone who seemed normal and kind.
~~~

"Maryland. Really?" Julian stopped while scooting his chair up to the table, turning to stare straight at him. It took a second, but Levi finally glanced over at Julian who had stayed in that exact position for several long moments. Levi's brows slid together in confusion, unsure of Julian's point, and looked back at his phone only to immediately glance back at Julian.

"What's wrong?" Levi asked when Julian still hadn't moved.

Julian continued to sit there, staring at him with his meal forgotten. "What's his name?"

"I met him through Johns Hopkins. His name's Nathaniel—very formal. He's part of the give-back program from the alumni. It's a mentoring program. He's been helping me get everything in order for when I return," Levi explained and went back to finishing the quick message before hitting send.

"Nathaniel graduated from Johns Hopkins?" Julian asked.

Levi lowered the phone to the table and turned more fully to Julian. "Yeah. Why? Do you know him?"

Julian looked away, scooted the rest of the way up to the table, and started to take a bite, but stopped with the fork midway to his mouth. "Do you know him?" Julian finally asked, turning back to Levi, looking every bit as confused as Levi felt.

"Sort of. He seems fine. Like a normal guy. Why're you being weird?" Levi asked.

"Why aren't you being weird?" Julian shot back, studying Levi.

Julian made no sense. Levi scrunched his face, mimicking Julian who looked genuinely confused. Levi could only shake his head, feeling like he was missing something monumental as Ricco came to the table and set his plate down on the other side of Julian.

"You better get up there, Red. The rolls are running out."

Levi had earned that nickname Friday night when one of the guys had noticed how much the brown lowlights had begun to fade in his hair. It certainly wasn't the first time he'd been called that name, but it was the first time it had taken hold so quickly. He'd been Red ever since. Ricco left his plate on the table and headed back toward the buffet as Levi pushed out of his seat.

"Do you have a picture of Nathaniel?" Julian asked, turning his head, tracking Levi as he started to walk away.

"No. It doesn't really work like that. If you have other social media accounts, they'll link, but he doesn't do social media."

Julian seemed so concerned that, when Levi started to walk away, he backtracked to the table, coming to within a foot of Julian's chair. Whatever the guy knew, he needed to just tell him. They stared at one another while Julian held a look of utter disbelief.

"Huh," Julian muttered, finally looking away, before taking a bite.

"What're you thinking?" Levi couldn't let it go, but Julian just shook his head and took another bite.

"Go eat." His boss waved a hand over his shoulder, dismissing him.

"He's just turned out to be a pretty good friend, that's all. He helped me with my housing issue and put a bunch of student services in front of me that I didn't know about," Levi said, staring at the back of Julian's head.

"It's good to have someone on the inside," Julian said, nonchalantly, without looking back at him. Levi still just stood there. He was clearly missing something big. Maybe it had to do with Julian's accident...

"You're acting like you know something," Levi finally muttered.

"I know enough. Now, go eat." Julian waved his fork toward the buffet as Ricco came back, followed by Chase, taking a seat on the other side of Levi's chair. Still unsure what had just happened, Levi finally took off toward the food line, looking back over his shoulder at Julian one last time.

CHAPTER 20

Bacon. Okay. Everything had bacon.

Furrowing his brow, Levi quickly scanned the menu, reading over the names of all the entrees. After the hasty run through, he guessed the name of the place made sense now. They'd called it the Baconator, after all. Not the play on words he'd originally imagined. Levi refocused at the top of the one-sided menu and started over, reading from top to bottom again, trying to find anything remotely healthy to order.

Yeah, it wasn't going to happen. Even the condiments were loaded with bacon. Huh. All right. The Friday night crowd hadn't thinned out much. The place was packed, and they'd waited an hour to get their table. No way would he dare suggest any place else after that long wait.

Levi glanced over the top of his menu and studied Luke. His brother looked so excited, studying the selections with meticulous care as if he were doing some complicated trig problem where he had to get each step exactly right. Even with Levi's arteries clogging from just the thought of digesting all the greasy bacon, his brother's look of pure enjoyment made everything worth the effort.

Logan's girlfriend, Alison, sat in the seat directly across the table from Luke. Logan sat right next to her without as much as an inch of space between them. They read from the same menu, quietly talking about the different options. Levi shared a knowing glance with Linda who sat next to Logan. She'd spent more time with his brothers and Alison. She saw this caring, loving side of Logan, but this was a first for Levi. His own personality seemed more like Luke's, an introvert who was a little awkward around new people and new situations. Logan was the exact opposite. His brother was kind of a stud in instinctually knowing how to treat his girlfriend right. Levi had needed to see Logan so taken with someone who seemed just as over the moon with him. He'd worry less now.

"What about starting with the fried bacon mac and cheese balls?" Luke asked, never looking up from the menu.

"I knew you'd pick those," Linda said, laughing. She finally put her menu down while stating the obvious. "This is a heart attack waiting."

"Makes sense that Luke would love it then," Logan said, glancing up from the menu. They were now all focused on Luke who didn't even seem to care at all.

"Not just me. It won the best of the best award from the San Diego Herald." Luke extended an arm in a Vanna White style sweep of his hand, motioning to the packed restaurant. "I'm not the only one. The place is packed for a reason."

Levi sat back in his seat and nodded at Luke; his brother had a point. The waitress came to the table, and he waited until drinks and appetizers were ordered before he asked, "You guys are part of Dishology, Inc., right?"

"Yep," she answered, never looking up as she wrote on her pad.

"I work for the company. Do I get a discount here?"

"Yep, fifty percent," she replied, finally looking up at him. "Where do you work?"

Thankfully Luke's excitement got the best of him, before Levi had to answer. "No way!" Luke quickly lifted his menu to the waitress, pointing to an item. "We'll take the bacon cheese fries then too." That might be the most excited Levi had ever seen Luke in all his fifteen years. The whole table, including the waitress, laughed at his enthusiasm.

"All right. I'll just need your employee ID number."

"We have employee IDs?" That was news to him.

"I just need the number. It'll connect you in the computer and apply the discount," she explained, looking over her shoulder at the table next to theirs. She lifted a finger in their direction to get a minute.

"I'll have to get it," he said, tugging his phone from his back pocket. He'd text Julian to ask, praying he wasn't already busy at the club.

"If you have a check stub, it's on there too," she said, taking a step backward toward the other table.

"I do. Out in the car."

"Okay, I'll get your order started."

Levi shoved out of his seat. Before stepping away, he said, "If she comes back, I'll take the all-American bacon burger, medium well." He was off, hoping there might be a check stub in the glove box of their car.

~~~

Thane edged his way through the front doors of the Baconator and gave in to the momentary surprise. The place was packed. From the outside sidewalk, all the way to the hostess stand, there was standing room only. He worked his way through the crowd and didn't even care that they hadn't met their required greeting times. The restaurant was slammed but efficiently moving people in and out as fast as humanly possible. He could find no fault with that.

Thane skirted past the masses, heading inside the dining room. There was supposed to be a reserved table waiting for him. He stood in the middle of the aisle and scanned the area for the front-end manager. They were so busy he had no idea who was who, so he started to make his way to the kitchen. He got a couple of odd looks as he walked through the waitstaff area, and as he came out the other side, he spotted the only empty table in the place, a handwritten reserved sign sat on top.

Probably his space since they didn't normally take dinner reservations. As he started to make his way to the bartender to ask her to send over the manager, something drew Thane's
~~~

attention. He couldn't name the feeling, but it stopped him in his tracks. With his hand still lifted in the air, his gaze shifted from the bartender to a side table a few feet away. He instantly recognized Levi's little brother, Luke.

"Yes, sir?"

Thane's attention stayed transfixed on the table, scanning all the heads. That had to be Levi's family. Two spots were open at the six-top table—both next to Luke—and one empty space had a menu placed in front of the seat.

Was Levi here? Thane instantly began looking around, hopeful to spot the guy.

After the week from hell, could he seriously be lucky enough to have stumbled on Levi and his family having dinner there?

"Sir?"

He managed to turn toward the now clearly aggravated bartender. "I need your front-end manager please." Thane didn't wait for a response. Instead, he made his way to Luke's table, coming to a stop in front of one of the empty seats. He opened his mouth to speak and froze, at a complete loss for what to say, as all but the older woman's eyes landed on him. This was important. He needed them to like him. When nothing readily came to mind, he just smiled. Luckily, recognition set in Luke's eyes.

"You're Levi's boss," Luke announced, and the woman's gaze softened. Both she and Luke gave him an immediate smile that somehow eased his nervousness.

"Yes, I am. It's nice to see you," he said and loosened the death grip he had on the top of the chair in front of him.

"Do you work here?" she asked.

"No, not at all," Thane said while extending his hand across the table to Luke. The boy hesitated like maybe he wasn't exactly sure what to do, but he finally lifted his hand and shook Thane's. Thane then reached for Logan's hand as the kid unwound himself from the cute blond girl staring up at him with big blue eyes. Thane got a closer look at the brother he hadn't seen before. Logan was more mature-looking than Luke, manlier. "I'm Thane Walker. It's a pleasure to meet you."

"Oh, my bad. This is Logan, my brother. Alison, his girlfriend. This is Linda, and I'm Luke," Luke explained. Thane nodded at Alison, but it was the boys who held his attention. As much as he'd thought about Levi, he'd also considered both these guys. On so many levels, he felt like he already knew them, yet he didn't at all. When he was afraid he'd stayed silent longer than appropriate, he forced his gaze away from Logan and took Linda's hand. "It's nice to meet you all. Where's Levi?"

"He's out in the car, looking for a check stub. We get a discount," Luke happily added, like that was some sort of spectacular prize. Thane couldn't help the smile that tugged at the corners of his lips after hearing Luke's excited announcement. He nodded in response to Luke's enthusiasm as the waitress came forward to place the drinks in front of each person. He pulled his wallet from his back pocket, handing over his magnetic strip employee identification card.

"Does that mean when we move to Maryland that we could eat out all the time for half price?" The innocently asked question turned Thane's smile in to a full-fledged grin, and he chuckled at the idea. Heartfelt emotions landed on his chest.

He was completely taken with this boy's brother, there was no way around it, but he was quickly growing attached to Levi's little brothers. Luke was brilliant to come up with such a plan to help their family out.

"Their meal's on me," he said to the waitress.

She looked down at the card, her gaze quickly darted up, and her face instantly changed. "I've seen your pictures on the newsletters."

"Don't worry. I don't write all that mess. It's my assistant. Could you let the front-end manager…" Thane's words trailed off as he involuntarily looked toward the front door. That unexplained and somewhat unnerving inner pull happened again as Levi came through the front doors. The guy was stunning. A visual breath of fresh air, and like normal, any time Thane caught a glimpse of Levi, everything faded into the background. There was something inimitable about Levi Silva, and it drew Thane, like a moth to a flame.

"I'll get him," the waitress said, pulling Thane's gaze away from Levi just seconds after Levi's eyes landed on him.

"Are you dining alone?" Linda asked, extending her hand to the available seat. "We have an open seat."

Technically, he shouldn't crowd in on the family dinner, but he really wanted to spend time with Levi and get to know the Silva family. Thane found himself nodding his confirmation to Linda. "I'm eating alone. I don't want to intrude, but I'd love the company. I've been traveling for days."

"You aren't intruding at all," Luke, his new best friend, said. "Anyone who creates a restaurant like this is a friend of mine."

The sincerity in Luke's unguarded words caused them all to laugh.

"He can't stay." Levi's voice echoed over the laughter as he approached the table. Thane's heart skipped a beat, but the challenge he'd heard in those words cinched his decision. His whole week had been a clusterfuck. An unexpected late season snowstorm had grounded him for three days. His luggage had been rerouted to God only knew where, and his office files were MIA with the shipping company. Levi wasn't going to be the cause of anymore obstacles thrown Thane's way. He was behind in his get-the-guy mission, and he wasn't wasting a single second more. Besides, no matter how much the guy tried to hide it, Nathaniel knew for a fact Levi was into Thane.

"Oh, but I can. And I'd love to." Thane looked Levi square in the eyes and pulled out the chair in front of him, taking the seat directly across from Linda. Which also happened to be the one right beside Levi's. As he scooted himself up to the table, Levi came to an abrupt halt at the head of the table. Thane ignored Levi's reaction and looked between Logan and Luke. "Thank you. I eat alone all the time. This is so much better."

"Sit down, Levi," Linda said, somewhat scolding Levi's annoyed behavior after a moment of weird silence. Thane busied himself with his silverware and napkin, pressing his lips together to keep from laughing at the absurdity of this unexpected situation. Levi slowly made his way toward his chair, pulling it as far back as he could before scooting in, making sure to put as much distance as possible between the two of them.

"So, where did you get the idea of bacon everything?" Luke asked, scooting his chair over to accommodate Levi's need for space.

Thane turned toward the kid. "I confess it wasn't my idea, but when the owner put the business up for sale, it was three locations and one of my first ventures into buying restaurants. Everyone thought I was crazy. Hell, I thought I was crazy. Now there's a dozen or so of these locations and they're some of my most popular places," Thane explained. He didn't even have to lean forward to see Luke because Levi had seated himself a good twelve inches away from the table.

"The guys online talk about this place all the time. I think I'm trying the flamin' hot burger," Luke informed him, lifting the menu as if Thane could see his selection.

"Solid choice. My favorite's the beer cheese chili burger."

"Is that good?" Logan asked, drawing his attention from Luke. Of course, Thane noticed when Levi finally scraped the chair across the stained concrete floor to move closer to the table, still keeping a noticeable distance from him.

"It's one of my favorite burgers. There's a spicy burger in Texas that's like Luke's choice tonight, but they don't play around with the flaming part. I tried it on my last trip. I'm a little gun-shy now," he said, winking at Luke. That bit of information seemed to take Luke's excitement to the next level. With Luke, he had a feeling they could talk food for hours and never get bored. The waitress was back with a glass of water for him and the appetizers that had to have been prepared in record time. Good. This family deserved the VIP treatment.

When the waitress finished taking their order, the manager came to the table. "Mr. Walker, I'm James." With the limited space they had, Thane was forced to stand, stretch across the table to shake the guy's hand, but that also allowed him to reposition his chair closer to Levi, and out of nothing more than the need to touch Levi, he immediately rested his arm across the back of Levi's chair. He only managed the briefest of touches before

Levi's body jerked, his spine going ramrod straight, forcing his upper body closer to the table. "We reserved a table for you this evening."

"That won't be necessary. I'm good right here," he said happily, giving in to the urge to counter Levi's move, placing his hand on Levi's back. Thane never looked to see Levi's response. Instead, he kept his eyes trained on the manager, but when his palm made contact with Levi's back, he could feel the immediate ripple of muscle. "You can give my table up. I'll be dining here tonight. They've invited me to join them." Thane looked around the table. "Are we here for any specific reason?"

"Just having dinner out," Luke answered.

"We're glad to have you tonight, Mr. Walker. Let me know if you need anything."

"Will do." Thane nodded and sat back as the waitress did her thing. By the time she finished and refilled all the drinks, Thane decided to give the cheese fries appetizer a try and was astounded to find them already gone. Those must have been Logan's favorite with the way the dish was pulled closest to him. Neither boy seemed too concerned about saving any food for anyone else. He remembered those years of being a human food vacuum.

Levi's family was an open and hospitable group. After those initial few minutes, Thane found he didn't have to say much more; he felt included. He just listened as Logan, Luke, and Linda all kept the conversation going. Levi remained the only sore spot in an otherwise nice dinner. He didn't say a word; his face still held that passive expression, but his body was rigid, and he sat at such an awkward angle that Thane was absolutely certain the guy was going to have sore muscles from it. Thane grinned, thinking about offering the wound-up man his solution for that back pain later. He'd happily rub out any of the strain Levi had, especially if that meant he got some time to worship Levi's ass.

~~~

As out of sorts as he was, his hamburger shouldn't taste like the best thing he'd ever put in his mouth. Levi swallowed the last
~~~

bite, tempted to use his fingertip to gather up all the remaining crumbs. He resisted the urge, no matter how badly he wanted to, because every time he moved, he was reminded Thane Walker was currently pressed shamelessly against the side of his body, engaged in an active, animated conversation with his brothers and had even drawn Linda and Alison into the discussion. Getting Alison talking was kind of a feat in itself. She was incredibly shy or at least she'd been with him, but clearly not with Thane.

Levi guessed he'd taken her place as the quiet one. Levi hadn't had much to offer on their conversation. He dropped his hands in his lap as he tried to calm his nerves. It was hard enough fighting his attraction, never mind trying to think of something clever to say. Every single flex of Thane's thigh against his seemed to stiffen both his back and his cock. The heat from Thane's body bled through the material separating his skin from Thane's, and it was almost too much to contain his desire. Levi's body ached but the position kept him inches away from the back of the chair where Thane's arm rested, but he also couldn't move too far forward, Thane was there too, leaning toward his brothers, laughing at something Luke said. Levi was so unnerved by Thane's proximity that he'd missed what they'd been discussing. Certain that at any moment Thane would be in his lap with as close as he'd edged to his seat. How in the world would he explain any of this to his brothers?

"Can I take your plate?" the waitress asked from directly behind Luke. Levi started to move to the side when she slid an arm in to take his plate. Thane's hand skimmed down his side, before wrapping around his back, holding him right there in Thane's personal space. Damn, Thane smelled good. Intoxicating would definitely be an understatement.

With his body reacting so uncontrollably, Levi shifted, trying to keep from embarrassing himself. Thane stopped speaking and bent his head, his nose going to Levi's hair. He could have sworn Thane breathed him in. He looked over, their gazes locked, and all the anxiety coursing through his veins slipped away while at the same time something insanely intense gripped him.

The feeling was something new, powerful, and raw. He couldn't name it, damn sure didn't understand it, but he couldn't look away even as heat flushed his cheeks and his dick reacted to the desire darkening Thane's eyes. The oxygen raced from the room as Thane's smoldering gaze bore straight into his.

"You added the brown back into your hair." Thane's husky voice caressed his skin as that dark gaze slid over his face before lifting to his hair.

Of course, he'd notice something so simple. And why did knowing that cause an unnerving flip-flop in his chest? He could so easily lean the inch or two forward and press his lips against Thane's full, fleshy mouth, and oh man, did he want to do that. But he didn't. Instead, he blurted out the embarrassing truth.

"They started calling me Red at work. That means it's usually time," he confessed.

"I like the natural color."

Levi had no choice but to shift positions, his dick had grown painfully hard. He squirmed in his seat, trying to relieve the pressure. It wasn't until Luke nudged him in the side that he even connected to the laughter at the table. He looked at his brothers, who weren't even trying to hide their amusement, neither was the waitress for that matter.

"What'd I miss?" he asked Linda who wasn't laughing at all. Instead, she looked to be sizing Thane up.

"Dessert," the waitress answered from behind him. "I passed out dessert menus."

"I thought we decided to go to Moo Time," Luke reminded them, but whatever just happened between him and Thane had his brother's speculative gaze shifting knowingly between Levi and his boss before Luke started grinning like the Cheshire cat. It didn't take long before Luke was chuckling, waggling his eyebrows, and making a production of teasing him. Up until this minute, he'd been so relieved to see Luke happy. Now, he just wanted to punch his littlest brother in the face.

"Moo Time, like over by the resort?" Thane asked. The hand at his side slid to the center of his back, warm fingertips grazing lightly back and forth over the material of his shirt, sending goose bumps springing up on his arms. Damn. He had to get control of himself and his reactions to Thane.

"Yeah, we could see where you work," Logan added excitedly.

Oh damn. Shit! No! The word *work* caught his full attention. A whole bunch of *no fucking way* filled his head. He bit back his reaction, trying to remain level, but honestly, his brain might have exploded over that one simple comment. He'd been so caught up in himself and Thane's presence that it hadn't occurred to him that Thane represented work and his family had no idea where he actually worked.

"I've seen the Elvis out front. Never visited, always wanted to stop in." Thane rambled on, oblivious to the slight heart attack Levi'd just had.

"I haven't been either," Alison chimed in.

"You guys are gonna have to go without me. I'm stuffed," Linda said, rubbing her stomach.

With the waitress still standing there, Thane finally turned and lifted a hand toward her. "I think we're ready for the check, and I'll treat everyone to Moo Time, if that sounds all right?" Then he immediately glanced over to Luke and Logan and went on to say the words that guaranteed the trip to the ice cream store. "Unless, I'm wearing out my welcome?"

"No, you aren't at all. This has been awesome," Luke said, excitement flashing in his eyes. "You should definitely come."

His family wasn't going to make this easy. Levi's shoulders slumped in defeat. How would he make it through the night with Thane so close and keep his brothers from talking about work? Life sucked.

~~~

Thane scribbled his name on the bottom of the sales receipt at Moo Time, pushing the pen and paper toward the waiting clerk as Levi stepped through the front door, letting the bells rattle in his wake. Levi hadn't ditched him. He was just following his
~~~

brothers, but he knew Levi would cut him loose if given half a chance.

He hurriedly moved across the store, not paying near as much attention to his surroundings as usual. Fate had gifted him this unexpected night, and he wanted to make sure he took full advantage every single minute. Well, at least until the carriage turned to a pumpkin, ending the time with his prince, or however that fairytale went.

"It's a fun place," he said, coming to stand beside Levi. Instead of responding, Levi took a lick of the stacked waffle cone ice cream in his hand, his thick pink tongue leaving a path in the frozen cream. *Damn!* Thane had to push the image of Levi on his knees licking a wet trail across his dick out of his head before shit got serious. He took a deep, calming breath and asked, "Where are your brothers?"

"Over there." Levi pointed to a group of kids standing directly across the street.

"Friends?" Thane asked, dipping into the cup he'd opted for over a waffle cone.

"Yeah. They're playing a phone game. In this one, they do better in groups apparently," Levi explained. Thane wasn't entirely sure what Levi was staring at. He looked more lost in thought, not necessarily watching his brothers, but definitely not giving Thane any of his attention.

"Like earning points kind of a game?" he asked.

"I think so," Levi replied.

Maybe Levi wasn't so lost. Perhaps it was more an avoidance deal.

"Why won't you look at me?" he asked, moving to where he stood directly in front of Levi.

"Why are you here?" Levi's gaze finally met his. Thane saw so much reflected at him in that stare. Honesty… Maybe some accusation, but he also saw more misunderstanding and pain. Thane had caused all of that, especially the hurt. That had him taking a pause as he stared at this captivating man, deciding the best course of action would be to just tell the truth. Levi deserved the truth—he wasn't a game player on any level.

Thane took the bite of ice cream he'd been holding in a spoon then lifted the wad of napkins in his hand to his mouth, cleaning any remnants.

"I want to date you," Thane finally answered.

"What?" Levi had been pretty steadily licking his cone. And yes, Thane had been watching that skilled tongue dart out every few seconds, but now, the cone in his hand had been forgotten and the look of horror on Levi's face caused Thane to laugh.

"Levi, I moved here today. I've been trying to get here all week. The weather stopped…" That look of horror turned to something different as Levi interrupted him.

"Why in the world would you move here?" Since he was naming all Levi's emotions tonight, he dubbed this latest look as startled.

"To woo you." Thane took another bite of the sweet frozen concoction to hide his grin. At this point, it didn't matter how Levi felt about what he'd done. Thane wasn't going to give up on his goals.

Levi's eyes widened, and Thane winked as he took another bite of ice cream. God, he'd love to know what was going through Levi's mind, because his face wasn't giving any clues. He kept his gaze on Levi, refusing to drop eye contact. Finally, Levi just shook his head and stepped around Thane. He followed the move, tracking Levi as he went. It looked like Levi was going to toss his cone in the trash bin, but at the last minute, he stopped and just the napkin he held was thrown away. "I'm not into those kinds of relationships. I don't hook."

His heart sank. How did they always end up right back here? "Please, Levi. I need you to stop throwing that in my face. I made a mistake, but I know who you are, probably better than you know yourself."

"And what's that?" The pain was back in both Levi's voice and reflected in the glance he gave Thane over his shoulder.

Reminding himself to keep it casual, Thane tried to consider each word he could use to describe his feelings for this man, and at the same time, keep it light. They were in front of an ice cream shop on a crowded street with his brothers not fifty feet away. It wasn't the time to go so deep.

Thane stepped closer to Levi, close enough he could feel the heat of Levi's back. "I'm attracted to you, Levi. You're so special and don't even realize it. You have integrity down to a science. You're loyal, smart, handsome, and funny. Well, not real funny tonight, but I've witnessed it, so I know it's in there. You're damn near perfect."

"This isn't a joke, Thane," Levi countered, turning toward him. The move put them almost chest to chest. The ice cream in Levi's hand dripped down the side of the cone and rolled seemingly unnoticed over his fingers. Thane didn't feel any anger reflected toward him, just that pent-up intensity that was all Levi Silva.

"I know." From the corner of his eye, he spotted Levi's brothers and cocked his head in their direction. "They're on the move. Wanna trail?"

Levi reluctantly turned away, checked out the scene, nodded, and started in their direction at a much slower pace. Thane followed.

"We're moving across country," Levi blurted after they'd taken several steps in silence.

That statement had to mean Levi was considering the idea of their dating if he'd started outlining all the roadblocks that lay between them. Thane took that as a good sign. "Not for a while though. So, it'll give us time to explore whatever this is between us." Thane shoved the bundle of napkins in Levi's hand. "Eat your ice cream. It's all over your hand. It's too good to waste." Thane looked around, scanning the crowd filling the street. "I can't believe this is within walking distance of the resort and I've never been here."

Levi took the napkins and adjusted his course, going for another trashcan. He tossed the ice cream away and began cleaning his hand. "I don't know, Thane."

"Yes, you do. We're good together. Hell, we're better than that, we're incendiary. I'm so attracted to you." Thane took the few steps, closing the distance between them. Levi held his ground. He didn't retreat as Thane came within inches of him. "This chemistry we have together doesn't just happen. It's rare and you know that."

As they stared at one another, Thane held his breath in anticipation. Levi's phone began to ring. On the third ring, he tore his gaze away and pulled the cell from his pocket, answering with a swipe of the thumb. Thane could only hear one side of the conversation, but Levi turned, looking over his shoulder toward his brothers. Logan was across the street, staring at him.

"Luke, too?" Levi asked. Levi glanced back at Thane then back at the boys. "I think Luke needs to be in at a certain time. Dad wouldn't let him stay out past midnight."

Thane smiled and took another bite of his melted ice cream before moving the step or two to dump his bowl in the trash. Luckily, he'd grabbed some wet wipes and fished those packets out of his front pocket.

"Okay, well, one o'clock then. I can leave the car for you and Uber home. Remember to jiggle the ignition to get it started," Levi said. When Levi lowered the cell, Thane handed a wipe over. The guy's hand had to be sticky.

"What's going on?" Thane heard footsteps and saw Logan jogging up behind him.

"They're staying with the guys. I'm gonna catch a ride home," Levi explained, using the wipe to clean his hand.

"Thanks again for dinner and the ice cream," Logan said to Thane, extending his hand to his brother for the keys. The car keys were placed in his palm, and Levi brushed past Thane to throw the wipe away.

"Thanks for this evening. I had a great time with everyone," Thane said.

Logan nodded. Clearly, he was ready to get back to his friends. He offered a well-mannered, quick-stated good night and was off running back to the group. Thane waved at Luke and Alison who had remained across the street. Both lifted their hands.

"Come back to the hotel with me," Thane said before ever turning back to Levi.

"Thane, I can't."

"Sure, you can," Thane responded immediately. Absolutely Levi could. Nothing was holding the man back except for his own hardheadedness. "We have three and half hours before they have to be home. Come with me. It's a ten-minute walk," he explained, hooking a thumb over his shoulder in the general area of the resort.

"This isn't a good idea," Levi said and took a step backward, creating distance.

"It's a great idea. I can even drive you home so you don't have to hire an Uber," Thane offered and that had Levi taking another two steps backward.

"No. You're not driving me home." Levi's tone was final. He frustratingly threw his hands in the air and turned, bumping into a couple walking past them. He gave a quick word of apology and moved ten or so steps away until he turned back to Thane and stared at him from across the walkway. Thane got the feeling he'd be doing this a lot with Levi if he ever managed a relationship. He always felt a step or two behind in whatever was going on in that gorgeous head of his.

"Why?" he finally asked, knowing that wasn't the proper response, but he just flat didn't understand.

"I'm poor, Thane. You shouldn't have ridden in my car to the ice cream shop. You can't be at my house." Levi became so frustrated he shoved his fingers through his hair. "You weren't wrong in thinking I was for sale."

Oh man, Thane was even more confused now. Did Levi just admit he hooked? And if he hooked, why the hell wouldn't he have just…

"I can be bought. You're already buying me. You pay my rent, you sign my paychecks…"

"Technically that's a printed signature," Thane interjected, and he wasn't sure why. He just wanted the pain in Levi's voice to go away. He wanted them back to where they were five minutes ago. Strolling down this street together, eating ice cream. Outrage hit Levi's face. He fumed as he pulled out his phone and began working the screen. "Levi, please don't leave. I was joking.

Your work and the EAP program are not what we're discussing, and they have nothing to do with me."

When Levi kept texting, Thane moved closer, placing a hand over Levi's phone. "Please, listen to me. Just go out with me. I'm not asking for commitments, so stop putting barriers between us. Who knows if we're even compatible outside the bedroom."

Levi gave him a ridiculous look. "We're compatible. You know we are. It's the other stuff that gets in our way."

Thane's grin spread slowly across his face. He had him; he just needed to close the deal. "Then don't let the other stuff get in the way."

"It can't not get in the way. You're successful and sophisticated and refined. I'll embarrass you. And I'm moving. There's no question. I can't let anything get in my way and you'd get in my way," Levi argued, listing all the manufactured reasons why this wouldn't work between them.

Thane stepped into Levi's space, taking the cell phone from his hand. He wrapped his arms around Levi's waist and tucked the phone in Levi's back pocket. "I'm not what you think you see. I had a regular childhood, made worse by my parents' divorce. They were educators. Neither made much money. And I'm saddened to be the one to tell you, but you're a reverse snob. Lucky for you, I'm here to help with that."

"Thane…"

"Come back to the hotel with me. Just for a few hours." Thane tightened his hold, drawing Levi's broad frame closer. He stared at Levi's lips as his hands traveled lower, the round firmness of Levi's ass cheeks filled his palms. He ground his erection against Levi's equally hard dick. "I only want you, Levi. I haven't had sex since the last time we were together and that was way too long ago. Tell me all the reasons why this is a bad idea, but let's have this conversation in my suite."

"Thane…"

"In the suite. Tell me in the suite." Thane loosened his hold, only to wrap his hand around Levi's forearm, drawing him to the street as he lifted a hand calling a taxi waiting on the road.

"I thought we were walking," Levi said as Thane pulled him toward the taxi. Thane opened the back door, pushing Levi inside. He followed, sticking his leg in before Levi could get fully seated. He gave quick instructions to the driver and took Levi's hand in his. Luckily, his driver seemed in as big a hurry as Thane. The guy whipped the car around, doing a sudden, squealing U-turn in the street, passing the group of kids. Thane lifted his hand at Luke and Logan who appeared to be transfixed by their whole exchange.

"They know what we're doing," Levi said, his face turned away, watching out the window.

"They aren't dumb," Thane said, looking over at Levi. He scooted closer. It was dark and he smelled so good. Thane lifted a hand to the back of Levi's neck, drawing him around until his lips were able to press against Levi's. This gorgeous, honorable, hardheaded man owned him, body and soul, whether he realized it or not. Being with Levi gave him peace and wrapped his heart with love. As Thane deepened the kiss with Levi readily following, he knew there was no turning back. He was home.

CHAPTER 21

Seriously, how in the world was he back inside this hotel room? Levi had promised himself never again.

Everything about Thane lowered his defenses, especially those two perfectly pouty lips. They were deadly to his resolve, and here they came again. Thane backed him against the suite's door as his palm hypnotically massaged Levi's traitorous, weeping dick. All he could manage was a slow exhale of breath as his eyelids slid closed and he gave in to the moment. His hands found Thane's belt buckle, and he fumbled with the clasp.

Thane deepened the kiss at the same time the man's strong hands slid inside Levi's jeans, gripping his dick and moving lower to cup his sac. Thane's relentless tongue eagerly swept over his, mimicking the gentle yet thorough caress of his hands, making Levi lose his ever-loving shit.

His hips rolled, and he tilted his head to change the angle and return this man's kiss. Dear God, if Thane didn't take advantage of both. Levi forgot all about the belt. All he wanted was to never lose this warmth spreading inside him. Thane completed him, made him whole. He filled in all the cracks and broken edges that his life had created. He had a taste of love and knew without question this was exactly how he wanted to spend the rest of his life.

Wrapping one arm around Thane's waist and the other around his shoulder, he held the back of Thane's head and kissed him. He kissed him like he had never kissed another human being in his life. He put everything he was into that kiss and gave himself over to Thane. Every single bit of desire he'd battled against, all the wanting he'd refused to allow, combusted inside him. In one swift move, he spun Thane around and pinned him against the door.

"I want you," Thane gasped, wrenching from the kiss. "I'm making love to you tonight…" But Levi had other things planned. He reached for Thane's chin and palmed his jaw, drawing those full kiss-swollen lips back to his.

"Is that so?" Levi drove his tongue back inside Thane's mouth as he ground himself against Thane's arousal. The little whimper Thane gave caressed his cock and squeezed his balls.

"It is." Thane panted into his mouth. "Come to the bedroom and I'll show you."

~~~

As soon as they stepped into the bedroom, Levi had him pinned against the armoire. Thane had kissed Levi until his lips burned. He clawed at Levi's clothes, frantic to have Levi naked.

"Let me feel you," Thane begged desperately against Levi's lips. The pressure of Levi's fingers holding him roughly by the neck flipped his switch and had him reexamining his earlier declaration. Right now, all he wanted was Levi's hard body pounding into him.

"I want that, too." Levi's hips rocked against his, and he could feel the swell of Levi's cock pressing against his.

"Need you naked." Thane slid his hands under Levi's shirt and pushed up. Levi broke away from him long enough to tug it over his head and drop it on the floor next to the love seat.

Those strong fingers were back on his jaw as Levi's mouth covered his. Levi's warm tongue swept across his and he deepened the kiss. The button on Levi's jeans got hung up as he rushed to get the sexy guy's cock in his palm. It seemed as if he couldn't get the other man out of his clothes fast enough. Levi finally broke from the kiss to shove the jeans down his muscular legs, and he started tugging at Thane's, undoing them as he stepped completely out of his. Thane drew his shirt over his head
~~~

and let it fall next to Levi's then rushed to shed the rest of his clothing, his gaze fixed on Levi's body.

"You're beautiful, Levi," Thane praised as he took in the sight before him.

Levi licked swollen lips, his light green eyes dark with desire. "I feel that when I look at you, too."

His heart beat heavy in his ears as Levi dropped to his knees and took Thane in hand and sucked him roughly into his mouth. Shallowly, Thane thrust, fighting the urge to speed up his hips and lose himself in the warm, mind-blowing draw of Levi's demanding mouth. He pushed his hands into Levi's thick hair and scraped his nails against Levi's scalp. The sexy man moaned around him. Thane's knees buckled and his hips thrust forward, his cock hitting the back of Levi's throat.

"Fuck, baby."

Levi's strong fingers dug into the side of his hips, forcing Thane to fuck Levi's mouth in crude deep thrusts. He bumped the back of Levi's throat over and over. Levi's watery eyes lifted to his, and Thane had to stop or he'd certainly come.

He gripped Levi's thick dark hair, stilling the bobbing head as he hoarsely whispered, "Fuck me."

The maddening suction stopped when Levi pulled back, releasing him. Levi mouthed the skin on Thane's stomach, leaving a wet trail of kisses up his abdomen, his tongue dragging across his chest as Thane pushed his body into Levi's mouth. The sting of Levi's teeth on his nipple sent a rush of pleasure spreading up his spine and wanton need pooling in his balls.

"Kneel on the bed." A deeper thrill pulsed in his aching cock at the sound of authority in Levi's tone. He went straight to the bed and crawled up on the thick comforter, his knees sinking in the soft mattress as he watched Levi walk to the nightstand and remove everything they needed.

Levi moved in behind him, dropped the lube and condoms on the bed next to him, and smoothed his large hand over his ass.

"I'm glad you talked me into coming home with you." Levi ran his fingers down the underside of Thane's balls then bent in and kissed the back of his thigh. "You're like a drug. I don't know how to say no to you." Levi nipped the sensitive flesh where his butt cheek met the back of his leg. An electrified shiver racked his body as Levi's stubble scraped across his skin.

Thane arched his back and spread his legs for Levi. Levi's fingers wrapped around his cock and hot breath blew against his hole. He almost jacked up off the bed when Levi's wet, moist tongue swiped against his most intimate place.

"Feels so fucking good."

Levi's mouth and persistent tongue were going to make him come. Levi lapped at him. His thumb dipped into Thane as he pushed his cock through Levi's tightened fist, the friction setting his nerves on fire.

"Oh damn, Levi. I need…" Thane couldn't get the word's out fast enough.

The sweet pressure in his ass relented as Levi pulled away. "I've got you."

Thane heard the sound of the condom wrapper being ripped open and the distinct snap of the lid on the lube closing before Levi's hands were back on him. Levi swiped his fingers across Thane's hole, teasing him as a thick finger slid inside him. He pushed back against the digit and rolled his hips. Levi spread him, working him open, slowly adding one finger at a time. Thane fucked himself wildly on those fingers. They filled him and stretched him and he loved the burn. Damn, when Levi curled his finger and brushed his prostate, he made sounds he didn't know he could make.

"You want me?" Levi growled, and warm lips brushed down his spine.

Thane nodded, anticipation holding his tongue.

"You want me to fuck you, Thane?" Levi ground his hips forward, the fine hair on Levi's legs tickling the back of his thighs.

"Yes!" Thane panted as Levi's thick cock pushed against his hole. He rocked back, and Levi dug his fingers in his hip, sinking into him in one powerful thrust that had them both moaning. Every nerve ending in his body sparked as he adjusted to Levi's girth.

"You good?" The tone in Levi's question made him smile. Always the gentleman even when he was getting ready to fuck him senseless.

"Perfect." Oh, and it was…so damn perfect. He canted his hips and began to impale himself on Levi's cock. His eyes rolled back in his head when Levi finally caught on to his rhythm and grabbed him by the hips, fucking him just like he wanted.

He strained against the electrifying pleasure as Levi's thick cock brushed across his prostate. He dropped his chest to the cool comforter while Levi's hands gripped him tighter, his hips sped up and his thrusts became harder. The familiar warmth blanketed his body. His blood sizzled in his veins, and his heart beat faster with every snap of Levi's determined hips.

Raw and dirty, Levi slammed into him. Sweat dampened Thane's skin as his lover drove the breath from his lungs. His balls tightened when Levi fisted him and stroked him roughly. Pleasure surged through his body, and he begged Levi to fuck him into the mattress.

"Stroke yourself." Levi seemed to know exactly what Thane wanted when he released his cock. Firm fingers dug into Thane's hips as Levi drove wildly into him.

"Harder, Levi," he pleaded. Nothing felt better than Levi's cock moving inside him. He was so far over the edge and halfway in heaven, completely helpless against his release when it slammed violently into him. "Yes, Levi…" Thane screwed his eyes shut, his body quivering as Levi held his hips hostage, fucking him through his orgasm. The muscles in his body froze in place as he unraveled on Levi's cock. Bright spots danced behind his eyes as he came.

Levi collapsed onto Thane's back, his full weight pressing him snugly into the mattress. Levi carefully pulled out of him before he rolled them to their sides. Thane snuggled comfortably against his lover. His soul was more settled. Always seemed to be that way when he was with Levi.

~~~
~~~

Don't linger. But he did.

Get your ass up. Yeah, that didn't happen either.

You're an idiot. Calling himself bad names did nothing but make him want to cuddle more.

It's what scared Thane off last time. Get your ass up. Yup. That did it. With an exhausted huff, Levi rolled out of Thane's lax arms. The sudden roll, almost made him fall off the edge of the bed, barely landing on his feet as opposed to hitting the floor with his ass. He blamed that stupid super-sated thing that was unique to being with Thane.

Man, he loved being with Thane. It didn't seem to matter how aggressive he got, Thane always took everything he gave and begged for more. Damn, that man was insatiable. No one had ever let him explore and do what he wanted to do. Not like Thane did.

Once he was steady on his feet, Levi rounded the corner of the mattress to find Thane's arm extended, reaching out, trying to catch him as he walked by. "Don't go." Thane tried to rise to one elbow, but his arm gave out and he fell back onto the bed. "You nailed me so good I don't have the energy to move."

Levi didn't utter a single word when he went into the bathroom or when he left the bathroom in search of his clothes. He dressed in the darkness of the living room, staring out at the open balcony. He was so relaxed; the ocean easily mesmerized him. But not nearly as much as that man who was still lying in the bed where he wished he could be.

"You're gonna make me work for this," Thane said, pulling him from his distracted thoughts.

Levi looked over to see Thane standing in the doorway, staring at him. Thane was so damn sexy. He turned away from the tempting sight, drawing his jeans up around his waist and gathering his wits before looking back. "I don't know what that means."

Thane barked out a laugh as his shoulder hit the doorframe.

"We're dating," Thane declared as Levi took a seat on the edge of the chair, reaching for his socks.

"So, dating means we go out occasionally, and I suspect, that means to you that we'll have regular sex," he stated, maybe wanting to understand the specifics, at least as Thane saw them.

He reached for his shoes and began toeing them on. He struggled to get his foot in. Levi bent, using his finger to help pull the heel on, and it still took a second. He was so tired, and more than anything, he needed a good few minutes alone to recover from their amazing round of sex. When Levi stood, stars sprinkled his vision, causing him to give in, dropping back down on the chair, resting his head against the back, closing his eyes.

He hadn't heard Thane move. Didn't realize he'd come closer until he took the seat directly beside him and said in a husky, deep, satisfying voice, "No question, I do enjoy making love to you almost as much as I like spending time with you. Your family's incredible. I thoroughly enjoyed myself tonight, even if you were in that weird made-of-stone, silent-in-all-your-indignation mode at dinner."

Levi didn't respond to any of that, because seriously, what could he say? He'd been exactly all those things. Thane always threw him off his game, made him so damn nervous. "So how about Thursday after I get—"

"Levi, that's six days from now." Thane immediately cut him off. All his good-natured teasing vanished. His tone turned from sultry to hard and questioning in seconds.

"Then Tuesday," Levi countered, opening his eyes and turning his head toward Thane.

"How about Monday, Wednesday, Friday, and Saturday," Thane said, proving he'd put some thought into this. Thane was always going to be a force to be reckoned with.

"I can't commit that much. It's too much time away from my brothers. I don't know why you want to do this with me. I have responsibilities that tie me down." Levi pushed forward in his seat as he realized the true logistical nightmare of having a relationship with anyone, let alone someone like Thane, who was used to having no restraints on his time. "You do understand that I'm their legal guardian. I have to be home with them. They have no one but me to depend on, and we're leaving California in a few months and moving to the other side of the country."

The humor was back in Thane's voice as he leaned forward, bending enough to look him in the eyes. "You're not scaring me, so quit trying. How about, Tuesday night when you get off, we'll have a quick dinner then you can go home. We can also go out Friday and Saturday night. One night alone, and one night we'll take your brothers with us, so you can be with your family."

Levi remained at that awkward angle in his seat, just staring at Thane. He so didn't need this in his life right now. He couldn't even focus. His brain was scrambled and the too handsome and even more charming Thane Walker was hard to resist. Levi shook his head, trying to clear his thoughts of the craziness while his dick began to stir. No, he'd be hard in a matter of seconds if he sat there staring at Thane like this.

Levi hoisted himself up, moving for the door on unsteady legs as a full-fledged hard-on built. He patted his jeans for his wallet and phone. Both were there, and he fished out his cell to find the nearest Uber driver. He made it as far as the door before Thane's palm hit the metal and kept the door closed tight. The man's warm breath on his neck and husky voice stroking his eardrum sent goose bumps springing up along his arms. "You've gotta stop making me pay for my misstep. I'm really into you. You're all I think about. Please, let me try to show you I'm not a bad guy."

As much as Levi wanted to bang his forehead against the metal door, he didn't. Instead, he just rested his head there and spoke honestly. "I know you're not a bad guy. I get that I'm lucky to have someone like you interested in spending time with me. I'm just too basic for a man like you. I don't play all those sophisticated games. I'm very…uninteresting."

Thane turned him around, but caged him in, not leaving any space between them. "You've used the word sophisticated twice tonight to describe me. What does that mean to you?"

He couldn't make eye contact as he spoke. "It means that my heart gets in the way. I've never been one who can easily go from person to person. I like sex. Love it. I do. But that's just it, we have to keep it only sex. All this other stuff you're doing and saying confuses me, and my emotions get involved. I can't turn them on and off. People like you…" He let out a deep sigh and finally lifted his eyes to Thane's. He was saying too much, giving up too much of himself. So instead of finishing the thought, he shook his head and tried to turn away.

He needed to leave, get out of there. This was exactly what he'd been talking about. At this point, they might as well be cuddling in that bed for all the sentiment he spewed. Giving Thane the upper hand would ensure Levi's demise. He'd be crushed. He was barely hanging on as it was. Thane's body pressed against him, taunting him, reminding him exactly why he needed to get away. He had no willpower when it came to Thane.

"Levi, finish your thought. Please."

Thane lifted his hand, warm fingers grazing Levi's jaw, his dark gaze imploring Levi to continue. It still took several long moments before he could find the words to make Thane understand. "You schedule your life."

"That's true on some levels. Keep going," Thane encouraged with a small nod.

"I connect with my life." There was silence between them as they stared at one another for another long pause. Levi could tell Thane tried to understand. The guy opened his mouth to speak, said nothing, and closed it again while continuing to stare at him.

"Okay…that makes sense. About me, up until a few days ago, I'd agree with you. But are you saying you're falling for me?" Thane asked, giving no clue how the man felt about the possibility. All Thane did was study him closely, waiting for his answer. And since Thane hit the nail on the head but showed no outward expression, Levi panicked. Pain coiled its doubtful fingers around his heart, stealing Levi's breath. Insecurity hit an all-time high. Levi shoved away from Thane's hold. He needed air. Being near Thane was too much; he felt caged and moved back into the living room.

"No. No." Levi let out a groan and tossed his hands in the air, circling back around toward Thane as the lie rolled off his tongue. He was unprepared to have Thane less than a foot away from him and took a giant step backward, creating the distance he needed. "Okay, maybe. And I'm only confessing that much to show you how basic I am. My life's much bigger than just me. Logan's gonna be gone in January, but Luke's with me for many years, and even when they're gone, I've got to remember birthdays and holidays. I have to be there for them forever. I can't get messed up. I've got to stay focused."

Frustrated, Levi just stopped speaking, knowing he wasn't explaining this correctly. His brain scrambled for something that might help Thane understand what he was saying and the importance of his needing to stay level and focused in his life.

He'd been pacing in all his agitation and whirled back to Thane. "It's like this. I'm a domestic beer. Maybe even a domestic generic beer like a Keystone and you're an Antarctic Nail Ale that everyone wishes they could have."

A smile touched Thane's handsome face, and he took a step forward. Levi retreated two, trying to keep distance between them.

"You've got some serious class hang-ups. You don't see either one of us clearly. All I'm asking for is a date… Tuesday, Friday, and Saturday." In an unexpectedly swift move, Thane swept forward and caught him, pulling Levi against him, briefly pressing their lips together before he spoke. "But I like our jumping ahead, defining things between us, because whether you believe it or not, I'm falling for you too."

That shocked Levi, and Thane laughed at whatever look he had on his face before taking his hand and tugging him toward the suite's door.

"So, we're set. Date nights are Tuesday, Friday, and Saturday. And we're giving ourselves time to let you get comfortable with us, right?"

"Okay," Levi said, not completely certain what had just happened. Thane opened the door and stood there, no care that he was still completely nude, and Levi found he really didn't want to leave. In one well-placed sentence, Thane had quieted the desperation inside him. When Levi hesitated, something speculative passed over Thane's face. He stepped closer, pulling Levi forward, his chest bumping Thane's.

"I don't want you to go. If you must leave, I wish I was driving you home, but I'm trying to show I'm mindful of your obligations and wishes. So, you better go before I drop to my knees and take care of this." Thane's palm cupped his arousal. "You've made me happy tonight. I like that you have feelings for me, Levi. I like it more than you could know." With that devastatingly sexy grin, he leaned forward and whispered against his lips. "Goodnight."

"Goodnight."

Thane gently pushed him out the door, but Levi left feeling more settled than he had in a long, long time.

~~~

The day had started out good, he guessed. Saturdays were set chores days. If he had the morning off, they usually started early, working together to clean the house, do laundry and yard work. Sometimes even having enough time for a grocery store run. Homework and the PT clinic were typical culprits in not getting everything done on Saturday. But they tried, because getting everything done on the weekends made the whole week easier.

Now, three hours into the scheduled cleaning day, Levi stared cynically at his brothers' closed bedroom door as he pushed the mop over the kitchen floor. He wasn't sure why his brothers would think today would be any different than every other Saturday they'd shared together in months.

So yeah, they'd had a late night. He'd made it home about twenty minutes before his brothers, but they'd all gone to bed by two. Still coasting on all those warm Thane feelings, Levi had even let himself sleep in this morning. Logan and Luke knew he wasn't scheduled at the clinic today, and they'd all agreed upon a nine o'clock start time this morning. Yet, it was almost noon, and Luke and Logan were still sound asleep. In the beginning, he'd decided to give them the extra sleep. Now with the housework and laundry almost done, he'd changed his tune,
~~~

deciding they were punk-asses who had strategically planned to sleep in, leaving him with all the work. He totally called complete bullshit on any oversleeping excuse.

Finishing the floor, he set the damp mop to the side of the kitchen entrance and went straight to his brothers' bedroom door. Past the point of being the nice, considerate brother, Levi busted open the door, letting it bang loudly against the wall and flipped on the overhead light. "You guys suck. You know it's past time to get up. I heard your alarm go off twice."

Luke stayed bundled in his ball, not moving a muscle. Logan did little more, but at least he wore a sheepish grin. "We figured you'd be happy this morning since you got some last night and you'd give us a break… We'd all sleep in."

"Our bad," Luke mumbled, still not moving. Both had their eyes closed and Logan let out a loud, jaw-cracking yawn.

"What I do or don't do plays no part in our chores. Get your butts up," Levi ordered and reached for Logan's blanket, jerking it off his body. He wadded the covers into a ball and threw the bundle at Luke before storming from the bedroom. The buzzer on the dryer beeped, and Levi headed that way. As he tiptoed across the possibly still wet floor, a sinister plan came to mind. He'd make his brothers do all the yard work on their own…

"I like Thane. He's cool," Luke mumbled, dragging into the kitchen all sleepy-eyed. He went straight for the cereal, passing by the mop-in-the-door indicator, not even caring the floor might still be wet.

"Be careful. Don't make a mess," Levi said and started to pull his T-shirts from the dryer.

"He bought our dinner just because we let him sit with us," Logan added, trailing behind Luke. Levi looked up to see Logan grabbing two bowls and spoons before taking a seat opposite Luke at the kitchen table. He swore they'd live off Froot Loops if given the chance.

"He's not like us. He doesn't understand our way of life," Levi said, watching Logan take the cereal box as the milk sloshed out the side of Luke's bowl.

"I'll clean it up. Don't worry," Luke immediately said before Levi had a chance to speak.

"What's that mean that he's not like us? Dad always said we're who we are, not where we're from or how we look," Logan said, mimicking one of his father's favorite expressions.

"Yeah. I've found that doesn't always translate in the real world." Levi sighed, eyeing Logan as milk spilled from his bowl too. What was wrong with his brothers that they couldn't pour milk into a bowl without spilling?

"But Thane didn't seem to think like that. He was cool and he got tiramisu and double dark chocolate. Anyone who eats that combination of flavors together doesn't live by society's rules," Luke stated emphatically.

It took a second to connect the dots until Levi finally laughed at the connection of ice cream flavors Luke had put together. "What? That's dumb."

"No, it's not. Double dark chocolate is normal, maybe a little different, but tiramisu ice cream is like, wow, okay, I'm here, take me like I am," Luke explained then put a huge bite of cereal in his mouth, nodding at Levi like he'd solved the problem of world peace.

Somehow Luke's assessment eased some of the irritation Levi had built, and he bent forward, taking the last of the clothes from the dryer. "You're dumb."

"Kind of I'm not. My IQ's higher than yours," Luke pointed out before adding another bite of the brightly colored cereal to his mouth.

Logan barked out a laugh, and Luke sat there, chewing, looking like he hadn't just completely owned Levi. How could he counter that honest and very accurate argument?

"Well, I guess it's a good thing you're into him because he wants to take us out again next weekend." When he finished folding all the clothes, he realized all he'd gotten was silence from his announcement, and he stopped in mid-motion of picking up the stack of T-shirts to look back over his shoulder. Both boys just stared blankly at him until Logan lifted a single eyebrow in a severe arch. "What?"

"So, it wasn't a one and done?" Logan asked.

"You just said he wasn't like that," Levi shot back, lowering his brows at his brother.

"We just assumed it was a one and done, and we were trying to make you feel better. We planned it last night," Luke explained, both boys still gawking at him. Levi stared back, his eyes darting back and forth between the two boys. Had they just insulted him? Totally doubted his ability to get a guy like Thane?

"I think I'm offended," Levi finally said and turned back to the washer, pulling the wet clothes free. Levi didn't consider himself a bad-looking guy. He had a college degree for God's sake. He could get someone like Thane if he tried. By the time he slammed the dryer door, he'd managed to work himself up and added, "So you're saying I can't get someone like him?"

"I guess." Logan reached down, pulling his socks off his feet. He bundled those, and they came flying for the empty washing machine, bouncing off the side, hitting the floor.

"Thanks. You two are great at building a guy up." Levi grabbed the folded laundry, ignoring the dirty socks while trying to hide his waning confidence.

He might be able to do a guy like Thane, but they were right, he was totally out of Levi's league. Even with the whole *I connected, you connected* thing last night, this wouldn't last. Thane's life and his were miles apart, and no matter how hard he wished it weren't that way, it was.

Leaving the kitchen, he said over his shoulder, "You guys get the yard work today."

"If he really does call, can we go back to the Baconator on Friday or Saturday?" Luke called out, and Levi didn't think he was teasing. God. His brother needed a lesson in how to read a room.

"Never again. I'm never going anywhere you ever want to go," Levi tossed back, taking his laundry into his bedroom. Maybe it had been a good thing he'd let them sleep. He'd had a solid three hours with no doubt clouding his judgment. Now, in less than ten minutes of his brothers being awake, he was right there with them. What was Thane trying to pull?

~~~

The silence of the darkened bar was eerily loud. The lack of windows on this end of the club made the darkness even worse. By design, the club's main purpose gathered people together, so all this weird silence felt wrong. Thane's eyes hadn't had time to adjust as he reached out for the wall and stumbled along until the stairwell leading up to the office tripped him up. Thank goodness, the light switch was near the stairs. But rather than help, the sudden flood of light blinded him almost as bad as a camera flash.

By the time he got to the office, he felt a little beaten. All he wanted to do was text Levi. He'd actually started a message on his cell phone, wanting to point out that Saturday night was date night. He'd almost pushed send on the text only to remember his cell phone was designated to the Johns Hopkins social media site and what if Levi had somehow seen his number? His deceptiveness had gotten in his way.

He'd almost gone out and bought a new cell phone, but that seemed dumb. He needed to man up and tell Levi the truth, but that needed to be done face-to-face, probably in the privacy of his suite. That way he could do whatever it took to make this right.

Luckily, he remembered the loaner phone at the club. It had been an odd expense, something Julian had felt was needed.

"*Papi* or is it Nathaniel?"

Thane didn't even need to look up to know who had instantly grated his last nerve.

"Don't call me that," he said and began opening desk drawers to rifle through the contents.

"Why? Isn't that the name your parents gave you?" Julian stepped closer, the look in his eyes daring him to deny it.

"You know, you're a pain in the ass," Thane said, closing one drawer and opening another equally filled drawer. Freaking Julian saved everything.

"Old news. I've been told that a time or two. Mostly by you, but others have shared that sentiment too. Let's talk raises instead," Julian said. From the corner of Thane's eye, he watched
~~~

Julian move to the edge of the desk to lean forward to see what he was doing.

"Do we still have that loaner phone?" he asked, tilting his head toward Julian.

"Can't communicate with Levi from your phone now, can you?" Julian replied, stating the irritatingly obvious problem. Except how did Julian know he wanted to text Levi? He'd just gotten to California yesterday. Had Levi told him about last night? And if he had, a more important thought came to mind. What were Levi's thoughts about how they'd left things?

"Whaddaya know?" Thane asked, pausing his search.

"A long time ago, I learned the value of tipping the bellboys to give me the heads up when my moody boss showed up unexpectedly. The guys in the south entrance saw you entering with Red last night," Julian answered smugly, acting like he had all the answers in the world.

Thane just stared at him, letting out an irritated *oomph* before moving to the other side of the desk where there were more drawers to search through.

"So, you already got him in your bed less than ten hours after arriving. Pretty impressive, even for you," Julian said.

Thane never looked up. He wasn't going to dignify that stupid remark with any kind of acknowledgement. They had well over seven hours before the bar opened. He knew they were stocked and ready to go. Julian would have insisted on that last night during closing duties.

"Why are you already here? You have hours before we open." That had Thane narrowing his eyes, his brow crinkled, and he glanced over at Julian, taking a good, long look at the man. Julian looked really good. Great, actually. He seemed like a man full of life. Even the scarring on his face was almost undetectable. Thane's gaze lifted to study Julian's eyes... "Are you okay?"

"Dr. Phil you are not." Julian snapped his fingers at Thane as he spun on his heel and headed for the office door. Under normal circumstances, Thane would have acknowledged the only topic that ever sent Julian packing, but not in this case. Instead, he had a sense of relief that Julian was leaving him alone to text Levi.

"Nope, not doing this today with you, *papi*. Loaner phone's in the bottom right hand drawer. Tell your boyfriend hello."

Before going for the phone, he picked up his cell phone and made a note to himself to explore Julian's behavior later. Julian probably needed more counseling. Something wasn't right, not terribly wrong, but not quite right either.

Within minutes, he had the loaner phone in his hand and a huge smile on his face as he sat back in the office chair and began to text, saying the words he'd wanted to say all morning.

"Hello, handsome."

~~~

Levi fished the phone from his pocket as he placed the last folded pair of socks on the coffee table. Before he looked down to see who had texted, he looked out the front window. Logan mowed the last stretch of the front yard while Luke used the weed eater. They were almost done. He should get ready to go to the grocery store. They could get all this crap done today. What he hadn't told his brothers was that he disliked chore day every bit as much as they did.

He glanced down at the screen, registered the unknown number, and opened the message with a slide of the thumb.

"Hello, handsome."

The relief those two words brought was insane. It amazed him how quickly Logan's and Luke's doubts had taken hold. He was insecure as hell, and with a huge grin spreading across his face, Levi quickly typed back, *"I'm sorry, do I know you?"*

Thane instantly replied, *"You do. I'm your date for tonight."*

Levi pushed back on the sofa, taking a settling seat as he replied, *"I thought we agreed Tuesday was our next date."*

Thane was on his texting game, because less than a minute later, he responded. *"We agreed to Tuesday, Friday, and Saturday. It's Saturday. I want my date."*

Yep, that had slipped passed Levi. He thought about that for a second. Looked at the time. Two o'clock. They could really get
~~~

everything done today and use tomorrow to rest, hang out around the house, do homework until his shift… Besides, if Luke and Logan were right, he probably shouldn't come on as overeager. Right?

Reluctantly Levi typed, *"That slipped past me. I'm sorry to already bail on our arrangement, but I can't tonight."*

"Why?" How could he read irritation in the one-word response he got back?

Before he had a chance to respond, the phone started ringing. Thane's number appeared. Of course. The guy absolutely *did not* like not getting his way. Levi answered. Foregoing any greeting, Thane blurted, "You agreed on three nights. I wanted seven. So, why're you already backing out?"

Levi laughed at the annoyance lacing each of Thane's words. He'd totally guessed his reaction correctly. "I'm gone so much at night that I hang out with my brothers on the weekend. Luke's struggled a lot lately, and he's just getting back to himself. I shouldn't just leave…"

Thane cut him off in mid-sentence. "Bring them with you."

That surprised him into silence. He took a lengthy pause before speaking honestly. "I'm not sure two nights in a row is a good idea. They already gave me a hard time this morning. They got the idea we're a one-night—"

Thane cut him off again, this time with humor in his voice. "Are you always this difficult or just with me? Bring them. Come hang out at the resort. They can swim, have dinner, watch movies. I think there's a movie theater here. You guys could even spend the night. I have two rooms in this suite."

"A sleepover's more than a date," Levi said.

"Come over now and quit overthinking things. I've got nothing going on. My luggage and office equipment are MIA. So, that means I've got nothing but time today," Thane said.

Levi didn't respond. Instead, he looked over his shoulder toward the kitchen as the guys had come through the kitchen door. They were sweaty messes, and Logan already had his nose buried in the screen of his phone. He dropped down in the chair next to Levi, not caring about the amount of dust and grass clippings that he had on his dirty body. Luke on the other hand dropped to the floor, stretching his long body out. Manual labor wasn't either of their thing.

"Say yes," Thane pleaded.

The boys didn't get out of the house like that and most certainly had never seen anything as nice as Escape Coronado. If nothing else, they could swim for hours or maybe go to the ocean. They lived in San Diego and rarely went to the beach.

"Thane's invited us to go to the resort today and spend the night. We could swim and eat there. He says there's a movie theater. I think I heard it goes all night. And he has an extra room to sleep in so we can stay if it gets too late," Levi said. Logan didn't look up from his always moving thumbs on his cell phone. It was Luke who jackknifed up, sitting straight, showing real interest.

"I'll go."

"You mean you'd allow us to do something other than our Saturday chores. Oh no, the world might fall apart," Logan deadpanned, still not looking at him.

"We're finished. All we have left to do is go to the grocery store. We can do that tomorrow before my shift. What'd you say? He's waiting," Levi said and pointed to the phone stuck to his ear.

"Let's go, Logan. The new Marvel's out," Luke said excitedly.

"Yeah, I'll go. Alison has to go to dinner with her brother's girlfriend's parents," Logan said, sounding somewhat discontent.

Levi didn't hesitate. "They're in." His leg started bouncing, his anticipation growing. His emotions ran deep where Thane was concerned, deeper and more meaningful than he wanted anyone to know. "We're doing laundry and just finished with the yard work."

"Sounds like a titillating time you're having. Bring swimsuits and a change of clothes. We can have dinner downstairs or in the room, whatever you want. There's enough to do that they'll stay busy all night and never get bored."

"I'll text when we're on our way," Levi said and ended the call. He sat there a minute. The happiness that had dimmed after his brothers' comments this morning was back in full force. When he finally looked up, both boys were staring at him.

"Is it serious?" Logan asked.

"No, probably not, but we all need some fun, right?" Levi answered somewhat honestly. Luke shoved off the floor, grabbing a couple of stacks of clothes off the coffee table before heading toward his room.

"We could go to the beach too. We haven't been to the beach since we took Dad. For the future, I'm totally in for anytime he wants us there." Luke disappeared behind the door.

"Put your clothes away. I'm going to shower," he told Logan and grabbed his stack of clean clothes before heading back to his room. He fought against all those warm feelings coursing through him. It didn't do any good. He was over the moon for Thane.

CHAPTER 22

"I love the scent of your cologne," Thane whispered in Levi's ear as they slowly swayed back and forth to "Demons" by Fatboy Slim. Macy Gray's voice was sexy as hell, and Thane was certain this was the best dance floor in all of Coronado. He'd planned to take Levi back to where they'd started, try to rewrite their first date. As far as he could tell, the place held the same allure as before. He and Levi were magic together, everything Thane remembered from their first night together.

"Mmm," Levi muttered. Levi had managed to seal himself inside Thane's heart tonight. There was no turning back. Tonight, Levi had drunk more, gotten more comfortable, and let his hair down, so to speak. Perhaps Thane had encouraged Levi to drink a little more; he certainly hadn't let Levi's glass go empty once he realized Levi was a happy, agreeable drunk.

Now, Levi's eyes were closed, the man's thick body pressed against the length of his, letting Thane guide their movement. Thane held on tight, kept Levi right there locked against him, as they moved seductively to Macy's unique voice. The song was as magic, erotic, and sensual as the man in his arms.

"This needs to be our new song," Thane said, dropping his head so his lips were close to Levi's. Every so often Levi would lean in and press his lips against Thane's neck in the sweetest possible caress. Next time, he wanted that kiss to land on his lips. "Babe, when this color grows out, don't add more. I like your hair's natural color."

"They call me Red," Levi whispered as if that explained anything. Thane let the words bounce around his head, tried to understand, but didn't really grasp their meaning.

"Over the last few weeks, I've often thought of you as my redhead," Thane confessed. "My sexy redhead." Thane felt Levi chuckle and start to pull away. Thane wasn't ready to let him go and reached a hand up, encouraging his head back down. "Just dance with me. Let me hold you and pretend I didn't fuck this up in the beginning. That you're as into me as I am you."

Levi's warm breath slid over his skin as he snuggled his face into the crook of his neck, tightening his hold. "I hope I remember you said all that in the morning."

"I hope you don't," Thane said. They had come to a standstill on the dance floor, no longer moving, just holding each other. "I'm afraid you'll run away scared."

Regretfully, Levi's head came up, looking at him with less than two inches between their noses. "I'm not scared. I'm practical."

Thane stared at Levi and contemplated that declaration. Instinct more than any well thought out plan had him answering before he thought better of it. "You're scared."

"You're really nice to look at." Tipsy Levi was really random. Thane busted out a laugh at Levi's compliment.

"Well, I have something to confess to you. Something I should have told you before now, but on my honor, when it happened, I truly didn't understand that you didn't know."

Levi's gaze turned speculative and locked on his. Thane's heart began the slow steady build of nervous anxiousness. Who the hell was he kidding? He was the scared one.

"But first, I think you need another drink."

"If I have another drink, you'll be carrying me to the room," Levi answered.

Whatever Levi saw caused him to stand a little straighter. Levi didn't move away nor did he let go of his hold, but Thane could tell he sensed something substantial coming. Thane swallowed the lump that formed. He just couldn't justify another day with this hanging between them. Until he told the truth, he'd never know for sure if they were able to move forward and make a go of this relationship.

"My name is Nathaniel Walker. I'm from Baltimore, Maryland, graduated from Johns—"

Levi finished his sentence. "Hopkins University."

Thane gave a single slight nod and his arm locked around Levi's waist. They stood there, staring at one another for maybe a dozen seconds. Hell, he couldn't be sure, time stopped for him as he waited for the fallout. The quiet between them felt mind-numbing. Thane's guilt grew as he watched Levi's complete non-reaction. Maybe he needed to explain.

"When I first reached out to you, I didn't know you couldn't see my nickname on my profile. I just enjoyed talking to you, getting to know you. You're a fascinating, intriguing man. After I realized it, I honestly didn't think you'd open up if you knew it was me…"

Levi's warm hand cupped the nape of his neck, and his gaze dropped to Thane's lips. He said nothing as he drew Thane to him and took his mouth at the same time his hips rolled forward and their erections met. Levi went straight for total domination. The kiss was possessive and urgent. Thane was so caught off guard that it took him a second to catch up. He found himself in the middle of the most erotic kiss he'd ever had and was struggling to process what just happened.

The sound of the music faded. The lights, the people, everything melted away as Levi tilted his head and deepened the kiss, rocking his world. He was thoroughly kissed, body and soul, as his heart leaped from his chest, landing in Levi's caring hands, and Thane was helpless to stop it.

Thane wrapped himself around Levi and tried to give back what he'd gotten. Just as suddenly as Levi began the kiss, he ended it, backing off, but not out of the hold. More dazed than he'd ever been in his life, and that said a lot because Levi left him regularly stunned, Thane tried to follow Levi's mouth, to bring him back to the kiss, but Levi dodged him, moving his head back even farther.

"Listen to me." Those words came out slurred as Levi's brows came together and he cleared his throat. "Listen. I wanted to be attracted to Nathaniel. I knew I needed someone like him in my life, but it was you. I was always thinking about you."

Astonished by Levi's sudden confession, Thane was on cloud nine. "You've never said anything like that to me before. You fight me at every turn—"

"I think I'm drunk." Levi leaned in, kissing the words from Thane's mouth in a quick brush of lips.

"I know you're drunk." Thane followed again, kissing Levi in a long, lingering kiss. "Will you remember this in the morning?"

"If I don't, remind me when my brothers aren't around. You'll be getting that fucking you like so much," Levi said loudly and laid his head back on Thane's shoulder. Thane looked around to see who might have heard. He got several disapproving stares. It was still relatively early in the night, and they had probably pushed the boundaries of acceptable behavior, but he couldn't care less. Levi's arms tightened around him, those lips touched his neck, and dear God, if he wasn't completely lost to this man who slurred the sweetest words. "It was you this whole time, and I didn't know, and I'm definitely scared."

"I have more to say, but let's go upstairs," Thane whispered. They had gelled too well tonight. As much as Thane wanted Levi alone in his bedroom, he also recognized the bigger implication; he wanted these moments with Levi every day. He began to envision scenes like Levi on his patio, hanging out with Corey and Erin. She'd love Levi as much as he did. Maybe, if his parents were serious about being a family, he could let go of the past to give Levi and his brothers a strong family foundation, more than just each other.

Reluctantly, Thane loosened the hold, but not completely. It seemed the idea of not letting Levi go applied physically as well as emotionally. He stepped backward, taking Levi's arm when he wobbled a bit and gave a long, drawn-out yawn.

"You okay?"

"Not really," Levi answered and reached out, wrapping an arm around Thane's waist to help keep himself steady on his feet as they headed back to the table. "I don't normally drink this much. I think you kept ordering on purpose."

"You can let your hair down with me," Thane teased, laughing as Levi downed the last of his beer while Thane closed their tab.

That last drink may have tipped the scale because Levi stayed plastered against his side as they went through the lobby. In the elevator, he started losing Levi. His eyes began to droop; his body slumped forward. At the suite, Thane had to hold Levi propped against the wall before he could get the door open.

"Come on, babe. Just a few more feet."

Levi managed to somewhat help get himself to Thane's bed, but he fell fast asleep before his head hit the pillow. Levi was still fully clothed, his body partially hanging off the bed. Thane needed to remember this. Levi had only seemed somewhat tipsy; he'd held his alcohol well until he passed clean out on him.

Thane adjusted Levi, trying to arrange him in a more comfortable position, before pulling off his shoes, and had just started on the belt buckle when he heard the suite door open. Logan and Luke were talking then went into complete silence. Thane listened closely, heard nothing, and couldn't resist the quick kiss he left on Levi's forehead, curious as to why things got so quiet between two boys who never seemed to stop talking. He looked around, didn't see either until he spotted both gathered in a corner of the balcony, looking over the railing.

Shit. He hadn't considered…

"Guys, come back in here."

"They're naked," Luke hissed, never tearing his eyes from the scene below.

"I know. This is adults only." When Luke didn't immediately move, Thane playfully grabbed the back of his shirt, pulling him away from the railing. "Luke, you're eighteen if anyone asks."

"Yeah, we figured that out already," Logan replied. Technically, he was near old enough, but Luke was nowhere close. The kid finally turned away from the beach to face Thane.

The grin plastered across his face said it all. Logan was enjoying the idea of adults only. Thane drew them fully inside the suite and closed the back walls, locking them in place.

"Next time, I'll make sure we're in the family section. Your brother wouldn't like this at all," Thane mumbled, going for the thermostat.

"He used to not be so strict," Logan admitted, already so comfortable around Thane that he had no problem plopping down on the sofa, grabbing the remote.

"He's trying to keep us together," Luke challenged, knocking Logan in the arm as he came to his oldest brother's defense. Thane caught the stern look Luke gave Logan as he stole the remote out of his brother's hand. "None of us are the same as we used to be."

"I wasn't throwing shade. I was just sayin'," Logan explained to Luke, defensively. Thane sensed a fight coming on and quickly inserted his two cents.

"Your brother's crashed in there." Thane pointed to his room without using the word bedroom. It seemed to help him justify that he'd put Levi in his bed. "We had a nice time tonight. He drank too much."

"Levi doesn't really drink," Logan answered, the fight forgotten as both boys lifted their heads in his direction.

"Yeah, I figured he doesn't drink too much." Unsure what to do now, Thane paused then continued using his hands to talk. "So, I'm going to bed too." Again, he hooked a thumb over his shoulder toward his room. The awkwardness of the moment increased for him. "Whatever you can find to eat, you can have." Thane went to a cabinet where he'd stocked up on chips and junk food from his restaurant downstairs. "The TV has everything you could want. Get whatever movie you want. Stay away from the porn because I want Levi to feel comfortable in bringing you back, and I think he'd think that was bad, and I have no idea how to block adult channels, so just don't watch. And probably don't leave. And stay off the balcony. And go to bed at some point. And don't do anything you're not supposed to do."

After he decided that last sentence covered anything he missed, he gave a thumbs-up before remembering Iris. They'd probably get a kick out of her. He looked around, judging where she'd drop down from and moved a step over. "If you want room service, or have any questions, you can call Iris, she's the virtual assistant." Before he ever got finished saying the sentence, she dropped down from the ceiling. Both boys went nuts with their no-ways and oh-mans. He chuckled as she smiled at him.

"Yes, sir?"

"I was just showing them how you work. I must have said your name too loudly."

She looked around, seeing the boys and smiled. "I believe that's a problem they're experiencing. My calling instruction will be changing soon. Is there anything you need?"

"No, we're good. Thank you."

When she vanished, it was Luke who jumped off the couch and stood looking up at the ceiling. "Can they see inside here?"

Good question. Thane looked up at the camera device. He had no real idea. Luke didn't give him a chance to respond.

"What if she drops down on top of you?"

Logan immediately shot back a quick, "She's a hologram." The tone totally implied dumbass, but he impressively didn't use the actual word. Still, Luke moved out of the way.

"Can I use your laptop?" Luke asked, abruptly shifting topics.

"Sure." Thane went for his desk, thinking about the split-second change in conversation, and handed over his laptop. "The password is *password* and stay out of my office programs. If you get notifications for me, leave them unopened. I'll take care of them tomorrow."

"Thanks," Luke said with the biggest grin on his face. He was just so easily pleased. Thane looked over at Logan who had his phone in his hands, typing away.

"No more balcony," Thane said again at his bedroom door, relieved they seemed to have no problem with Levi's sleeping in his bed. They were great kids—well behaved and easy to be around. Thane shut the door to a loud snore from Levi. He chuckled as he started to undress.

~~~

Something was really very wrong. Levi lay utterly still, taking inventory of his body. It wasn't the vile taste in his mouth or the spike of pain in his head that had apparently awakened him. No, he needed to use the bathroom. Like in a big, immediate way. Rolling from the bed, he found himself still almost fully dressed. Levi stumbled around the bed straight toward the bathroom, leaving the door open and the light off, squinting just enough to see the toilet as he hurriedly unbuttoned his pants, and shoved his underwear low, his morning wood greeting him. He leaned over the commode and held his rogue cock at an angle and waited. For as bad as he had to piss, it was taking him forever to get started. Finally. Relief swamped his body as he tried to remember what he'd done last night. The four of them had gone swimming; they'd had dinner together at one of Thane's restaurants in the resort. Logan and Luke had gone to the movies, and he and Thane had gone to the same bar they'd gone to that first night.

Thane hadn't let his glass get empty.

That was where things got fuzzy.

Did he know if Luke and Logan made it back to the room? He wasn't certain. Dammit, he couldn't think straight with this vile taste in his mouth.

He had no idea of the time and stuck his head out the bathroom door, looking for an alarm clock. He didn't see one, so he looked at the windows. No light shone from around the edges of the curtains. Maybe still nighttime? Levi quietly shut the door and flipped the bathroom lights on as he pulled his shirt over his head. The light blinded him as he tossed the material toward the counter. The pain in his head spiked again, and he stood there with his eyes closed, absorbing the pain.

"Damn," he murmured and reached out with his hand, trying to find the sink.
~~~

Slowly his eyes adjusted, and he opened them to find a toothbrush, Advil, and a bottle of water. His shirt was on the floor, at least a foot off its mark of the sink counter. He quickly swallowed the Advil before starting on his teeth. He scrubbed them for a good long time, hoping to rid himself of the taste, then splashed cold water on his face. Reaching for the hand towel, he saw, on the other side of the counter, a can of Sprite with a note.

Levi,

I like a carbonated drink after drinking too much.
Wake me if you need anything.
Thane

He barely got his face dried before reaching for the soda and popping the top. He downed the Sprite while looking at himself in the mirror. His bedhead was extreme, and he searched for a brush to try to tame the mass. When he decided this was just as good as it got under the circumstances, he reached for his shirt, leaving his jeans undone as he went back into the bedroom. This time, a lamp was on. Thane lay on his side, resting his head on his hand with his eyes closed.

"I'm sorry I woke you," Levi apologized, heading for Thane's side of the bed where the alarm clock was turned facing the wall. It was four thirty in the morning.

"No problem. I can be a light sleeper," Thane said and reached for Levi's hand, bringing him to sit on the edge of the bed as Thane rolled to his back, pushing a pillow under his head. "How do you feel?"

"Hungover. Thank you for that stuff in there. Do you know if my brothers got in okay?" he asked, scrubbing a hand over his face. Luckily his headache had started to ebb, allowing him to think a little clearer.

"Yeah, I made sure and just checked on them. They're passed out in the living room. Didn't make it to the bedroom," he said, drawing Levi's knuckles to his lips.

"I'm sorry. I can go move 'em."

"No, leave them. I'm glad they're comfortable here," Thane said and started to scoot over, moving to the middle of the bed. "I pulled out blankets, and they had their pillows. Each has a sofa.

They'll sleep awhile. Come back to bed." Thane patted the mattress next to him, and Levi didn't need to be told twice. He pulled off his jeans, grabbed the shirt he'd set on the bed and tossed them on a nearby chair before crawling in the warm spot Thane had just vacated.

"I like both of them, but I have another confession," Thane said, adjusting himself until Levi was lying on his back with Thane wrapped all around his left side. "They found the adults-only swimming pool below."

"Oh no. I didn't think about that," Levi said. His first thought was that he needed to remember to tell Luke not to say a word; their social worker probably wouldn't be too keen on that judgment call.

"Me neither, until Luke acted shocked and excited all at the same time." Thane chuckled and reached across Levi to tap the lamp, plunging the room into darkness. "I'm gonna ask for different rooms tomorrow."

"You don't have to do that."

Thane pulled at the pillow under his head, moving to where they now shared one. Thane's leg hooked over both of his, pulling them closer together. Thane stared at him. It was shocking how comfortable they were together, when it was just the two of them, nothing else in the world seemed to matter. Even all the worries and fears that bombarded him every day seemed to take a backseat to Thane.

"Of course, I do. I want you guys to come back. They seemed to have had a great time." Thane stared at him for several long seconds before lifting a hand to his face, his thumb moving slowly back and forth against his cheek. "Luke's loyal to you."

Levi chuckled, not missing the absence of Logan's name in that thought. "He's gay. At least, I think. Did I tell you?"

"I wondered. Does Logan know?"

"Logan's always been the classic middle child. He's the victim and the aggressor all at the same time. He's been real steady throughout this adjustment period. Logan's a good guy. He takes things in stride a little better than either Luke or I do, but I'm betting he doesn't know, even though they've always been close," Levi said. Dropping his gaze to Thane's lips, he brushed his thumb across them. He loved touching this man. Levi took the feel of Thane's skin, the texture of his lips, the coarse stubble of his beard into his mind and wanted to always remember.

"They seem like they're close," Thane replied. "Do you remember what we talked about at the bar before we left?"

Levi struggled on that one. They'd talked about everything tonight. They were comfortable together in conversation, nothing seemed off limits. Work, religion, politics. Goals for the future, movies, books, music… He looked up at Thane who stared at him and waited. He had to think, something needling around the edges. "The name thing?"

"Mmm," was all he got from Thane.

Again, he had to concentrate which seemed to bring the headache back. "I remember a fantastic kiss. Did we get kicked out for being obscene?" Based on his sketchy memory, that was a viable option. He could have done Thane right there and never been the wiser. "Were the police called? If they were, they'll notify the boys' social worker."

"They have a social worker?" Thane asked, his face changing into one of concern.

"Yeah, two actually, but one's more an advocate, just making sure everything's functional for Luke," Levi explained, trying to make the situation seem less overwhelming. They barely ever saw her. Their protective service worker had stopped by once a week in the beginning, but she switched them to quarterly visits now. As long as they held it together, there wouldn't be a problem.

"You have a heavy load. I admire your tenacity," Thane said and leaned in to kiss his lips. Levi didn't say a word. It didn't seem so heavy, at least not any more. "We weren't kicked out. Police weren't called. However, we did share a naughty kiss and you told me you've wanted me for a while. Umm…and that I was nice to look at."

"Mmm," Levi repeated, making Thane laugh. "So, you were actually the one getting my paperwork pushed through at school?"

"Not really. My father's name helped. He's a professor—"

Levi placed two fingers on Thane's lips, stopping him in mid-sentence.

Strangely enough he wasn't mad or pissed off. He had needed someone on his side and that someone turned out to be the man holding him in his arms.

"Thank you for doing what you've done. It helped me. I was struggling with you, with money, Luke's depression. I just had a lot coming at me and you helped me. I needed Nathaniel. I needed a friend more than anything, but don't ever lie to me again. I get what happened, just not again," Levi said, looking Thane straight in the eyes.

"Never again, but in my defense, technically I only omitted a part of the truth." Thane moved Levi's fingers from his lips, threading their fingers together. "Can I ask one thing that I shouldn't? If I were smart, I'd just leave this alone." He stayed absolutely silent, listening to Thane. "I expected something different when I told you. Instead, you seem almost relieved. Explain that to me. I want to be what you need, if that makes any sense."

Thane's declaration embraced his fragile heart. The man was coming on strong, and Levi couldn't find it in him to resist and was even long past the point of trying.

"When I was talking to Nathaniel, we had this same weird connection that you and I have—at least that's how it felt to me." Levi's anxiety rose, and he dropped his gaze to the light gray pattern on the sheets.

"Don't do that," Thane said. He slid his strong fingers under Levi's chin and forced his head up. Levi met Thane's sincere gaze. "You know I feel this connection. I've moved across country to be near you."

Just hearing Thane's words made his stomach flip, sink, and flutter all at the same time. Levi let out a quick, deep breath, and continued, "Nathaniel and I clicked. I don't always click so well with people. So, I hoped that meant that maybe once I got through school and turned my life around, that maybe I could find someone special to share my life with. Nathaniel gave me hope. I felt accepted, but I always wished it were you. I'm really attracted to you, but felt safe talking to him." There, he'd just laid his heart out on the line, no longer hiding. The honesty he had with Nathaniel bridged the undeniable pull he had with Thane, adding a new dimension to what they shared.

Thane's weight shifted and his lips touched Levi's chest in the briefest of kisses. Levi pressed himself closer; a slow burn heated his insides as Thane's lips trailed along his skin, teasing him with wet nips and licks up his neck and on his jaw. He wanted Thane to make love to him, hold him, take his mind off everything that had happened in the past. He needed to lose himself in Thane and forget about the rest of the world if only for a few minutes.

Thane's mouth found his and his whole body ignited. Levi sucked Thane's fleshy bottom lip between his own, opening when Thane's tongue pushed inside his mouth and skilled hands began to roam every inch of him, heating the blood in his veins. Wanton, burning pressure rushed deep, filling his balls, as Thane's hand pushed into the waistband of his underwear. Levi arched his back then lifted his hips when his lover's thick fingers wrapped around him and tightened so perfectly. He thrust into the grip.

God, he wanted them both sweaty and straining as Thane's girth stretched him, filling him till everything faded into the background but the two of them. His ass clenched at the thought.

"I know we're not alone. My brothers are in the other room, but I want you, Thane. Make love to me," Levi whispered, moving his hand to Thane's, urging him to stroke his aching erection. His dick throbbed, definitely on board with the decision as Thane's thumb spread the need leaking from the tip of his dick.

"We'll have to be quiet. Roll to your side." Thane changed positions, disrupting the bedcovers as he helped rid Levi of his underwear while assisting him to his side. Thane pulled him closer, and Levi snuggled back against Thane as the man tugged the blankets up around them both. This moment was so right. Thane's lips pressed against his shoulder as he tucked one arm under Levi's pillow and wrapped the other around his waist. Thane's arousal nestled perfectly against his ass. Thane's stubble skimmed across his neck and shoulder, making the hair spring up on Levi's arms. He couldn't help but cuddle back against Thane. "Since we're being so honest, I have something else to say."

"What's that?" Levi whispered. Excitement and anticipation tensed his muscles and he closed his eyes. That husky tenor, Thane's hands moving on him, and that trimmed beard scrapping over the crook of his neck, fisted his balls and squeezed. He was having a hard time concentrating, but he tried. The scent of Thane's cologne on the pillow surrounded him, making it almost impossible to listen.

"After the first night we were together, I took the pillow we shared home with me. My neighbor helped me identify your cologne." Thane nipped at the area he'd just scraped with his beard and a shiver raced down his body. "I have a bottle now."

"That's not true," Levi finally challenged after a moment of trying to process Thane's words while his fingers toyed with Levi's nipple.

"It's very true. Your cologne's Armani Code, but it's not quite the same without your body's scent mixed in." Thane's palm flattened over Levi's stomach then slid down to his rigid dick. Levi sucked in a breath as strong fingers curled around his aching shaft.

Levi glanced back over his shoulder at Thane, trying the gauge the truth from any possible fiction. He seemed serious. Levi settled back down, placing his hand on Thane's hip, drawing the man closer, closing any space between them. He didn't say a word, just thought about Thane's words—what they meant, how telling they were. Thane was coming on strong, and Levi was already struggling to keep his perspective. They needed time, no question there, but maybe Levi also needed to lighten up, quit being so doubtful and skeptical. Go with the flow instead of being suspicious of every one of Thane's actions.

"I'm scared," he said truthfully. He could feel the movement behind him. Thane lifted his head enough so that his warm breath tickled Levi's ear.

"You said that earlier. Tell me what scares you?" Thane's hand moved tenderly to his hip then up his back to caress along the line of his shoulder. It was that right there. They were already so much more than just the sex they had.

Levi sighed, closed his eyes, and spoke from his heart. "Of this. Of what you're doing, what you're proposing between us, and how much I want it to work."

Thane's palm cupped his shoulder, his fingers sinking in the tight muscles in his neck and upper back before traveling back down his spine.

"I get it. I was scared too. You blindsided me that first night, and I did the only thing I knew how. I ran. I'm sorry it took me so long to figure everything out and get back here." Thane's lips touched the back of his neck before he continued, "I never wanted to leave you in this bed that first morning, and I haven't forgiven myself for being such a coward. It was my fear of how amazing this was between us. That feeling had me running scared. I was afraid of what I felt, how fast it happened, and how fucking real it was. I didn't know what the future would hold for us. I've been alone most of my life. At least I consider myself a loner. I've never connected with anyone like this before."

Levi considered himself a loner too. Not by choice maybe, but circumstance.

"It's the way you handle me. You dominate me. You take charge. I can only step so far, move so much—no one has ever had power over me like that. You're the only one. It's weird to admit it out loud, because you confuse the hell out of me, but it also turns me the fuck on when you take charge and own me," Thane said.

"I can't control my urges when I'm with you," Levi confessed, angling his head.

"God knows I love our sex and how rough I like it with you, but no, I wasn't talking about sex. It's in everything we do—you control everything whether you realize it or not. And when I can get you to give in, it's like an aphrodisiac."

Levi nudged Thane as he tried to turn and look him in the eyes. "We're leaving here at the end of the summer. There's no question about that. I have to get them away from here and give them a new start." Levi explained what he and his brothers had planned, what they were working so hard to achieve.

"My offices are actually there—not thirty minutes from the JHU campus. We're jumping too far ahead, but I've told you very clearly, I'm only here in California because you're here. We can see each other in both places," Thane said.

"Thane, once we get there, I'll have to work as much as I possibly can. I won't be able to make the money I can at Reservations. School'll have to be my top priority, and I also have no idea how to be a father, but I kind of am one now. I'm trying hard to navigate the things I've never done before. It's been rough for me and for them. They have to come first. Luke absolutely has to come first. I need to be a home base for both of them forever. My dad asked me to take care of them, and I gave my word. I can't let him down," he said, laying everything out between them. Thane had to see that he wasn't purposefully trying to control anything. Some things just had to be the way they were; he had obligations now. Time restrictions to the extreme.

"I know. I have a full understanding of what I'm walking into. Only because we're being candid…when I decided I was going to pursue you, your situation and commitments made me pause, but only for half a second, wondering if I was good enough to help raise your brothers. I haven't been around kids ever, but my eyes are open and I'm trying. I hope you see that."

Levi searched the man's eyes before again turning and fully giving Thane his back.

His heart was so full. He wanted Thane's words to be true. Levi closed his eyes and fought all the deepening emotions. He'd truly thought he'd be alone forever, especially with his responsibilities. Fear was there, lurking below the surface, but also hope and a sense of happiness. The future felt foreign yet almost tangible in the form of Nathaniel Walker, and that was something he wanted to grab on to, and hold forever. "So, you really want to date me?"

"Yes. That's what I want more than anything." Thane caressed his ass again, and this time, his fingers slid along Levi's crack. Levi pushed back against him. Thane's digits slipped between his ass cheeks and began circling his rim.

"Please," he moaned and brought his knee forward, opening himself.

Right now, having Thane moving behind him, whispering everything was going to be okay was all he really wanted in the world.

"I locked the door. We'll have to keep it down. They're sound asleep," Thane said huskily from behind. He heard the snick of a lid opening seconds before Thane's slick fingers breached his hole. His lover's skilled fingers brought instant pleasure as they circled his hole then dipped in slowly, pressing and probing, massaging and retreating. Levi closed his eyes and lowered his chest closer to the mattress, spreading out as far as he could go. "I want you. Do you want me, Levi?"

Thane pushed two fingers inside his channel, easily finding his gland.

Oh God, yes, yes, yes. His body tensed as he absorbed the instant rush of hunger that swept through him.

"Answer me, babe," Thane whispered right inside his ear, sending shards of tingles and goose bumps springing up on his arms.

"Yes," he managed, gripping the edge of the pillow with his fist.

~~~

He'd waited forever to make love to Levi, and he needed to calm the fuck down or the experience would be over before he even started. Thane cast his gaze down, taking in the way Levi's muscles flexed and moved under his touch. He followed the trail,
~~~

kissing his way down Levi's body, eager to get a taste of that perfect ass.

Gently, Thane pushed at Levi's hips, rolling him forward just a little more so that Levi was on his stomach and more open. Thane bit at the perfect globes of Levi's ass, kneading the firm flesh in his palms. He spread Levi's butt cheeks and admired the view. Thane dipped his head and licked across the wrinkled pink flesh, Levi's sweetness mixed with the coconut-flavored lube intoxicated him. The younger man groaned and shifted his hips back against Thane's tongue. Thane took that as all the permission he needed and buried his face in Levi's ass. His fingers joined in with his tongue to pleasure and relax Levi. He was drunk on everything Levi Silva, and from the whimpers coming him, Levi was just as strung out as he was.

"Thane, please. I need more…" Levi squirmed on the bed as Thane held him exactly where he wanted him, eating his sweet ass like he'd dreamed of doing for so long.

Levi's hips bucked roughly. "Oh, God… Please, Thane."

Thane loved the way those words sounded coming from Levi. He eased up on his oral assault, lightly kissing Levi's butt cheeks, and maybe a little along his spine as he positioned him back on his side.

Thane rolled over and grabbed for the condoms and lube from where he'd dropped them on the bed earlier. He tore the foil wrapper with his teeth then rolled the condom down his aching shaft. Using a generous amount of lube, he coated himself and made sure Levi was slick and ready before gripping himself and shifting Levi's leg forward to change his angle.

Thane closed his eyes as he lined himself up and pressed the tip of his cock to Levi's hole. White-hot heat engulfed him as the head pushed passed the tight muscles resisting his efforts. They both tensed at the sensation of him sinking into Levi's body.

"So fucking tight, baby." Thane adjusted his hips and ran a comforting hand along Levi's spine, allowing his partner to become accustomed to being breached. Levi relaxed and pushed back against him as Thane kissed the nape of his sexy lover's neck and mumbled sweet promises against his skin.

"Please move, Thane. I've waited too long."

Thane agreed. He'd definitely waited a long time for this moment. He just wished he had the time and the privacy to pleasure Levi like he deserved.

Levi whimpered when Thane slowly withdrew from his body. He gripped Levi's leg and pushed back in deeper than before and pulled out again. He repeated the motion over and over, going deeper each time.

"Feels so good, Thane." Levi lifted his leg as Thane adjusted their position and rocked his hips into Levi. Thane pulled Levi against him and thrust into him harder and harder each time. Levi groaned and reached back, grasping for him.

"Right there…so close." Levi's words came in gasps, his upper body twisted so his shoulder was partially on the rumpled pillow. Levi's lips parted, and Thane lowered his head to take Levi's lips with his. Levi's tongue greeted his in a languid kiss. His kisses were like a drug, and Thane craved them like the junkie he was. He ate at the other man's mouth, lost in the pleasure and bliss of the moment.

He must have died; Levi's body was heaven, and he didn't want to ever leave it. Thane held Levi's leg steady, while digging his foot into the mattress for leverage, fucking Levi hard and fast.

Heat lapped at his spine and burned like fire in his balls. He was so close, but he refused to succumb to his pleasure. He released Levi's leg in exchange for his cock. Levi immediately pushed into his fist. He stroked Levi's swollen shaft the way he knew drove Levi crazy.

"I love being in you," he panted into Levi's mouth. Levi's eyes opened, and that piercing green stare locked on to his. He swallowed Levi's moan with a kiss.

The feel of Levi's body quivering around him set him off, and he fell willingly over the edge. Levi's cock twitched in his grip and thick ribbons of come hit Levi's chest and neck. His own dick pulsed wildly in time with his heartbeat as his seed filled the condom buried deep in Levi's ass.

He let himself melt into Levi, gathering him in his arms as the vibrations in his body quieted and his breathing returned to normal. He lay there even longer, comfortable holding Levi, who threaded their fingers together, clinging tightly to his hand. Neither slept nor spoke. Thane had no idea how much time passed before he kissed the back of Levi's head and whispered, "Come on. We need to shower before the sleepyheads wake up and want breakfast, or even worse, decide to sneak down to the adults-only beach."

CHAPTER 23

Four weeks later—June 2017

"Why tonight?" Thane pouted, making Levi laugh as he ran his gelled fingers through his wet hair. Luckily, a Friday night shift had opened, and Levi just happened to be there when Chase told Julian, giving him the opportunity to swoop in and offer to cover the shift before anyone else got the chance.

Thane didn't like the idea, not one bit. Friday nights were their pre-scheduled date nights, per Thane, and the guy had been complaining for over an hour about the inconvenience.

"The money's too good to pass up." Levi turned on the hair dryer to help drown out Thane's continued whining. The smile that had been etched on his face for weeks now only grew broader. Even through the gradual decrease in hours at the PT clinic that had eventually resulted in companywide lay-offs, including his position, this afternoon, Levi had managed to keep a genuine grin on his face. He was finally really happy, and after such a dark time in his life, happy felt amazing. He'd find other work to fill his daytime hours. He'd figure it out and that sense of self-assurance felt great too.

Levi watched in the mirror as a nude, disgruntled Thane came through the bathroom doorway, his stern gaze meeting Levi's in their reflections. When he got within reach, Thane took the dryer out of his hand, pressed the off button, and tossed the thing on the counter without a care before propping a hip on the edge of the counter and crossing his arms over his chest. "You did that on purpose."

Of course, he had. How many times could he say that Friday night shifts were too good to pass up? So yeah, turning on the hair dryer had been strategically designed to avoid further discussion. Absolutely.

"I came over early," he countered and focused on his image in the mirror, using the brush to help keep his hair flipped back off his forehead. "I thought that'd meet our contractual obligations," he added, now trying to keep a serious look on his face and hoping he could hold his laughter inside at his outrageous statement.

Levi pushed past Thane, placed the brush in the drawer before leaving Thane standing there as he headed to the bedroom. He needed his backpack, but he didn't see it. He completed a full circle in the bedroom before remembering he'd left it in the living room and taking off in that direction. He dug through the pack and pulled out the uniform, dropping his towel before stepping into the underwear and sliding it up his thighs. He heard a faint moan from across the room, and he couldn't help but allow his grin to grow. Thane was insatiable.

"You're killin' me, babe. I just don't get what you don't understand. We agreed Tuesday, Friday, and Saturday, Levi. I had great plans in place for you tonight. Arik and Kellus are here. We're meeting with my chef about the oils then going to dinner and dancing. This is the only night that you can stay out late," Thane explained. Levi looked over his shoulder at Thane who still hadn't felt the need to dress. The man was so damn sexy it wasn't fair. Levi adjusted himself. He was learning that Thane wasn't shy. In fact, he was most comfortable in no clothes and chose that look very regularly when they were alone together, which made it very hard to leave the man.

"Well, first, it should probably be said that your Tuesday, Friday, and Saturday has changed to include Sunday and Monday morning too. Then we need to factor in you sitting in my section Sunday through Thursday nights. So, technically the three-day thing really ended before it ever got started." Levi reached for his shorts and began pulling them up. "As for Arik and Kellus...go with them."

"No, if that were true, the extra time is extra. This is Friday, our designated night," Thane interrupted.

"You're so hardheaded. Go to your meeting. Go to dinner. Come dance at the club afterward," Levi suggested and reached for his button-down. "I have to work. I have bills to pay. I have college to pay for. I tried to explain all this to you from the very beginning."

"If you'd move in with me, that'd alleviate a lot of your struggle, so who's the hardheaded one now?" Thane accused, becoming visibly frustrated.

Levi's smile faltered. He looked closely at Thane, then narrowed his eyes. They had never discussed moving in together. No, certainly Thane didn't mean that. He was just being the force of nature that was Thane Walker.

"You're being ridiculous," Levi finally said, shoving each arm through a sleeve.

"I'm not being ridiculous at all. I love being with you. You promised me Friday and Saturday nights were mine, and the first chance you get, you bail. If you guys lived here, you wouldn't have to take this shift. Can't you see? It's the perfect solution." Thane threw his hands out and used his arms to speak, circling Levi as he paced. "If you were here, I wouldn't be so hurt that you ditched me so easily."

Oh Lord, Thane was being overly dramatic now, working himself into a frenzy. They hadn't even officially discussed being boyfriends or said the words *committed solely to one another*, and now Thane had his feelings hurt because Levi didn't live there?

Thane would do or say whatever was needed in order to get his way. The guy loved the fight. Levi decided his best course of action was to refuse to even acknowledge such a ludicrous suggestion, so he began toeing on his sandals, ignoring Thane altogether. With a glance at the clock on the wall, he saw he had a little over twenty minutes to walk about a quarter of a mile to the bar. He needed to get going soon.

"So now I'm gonna have to cancel all my plans and spend the next four or five hours in that club, watching all those men ogling you," Thane said.

"You ogle me."

"Guilty as charged." Thane flashed him a sheepish you-caught-me smile then narrowed his eyes. "Well, do you know how much money I lose by sitting at a table all night?" Thane questioned, changing his tactic.

"I tell you not to tip me." Levi reached for his backpack, slung it over his shoulder, and left Thane pouting as he went for the door. Thane followed, right on his heels. Levi took some of the blame for Thane's attendance at the club every night. When they'd first started doing this, Levi had encouraged Thane to come spend time with him in his section. Just like with everything they did, that seemed to become every night really quickly. Now, Thane was a standard fixture at one of his tables while he worked. Levi liked Thane there. Enjoyed being able to look at him anytime he wanted, and when things got slow, he always spent the free time at Thane's table, talking.

"Levi, that's not it. Every time you work, I lose the money for that table I'm sitting at. Julian's pissed off and wants to charge me to sit in my own damn club. The fucker presented me with a bill this afternoon. You're a top earner. You make money for us, and I'm messing that up by occupying a table. Just imagine what they'll miss with me taking a table tonight." At the front door, Levi turned back, looking at the beautiful Thane Walker who was still nude and only a foot or so away.

"You don't have to come, Thane."

"It's the only way I get to see you." Now, Thane looked like he didn't have a friend in the world.

Yeah, he looked sad because he wasn't getting his way.

"That's not true. I'm here now, aren't I?" Levi asked, gripping the doorknob.

"A quickie doesn't count. Besides, that Marlboro Man has his eye on you. I gotta protect my territory."

Levi laughed right in Thane's face. Like Thane had anything to worry about. Levi knew the Marlboro Man was more interested in his manager than him. Besides, Levi was so hung up on Thane that no one else existed. The realization immediately caused a sense of fear to start to edge in, but he squashed that right there.

He refused to consider how closely he'd tied himself to Thane in such a short period of time.

They stood there, staring at one another, neither saying a word. Great, they were in a standoff.

After a second, Levi decided to change his tactic. He dropped his backpack and went straight back to the bedroom.

Thane couldn't possibly be serious about the Marlboro Man who was a late thirties, early fortyish, drop dead gorgeous cowboy who had made his money in oil. The guy was about as comfortable being gay as Levi was being the father figure to his brothers. Walking into the club had been a big step, and Levi was certain the only reason he'd become a fixture in his section—much like Thane—was because Levi didn't hit on the clientele like the other waiters. He kept it friendly, but that was as far as it went. It also hadn't escaped his attention that the Marlboro Man had a thing for Julian—a quiet attraction from afar. Levi only knew because of the long stares and absolute silence the man went through anytime Julian was around. He'd also noticed that fiery spark in his manager's eyes when Julian caught the Marlboro Man watching him.

Thane was way off base if he truly believed that about the guy and needed to get over that fixation. Besides, Levi wasn't buying any of Thane's excuses. He knew the true reason Thane wanted Levi alone tonight, and it had to do with the contents of the special drawer in Thane's dresser. Levi went for Thane's room and opened the newest addition, a drawer dedicated to sex toys. Levi wasn't so naive that he didn't understand all the different devices, but he also hadn't used any of them before. Some actually made him a little nervous. Under lots of heavy and hard carnal persuasion this afternoon, he had agreed to use them all, but only after Thane tried each one first. Now seemed as good a time as any.

Levi scanned the selections until he found what he wanted and grabbed the one labeled Hush—a wireless remote-controlled plug—along with a new bottle of lube. Levi grinned at his choice; yes, this would do nicely tonight. He hurried back to Thane, his handsome face lighting up when he stepped into the room.

"Yes, perfect idea. Let me have that," Thane huskily demanded and started to grab the plug out of his hand. "That way you know who you belong to."

Levi smirked, amused by Thane's bossy attitude. "Oh, is that the way you see it?" He dodged to the left, then darted backward several steps, keeping his hand out of reach as Thane continued to follow, trying to grab the device. When Levi stopped, Thane bumped against him, their lips only inches apart. He leaned closer and watched as Thane's eyes darkened and his chest rose and fell with his quickened breath. The air around them thickened. Levi deliberately licked his lips. Thane's gaze darted to his tongue, and in that moment, he knew he had Thane.

Levi lifted his chin and moved closer to Thane. Right before their lips met, Levi shook his head and gave a *tsk*. "Not tonight, caveman. This is for you."

Thane had what Levi could only describe as a comical array of emotions playing across his extraordinary face. Levi leaned in and kissed those tempting lips. When he pulled back, he had to force himself to turn and walk to the couch, not laugh at the confusion he saw reflected back at him.

"You ravished my ass today. I'll be feeling you all night," Thane said, trailing after him, but Levi could tell by the raw sound of Thane's husky voice he was intrigued with the idea and already completely turned on.

"Exactly what I'm hoping for." He set the plug on the coffee table and turned to Thane, sliding his hands over Thane's ass then pulled Thane between his legs as he lowered to the couch while fisting his guy's hard length. Levi scooted forward and pressed his lips to Thane's firm stomach as he stroked the thick cock in his palm. His pants suddenly felt two sizes too small as he greedily licked up the length of Thane's shaft. Thane's hands dropped to his neck, and strong fingers slid up into the hair at the base of his skull and twisted. Salty sweetness spread across his tongue as he took Thane to the back of his throat and swallowed around him.

"*Fuuuccckk*," Thane moaned.

Kneading the globes of Thane's naked ass, Levi curled his tongue around the smooth head of the man's delicious cock and selfishly swallowed him to the root one last time before looking up, releasing Thane from his mouth, and nodding for him to turn. Levi would love nothing more than to ravish Thane's ass again, but that would have to wait. Right now, he needed to give Thane something to keep him occupied.

"Hands on the coffee table." He nudged Thane's leg.

"You're really serious?"

Levi let out a low moan and shifted in his seat as Thane slowly bent forward in front of him, exposing himself fully. After he coated his fingers and the butt plug with lube, Levi took full advantage of the situation and fingered Thane till his guy was begging and his own cock was aching, pushing painfully against his shorts.

Levi teased the toy around Thane's opening, watching as the man's hand lifted to his cock.

"Don't touch yourself. You can't come. At least…not till I do," he said, encountering a little resistance as he pressed the lubed toy against Thane's entrance. Thane whimpered as it popped past the outer muscle and slipped inside. "There we go. Now, how's it feel?" Levi asked wiping his slick fingers on the back of Thane's thigh as Thane pushed off the table and stood.

"Did you just wipe left over lube on me?"

"You caught me," Levi chuckled, looking up at Thane. "Now, how does it feel?"

"I'm not sure." Thane's face told him everything he needed to know. His guy liked it; he just wasn't going to admit it.

"Hmmm, let's see if we can fix that." Levi got to his feet, brushing a quick kiss to Thane's lips as he grabbed his phone to connect the device. As soon as the devices were paired, he pressed the button. Thane's body tensed, his eyes closed, his lips parted, and his dick twitched. Levi's pulse amped up and his balls filled just watching Thane. Levi released the button and Thane sucked in a breath as those mesmerizing eyes found his.

"You have to be kidding me," Thane said incredulously. "You can't expect…"

Levi grinned. "I've really got to run. Julian's gonna be mad if I'm late." He hurriedly gathered his things, carefully placing his phone in the front pocket of his bag. "I'll see you in a bit. Don't remove it. I'll remove it when I'm ready. And remember, no touching yourself." Levi winked at Thane as he stepped out the door and pulled it shut behind him. Tonight just got way more interesting.

~~~

Thane had come up with the brilliant toy idea three days ago. The following day, he'd begun one-clicking. He'd had everything charged and ready to go before he'd ever said a word to Levi. And Thane's plan for the evening had been to explore and prod every inch of Levi. He'd planned to use them on his guy, give Levi a little bit of the decadent pleasure Levi gave him so willingly.

There would be alcohol involved, also probably lots of bartering, swearing to do whatever Levi wanted for all of eternity, then on to lots of toe-curling pleasure. But that perfect plan had blown up in his face, and he sat, downing one vodka after another, trying to dull the hard-on he'd been sporting all evening.

Surprisingly, butt plugs worked really well, and that completely sucked. Well, in this situation, it sucked. He was fucking hard as hell, and Levi kept teasing him, brushing against him, and twice that night he'd conveniently dropped a napkin right in front of him then proceeded to bend over and pick it up in a lewd manner. Oh, Levi knew exactly what he was doing.

Levi would pay for every time he pushed that damn button on his phone. Thane was certain. He tossed the remaining ice cubes in his mouth and stared at his boyfriend who didn't seem to understand that he was in fact Thane's boyfriend. What the hell was that even about?

Thane had spent a month now trying to show that man how much he meant to him, and Levi had seemed stunned silent at the idea of moving in together. How could that even be? Hell, they didn't spend Tuesday, Friday, and Saturday together—they spent
~~~

every single evening together and two, sometimes three, overnights a week together. Things had only gotten better between them with time. Well, at least for Thane. Clearly, Levi wasn't at all on his same page.

Upset, which technically might border pouting, Thane spotted Levi chatting with the Marlboro Man. Thane didn't have a history of ever being jealous. Not really. He was the opposite of jealous, but Thane had grown to sincerely dislike that man. Three times in the last two weeks he'd considered pulling the guy's membership. There was no question that man wanted Levi, and fucking hell if he didn't think Levi turned it on a little too strong. All those smiles he gave that man. Levi was usually stingy with his smiles. Dammit, unfounded jealousy was hard to tame.

"Hey, *papi*," Julian said, coming to the table. "How's married life?"

"Stop saying tha—" He hissed, electricity jolted through his body, his ass cheeks clenched together as he grabbed for the edge of the table and ground his jaw. Halfway through his sentence, that on edge feeling started buzzing then suddenly and powerfully rushed through him. *Motherfucker*. Fucking hell and every variation of the word *fuck* applied right then. He was going to lose it. His body quivered as he tried to remain poised. Who knew he'd have such a reaction to that damn vibrating butt plug?

Everything around Thane faded except the pulsing in his ass. Damn it, heat washed over him. He screwed his eyes shut and absorbed the vibration. The damn thing lit him up as if it were Levi's own finger teasing him. His dick was so hard it hurt and his balls so full they ached. Thane flexed his ass cheeks, loosening his grip on the table and letting out a pent-up breath as the pulsing slowed. His body calmed, and he quickly tried to regain his composure as he glanced over at his smartass manager.

Julian's brows lifted and a knowing gleam flashed in his eyes. "What just happened? That's your 'O' look. Care to let me in on whatever it is that has you so coiled up?" Julian asked.

Thane couldn't even answer as he lowered a hand, pushing the heel of his palm into the base of his hard-as-stone cock. Too many more of those unexpected moments and he was going to blow his load right there.

When he gained a little more control, he turned and scowled at Levi who was walking away from the Marlboro Man, looking hot as hell in nothing but those skimpy black briefs. Levi smirked at him before walking up to the bar beside Quinn. Thane tracked his feisty waiter the whole way, tempted to get off his stool and drag Levi to the office and fuck that smug grin off his handsome face. He almost did when Levi leaned across the bar and stuck his ass out. His guy even had the audacity to glance back over his shoulder and blow him a kiss. Yeah, Levi would pay.

"Butt plug?"

"He's fucking driving me insane. I don't know if I'm coming or going. I can't fucking think of anything but him. I'm messing up all parts of my life because I'm so fucking jacked up over him, and now he does this. What the fuck is wrong with me? He's got me so turned on all the damn time. I would fuck him right here if I could, and he knows it. He's toying with me." Thane looked over at a somewhat stunned, but mostly amused Julian. *Shit*! His stomach muscles tensed up, he bit his bottom lip to keep from moaning. Damn it if Levi hadn't lit him up again, this one lengthier than any before.

Thane gripped the side of the table, closed his eyes, and fought to keep his hips from bucking. The waves that pulsed through his body started to ebb. That was some intense shit. Who would have ever known he'd be so turned on by the damn toy? He'd been missing out by being the one to always handle the remote. But this was neither the place nor the time to explore the joys of a vibrating butt plug.

Thank God it was only Julian who had noticed. He didn't need anyone else finding out. Shit, he looked frantically at Julian. That had been two jolts in a row. Why two in a row? Then it dawned on Thane. Anytime he talked to anybody tonight, he got zapped. Levi was possessive. How had he not figured this out before?

"You gotta go, Jules. I gave him a hard time about the Marlboro Man, so I think he's getting me back. Every time someone comes and talks to me, he lights me up and he's relentless. He's got me so fucking hard I can't take it." The words rushed out. Hell, he was still recovering from the latest hit. Another hit like that and he'd come in his pants.

Julian started laughing. "Damn, who'd have thought. Sounds like Thane Walker met his perfect match."

"Cut him first," Thane demanded as Julian moved off the stool. "And stay out of the office."

"Not gonna happen tonight, boss man. He's closing." Julian smugly singsonged those words as he walked away.

"Cut him, Julian. He's got something to take care of before he heads home." Either Julian was cutting Levi or he would. His dick needed attention and then this thing was coming out of his ass. He couldn't take much more.

<div style="text-align:center">~~~</div>

Levi watched Thane climb off the stool. His heart skipped an excited beat when those piercing eyes locked onto his. They stared at one another for a second or two before Thane lifted his chin and gave a nod toward the office and started that way. Julian had just cut him. He was supposed to stay for the night, but watching Thane the last two times he'd pressed the button, he knew the butt plug was more effective than he'd ever thought possible. His dick grew so hard from watching the expressions flash across Thane's face as he held the button down. He loved that heated look. Thane was gorgeous to look at, but Levi also enjoyed watching him squirm.

As he waited for his customer to pay, Levi stuck his hand in his pouch and pressed the button again. It was wishful thinking, the music was too loud to have actually heard anything, but he still swore Thane yelled a string of profanities directed at him while climbing the stairs.

With record-breaking speed, Levi cashed out his tickets, performed his end of shift duties as efficiently as possible, and rushed to get to Thane. After everything was in order, he almost ran to the locker room to grab his clothes then took the steps up to the office two at a time. On the third step from the top, he couldn't contain his satisfied smirk as he hit the remote from his phone again.

The string of curse words Thane so artfully put together had him standing just outside the office preparing to push the button again when the door was abruptly yanked open. Thane reached out, cupped his neck, and tugged him forward. He thought it was to draw him in for a kiss.

Oh no. He laughed as a gloriously naked Thane spun him into the interior of the office just enough to shut and lock the door while simultaneously pushing him to his knees.

Just knowing Thane had been naked, lying in wait, ready to ambush him as soon as he opened the door gave him a lusty adrenaline rush and made his dick twitch with joy. Levi didn't hesitate and had Thane's cock in his grip stroking him roughly as soon as his knees hit the soft rug.

"Baby, please, suck me. I'm going fucking crazy here." Thane's hips tilted forward. Levi buried his face and nose against Thane's neatly trimmed pubes, breathing him in. Filling his lungs and surrounding himself in Thane.

"You're not the only one. I've wanted to get you alone all night." Levi nuzzled Thane's cock and squeezed, licking the bead of moisture seeping from its tip. Unable to resist the temptation, he deliberately dragged his tongue along the underside of Thane's rigid length, before swallowing him the back of his throat. He pulled Thane's thick cock from his mouth, lapped at the glistening crown, then quickly sucked him back into his mouth. Levi bobbed his head, hollowing his cheeks, sucking and laving Thane with his tongue while he discreetly reached down, found his phone in his money bag, and pressed the button with his thumb.

"Agghh. Shit!" Thane's fingers tightened in Levi's hair.

Levi had to reach up and grasp Thane's hips to steady his lover's wild thrusts. Thane's hips slowed at his touch before abruptly stopping the movement. At the same time, Thane clamped his fingers around the base of his shaft.

"That was too damn close."

Thane pulled away from him, stalking across the room toward the sofa. He climbed on, putting both his knees on the cushions. With purpose, Thane spread his thighs and leaned across the back of the couch.

"You owe me big, so get over here and take this thing out of my ass then give me your cock."

The tables had turned. Levi almost came at the sight of Thane's long body spread wide for him, smoldering hot, all dark with muscular model good looks. The guy had the most perfect ass he'd ever seen and was currently waiting for him. Levi couldn't get to his feet fast enough, the phone clasped tightly in his hand as he stood. Levi shoved his briefs down his legs and stepped out of them on his way to take Thane up on his offer. Thane reached over to the side table and produced a bottle of lube and strip of condoms, dropping them on the cushion next to him.

Levi wasted no time. He quickly rolled the condom on and had his cock lubed. He held the phone in the palm of his hand and gripped the head of his cock, lightly pushing it against the silicone toy in Thane's ass. He hit the button on his phone more out of curiosity than anything. A sharp jolt shot down his dick and tensed the muscles in his stomach.

"Holy fuck!" Thane's back bowed. The vibration at the tip of his cock had him dropping the phone and rushing to ease the plug from Thane's ass. He dropped the toy on the floor—he'd deal with that later—and pushed two fingers straight into Thane. He wasn't sure how long he was going to last. He was so turned on he couldn't bury himself in Thane quick enough.

"Levi, babe…just fuck me." From the sound of Thane's voice, he didn't think either one of them would be breaking any hours-long endurance records tonight.

Levi withdrew his fingers and changed their position. He sank down on the office sofa, pulling Thane across his body so the gorgeous man straddled his lap. Thane's dark hungry eyes met his and their mouths crashed together. Lips, teeth, and tongues collided as Levi kissed Thane with everything he had. They were explosive together, had been since day one. His breath hitched when Thane's warm fingers found his cock. Levi's hands instinctively moved to Thane's hips to steady him.

Incredible tightness surrounded him as Thane slowly impaled himself inch by inch until his perfect ass was flush against Levi's thighs. It took every ounce of energy he had to remain still and let Thane make the first move.

Thane started to roll his hips. Levi lifted his to push deeper into Thane, picking up the rhythm. He thrust his cock into his man, swallowing the little sounds Thane gave him every time he slammed up into him.

Thane clawed at his shoulders, breaking from the kiss to lean back, working his hips as their bodies frantically slapped together.

"Don't stop...don't stop...don't stop," Thane chanted over and over as Levi pulled him down on his cock.

Levi pumped into Thane's grinding hips, determined not to come. The feeling of Thane's body surrounding him made that decision nearly impossible as Thane picked up the pace. The heat that started in his balls spread quickly throughout his body as he watched Thane bouncing on his cock, eyes closed, mouth slightly open, all that sexy skin on display, his cock bobbing with every thrust.

Perfect.

The blissed out sexy expression on his lover's face made him want to crawl in deeper and never let him go, the moment so beautiful, so real that Levi committed everything about it to memory. Levi leaned forward and sucked Thane's nipple between his lips then teased it with his tongue.

"Babe..." Thane moaned.

Levi took hold of Thane's swollen cock, and as soon as his finger dipped in the slit, Thane's ass clenched around him and Levi ground up into the vise-like grip Thane's ass had on him and followed his man over into sweet oblivion. His legs were on fire and his lungs burned from the exertion. Their muscles strained together, both caught in the ecstasy of their orgasms.

"God...Thane." He thrust his hips a few more times, needing to be deeper as Thane's warm come landed on his chest and chin, and he filled the condom in Thane's ass. The force of his powerful release held his body in complete submission. After the last spasms subsided, Thane licked across his chin then kissed him like he owned him.

"Damn." He panted breathlessly, still trying to recover.

"Oh my God, that was intense. I don't think I'll ever catch my breath," Thane gasped against his lips.

A small towel Levi hadn't even known was there landed on his chest before Thane reached underneath himself to hold the condom in place before lifting off him. He dropped to the office floor and rolled to his back, his chest heaving with every breath. Levi pulled the condom off and tied the end before tossing it into the trash can beside Julian's desk. He started to stand as he wiped the cloth up his chest, but he didn't have the energy. His legs were like spaghetti noodles, so he slid down on the floor to join Thane.

~~~

"There's no chance we could go pick up your brothers and you all stay at my place this weekend, is there?" Thane said, trailing his fingertips up and down Levi's arm. As far as Thane was concerned, the uncomfortable floor of this office and the ache he was sure to have in his back tomorrow were worth every bit of discomfort if it meant Levi stayed here with him a little longer.

Levi had tried twice to get up. Thane was sure his guy worried about being in the office of the club. When he started to speak, Thane stopped him by placing two fingers on his lips.

"Shh, don't say no. Not yet. I've never felt like this. I didn't believe this was possible. You're so hardheaded you challenge me. I've never met anyone like you before." Thane craned his neck and brushed his fingers under Levi's chin, lifting Levi's face to look him in the eyes. "To me, you're so much more than what the label boyfriend represents, but you are my boyfriend. Got it?"

"That was a strange pairing of sentences."
~~~

Thane chuckled and dropped his head back to the floor. Levi never gave him an inch. Not ever and his arms tightened around his mister.

"Doesn't surprise me. I was telling Julian you have me all jacked up. I can't think straight." Thane scrubbed a hand down his face. "I'm making mistakes all the time. I'm dropping my balls. I never drop my balls," Thane said, feeling his inner Beavis snickering at the reference.

"I'll catch your balls." Levi smirked, crawling up his body to press a kiss on his lips, looking down on him as he spoke. "The boyfriend thing makes me oddly secure."

Thane lifted a hand, caressing Levi's cheek. Levi was so solid, so much in control of himself, that it always surprised Thane to hear words like insecure and nervous come from his guy's mouth. "You're all I see, Levi. It's been that way for months now, probably since the first night I laid eyes on you," Thane confessed. "It's only growing stronger for me."

Levi bent, kissing Thane's lips. "Just tell me when you're done. You don't have to worry about me, just always be honest about us." Levi's hand came to his cheek, and his thumb traced his bottom lip.

"I wish you were staying the night. I like it when you stay with me."

"Linda's with Logan and Luke tonight. I can stay."

Thane lifted, dislodging Levi as he judged the sincerity of Levi's words. Within seconds, he was reaching for his pants.

"You didn't tell me," Thane said, grabbing Levi's backpack, tossing it to him as he rose to stick one foot inside the leg of his slacks.

"You didn't ask. You were just mad I had to work," Levi explained, laughing as Thane stumbled while balancing on one foot. Those words immediately fired up his need to argue until Thane stopped while tugging his shirt on. Levi was right. He'd just accused, nothing more.

"I'll cook for us. That was my original plan for the evening. I got the stuff for the enchiladas you liked so much…"

"You said we were going to dinner with Arik and Kellus." This time Levi stopped and stared at him midway through pulling on his shorts.

"Yeah, about that. They did ask us out to dinner, but I didn't accept…" Thane hesitated, trying to give an apologetic look.

"You're sneaky," Levi said, pointing a finger in Thane's face.

"No, I'm desperate. There's a difference." Thane tugged his shirt over his head. "What time are they coming tomorrow?" Thane asked, calculating how much time they would have alone and all the things he could do during that time. The weekend was a big celebration, and one Thane was extremely pleased to be included in. It was Luke's and Logan's birthday celebration. Both had birthdays in the next few days. Thane's gifts to them were new cell phones. Luke's first ever cell phone and they had also been given tickets to a concert festival the resort was hosting.

"Ten tomorrow. They're on cloud nine, telling everyone they're going." Thane stared at Levi's hands as they worked the front buttons of his shirt. Even such a simple act as sharing time with Levi while he dressed seemed to bring Thane joy. He was so hopelessly in love. The love never faded, only grew in intensity until nothing else mattered. He couldn't imagine a life without Levi.

Instead of saying all that, he righted the furniture that had been shoved around in their sexual quest and stuffed Levi's sexy briefs and the butt plug in his backpack. When some of the overwhelming emotion ebbed, Thane finally spoke. "Let's go. I'm starving."

"You eat all the time." That was just what he needed to lighten his serious mood.

"Yes, I do."

CHAPTER 24

Six weeks later

The doorbell rang and all three guys lifted their heads, staring in the direction of the front door as if they could see who stood there from their spots at the kitchen table. "Can't be Aunt Linda. She won't be home until later," Luke said.

"Why would she use the front door? She'd come to the back," Logan added, and Levi looked over at the clock on the microwave. It was a little after six. His shift didn't start until eight—he closed tonight, so he and his brothers had prepared dinner, opting to eat together. Levi scooted back from his seat, shoved the bite of chicken into his mouth, and went for the door.

"Hang on," he mumbled toward the front door when another knock came. He looked through the peephole as his hand went for the doorknob and he froze. It was Mrs. Gathright from the Department of Human Services. Levi searched his head to remember if this was a scheduled appointment. He couldn't recall, and he quickly looked around the living room, making sure everything was picked up as he tried to swallow the large bite.

He caught her with her fist rising to knock again, and he tried to speak, but the bite wasn't going down easily. When no words came, he extended a hand, inviting her in before lifting a finger to his throat, and guided her toward the kitchen to his glass of water.

"Hi, guys," Mrs. Gathright said.

Levi watched Logan and Luke have about the same reaction he had. It happened every time she came, whether unannounced or scheduled. He didn't know why it made them so nervous, maybe because she held power over them. She was the warden, the gatekeeper, and had the ultimate say over the three of them staying together.

Levi knocked Logan in the shoulder as he reached for his glass, taking a deep gulp. Luckily, that jarred his brother into talking.

"Hey, Ms. Gathright," Logan said and scurried out of his seat to stand. Levi knew it was manners that had Logan standing, but he also watched Luke become even more anxious, looking between Logan and Levi before he put his fork on the table and slowly slid out of his chair.

"Am I supposed to stand too?" he asked Levi.

Mrs. Gathright laughed, which weirdly eased at least Levi. "No, sit down. I didn't mean to interrupt while you're having dinner. I was getting a lot of chatter about you guys, so I'm early on my visit, but everything looks promising, so I decided to stop by and see for myself. Can I join you?" she asked, pointing to the empty chair.

"Sure," Levi nodded. When Mrs. Gathright started to take her seat, he quickly nodded to his brothers to sit down and keep eating.

"Can I get you a plate? We have extra," Levi said and started for the stove.

"Oh no, thank you. I brought a bottled water," she said, digging through her purse, placing the water on the table before opening her portfolio. He took a seat and picked up his fork, but his appetite was waning. "I'll start first so you can keep eating," she said, writing on her tablet. When she looked up, none of them had started eating. Instead, they were all staring at her. "Eat. Really, this is a good call. The first thing I want to talk about is Logan's changes in high school. I talked to your counselor, and you're finishing school at the end of summer instead of the winter break. You're still going to University of Virginia in January, correct?"

"Yes, ma'am," he said, nodding vigorously.

"Is there a reason you're graduating early? Is it a financial decision, because if so, we can help," she said, and Levi lifted a hand to stop Logan who started to speak.

"I sent over the relocation paperwork. Do you have that?" Levi asked.

"No, I haven't seen that," she said, her brow wrinkling as she sifted through the stack of loose papers in her portfolio. Levi rose, going to the place in the kitchen that held all their bills and paperwork. Luckily, he'd copied his forms before he sent them. He gathered those and handed the stack to her.

"I've been working with Johns Hopkins, and they've got an on-campus apartment for us for the fall term. It's two bedrooms, and they've offered me an on-campus job. We're planning on going at the end of August after Logan graduates. Luke's grades are up; Mrs. Underwood's working his transition paperwork herself. We've been saving money…"

Mrs. Gathright was writing, but when he said the word money, she interrupted, spreading several pieces of paper from out around her, searching for one in particular.

"I saw you guys opened a bank account."

"We've been socking away money. I was able to put all the back payments from social security in there," Levi said, pushing his half-eaten plate forward several inches, and rested his forearms there as he spoke.

"And you're working two jobs still?" she asked, lifting her very direct gaze his way.

"Yes and no. At the beginning of June, I got laid off at the clinic. Medicare cuts forced the clinic to downsize about three-quarters of the assistants. Linda—" He hooked a thumb toward her house next door. "Her company needed some temp work. I've been doing that four days a week, about twenty-five hours or so a week. That's coming to an end, so I'll find something else to do until we leave."

"But you're still at the club… Is it Reservations? Is that correct?" she asked, back to writing on her tablet.

Luke's head jerked his way. Levi hadn't been truthful with his brothers about which restaurant he worked at. He had led them to believe it was a dining restaurant. Since Thane had four different locations at the resort, he'd just stayed vague. Levi gave the slightest shake of his head toward his brother and pointed to Mrs. Gathright. They'd talk about this later.

"Yes, ma'am."

"I'm getting a job at the Baconator. They already hired me, and I'm working, but I need my social security card. Levi's got it coming for me, so I'm gonna put all that money up too. Then me and Levi can transfer in the company when we move to Maryland," Luke explained, dropping that information out of nowhere before turning back to Levi for verification. "Right?"

Levi nodded at Luke while looking at Mrs. Gathright. She'd stopped writing when Luke started speaking, focusing her gaze on him. She fought her smile when he turned his question to Levi, ducking her head, jotting down more notes.

"I've been working some weekends at Castelli's," Logan said, leaving out that it had only been a few times over two months. Logan's school courses required too much homework to do much more than a few hours here or there. "It's how I paid for my DC trip. I'll start working for the company when I graduate. Levi knows the owner."

Luke threw out a not so helpful, "They're dating. Right?"

All Levi wanted to do was lean back in the chair and cover his face with his hands while telling his brothers to stop talking. They had to work on Luke's manners and the concept of *less is more*. Damn.

"We are." Levi finally nodded.

Mrs. Gathright lifted her head, stared at him for several seconds then looked between the boys, her face growing serious. She started writing again in her journal. She never gave any clue how she felt about him dating anyone, let alone the owner of the company they were all going to work for.

"How'd you like DC, Logan?" she asked, never looking up from her notes.

"It was good. Luke's gonna like the food. We had this lobster roll thing. We're gonna try it when we move," Logan said, then as an afterthought, he added, "We didn't win. Didn't even place."

"I'm glad you enjoyed yourself. All right," she said, finishing her notes. Before she closed her portfolio, she looked back at Levi, lifting the paperwork he'd given her. "Can I take these? I'll make copies and get them back to you."

"Sure," he nodded and finally let out the pent-up breath he'd been holding since the Thane revelation.

"Everything looks in order. I'm proud of you all. It looks like you're keeping up, and I appreciate your keeping me informed," she said, tapping the papers Levi had given her. "I'll need to call Johns Hopkins, but I'm impressed with how well you've done. I wish all my cases were this easy."

Mrs. Gathright gave a genuine smile, looking between them all. It was such a relief that Luke leaned back in his seat and gave an audible exhale, so loud that she laughed.

"I never know how to ease people."

"You're fine. It's us. We're trying hard to keep it all together," Levi confessed.

"And you can tell you are. In the beginning of August, I'll transition your paperwork to Maryland. They'll be required to follow up like I do. Luke's technically a ward of California. They'll do these same types of visits a couple of times a year. I'll get you the name of your Maryland case worker as soon as it's assigned." Mrs. Gathright unscrewed her bottle of water, taking a long drink before placing it back in her purse. "And, Levi, there's an internship we do in six week intervals. The new session's starting soon. Fill out the application online then let me know you did, and I'll go talk to the department head. I'm sure you'll get the job. It pays twenty dollars an hour, and it's twenty hours a week."

"Thank you!" he said, getting to his feet as she did. That would be enough to allow every single bit of his tips to go into savings.

"What about me? What happens to me?" Logan asked, rising to his feet.

"Well, you're eighteen and soon to be a graduate," Mrs. Gathright said, putting her purse over her shoulder. "You're an adult. Levi's got custody of Luke, so you'll be left out of the mix when the files transition to the new state, but I'm always here if you need me for anything."

Again, Luke was the odd man out. It took a second, and required an encouraging nod from Levi for his brother to hurriedly leap to his feet.

"I'm sorry to interrupt your dinner. I stopped by on Saturday and no one was home."

"We were at Escape in Coronado," Luke added proudly, and all Levi could do was stare at him. What the hell was wrong with his brother? She was leaving, and instead, turned back toward the table, interested in Luke's comment.

"Escape. I haven't been there. I hear it's nice," she said, clearly encouraging Luke to say more.

"It's real nice, isn't it?" Luke said, nodding at Logan who remained absolutely still and silent looking every bit as concerned as Levi felt. "Levi's boyfriend has a suite there, and he invites us all the time. The hotel's right on the beach, and the back wall in all the rooms open all the way up. There's no wall. It just goes from the living room to the balcony, nothing stops you. It's all decorated the same, but each suite's a little different."

Levi had moved, closer now to the social worker. He looked at Mrs. Gathright, who was staring at Luke. He quickly raised a hand, giving a cutting motion at his neck. Luke needed to shut the heck up. His younger brother gave a startled look and just closed his mouth, becoming silent and ducking his head.

"That sounds really nice," Mrs. Gathright said. She looked confused, probably because the unusually animated Luke had just stopped talking so abruptly. Levi just gave her a shrug and immediately started ushering her toward the door, Logan following behind him. "Okay, well, if I don't see you again, then keep doing as well as you are now. Levi, I'll be in touch. I'll get these back to you in the next few days."

"Great. Thank you," he said, taking hold of the front door that she had opened.

"Let me know if you apply for the internship. Bye, guys," she called out and gave a quick look over her shoulder, waving before heading down the porch steps. When the door shut, Levi turned and leaned back against it, closing his eyes, the relief strong.

"Luke, dude, you say too much," Logan said, going back to the kitchen.

"What'd I say wrong?" Luke asked defensively.

Levi went back into the kitchen, dumping his paper plate in the trash. "You had to say I'm dating the owner of my company?"

"What? You are," Luke said, becoming as frustrated as Levi and Logan, pushing his not quite empty plate to the center of the table.

"That breaks about every employment law on the planet. Less is always more," Levi explained, coming to stand directly by Luke's chair. "And anytime a woman enters a room, you're supposed to stand."

"How am I supposed to know that?" Luke asked, throwing his hands in the air.

"We learned that in elementary school," Logan said.

"I didn't," Luke shot back, and Levi sensed a fight coming on.

"What time is it?" Levi asked, fishing his phone out of his pocket.

That distracted quick-draw Logan, and he read the time from his phone before Levi ever got his phone out. "It's seven twenty."

"Crap, I'm gonna be late." Levi started texting Julian that he'd be there as soon as he could while he went to finish grooming. He thought about texting Thane. If CPS called Johns Hopkins, would they need to be prepared? As he went for the bathroom, he pulled his T-shirt over his head and reached for the hair gel.

"So, I thought you worked in the restaurant," Luke said, coming to the bathroom door, leaning a shoulder against the frame. Of course, Luke wouldn't skate past that. Levi squirted the gel in his hand and started working his fingers through the ends. He didn't readily answer because he didn't know what to say. So much had happened to him over the last six months—actually, even longer than that. Both his attitude and perspective had changed. It didn't seem quite so bad to be working at a club like Reservations. Those were some of his best friends, and Thane had lived that life for years. The thought of others exchanging money for a hookup didn't completely freak him out anymore. It also didn't put people in the category he once thought it did, but how did he explain that to Luke?

When Luke continued to stare at Levi's profile, Levi reached for the towel to wipe off his hands and finally turned to look at his brother. Luke had so much to learn, and Levi just needed to make sure he was there to teach him, help guide his brother. If Luke stayed true to himself and kept an open mind, he wouldn't struggle like Levi had.

"I was embarrassed in the beginning. It felt like I was resorting to things I never wanted to do, so I led you to believe something else. I was wrong about it all. I prejudged the situation. It's not at all what I thought, but I still kept it from you and Logan because of the stigma."

"Logan said he figured it out a while ago, and it's a gay dance club," Luke said as Levi tossed the towel over the curtain rod.

"That's what it is. I met the manager at the clinic right before Dad died, and he offered me a job when the coffee house went out of business. I only told Mrs. Gathright because I knew your counselor was going to eventually talk to her, and when she started poking around, I didn't want anything to get in the way of you and me," he said.

"So why were you embarrassed?" Luke asked.

"Because I'm dumb, and I think about all that crap out there, right outside our door," Levi explained. He grabbed the brush and turned back to the mirror to rake it through his hair. "You're such a better person than I am, Luke. I needed money for us, and I thought I was lowering my standards, but I wasn't. Those are really good people, and I think you would have seen that before I did. They've been great to me. Honestly, they were the best thing that could happen to us."

"You make great tips," Luke added.

"I do." He nodded at Luke in the mirror and grabbed the hairdryer. "I have to wear underwear as my uniform, though."

Logan came around the corner. "No wonder we aren't allowed to touch your laundry."

Levi rolled his eyes, like they would ever voluntarily do his laundry.

"Like just underwear?" Luke asked.

"Yeah," Levi said, watching Luke's smirk.

The bathroom wasn't large, and they were having a family gathering right there while the gel hardened and time slipped away, but Levi still paused, letting Luke ask anything else he wanted to know.

"I bet Thane likes that," Logan teased, pushing away from the door, going back toward the living room. "And that spray tan you keep getting."

"Wanna know anything else, Luke?" Levi asked.

"Don't lie anymore. I'd be getting some lecture right now if I lied," Luke said and left him there alone. Levi grinned at the reprimand, because Luke was right. He chuckled and turned on the hairdryer.

~~~

Thane walked the distance of the outside walkway to the employee entrance with his phone stuck to his ear, listening intently to his Realtor explain the final details of the counteroffer to the counteroffer to the counteroffer of his offer on the house he'd wanted in Ellicott City. As suspected, they'd come way down on price, but now they were penny-pinching, trying to get every last cent they could.

Since everything in Thane's professional life seemed to be suffering, Thane had started counting the days and his dollars until he could get back to Maryland. All parts of his life were behind, and his company's bottom line reflected his absence. They had a little over a month left, maybe six weeks, until Logan finished his last class mid-August, and if he played his cards right, maybe they could be back in Maryland soon after.

The complicating factor was with the current homeowners—they had to quit stalling. No way could he take Levi and the boys
~~~

back to his one-bedroom townhome, and at this rate, that would happen if he didn't get this purchase nailed down.

Distracted by that Levi-is-near feeling washing over him, Thane grabbed the door as a shadow cast over him from behind. He pulled it open wide and stepped back, hoping to finish the call before going inside.

"Make it happen with the title company. Keep tomorrow's appointment. I don't want to have to come back there in a week. If I can't take possession in the morning, I want access to the place. I've got meetings with my contractor and designer scheduled…" Thane abruptly stopped speaking as Levi grabbed his waist and whispered *boo* in his free ear. His guy slowed long enough to give a teasing flip of his finger up over his lips to nose. "You're late."

"I am," Levi said, now walking backward. "Our protective service worker stopped by the house."

That had Thane forgetting the call as he lowered his arm. "Why? Something wrong?"

"Nah, I don't think so. It was a drive-by. That's what we nicknamed 'em, but they gave us the thumbs-up to move, and she thinks I could get a job as an intern for the next six weeks. It's part-time, but pays good."

"We talked about this, Levi. Why're you working another job?"

Levi stunned him by taking steps back toward him and leaning in to place a quick kiss on his lips. If the goal was to shut Thane up, it worked.

"I gotta go get changed. And Luke knows all about Reservations." Levi winked at him and left him standing there after dropping all those possible little bombs. Levi didn't seem upset. Thane watched him go before remembering his Realtor was still on the phone.

"I'm sorry. I got distracted. Where were we?" Thane said, not even sure what they had been discussing. Levi had voluntarily kissed him without being encouraged. That meant something special, and Thane ducked his head, grinning from ear to ear as he absorbed the impact to his heart.

"It sounds like a party." He registered her laughter, at least he was paying that much attention.

"Yeah, I guess it is." He struggled for a second more, trying to remember—oh, the house. Right. The house that just got monumentally more important. "So, I'll be there tomorrow morning. Push this through for me."

"Not a problem. I'll send confirmation to your email."

When Thane ended that call, he sent a message to Jenna to confirm appointments with Layne Construction and the interior designer she'd hired who specializes in lived-in looking homes. He wanted someplace functional and nice for Levi and his brothers.

He looked down at the ground as doubt needled at him. Reason dictated he should lock Levi in before going to all this trouble. But Levi had the personality of someone who needed to be eased into things, guided with a careful hand. That time would come. Nodding, he pushed send on the email and entered the club.

His new home away from home.

~~~

For a Tuesday night, they'd stayed busy longer than normal, but it was still a little before midnight when Levi cashed out his last guest. Thane sat at his normal table, nursing a drink he'd had for well over an hour when Levi took the chair next to him, as Thane let out a loud yawn. "You should've gone to bed hours ago."

"I can sleep on the plane," Thane said, reaching across the table, taking Levi's hand in his.

"What time do you leave?" he asked, feeling a little bad about not asking before. Since he'd found out that Thane was planning a trip back home for the re-grand opening of their corporate offices, Levi had worked at keeping his insecurity at bay, not letting Thane know how badly he didn't want him to leave. They'd gotten into a groove, spending parts of every day together. Levi was going to miss Thane like crazy.
~~~

"In about three hours," Thane, said, looking down at his phone.

"Do you need a ride to the airport?" Levi asked, lifting their joined hands, threading their fingers together. "I'm off. I can take you whenever you're ready."

"No, I didn't want to put you out. I have a car scheduled to be here in about an hour. You could pick me up though. I'll be back early Friday morning, around this time. I'm taking the red-eye."

"I will, for sure," Levi confirmed, nodding. Thane wrapped his free hand around Levi's bicep, drawing him in for a kiss that lingered. He wasn't one for PDAs in the club. Well, except for Thane patting his ass on occasion, but dammit, he already missed Thane, and he hadn't even left yet.

"I'll leave my key fob in the suite. Drive my car while I'm gone. That battery thing's getting worse on your car," Thane said, and Levi decided not to buck him. He wouldn't drive Thane's car, but he didn't fight it out either. They were turning a corner, building a true relationship. They felt genuine and real. He'd let Thane have this one. "Tell me about the social worker stopping in."

"The lady that stopped in was our protective service worker, and the change in Logan's school plans instigated her visit. She didn't get our relocation paperwork, so I gave her my copy. She said she was good with everything, and she's forwarding our case to Maryland in August. I'm taking that as a thumbs-up," Levi explained.

"Why do you have a social worker watching you?" Thane asked, his warm fingertips gently caressing across the top of his hand, the compassion he had for the situation on his handsome face.

"I think because I'm so young they want to make sure Luke's taken care of. It hasn't been a problem. We get nervous when she shows up, but we shouldn't. She's always been good and helpful," Levi explained.

"Do they know about me?" Thane asked.

"Luke told her. I've gotta work with him on over-talking. He was all chatty. He told them about the job at Baconator." That caused Thane to smile. He and Luke had built quite the bond over food. Thane was a self-taught chef with a knack for blending spices and ingredients. Luke had a love for anything Thane created. Even sometimes just standing in the small kitchen in the suite, watching Thane prepare their meal. It seemed to make both of them insanely happy to talk food.

Thane smiled. "Luke's so excited about that. He asked me again if he got half off his meals. He can eat like nothing I've seen before."

He grinned too, looking down at their joined hands. He firmed his grip and lifted their hands. This time he kissed Thane's knuckles then took a deep breath and tackled the subject he'd been thinking about since Thane told him he was leaving. "Listen, I've got something we haven't really talked about. I've been waiting. I didn't wanna mess us up."

"You're being very attentive tonight. Maybe I should plan to leave more often," Thane said and again drew him over by the bicep for another kiss. "What'd you wanna talk about?"

"That money you gave me that first night…"

Thane let out an audible groan and pulled away from Levi, sitting fully back in his seat. He kept his eyes on Levi and grabbed his glass, taking a long drink.

"No listen. I'm gonna leave it in the suite. I haven't brought it up, because everything was going so well and it feels awkward to give it back to you, so I'll leave it in the nightstand drawer."

"Levi, please, keep the money. Let it be my contribution to your savings account. Or better yet, put your car in the shop for professional maintenance," Thane suggested and then abruptly changed his tactic as he reached for Levi's hand again, pulling him forward, kissing the center of his palm. "Please. I've done everything you requested, but you're not looking at it from my perspective. I've refrained from buying gifts, we don't take trips anywhere, we don't have expensive dinners or really even go anywhere because the cost makes you uncomfortable, but it stinks for me to not be able to buy my boyfriend things I know he needs."

"I'm not taking that money. I'm not going to. I was never going to," Levi explained, and Thane clamped on to his hand as he started to pull away. "And I'm not taking gifts. That's not right. I can't afford to buy you things. You already pay for everything we do even when we're all together. We're very expensive when we're together."

"Baby. You're killing me," Thane whined leaning in toward him. Thane looked like he'd lost his best friend, and it did tug on his heartstrings, but he wasn't keeping that money. Levi looked over his shoulder when his name was called. Julian gave him the cut sign, a hand cutting across his neck. He lifted a thumbs-up and started to scoot off the stool when Thane clasped his hand tighter.

"Here's my counteroffer. If I take the money back, then I want you and your brothers to agree to move in with me. School's out, you guys are there a lot all ready. It's only a fifteen minute longer drive for Logan. That way you don't have to take that second job and you can save money on utilities, things like that."

That came so far out of nowhere that Levi stopped in mid-scoot, looking over at Thane, astounded. "We've been dating for three months. You can't move in with someone after three months."

"It's been five months. Our first date was in March."

"You work out of the suite. We can't be there all the time," Levi said.

"It hasn't been a problem," Thane countered.

"Thane, it's a generous offer…" Levi started. He moved off the seat and stood. Thane hadn't let go of his hand and tugged him around to his stool, drawing him between his legs. "Stay in the suite while I'm gone. We can start getting you packed up in our free time and another reason you shouldn't begin another job. I worry about you guys over there. And this can be a test run, see about making it permanent when you move to Maryland."

Levi felt his face go completely blank. Permanent in Maryland? Where in the world was this coming from? He may have managed a blank expression, but his heart began pounding in his chest. Thane lifted Levi's hand, threading their fingers together, and kissed his knuckles.

"Nothing to say to that idea?"

"You already know we fit well. That's never gonna be our problem."

"Then what's our problem gonna be?" Thane asked. His hands inched around Levi's waist then slid down, lingering briefly on his ass before ending up on the back of his thighs, drawing him closer.

"When you get tired of all my boundaries. They'll increase when we get to Maryland. You'll get bored," he answered honestly, but still wrapped both his arms around Thane's shoulders, stepping in close. Thane made him feel wanted. Let him think everything would work out. He needed that more than anything.

"I told you, my eyes are wide open. I know what it takes to get through medical school. It's long hours. You'll need help with Luke. I'm in, Levi," Thane said and rolled his eyes as he continued. "So in."

"Thane." Levi stopped himself from arguing and shook his head before leaning forward and pressing a kiss on Thane's lips. "You're a good man."

"You make me a good man," Thane murmured, drawing him back for another kiss. Levi laughed at the absurdity of such a notion.

"Cancel the car. Let me take you to the airport. We can wait together, maybe make out in the car before you leave." Levi pulled away from Thane, slowly backing away. "I'm going to change."

At least he got a little more time before Thane was gone. The next few hours started looking up. He'd get to make out with Thane. He was so in for that.

CHAPTER 25

"Hey, you," Erin said, drawing Thane's attention from the initial mock-up sent over by his new interior designer before looking down at his laptop again. The designer had spent the afternoon with the contractor, working out the details on the remodel, coming up with some preliminary ideas. She was spot on with what he wanted, something easy and casual while retaining the look and feel of the area. Surprisingly, there wasn't going to be a lot of structural repairs. The house was in better shape than he'd hoped. They were knocking out a wall or two, opening the house up with a pretty intense remodel on the kitchen and bathrooms, but other than that, they had some painting to do and furniture to bring in and that was about it.

Thane slid a finger over his computer's screen to take a closer look at the basement—

"Hey, you, again. Forget I was here?"

Thane looked up, chuckling. "I did. How are you?" he asked, giving Erin a side hug when she came around the kitchen bar. She had a small cooler in hand and lifted the lid for him to look inside. There were two bottles of Two Hearted Ale and two small bottles of wine. She'd done well by bringing such a treat, and he reached for a beer then twisted off the cap. "You always were my favorite neighbor."

"It's eight thirty. When you didn't come home, I had a feeling you might be here." He was still on California time and did the quick math. Damn, he'd planned to call Levi before his shift, and he didn't have long. Palming his phone, he searched for the FaceTime app.

"I need to check in with Levi before he goes to work," Thane said, working the screen until it rang through to Levi's phone.

"I wanted to know more about that, other than the cryptic messages you keep sending," Erin said, opening her bottle.

He watched until the call wasn't answered. Damn. He shot off a quick text of apology for the time slip and put the phone on the counter, drawing her gaze down with it.

"Are these the plans for our new house?"

Thane chuckled, tilting the bottle back. He took a long swig before answering, "About that."

"No. You have three bedrooms up here, don't be trying to get out of it," Erin said, her finger working the screen, looking at all the changes.

"Luke could live up here, but Logan's eighteen and needs his own space," Thane argued.

"And he's going to college. And with all these mouths to feed, you'll need the rent. Thane, don't squash my hopes and dreams," she said before looking up, her gaze floating around the room. "Yeah, that wall needs to go. Such a simple change makes all the difference."

He rolled his eyes, taking another long drink. Every person in his life was so freaking hardheaded. When his phone began to ring, he looked down to see Levi FaceTiming him.

"Hey," he answered, grinning at his handsome honey. Levi looked freshly showered, that long-on-top hair styled in place. His fingers itched to slide through all those silky strands.

"I was blow-drying my hair," Levi said. The man's grin made his heart flutter and his cock stir.

"Let me see," Erin said, grabbing his wrist to angle his phone in her direction. "Hey, Levi."

"Hi." As much as Erin knew about Levi, Levi had no knowledge of her except a few passing comments.

"Levi, my neighbor Erin. Erin, this is my boyfriend, Levi." He quickly made introductions, and Erin took the phone out of his hand.

"And your soon to be renter. You should see the place. You're gonna love living here. It sits high on the cliff—"

"Hey, hey, stop." Thane's brain kind of exploded, and he darted for the phone. Erin dodged him, turning this way and that, keeping the phone out of his reach.

"What?" Erin asked defiantly. "I wanna talk to him."

"I haven't told him." Thane lowered his voice as if Levi wouldn't still be able to hear him.

"What? You haven't told him about the house? Or what?" Erin asked, confused, stopping her game, giving Thane a chance to take the phone.

"What's she talking about?" Levi asked, looking really confused. Now that Thane had the phone, he didn't want it. Thane lifted a brow and let out a deep sigh. His life. He tried to be a good guy, he helped people, never cheated anyone. How did he always wind up right here?

"Babe. I didn't want to freak you out. I was already in the works of buying the place before we got together."

Levi stared at him, not saying a word.

"I bought a house in Ellicott City. It's maybe thirty minutes to Johns Hopkins. It's the town I told you about. The one I love to watch storms blowing in. Remember?" he asked hopefully.

"Thane," Levi started with that doubting tone he'd grown to hate.

"It's a great house, in a great school district. Luke'll do wonderful here. He told me how much he enjoys aviation. I found a program nearby…" Thane's words trailed off and his heart began to sink as he watched Levi's head slowly shake no. He could see the fight forming right there on his boyfriend's face.

"Babe," Thane said desperately, but Erin took the phone from his hand.

"You're very handsome. I can see why Thane's nuts about you," Erin rattled happily as if she and Levi were the best of friends. She even turned the phone, showing Levi the living room and kitchen while talking about the benefits of the area before disappearing upstairs. Thane scrubbed a hand over his face then lifted the bottle of beer to down the rest of the liquid in a few short gulps. It did nothing to fill the pit that had formed in his gut. He had to remind himself this was always going to be a fight. He was rushing things, but dammit, he was in. He knew what he wanted and time would do nothing to change any of his feelings.

When he heard Erin walking back down the stairs, still happily chatting, Thane went to rescue his hopefully still boyfriend by taking the phone back. When he looked down at the screen, Levi's face was inquisitive. He'd even been laughing with Erin.

"I was going to tell you," Thane said carefully.

"Yeah, eventually. She wants me to tell you they'd be great in the basement," Levi replied, grinning when Erin's head popped into the view.

"Great job. That sounded convincing," Erin said to Levi.

"Yeah, I'm pretty sure I'm never going to be friends with her again."

Levi just laughed at him as Erin playfully slapped Thane's arm.

"I gotta go to work," Levi started, but Thane quickly cut him off. He couldn't let this sit between them unanswered.

"Babe, I was gonna tell you. I was just taking it in steps. I wanted to make sure I got the place first. You know you don't like to be rushed," Thane tried to explain.

"Thane, we're just not there yet." Levi moved closer to the screen, talking softer like that would keep Erin or anyone else from hearing for that matter. "We have a long way to go. We haven't really talked about a future together. We're kind of just living in this moment."

"We're in a holding pattern because of Logan's school. Otherwise, we could already be up here," Thane argued, and that seemed to confuse Levi which almost devastated Thane.

"We'll have to talk about this later. I gotta go to work," Levi said after a moment of silence.

"Call me when you're off."

"It'll be late. I'm closing," Levi reminded him.

"Call me," Thane insisted, he didn't care about the time difference. He wouldn't be able to sleep anyway. Not after this uncertainty. Levi finally nodded at him, watching him for several beats before his eyes narrowed.

"It's gonna be weird without you at the club tonight. I know it's an inconvenience for you, and Julian bitches about you taking up precious real estate, but I like you there." Levi stopped speaking and stared at him. Thane loved hearing that, the words easing the concern that had gripped his heart. "I'll call you when Julian cuts me." Levi lifted a hand in a tentative wave, making Thane smile.

"Bye, Levi," Erin called out.

"Bye, Erin!"

Thane waited until the screen went dark before he turned and gave Erin a disbelieving glare. She lifted both hands, immediately on the defensive.

"So not my fault. You didn't tell me." She singsonged her excuse.

"Seriously? Do you think I'd be doing all this so frantically if he was in on the deal? He'd be here with me, picking the furniture he wanted," Thane declared, throwing his hands in the air.

"Okay, that's a point in your favor, but I have one in mine. He picked Luke's room. He agreed he needed the one with the better view since he'd be here the longest," Erin gloated, grinning wide like she'd handed him a winning lottery ticket as she extended a hand in a high five.

"He did not." Thane lifted his hand to give her a high five, but paused as doubts began to push away his excitement. Was she messing with him? Levi was never that agreeable.

"He totally did. And he also agreed we should move into the basement, because Logan's going away to school." Thane narrowed his eyes, staring at her as he considered that bit of information.

He reached over to close the lid to his laptop before shoving it in the bag. "Let's go home and talk this out. I want to hear every word he said. But first, I'm starving. What do you have for dinner?"

"Leftover spaghetti with that Italian sausage you like," she answered, waggling her brows, reaching for her cooler.

"Do you have fresh parmesan?" he asked, hanging his computer bag over his shoulder while pushing his phone in his back pocket.

"Of course I do." As if that were a given.

"That goes a long way toward making all this better." Thane turned off the lights and started for the door, laughing as Erin gave a squeak in the darkness and scurried toward him.

~~~

Levi had stalled long enough. He'd told Thane he would call, and he needed to, but he couldn't shake all the unwanted uncertainty that had messed with him all night long. He'd had a hard enough time keeping the brakes on his runaway feelings, keeping himself in check and not falling hopelessly in love with Thane on a daily basis, but to find out Thane was in Maryland, secretly buying a house big enough for him and his brothers to live in…that took this emotional roller coaster to all new heights.

No, he and Thane weren't to a point of making a home together. That took time of getting to know one another. So, without question, Levi really couldn't move in with Thane. He'd mentally conjured up point after point, listing all the reasons why it was a bad idea, all night long.

They'd known each other less than six months.

They'd never lived together before.

His school had on-campus living arrangements ready for them.

What would happen if he gave up the campus apartment and it didn't last with Thane? He'd have nowhere to go. He couldn't risk that for Luke. Also, something else to consider, his brother would have to change schools again if Thane put him out. What would that do for Luke's scholarship possibilities?

"Stop, Silva," Levi muttered as he went through the house, turning off lights. He listened at Logan and Luke's door, but no sound came from their room. That was good sign. They were staying up far too late with Logan having to be in summer school by eight in the morning. Levi headed to his room and shut the
~~~

door behind him. He undressed, putting off the call until he was stretched out on his bed. Levi pulled up FaceTime, dialing Thane's number.

The call went to voicemail. That was probably for the best, but dang it, all night long, he'd been doubting the probability of a long-term live-in relationship, and now he wanted to know why Thane hadn't picked up the phone. His guy had said to call. No, he'd actually insisted that Levi call him no matter the time. It was almost three in the morning California time so six in the morning Maryland time. Thane had always responded when he spoke as Nathaniel.

See? This was how messed up Thane made him. One minute Levi dreaded the call, and the next, he doubted Thane's intentions when he didn't answer. What was wrong with him?

His phone rang before he ever got the device on the nightstand. He automatically slid his thumb over the screen to see a barely awake Thane. The room was dark, and Thane was yawning. "I'm sorry. I knocked the phone to the floor, reaching for it."

"It's okay. Go back to sleep," Levi said, pushing up against the headboard.

"No, no. I'm up," Thane responded as his eyes closed and stayed closed several long seconds before popping back open. Thane shook his head. "Where are you?"

"At my house. I came home before I called. I had to close," he said, laughing at the second shake Thane gave. He was tired. Levi got it. He couldn't have slept much over the last forty-eight hours.

"I wish you'd stayed at the resort while I was gone. Stay tonight. Bring your brothers, but stay the night. I miss our routine." It was that right there that always snuck past Levi's defenses. Damn, if Levi's feeling weren't so deep for this man. Thane never faltered in making him feel wanted. "What's wrong? What happened?" Thane asked and yawned again, lifting to a sitting position. The lamp turned on, causing Thane to squint as he moved the phone closer to his face, staring at Levi. "I see that look on your face. What's freaked you out? Was it Erin tonight?

She shouldn't have said anything, Levi. You really shouldn't worry about any of that. I was already buying the house…"

"Thane, stop. Seriously. It's okay." Levi scrubbed a hand over his face, looked away, and took a deep breath before glancing back. "Did you want us to move in there like she said or was she jumping ahead because that's what she does?"

Silence fell between them while Thane opened his mouth to speak, then closed it again. A range of expressions crossed Thane's handsome face before his face scrunched up as he spoke, causing Levi to laugh at the silly look. "I don't want to answer that."

"Just tell me," Levi encouraged.

"I wish you three would move in here and forgo the on-campus housing," Thane confessed.

"Thane…" Levi started shaking his head.

"No. I don't like that tone, Levi. You use that tone when you're fighting me, but you're also fighting us…" Thane explained.

"Listen to me. I've known you a total of six months. What if this doesn't work? I'll have given up my campus apartment. Luke would have to change schools again…" Levi emphasized the two most important points that had come to mind consistently all night.

"But the same argument holds if in six more months we decide we want to live together. If we keep going like we are, I'd be staying in that apartment with you, or Luke would have to drive into Baltimore every day to go to school," Thane reasoned.

Levi hadn't thought about it like that. After a second, he dropped his chin to his chest. His stupid emotions were all over the place. Thane was serious about their moving in together, and for some reason, that just changed everything.

"Babe, my feelings for you are so deep. I have so much I want to say that I haven't, and I'm not going to on the phone, but I'm also not going to voluntarily walk away from you. What can I do to show you how serious I am?" Thane asked, his tone changing to one of concern. That always got Levi. He loved Thane's voice and had to close his eyes as the goose bumps raced across his arms, imagining Thane being there with him. He'd have moved into Levi's personal space by now, trying to find an answer to Levi's growing melancholy.

"I don't know, Thane," he answered truthfully.

"I do. Luke can walk everywhere here. I'll get him a job at Sweet Suds until I get a restaurant opened around here—which will be soon. He'll have friends here, Levi. If it doesn't work out between us, you can take the basement apartment, or I'll take the basement apartment until Luke graduates—whatever you want. I don't care, because I don't see us ending like that. I just don't. Neither of us went into this lightly."

Levi listened and about halfway through Thane's explanation, he lifted his head and stared at Thane. "Erin said she's moving into the basement. Her, Corey, and somebody named Brock or something like that," Levi said.

"Erin's on my shit list."

That made Levi laugh, knowing that wouldn't bode well for Erin. Thane didn't let go of his grudges easily. He started to speak when the alarm clock in Thane's room went off.

"Go start your day. I'll pick you up tonight."

"You go to bed. You look exhausted, and you'll need to save your energy. It's been little more than twenty-four hours, and I'm really missing you. I'll talk to you later. Text me when you wake," Thane said, pushing himself out of bed while trying to keep his face in the phone's view.

"I will. I'm sorry I'm always so difficult," Levi apologized.

"You aren't at all, babe." Thane stood and stretched, giving a solid yawn that was contagious. "You're perfect the way you are. I wouldn't change a thing. Go to bed. We'll talk more tonight. Dream of me." Thane blew him a kiss and grinned that super-sexy smile Levi loved so much before disconnecting the call. Levi was slower to lower the phone. He wiggled under the covers still dressed in his T-shirt and shorts. He was either going to have to be all the way in or end this completely. Thane was too much of a force. He'd have them married before he ever realized how incompatible they were.

CHAPTER 26

Levi pulled Thane's car right along the edge of the loading zone about the same time he got a text that Thane had already made it to baggage claim. It was late, or early rather, almost two o'clock in the morning. Levi put the car in park and checked all the mirrors then opened the door, stepping out to scan the area. There weren't many cars around; he also didn't see security anywhere, but he did see a group of passengers beginning to exit the airport just a few feet away.

He decided to take his chances. He clicked the key fob and jogged the few steps toward the front doors, spotting Thane coming through as he started to enter.

"Hey," Thane said, sounding surprised, coming to an abrupt stop in the middle of the door. Man, it was so good to see him even though he looked exhausted and disheveled—a rarity for Thane.

"I was afraid I wouldn't get here on time," Levi said, reaching for Thane's suitcase at the same time Thane leaned in for a kiss. The peck landed somewhere on the side of his head. Their normal fluidity and ease had vanished, and that was Levi's fault. Things had become awkward as they stared at one another in the middle of the entry, forcing people to move around them in order to exit the airport.

"Are we gonna be weird now? We've never been weird," Thane said in his normal direct way. There may have been hurt reflected in his gaze. That was the last thing Levi wanted. He forced a laughed, desperately wanting to lighten the situation. Levi took the suitcase that Thane had fought to keep and quickly moved them aside, much to the delight of the other passengers. When they got out of the way, Levi initiated the PDA, leaning forward to give Thane that kiss he'd wanted, then threaded their fingers together, tugging to get Thane moving the fifteen or so steps to where he'd parked.

"You drove my car," Thane said, sounding pleased.

"I left mine with Logan so he could get to school in the morning." Levi used the key fob to pop open the trunk.

"You're staying with me tonight?" Thane asked.

"I thought so."

Thane's face lit up, and he stepped in closer, wrapping an arm around Levi's waist, making it impossible to put the carry-on in the trunk. "You look amazing."

Levi's face heated. "Thank you. It felt like you were gone for weeks."

"I was hoping for a moonlight walk on the beach. We could finish our talk there. We've never walked on the beach at night before. The water calms you," Thane said, moving enough to take the case from Levi and toss it carelessly into the trunk.

Thane had done it again, mesmerized Levi while staying in complete control. Thane shut the trunk and leaned his ass against the car, waiting for Levi's answer.

"Whatever you want."

"Good, then let's go. And just so you know, you in that tight shirt is an image that's spank bank worthy." Thane pushed him toward the driver's seat, patting his ass as he went.

~~~

As much as he missed the seasons of the East Coast, there was something to be said for the calming effects of the always cool night air and the churn of the Pacific Ocean under a moonlit sky. At home, Thane never spent time at the beach, but that needed to change. He loved the feel of his bare feet sinking in the wet sand and the tickle of the water as it lapped at his ankles.

Maybe it was more Levi's warmth next to him and the grip of the man's hand in his. Levi held on tight like he'd rather do
~~~

anything other than let go. Whatever it was, the feeling of dread that had hovered around most of his activities today had finally dissipated, and his heart settled back in its happy place. His fear that Levi would think he was pushing too hard, moving them too fast, eased with every step they took together.

"The grand re-opening went well?" Levi asked after several minutes of comfortable silence.

"The place is beautiful. Layne Construction—the same ones that built this resort—did my remodel and did an outstanding job. They utilized the space so well. That's Arik's family's business. You can tell grandness runs in that family."

"They do smaller commercial jobs too?" Levi asked.

"Yes, and they do residential," Thane explained, kicking at the water. "They're doing the remodel on the new house. That's probably the other reason the office space seemed more efficient. I used to live on the third floor of my corporate office. Now that's converted into more usable office space. My office'll be up there. I figured I could use the exercise climbing three flights of stairs. Especially with all Luke and I tend to eat." Thane chuckled at the thought, cutting a sideways glance toward Levi who smiled, but otherwise stayed silent. The moonlight bathed them in soft light, and he didn't think Levi could be any more beautiful.

"Wanna talk about the house? Our possible living arrangements?" Thane asked. The farther they went down the beach, the more the lights from the resort faded. The cool ocean breeze and the gentle sound of the waves in the distance assisted the moonlight in creating magic, making everything a little more romantic.

"When were you gonna tell me?" Levi asked quietly.

"Tell you I wanted you to move in with me when we got to Maryland?" Thane waited for the clarification. When he got a nod, he straightened his spine and answered honestly. "After I worked up the nerve to tell you how much I love you."

Levi's steps faltered, making the uncertain tension Thane shouldered suddenly lift. Their steps slowed until they came to a complete stop close to a large outcropping of rocks. Thane turned toward Levi who continued to look straight ahead. His guy's broad chest heaved with every breath. Thane got it; he was pretty much freaking out on the inside too, but he pushed that feeling aside and took in the death grip Levi had on his hand.

"I have for a long time now. Probably since our first night together. It scared me and I freaked. That's the only reason I did what I did. I was scared. Everything about you has me all tangled up, Levi. Ever since the first time I laid eyes on you, I couldn't get you out of my head. Then, after our first night together, I couldn't get you out of my heart."

Levi had perfected being silent—had it down to an art. He did turn his head and assess Thane before he shifted and turned fully toward him. Thane resisted the smile he felt nudging his lips as he watched Levi's face shift through a constant array of various levels of astonishment, but he never released his hand.

Thane brought Levi's knuckles to his lips and kissed them, just waiting for him to speak. Levi's eyes tracked his movement; he took a step in, coming chest to chest with Thane as his free hand cupped Thane's neck, drawing him in. This kiss was different. Desperation and intensity fueled it. Thane purposefully tried to keep it light. Words needed to be said. Things discussed. Decisions made before he got lost to this man.

"Babe, tell me what you're thinking. Please," he said, pulling away.

"If it were just me…" Levi started then shook his head, looking away. No, Thane wasn't having any of that. Thane used his palms against each of Levi's cheeks, bringing those expressive eyes back to him.

"If this were just you, what?" Thane asked, only inches separated Levi's face from his. "You'd say I love you back to me?"

"Yes," Levi hissed like that was an absolute given. "God, yes. I would have already said it to you."

Thane's heart latched on to those words, easing, while at the same time filling with happiness that began to build in his chest.

"I've embraced your brothers, Levi. I know you three are a package deal," he explained, stepping in a little closer as he caressed the soft skin beneath Levi's eye. Levi's hands went to his waist, and fisted his shirt, drawing Thane forward until he was fully plastered against Levi from head to toe.

"But we can't move this fast. It's too complicated. Luke needs to finish high school in whatever school he starts in Maryland. Logan has five months before he starts college. He needs a steady foundation…"

They were starting the same conversation they'd had a hundred times now. Thane moved his fingers, covering Levi's mouth, cutting off his words. Thane spent the long plane ride preparing for this exact argument.

"So it's safeguards you need? Then we'll give you those. If this doesn't work out, I'll move to the basement with Brock until Luke graduates. I'll put it in writing."

"Thane, we've known each other for only a few months. You can't give me your house if we decide we don't want to date anymore," Levi countered, but his guy's hold only tightened, locking around his waist.

"This is so much more than dating, Levi. *Augh.*" Thane felt himself deflating, growing frustrated. In his heart, he knew Levi wanted all this with him. It was his own hard head that kept him fighting their inevitable future together. "Levi, if you didn't have your brothers, would you move in with me?"

"Absolutely. Of course," Levi replied instantly without any hesitation.

"Then stay in that mind-set. Stop putting obstacles that aren't obstacles in our way. Luke will have what he needs—a good home, a good school district, a million places he could work and hang out. While you're in school, putting in all those hours, I'll be home with him, helping with homework and hopefully easing that concern for you. Let me share that life with you. I want the whole package, Levi."

"It seems unfair and one-sided," Levi challenged.

"One-sided in my favor. You're all I want in the world. I want to create a life with you, a family with you. Stand by your side and have you by mine," Thane reasoned, and for the first time in this conversation, he sensed Levi giving.

"I'll need to pay our way," Levi stated matter-of-factly and adjusted his body, leaning against one of the large rocks, drawing Thane there with him, between his parted thighs.

"Or you could attend school and spend your free time with me," Thane countered, a small smile spreading across his face. He had him. Levi had just indirectly agreed to move in with him.

"Thane…"

"Levi…" Thane mimicked. "Do whatever you want. I don't care. Just do it with me by your side. It's not complicated… I'm actually saving money by being in this particular relationship because you won't let me buy you anything." He'd tried to lighten the mood, but a different emotion took hold as Thane gazed deeply into Levi's eyes. "I want to hear you say it."

"I love you. I do. I have. For just as long. It happened that first night. I've only ever been in love with you," Levi explained in a rush of rambling words. Thane didn't stop him. He needed the flow of that loving confession like he needed his next breath. Levi had been so hard to get to know, he'd kept himself at a distance, and now he fully understood why.

Thane gripped Levi's head, drawing him forward as he started to descend. Right before he opened for the kiss, Thane paused and drew back a fraction of an inch, staring Levi in the eyes. "I'm going ahead with the idea that you also mean yes to moving in. That you understand we're committed, that we're building a life and home together. That it's you and me against the world."

Levi slowly began to nod while staring at Thane's lips. "Kiss me."

And Thane did, hopefully a kiss Levi wouldn't ever forget.

~~~

Everything fell into place the instant Thane's lips touched his. Thane took his time, biting and sucking his tongue while lazily ravishing his lips.

Soft and slow, demanding and selfish.
~~~

Levi hung on to every little intake of breath as his fingers fisted in Thane's shirt. Thane deepened the kiss and Levi moaned his approval. His dick had been hard since he laid eyes on Thane at the airport, and now, Thane took his desire to the next level. He wasn't far from begging Thane to claim him right there on the beach under the moonlit sky.

The saltiness of the night air infused with Thane's sexy scent intoxicated him, while the lull of the nearby ocean centered his soul. The thought of being discovered excited and terrified him simultaneously. The only thing keeping them hidden from view was the large bank of rocks and the shadows cast by the passing clouds. His dick twitched as Thane's fingers inched up his thigh and teased him through his clothing. Thane licked at his lips and rocked his hips suggestively into Thane's hand. Thane's breath seared his lungs as he breathed him in, hungry for more. Their hips touched and their cocks rubbed together as Thane's tongue twisted dominantly around his.

The feeling of Thane's warm and very aroused body pressing him into the wall of rock only made him crave more. To be even closer. His heart raced in his chest as he thought about earlier. Thane loved him; he'd told him so. Levi tried to absorb everything and couldn't process anything except that Thane wanted to share a life with him. Levi was even more in love with Thane in that moment than he could have ever thought possible.

"Love me, Thane."

"Always and forever, Red." Thane's lips moved down his neck in stinging bites and moist, soothing nips. His skin burned everywhere Thane touched. He managed to release the button on Thane's jeans, and Thane moved out of his reach.

Levi unbuttoned his own pants, and Thane pushed them down his legs. Levi stepped out of his clothes, the breeze chilling his skin as he left his pants and underwear on the cool sand. He kept his shirt on only because Thane told him he looked sexy with the material stretched tight across his chest.

He glanced up and caught Thane watching him, a wicked glint sparkled in his eyes. A pack of lube and a condom were placed on the upper ledge of the rock structure before Thane stripped out of his clothing. Levi's stomach filled with a thousand butterflies as he processed Thane's predatory gaze.

He shut his eyes to calm his racing heart and to stop from flat out attacking Thane. His dick jerked excitedly, and he opened his eyes as Thane's strong fingers curled around him. Dark eyes met his. So many emotions and feelings building inside him, his doubts and insecurities began to fade at the sincerity and love reflected in Thane's eyes.

Thane worked his cock, stroking him and telling him how beautiful he was. Levi scooted himself up on the rock, it's slope the perfect height for him to wrap his legs around Thane, but he didn't, he just leaned back and flattened his feet on the little ledge, opening his legs wider to give Thane more room.

"You're so damn sexy." Thane growled and, with a dip of his head, swallowed him to the base.

Fuck! Thane cupped Levi's balls, and Levi slid his fingers through Thane's thick hair as he arched his hips and pushed his cock deeper into Thane's throat. The feeling of Thane swallowing around him forced him to elevate his hips even higher.

Levi groaned at the loss of Thane's mouth and roaming hands.

"Thane, please," he pleaded as Thane ripped open one of the packages. Levi gripped his own dick and started to stroke himself.

"I promise your cock'll be back down my throat in about three seconds, and I won't stop again until you come."

"Gawhh." His breath rushed from his lungs as Thane kept good on his promise.

Fingers pushed into him while Thane's mouth worked him at the same time. Levi held his breath as he arched into Thane's clever hands. His mind raced, and his body spontaneously combusted. It was brutal torture in the sweetest of ways. His world tipped on its axis. He was so lost in Thane.

Thane shoved his shirt up his stomach, and Levi yanked it the rest of the way off and tossed it behind his head. Thane swept his eyes over him and flexed his hips in short shallow thrusts, rubbing his hard flesh against Levi's sensitive skin.

Levi pulled Thane's mouth to his and kissed him before whispering, "I need you, Thane."

"I need you more, Levi." Thane growled into his ear. Those words and the awakening pressure as Thane pushed into him made his heart race faster. His legs quivered, and the muscles in his ass burned in the best possible way. Levi blew out a breath as Thane slid in deeper until his groin met the back of Levi's thighs.

"So fucking tight." Thane withdrew a fraction of an inch, then pushed back in, repeating the motion with a fluid flow of his hips. Levi sucked in a breath and absorbed the building sensation.

Thane lifted Levi's leg and draped it over his shoulder. Levi gripped the shin of his other leg and pulled it back and to the side, opening himself wider for Thane.

His focus grew along with his grunts and pants. He clenched his ass around Thane, which had Thane whispering rude things in his ear. Levi held Thane's mouth against his ear and let Thane have his way, as long as Thane kept fucking him like that. Levi surrendered, let go of everything, and gave himself completely over to his lover. Thane's fingers dug roughly into his thigh as he forced his leg back and leaned in to fuck him even harder. Levi opened his eyes to watch Thane. Their gazes collided. Thane pinned him with that smoldering stare, and Levi realized always and forever would never be long enough. Not with Thane Walker by his side.

"I love you." His voice was ragged with the overwhelming feelings flooding his heart and tumbling from his lips.

"I love you, too, Levi." The constant drag of Thane's thick shaft across his gland brought his nerve endings to life. His breath came in heavy pants as unintelligible words fell from his lips. Thane spread his cheeks and thrust up into him, hard and demanding, his thick cock rubbing all the right places.

"Wanna fuck you bare next time." Thane grunted breathily.

"Yes!" Levi sank his nails into Thane's shoulder at that thought. He wanted that too. No barriers between them.

Thane gripped his cock and stroked him in time with each thrust.

Unbearable pleasure hit him and raced down his spine, electrical currents coursing through his body and into his cock. His dick jerked in Thane's palm as his orgasm traveled through him. The intense gratification of Thane's hips pumping into him stole his voice and locked up his movement when Thane thrust one last time then collapsed on his chest. Levi wrapped himself around Thane, tightly holding him right there, his heart full, his body sated, his future promising as Thane took his lips.

CHAPTER 27

Levi stretched as much as he could with the full weight of Thane's body on top of his. It was Thane though who seemed to be moving with purpose. Levi grinned and spread his legs, waiting for Thane to settle between them and take his already hard cock in hand. But when Thane crawled completely over him toward Levi's nightstand, it confused him. He cracked an eyelid just in time to see Thane reaching for his old cell phone.

"It's going nuts." Thane's sleep-filled voice made him take notice. A second later, Thane's cell phone started ringing much louder than Levi's vibration. "What the hell?"

"It's seven in the morning," Levi mumbled and took his phone from Thane as he rolled to the other side of the bed.

"It's Luke," Thane said at the same moment he saw four missed calls from his brother. "Hello. Hang on." Thane shoved his cell toward Levi.

"What's wrong?" he asked as Thane turned on the lamp, and Levi sat up, propping himself against the headboard. He tried to follow what his brother was saying but Luke seemed to start in the middle of every sentence. "Slow down, Luke. I don't understand. Start from the beginning."

Thane moved from the bed, going straight to his closet.

"Mom's here, Levi. She's here and Linda's here and they're fighting on the front porch and mom's trying to get inside the house."

"What?" Levi yelled, immediately darting off the bed.

"It's bad. You need to get here. They're screaming. Someone's gonna call the police."

"Are you sure it's her?" Levi asked, going for his clothes.

"Yeah, that's what Linda said, and she looks bad. Real bad," Luke said.

"I'm on my way. Tell Linda I'm on my way," Levi assured his little brother as he anchored the phone on his shoulder and pulled up his pants.

"I can't go out there. Linda said for me to stay inside."

"Yeah, you stay inside. Tell Logan to go tell Linda. You stay out of it, Luke. Go in your room. Keep the phone with you. I'm on my way," Levi said, disconnecting the call while trying to pull his shirt over his head.

"What's happened?" Thane asked, tugging his shorts on while toeing on his sandals.

"Luke said my mom's there. I don't know what that means, but Aunt Linda said it's her, and apparently, they're fighting. Linda won't let her inside the house," Levi explained, pulling on his shoes.

"I thought she died," Thane said, tucking his wallet and cell phone in his pockets while going for the ball caps he'd brought home for Logan and Luke from Johns Hopkins. He tossed one to Levi then put the other on.

"She did, was…I don't know. I thought social services had confirmed it." Levi grabbed his wallet and cell phone and started for the front door, not quite able to wrap his head around the possibility that his mother was at his house.

Thane called out for Iris. He heard Thane's clipped voice requesting his car be delivered to the main lobby entrance immediately. Levi should have just told him he'd take a cab, but he didn't. His heart was racing in his chest, and he could really use the support right now. His mother had been gone for almost all of Luke's life. They had all believed for so long that she was dead. What other reasons would allow a mother to abandon her three young children? There were none that he could think of. No phone calls, no cards or letters. Year after year, birthdays and Christmases came and went and nothing, not a word from her. What the hell could she hope to gain by showing up now? Only one thought came to mind and that had dread coiling in his gut.

Thane was in the kitchen, chugging orange juice from the carton. He quickly replaced the carton with two cold coffee drinks while Levi pushed his hair back, putting the cap on backward, "Are you ready?"

"I should tell you I'll handle it," Levi offered, giving Thane the out, but his guy just shook his head, pointing his finger toward the door.

"We consummated our new relationship last night. I'll always be by your side. I'm not arguing this out with you. I just wish Logan and Luke had been here so they didn't have to deal with all this," Thane said, pushing open the door for Levi to walk through first. They double-timed it toward the elevator.

"I can't see anything good coming from this," Levi said, rubbing the sleep from his eyes.

"What's the worst-case scenario?" Thane asked as the elevator door opened. They were inside alone with Thane frantically pushing the close door button.

"She wants Luke," Levi answered. Saying it out loud had the dread multiplying inside him.

"Where's she been this whole time? She left all of you right after Luke was born. She won't get him," Thane declared, his leg bouncing with adrenaline as they watched each number above the doors light.

"I don't know that. If it's her and she's cleaned herself up and just found out about my dad, I could see it happening," Levi reasoned and closed his eyes, pressing his fingers in his eyes.

"We'd fight that, Levi. Luke doesn't need that kind of disruption." Thane huffed, his steely gaze landing on Levi.

"I don't think it would matter if we fought it. Maybe Luke's age might help, especially if he doesn't want to go with her," Levi said and edged closer to the doors as they got to the lobby floor and waited for the elevator to open.

"But it would stop the move," Thane said as the doors opened. They were out the doors; Thane right on his heels. When he started heading in the wrong direction, Thane reached out, gripping Levi's bicep. "It's out here."

They got inside the car, and Thane zipped across the parking lot. Levi stared out the side window, contemplating everything. He couldn't believe all the years she'd missed. She'd been gone a long time. Why would she surface now? Hope took hold. He remembered being in the social worker's office when she confirmed his mother's death. Maybe it wasn't her, maybe his brother had misunderstood Linda, but regardless, in no scenario did he see this ending well.

"I work in a gay men's club peddling drinks in my underwear. The court's gonna *love* that."

"Stop that, Levi. You're jumping way ahead; you don't even know the situation," Thane said, taking a turn a little too quickly while punching the gas.

Levi marveled at the speed and ability Thane had behind the wheel. The fifteen-minute ride took eight before Thane whipped the rental into the driveway. Levi stared at the scene. No doubt, it was his mother. She was sitting on the front porch step, cigarette in hand, and couldn't have weighed more than a hundred pounds. Linda stood by the front door with her arms crossed over her chest. He could see the frown on her face as she guarded that door. His mom would have to go through Linda before she got inside, and Linda's stance made it clear how likely that would be.

"It's her," Levi said, staring at his mother as she lifted her face toward him. His heart dropped to his stomach. He was so torn. He didn't have any special memories of her—only that she was always drunk or strung out, always running off with strange men. Love… He'd never really felt that from her. She'd treated him more like a chore she hated than a son.

He continued sitting there, looking at her haggard appearance and her hollow face. Nothing like the mental image he remembered of her or the pictures his father had kept over the years. She took a drag, blew the smoke out slowly, and continued to sit there, staring at him. Big sunglasses covered her eyes, but nothing hid the attitude she'd come packing.

"She's gonna ruin us."

Thane's hand came to his arm, gently squeezing before drawing Levi's attention to him. "Let's find out why she's here. We can't find a solution until we know more."

Levi slid his worried gaze back toward his mother. "I'm sorry…"

"Don't even start that." Thane pushed open his door, and with more anxiety than confidence, Levi did the same. He hadn't walked two steps before she shoved off the step, dropped the cigarette on the sidewalk, and put it out with her shoe.

"You're bigger than I thought you'd be." She stood there, swinging her hip out, putting a hand on her waist like she had all the right in the world to be standing right there.

"What're you doing here?" Levi asked, coming to a stop about three feet in front of her. Thane's hand reassuringly moved to the small of his back.

"I heard you like dick. I knew you would from the time you were three years old," she said. Thane moved closer to him. His mom removed her glasses, giving Thane a thorough once-over before putting them back on her face. "He looks like he's got some money. He your boyfriend?"

"What do you want?" Levi asked, forgoing all the other questions he wanted to ask.

"Aren't you happy to see me?" she said in mock indignation.

"We thought you died…" Levi said, but Linda started in from the porch.

"You hadn't showed your face around here in fifteen years and you think any of these children you abandoned wanna see the likes of you?"

Levi lifted a hand in Linda's direction, hoping to stop her tirade. He needed a firm understanding of what she expected, and they wouldn't get there if they all started fighting. "We thought you were dead. The social worker searched you and you came back deceased."

"I'm alive, Levi," she said condescendingly. She gestured dramatically up and down her body with her hands, showing that she was clearly really there. "You always were one to question everything," she said tersely. "Someone stole my wallet. I just let everyone believe what they wanted. I heard about your father, so I came. I know Luke needs a real parent."

"You thought you'd come sniffing around for the social security money," Linda called out, still perched by the front door.

"I've always hated you, you old hag. Stay out of mine and my kids' business before I come up there and whoop your meddling ass," his mother threatened, going as far as the top step, but no farther.

"You can try." Linda was unfazed. Right then, all the years of living in the wrong side of town came out in Linda. His sixty-year-old neighbor was ready to go toe to toe with his mother.

"Hang on. Hang on." Levi inserted himself between the two and spoke directly to his mother. "I'll ease your conscious. We're fine. Everything's fine. We don't need you."

His mother lost some of her attitude, deflating in what looked to be a pre-rehearsed act. His mother's theatrical skills were clearly lacking. He didn't buy a second of her remorse.

"I'm coming home, Levi," she stated, trying for meek. He watched her hollow gaze stay devoid of expression. "I heard about your dad, and I know Luke needs a parent in his life. You all do."

He ignored Linda who barked out a bitter laugh. "She just wants whatever money she can get out of this. She doesn't care a lick about any of you boys."

"Shut the fuck up, bitch." His mother's tone instantly filled with venom as she started toward Linda. Levi had to forcibly hold her back. "The first thing I'm gonna do is make sure you never see them again." She weighed nothing, but her arms and legs were all over the place, trying to get out of Levi's hold to go after Linda.

Thane came from behind as Levi struggled to keep hold of his flailing mother. Looking as if he'd done this before, Thane had no problem wrapping an arm around her waist, hauling her from behind back out into the yard until she turned her fight on Thane, scratching and kicking him.

"Keep your hands off me."

When Thane put enough distance between them, he let her go and his mother rounded back, screaming across the yard. "This is gonna happen. I'm back and that's my kid. I'm his mother. His social security goes to me."

Levi held his ground as his worst possible scenario played out in front of him.

"And you," she screeched, pointing to Linda. "You old cunt, you're done." His mother grabbed for her purse that had fallen when Thane released her. She was still yelling, this time her vengeance aimed at Levi. "Before this is over, that boy'll be mine. His money goes to me. You watch."

Levi stared helplessly as she forcibly slung her purse strap over her shoulder and started down the street, shouting at the top of her lungs as she went. Levi finally turned to Thane, completely shell-shocked by what had happened. This was so much worse than the humiliation heating his cheeks. He was scared, his life and his brothers' lives were going to be ruined. There was no way the state would let them leave now, not with his mother fighting for custody of Luke. Distress and desolation flooded his heart.

Whatever Thane saw as he looked at Levi made him pivot on his heels and take off after his mother. If it were even possible, things got worse for Levi in that second. Levi started down the steps, calling out to Thane, "No, let her go."

Linda yelled out in a stern voice. "Let him go, Levi. Go check on Luke and Logan. They'll need you."

Helplessly, he did stop, knowing she was right. As he turned back toward the house, he saw a visibly upset Logan standing right inside the threshold of the front door, Luke directly behind him. He went straight for them, wrapping an arm around Logan, pushing him back inside as his other arm reached out for Luke.

~~~

"Wait up," Thane yelled, jogging the distance to Levi's mother.

"Fuck you," she called out, looking back over her shoulder as she stalked down the street. She was a mess. From behind, he
~~~

saw her clothes were dirty, hair greasy and tangled, the smell trailing behind her proved she hadn't bathed in a while. He knew her kind, had dealt with them in the restaurants when they walked out on the bill, begged for food, going through his trash bins, or claiming injury and lawsuit all the damn time. She wasn't interested in her sons, but she would turn their lives upside down to get a hold of the measly social security money.

Did he fear she'd actually get custody of Luke? Hell no. Would she change the course of their lives? Abso-fucking-lutely. And thereby change the course of his life. Thane ran past her, stopping her retreat as he pulled his wallet from his back pocket. He fished through the folds until she came to a stop, cocking that hand on her waist, staring him up and down.

"I want some of that," she said, pointing to the cash in his wallet. He ignored her and handed over a business card.

"Give me ten minutes, then call my attorney to set an appointment." He handed over the card. She eyed him, then the card before flipping it back at him.

"They done pissed me off. I'm those boys' mama. I control this show," she said with certainty.

Thane let the card fall to the ground. "Stop. We both know this is about money. You can call that number and schedule an appointment or you can call social services, but know, if you choose that route, you're fighting me and you won't win."

Thane left her standing there while he jogged back across the street. The front door was open. Linda was watching his whole exchange, and he could see Levi standing inside, his arms wrapped around his brothers. Luke stared at him over Levi's shoulder. Thane leaped up over the steps, meeting Linda's direct stare as he slid past her to enter the front door.

"Get packed," he said with authority as he took in the fear and despair before him. "Logan, you should get to class, but take a minute and gather your things. We'll take them back to the suite with us." Thane stepped around them, looking through a doorway, seeing the kitchen. He went straight there, opening cabinets, looking for a glass. He needed water. Something to rinse the vile taste of Levi's mother away. "Take as much as you can now, and we'll come back and get the rest later. You're all staying with me indefinitely."

"Thane…" Levi started. The cupboards were close to bare. He counted four plates, four bowls, and a single serving dish in one. Thane had more in his tiny suite than these three did. When he finally found the glasses, he grabbed one and went for the faucet.

"No, it's not open for discussion." Thane glanced over to see Logan and Luke standing right behind Levi. Linda's shorter head moved through them to stand beside Levi. "This is as good a time as any. Since I have your attention, your brother and I committed to one another last night. We're a couple and plan to be one for a long time. I'm part of this family, and I'm done with all this bullshit." He pointed a finger in the direction of where Levi's mother had stood. Thane drank several satisfying gulps of water, before dumping the rest in the sink, placing the cup on the counter, certain Levi would have it washed and put away before they left the house. "Had you been at my place like I wanted, she would have never found you. Go pack everything you need for the next few days. We'll figure out the rest after I make a phone call." Thane pushed past Levi, going for Luke and Logan, turning them toward their rooms. They were hesitant to go, looking every bit as worried as Levi. "Please go pack. Let's get out of here."

Still ignoring Levi, he turned to Linda. "I can get you a room at the hotel so you can be close to them."

She shook her head, her gray curls bouncing as she fiercely said, "I'll stay here, keep an eye on things." Linda kicked into gear, shooing Logan and Luke, who stood right by their bedroom door, watching Levi, probably waiting for his nod of approval. "Come on, boys. I'll help you pack. Logan needs to get to school."

"I can miss," Logan started while disappearing into the room.

"No, you can't. We have to do everything by the book right now," he heard Linda say.

"Go pack, babe. We're not doing this *man unto himself* crap anymore, Levi. ."

When Levi didn't readily move, Thane went to him, taking him by the shoulders in a much gentler hold than he thought possible with all the aggravation rushing through him.

"I just had to watch the man I love in one of the most heartbreaking scenes I've ever witnessed. You're coming with me where you know you should be." He had no idea where Levi's room was, but that was all right. Since the kitchen took one opening, Levi's room had to be down the other. He guided them in that direction. Just as he suspected, Levi's room was spotless.

"What'd you say to her?" Levi asked, turning, following Thane as he left Levi standing in the doorway and went to the center of the small room.

"I just called her bluff. We'll see if she bites. For now, I need you to pack." When Levi hesitated, Thane's frustration grew. He had to remind himself that Levi was only being difficult because he wanted to pay his own way, handle his responsibilities himself. That helped settle Thane, and he stepped forward, placing both hands on Levi biceps. "I like this look on you with the bill of the hat turned to the back. Your face was made to wear ball caps like this."

Levi let out an unsteady breath, showing just how stressed he was.

"Don't get upset. Stop worrying. She doesn't want Luke; she wants his money and it's not much."

"You're right, it's not," Levi started, his head shaking back and forth as if he saw the ridiculousness in her thoughts. "He gets less than eight hundred dollars a month. She can't make it on that."

"I needed to know that figure. Babe, get your stuff. Let me go tell Logan to make sure he packs all his school work together. I don't want you guys coming back here ever, but certainly not for the next few days. We'll talk this all out back at the resort. I don't want her showing back up, and she might."

That spurred Levi into action. Thane left him there, calculating his next steps. That was far less money than he'd initially thought. He wouldn't even have to move money around to write that check. Once he felt reasonably comfortable in his strategy, he went to the car for some privacy. He needed to talk to his attorney, get his game plan set. Buy him some time to get these guys as far away from California as he could.

Thane arrived at his attorney's office forty-five minutes early, still surprised at how quickly his California legal counsel, Jason Hammer, had pulled this meeting together. Levi was in tow. He'd seen firsthand the dismal quality of Levi's wardrobe. His guy lived off vintage T-shirts and athletic shorts with a stack of hand-me-down blue jeans and sweaters he'd bought while living in Maryland. He had nothing but sandals and a single pair of tennis shoes for his feet. For some reason, that had been the catalyst to show Thane just how much Levi gave of himself to keep this family going. The best he could see, Levi's only splurge was his used smart phone on a cheap month by month plan. Saints had nothing on his guy. The knowledge incensed him more that his mother would try and take from her children who lacked any sort of real foundation due to her own negligence.

Levi looked as uncertain as he'd ever seen him as they walked toward the reception desk. "Hi, Thane, Jason's expecting you. Let me tell him you're here."

"Thank you."

"Do you think he'll really scare her?" Levi asked for maybe the hundredth time today.

"I do," he said, running his hand down Levi's arm, hoping to give him reassurance.

"I'm underdressed." Levi looked around at the grandeur of the attorney's office then down the length of Thane's body. He had worn a suit and tie, his standard dress, except Levi didn't really know that. Since he'd been in Coronado, he'd kept it casual. "You look like you did when I first met you."

"I don't know if that's a compliment," Thane teased, drawing Levi's eyes straight to him. "Now, listen, I brought you here today so you can read the terms we've put together, see what we may have missed, and so you'll know exactly what's going on, but please don't start that fighting thing you do with me. Not in there. We're united."

"We are united, but I don't want you giving her money." Levi immediately started to argue, and Thane laughed, never taking his eyes from Levi.

"Exactly that. Don't do that," Thane teased. Jason came through from the back, his grin splitting his face from ear to ear. He was a large man in every way, at least six feet, six inches tall and a combination of brawn and good looks. His loud booming voice sent a chill down the spine even when he was jovial, like right now.

"Well, I see you got your guy," Jason said, laughing as he stuck out his hand first to Thane, then to Levi. "I've been to the club a few times. I was there the night you shot him down. It was very enjoyable to see Thane getting some of what the rest of us get regularly."

"Hey, hey, hey," Thane said, grinning back at Jason. "We don't need to remind Levi of my shortcomings."

"I don't know, I'm kind of enjoying this, but since we have thirty or so minutes before she arrives, we can continue when you buy me drinks tonight."

"I'll buy you drinks if you get this settled for us," Thane countered, following Jason through the door. Levi had suddenly become quiet, not uttering one single word. He was unsure. Thane did nothing to relieve Levi's uncertainty. Instead he hoped Levi remained quiet like this for the next couple of hours because it made his boyfriend appear agreeable. Thane gripped his hand, threading their fingers together, tugging him along.

~~~

Levi tried. Lord knew he did. He stayed silent through the terms of the agreement Thane's attorney had quickly drawn up. Hell, it hadn't been seven hours since his mother had been at their house. How Thane had gotten Jason to stop everything and draft this agreement was beyond him. That was the first most impressive feat. The second came when Jason outlined all the
~~~

requirements his mother would have to live by. The most important one to Thane was zero contact with Logan or Luke. If either boy wanted to know her, Thane or Levi would readily give her information to them, but she was to stay away from both boys for the rest of their lives. She also had to stay away from social services. That was said very carefully, but still stated clearly. If she broke any of the terms, future payments would end, and she'd be expected to pay every dime back. That was where things got tricky for Levi.

Levi zeroed in on the payment portion of the agreement, and he immediately started shaking his head, looking up at Thane, whispering as if Jason didn't sit just feet away, "I can't afford this, Thane."

Thane's hand came out, taking the agreement from Levi, while the other clasped his hand. "Don't worry about that, babe. I'm guaranteeing that payment."

Levi's head might have actually exploded right then. Heat flooded his cheeks as he spoke much louder this time. "You can't pay for her."

Thane rolled his eyes, and Jason busted out with a booming laugh. "I wasn't sure about him. I wondered if that was an act."

Thane answered, "It's frustratingly not at all an act."

Levi sighed dejectedly, staring between both men that had just blown him off. He wasn't certain what he had expected by coming there today, but the small amount of hope he'd hung on to all morning slowly began to slip away. An anxious desperation took hold. It would take everything and then some to keep his mother away from Luke.

Jason's office door opened, interrupting the steady build of fear growing inside Levi. "She's here, but she's refusing to give me her full name."

"Levi, do you know her full legal name?"

Still stuck on the three tier payment schedule, coming to a total of forty thousand dollars his mother would get over the next two years, he completely missed the question directed to him. That was more than double what Luke would be paid through social security.

"Levi, answer the question," Thane encouraged. It took a second as he looked between the three expectant faces to remember the question he'd been asked. Name. His mother's name. Right.

"Teresa-Jane Silva. It's hyphenated. No middle name."

Jason turned back to the assistant, letting her know there were no other changes. Thane started to stand, motioning for him to follow. He did, still lost in the possibilities of how in the world he could afford those payments. They were led through a side door into an empty conference room. Thane flipped on the lights and drew Levi farther inside. An oversized table with six leather office chairs filled the center of the room.

"I want you to stay in here no matter what you hear. I'll come get you when it's over."

"Thane, you can't do this. I can't pay that, and I won't let you pay that to her," Levi said, rounding to Thane, cutting him off. Thane eased forward, kissing his lips. Not necessarily a romantic kiss. He got the feeling it was an appeasing him kind of kiss to help stop his objection. Levi's eyes narrowed, realizing Thane did that move quite a bit.

"No one's ever watched my pennies as closely as you, Red. Promise me. I know if you promise, then you'll stay in here, but if she sees you're distraught, she'll know she can get more from me. Promise," Thane said right in his face, turning serious as he spoke.

"I'll wait, but I don't agree with this," Levi added, crossing his arms over his chest.

"Noted." Thane disappeared behind the door, and Levi edged back against the table, staring at the now closed door. He stayed just like that for a good thirty minutes only gathering bits and pieces of the conversation. When the big gentle bear, Jason Hammer, viciously raised his voice a couple of times after his mother did the same, Levi got Jason's intimidation factor. Outside of that, he heard nothing he could make any sense of.

At times, he couldn't even be certain they were still inside the office. He dropped his chin to his chest and closed his eyes. He hadn't even let himself dwell on the heartsick emotion of seeing his mother, knowing she'd kept some kind of tab on him. She had known he was gay. She'd stayed in San Diego, but never came back to see him or his brothers. That hurt, knowing she was in the same city as they were all these years and never even bothered to pick up a phone… The knowledge threatened to crush him. It had to hurt Logan and Luke, and it had to have gutted his loving father. He wondered how much his dad had known. Levi suspected he probably knew the truth, lied to protect Logan and Luke.

The door opened, and Levi looked up to see Thane. He looked tense and rolled his shoulders as he opened the door wider. "We're done."

"She agreed?" Levi asked, not budging, his knuckles digging into the table.

"Yes. How are you?" Thane asked, moving closer.

"I'm not sure," he answered honestly. Thane sighed and came toward him, stepping between his legs.

"This has to be hard to deal with," Thane said, gently putting his hands on Levi's waist.

"As I waited in here, listening to her voice, there were so many unexpected layers to her just showing up like this. Part of the reason I'm like I am is because I taught myself to be the best person I could be so she'd come back home. She hated cleaning house. From the day she left, I always kept our house clean just in case she came back, she'd see I wasn't messy anymore. I wanted her back so badly."

Thane said nothing. He just wrapped his arms around Levi and held him. Exactly what he needed. Levi closed his eyes and melted against Thane. Minutes passed in their silence before Levi said, "I'm worried about how you can afford everything you're putting out while taking us on. I'll work. We saved…"

Thane pulled away, moving back to look Levi in the eyes as he interrupted and said seriously, "We'll be broke."

Levi widened his eyes, and the relief running through him caused him to speak without thinking. "That's okay. Maybe even better for me. I was uncomfortable with all the money you have…"

Thane lifted a hand, pressing a finger to Levi's lips, silencing him. A grin tugged at the corner of his mouth. "Wait. Don't get your hopes up, Red. We're broke like getting you a reasonably loaded XT5 instead of a fully loaded Escalade, which I really wanted you to have to drive back and forth to school."

That silenced Levi. He lifted his brows, causing Thane to chuckle as he placed both his palms on Levi's cheeks, holding him in place.

Levi pressed his lips to Thane's expecting to be brief, but this man made him complete. Thane had given him the world.

Thane slanted his head, his tongue sliding along the seam of Levi's lips until he opened, and let him slip inside. Had they been alone, Levi would have taken full advantage of this moment, but they weren't—not really—and he reluctantly pulled away. "I love you."

"I love you, too."

Jason came through the door. "I don't want to rush you two along, but my next appointment's here."

"Come on, baby. Let's go home."

CHAPTER 28

That night, the music thumped while Levi gyrated enticingly against Thane. Being the owner of Reservations had its perks. His reserved table was right off the dance floor, not in the VIP section, and as far as he was concerned, it was the best table in the house. Thane held Levi's glass as Levi took a drink from his celebratory martini and continued to move; his guy never lost his groove as he swallowed the gulp down.

Thane handed the empty glass over to Jason, who was there with them, celebrating their victory. With nefarious intent, Thane lifted the hem of Levi's shirt, pulling it over his lover's head, tossing that in Jason's direction too. Levi turned and backed his perfectly round bouncing ass against Thane's rigid cock then looked back over his shoulder, giving him that tipsy, irresistible grin. Man, he was so in love.

He kept the beat, moving in time with Levi even as Chase came forward, abandoning his tables to begin dancing with Levi, effectively sandwiching Levi in between the both of them. There was a split second of jealousy that soon died as the cheers of the tables around them started, and Levi turned in his arms, pressing himself head to toe against Thane before kissing him. His guy wasn't the least bit interested in the other waiter. Chase didn't seem to care; he kept moving like a trained dancer to the delight of the entire room.

"Wanna break, handsome?" Thane yelled.

"Yeah and some water. You're getting me drunk," Levi yelled back, already moving from his arms to go back to the table. The club was in rare form tonight. They were packed full, which was nothing new. Much to Julian's dismay, Thane had just ordered the entire club a round of Redheaded Slut. A shot he'd chosen in honor of his mister. Levi had laughed about the name, but leaned in when no one was paying attention and promised to show him exactly how slutty he could be when they were alone. Thane was so looking forward to that promise he'd almost taken Levi back to the room early.

They were having too much fun and had partied so much tonight. The club members thought it was their new status as life-partners they were celebrating. For Thane it was so much more. They were free of all the ties that bound them.

This afternoon, Thane officially became part of the family. He, Levi, Luke, and Logan all sat down for their first family meeting, unanimously agreeing to forgo the on-campus apartment, and move straight into Thane's new home in Ellicott City.

They planned to move the Silva brothers out of their home in San Diego next week. Thane wasted no time in having Jenna purchase all their airline tickets to Maryland the afternoon of Logan's last day of class. That had earned a tearful Alison a night out with Logan. Thane pulled some strings, giving the young couple the VIP treatment at Castelli's by themselves tonight. Luke was happy to stay at home on the new gamer laptop Thane had impulsively purchased after leaving the attorney's office. Luke needed something special of his own.

Thane had finally gotten his guy and had two new brothers in return. Thane wrapped an arm around Levi's waist as he scooted up to the table, gulping down the cold water that had been left behind. When Thane kissed Levi on the shoulder, his guy stopped drinking, instinctively offering the drink to him. It was a sweet gesture; he took the glass and finished the water.

"You need to get out there and dance," Thane yelled across the table to Jason.

"I'm not the dancing kind."

Chase obviously heard the exchange, or watched Jason's resistance, and immediately came over, gyrating in front of Jason before pulling him right off that chair.

"Come on, Daddy Bear. You're dancing tonight," Chase said matter-of-factly, refusing to take no as an answer.

It took a little more prompting, but Jason did get out there on the floor, and he wasn't half bad.

Thane ran his fingers through Levi's hair, drawing his redhead's face back so he could lean in and kiss him, first a simple brush of the lips that lingered then turned X-rated. That was Levi's fault. Levi kissed him like he had a right to be there. Thane always lost his mind when Levi dominated him. It wasn't until he was knocked in the arm that he broke from Levi to see Julian placing two fresh glasses of water in front of them. It kind of pissed him off. Water wasn't enough reason to interrupt such a kiss…until his club manager stepped aside and he saw Linda standing there.

Her grin spread from ear to ear. When he'd planned this impromptu celebration, he'd called her. Her presence definitely broke the rules, but no Walker-Silva gathering would be complete without her.

"I come bearing company," Julian announced with sass.

Thane grabbed Jason's seat for Linda. "I'm glad you came."

"It's so much fun here," she said, both he and Julian started snapping fingers, drawing waiters from every direction to give Linda the VIP treatment.

Julian suddenly grew quiet, which wasn't often. Thane watched with amusement as his manager stood dumfounded by the Marlboro Man. The ruggedly handsome guy had finally gotten bolder and moved just feet away, to the outside edge of their tables, locking eyes with Julian. Thane felt the chemistry of their non-verbal communication. He could easily read his manager's body language, and no question, Julian was definitely interested. Something Thane hadn't seen since Julian's attack. Thane nudged Levi in the arm so he didn't miss the interesting exchange between the two men.

"You sure stare a lot. Is there a problem or something?" Julian asked huskily.

"Or somethin'," the good-looking guy drawled, the corners of his mouth slowly tipping upward as his gaze dropped to

Julian's lips and lingered briefly before lifting back to his eyes. "Surely, you have to be used to men starin'. You're gorgeous."

"Oh, direct and smart. I like that in a man," Julian purred, wrapping an arm around the guy and tugging him to the dance floor. That was the first time in almost a year Thane had witnessed Julian react to a man in that way.

Tristan bumped his shoulder. Thane grinned brightly at his friend. He'd called and invited Tristan and Dylan down for the celebration. Thane reached out, shaking Tristan's hand. "I'm so glad you could make it. This is Levi."

Tristan moved closer to Levi. "It's nice to meet you. I heard you two were getting married," Tristan said, loud enough for everyone in their circle to hear.

Thane whipped his head toward Levi, and there was what could only be described as a look of horror on his man's face, but with the way Tristan started laughing, luckily Levi caught on to the joke and also gave a smile. Linda gave a boisterous laugh. She knew how Levi was.

"Julian made me say it. Said we'd get free drinks," Tristan declared.

Thane feigned a scowl as his gaze moved to the dance floor. He pointed a finger at the laughing Julian. No way the guy could have heard Tristan; he'd just seen Levi's reaction.

"What? You don't want to marry me?" Levi called out to Thane, making sure he was heard over the crowd.

Thane could only laugh at such boldness. Levi was clearly growing more comfortable with them as a couple. Thane moved closer, bending to place a kiss on those upturned lips.

"In due time, handsome." That earned him a sexy blush and Thane bent in again, this time to kiss Levi's already puckered lips.

Quinn was there, taking drink orders, pulling stools from the back to accommodate their growing party. Thane made introductions with Tristan, Dylan, and Linda. It was Levi who surprised him again by taking Linda's hand and gently pulling her off the seat.

"Let's dance. I can twerk pretty good apparently."

"Well, we need to see that." Linda was moving out on the dance floor. Thane stared after them, watching as Levi threw his head back in laughter when Linda tried to mimic his moves. He loved the way Levi's eyes sparkled when he laughed. Damn, he was so in love with that man he didn't ever want to imagine a life without him.

"You know, the next step is marriage. You'll be marrying him before long," Tristan yelled, getting his attention. He smiled in Tristan's direction, but his eyes remained on Levi dancing and laughing with Linda.

"I can only hope," he said, probably sounding more enamored than he'd intended.

"That was pretty much how I felt. Weird, huh?" Tristan asked.

"It is, but it's so right," Thane replied, taking another drink of the water even when Grey Goose had been placed in front of him. After a second, Thane scooted off the seat, going for Levi and Linda. He could dance alongside Levi. It was the only place he wanted to be.

EPILOGUE

Thanksgiving HSN Special

"How much longer?" Thane called out, his attention split between the television and the appetizers he and Luke were preparing. He was a little anxious to say the least; today was the television debut of his and Arik Layne's joint venture. He cautiously hoped their exclusive line of premium organic oils, balsamic vinegars, and seasonings would be well received. Refusing to let his nerves get the best of him, Thane forced himself to concentrate on his task at hand, feverishly preparing the last dish for the party. He'd chosen his spot at the enormous center island that separated the kitchen from the living room so he could see everything in case the food took longer to prepare than he'd anticipated.

"Three minutes!" Erin yelled excitedly from the living room before everyone near the television burst out laughing. Thane glanced up, angling his head to catch a glimpse of Arik and Chef Ferico. The brief shot of the two was meant to promote and tease the next segment before a commercial break. Instead, it caught Chef Ferico diligently working over a pan of beautifully caramelized butternut squash. A crostini recipe Thane and the chef had spent time perfecting over the last few weeks of his stay in Coronado. As Ferico began crisscrossing the squash with a mix of whipped feta cheese and the perfect blend of za'atar seasoning and tahini, he still managed to look up at the camera and give a wink. Arik on the other hand took that exact moment to stuff his big mouth with what looked like something close to a chocolate brownie. An item that definitely wasn't on the list of recipes they'd all agreed would help promote their products.

In stunned silence, Thane watched as Arik turned toward the camera and rolled his eyes as if the food he'd just eaten was the best thing he'd ever put in his mouth while motioning for someone off screen to come try whatever he held. Thane would bet his house Kellus was on set with Arik, which broke all the rules of only having two company representatives onsite while filming.

"He's not even trying to sell the product. He's too busy stealing the food props off other peoples' sets," Logan said.

"Is that your business partner, Thane?" his mother asked laughingly, all her attention riveted to the television screen.

"Arik's hilarious, Thane!" Erin added, barking out a laugh. "You can tell he wants to talk, but his mouth's full. Oh my God. This is priceless."

Thane couldn't find the humor in Arik's actions; his stomach was too knotted up for that. Honestly, he'd only half believed Arik when he'd said he wanted to taste all the food HSN pimped on the Thanksgiving special. Thane had stupidly thought the real reason Arik wanted to be the one on camera was for bragging rights. When their joint venture did well, Arik would be the one to say he'd made a success of their business. From the looks of it, Arik had been absolutely serious about sampling *all* the food on the show.

"Want me to take 'em over?" Luke asked, drawing his attention away from Arik and the embarrassing display of the man's lack of focus in front of millions of viewers. Luke motioned toward the perfectly crafted platter of nachos as if waiting for Thane to give his approval.

"Looks good."

Luke grabbed the large tray and headed straight for the sofa, stepping over Corey's body spread out across the floor, to sit in his seat next to Thane's mother. As he'd hoped, his mother and father had taken to Luke and Logan immediately, doing this weird grandparent type thing to the boys, helping to ease any lingering resentment he had toward the both of them. More so,

Thane found he had a deep sense of gratitude toward his parents for pushing him to go to Coronado. Had they not, he had no doubt he'd have kept his distance from Levi, ruining any chance at finding this happiness.

Clearly proud of the food he'd made, Luke held out the tray, giving Thane's mother the first choice at the nachos, then stretched across Logan to offer one to Thane's father. Both eagerly took some nachos, praising Luke as if they'd never seen anything quite so delicious. Logan on the other hand seemed to have no care for the artistry of Luke's design. He shoved one whole nacho in his mouth and took two more before Thane's father was able to get his off the platter.

Thane reached for the dish towel, wiping away any crumbs he'd left behind before automatically wiping the rag over the counter. Luke loved to cook and was always there to give a hand in the kitchen when the need arose. He was proud of the progress Luke had made in such a short time, Logan too for that matter. They were all still settling in, working out the details as they went, but they were becoming a solid family.

His family. The thought warmed his heart and wrapped around his soul like a welcoming embrace.

Levi, Logan, and Luke had all stepped up to the plate and worked together, supporting Thane, even trying to lighten his load as he stressed about the official launch of this particular new line. God, he hoped everything went as planned. If the brand was as successful as Arik kept indicating, it would change all their lives. He could see Dishology BBQ and steak sauces, special seasonings, and maybe even branching out to frozen foods.

"It's about to start," Levi announced.

Thane shifted his attention toward his guy. Levi stood in front of the refrigerator, his shirt tight enough to see the muscles in his back flexing as he opened the door before glancing over his shoulder. "Need another beer? Or did you want wine?"

Their gazes collided and all his worry faded away.

The realization that Levi was his still stunned him. Thoughts of Levi regularly stole his breath and robbed him of his focus—something that had only intensified since they had moved to

Ellicott City. He rightfully considered himself the luckiest man on earth that he'd somehow managed to win Levi over.

Thane absently dropped the hand towel and started stalking in Levi's direction. His guy shot another questioning look over his shoulder before turning back to the refrigerator. A split second later, Levi darted his head back around. Thane watched the expression on his handsome face change as he got closer. Levi quickly stepped aside, letting the refrigerator door slam shut as he turned to face him, shaking his head with a big smile forming on his lips.

Levi tried to move around him. Thane grinned as he threw out an arm to block Levi's retreat.

"Everyone can see," Levi whispered, putting a palm to Thane's chest, using his strength to keep him at a distance.

Like that would ever keep him away. Hell, Thane considered that foreplay.

"Just one little kiss," he said, giving his first counterargument.

"He's right, son. Everyone can see," Thane's father added from the living room. Levi started to turn his head that direction, but Thane discouraged the move by placing his hand under Levi's jaw, keeping his redhead's focus just on him.

"Just a celebratory kiss. Hopefully it's gonna be a big day for us, handsome." Thane lowered his voice while he lingered over his lover's lips. "Daddy's 'bout to make the big bucks. You play your cards right, I'll buy you something really special." A chuckle welled inside Thane making it hard to get the words out with the look of horror crossing Levi's face.

"I think *Daddy* should focus on the current gift right now. The Escalade's too big for the driveway, and you're gonna have to build a taller garage to park that thing inside," Logan quipped, causing everyone to laugh.

Thane tried to press his lips to Levi's but only managed to catch the soft flesh behind Levi's jaw just below his ear when he dodged the move and tried to squirm out of his arms.

Thane's parents' presence made Levi nervous in the PDA department. Probably the only disagreement they'd had in the three months they'd been in Maryland. For whatever reason, Levi felt it was disrespectful to pack on the affection when Thane's mother and father were around and always shied away. Of course that became a game for Thane, doing everything in his power to get even the smallest of pecks from his guy.

"Yeah, Thane. The Escalade's a problem. In the lease agreement, we're allowed to park in the driveway in order to get around back for efficiency, but we can't get past the enormous ride. I think you need to knock some off our rent for the inconvenience," Corey teased.

With the talk of rent reduction, Thane finally turned, looking away from Levi to discover his mother and father, Luke and Logan, Erin, Corey, Autumn, Jared, and Brock, along with Linda who had insisted on being there via Skype, all staring their way.

"You know, I'll take that reduced rent too," Brock added. "I feel real inconvenienced."

"If you're paying people, we shut down Sweet Suds to be here today. I could use some cash," Autumn teased, Jared nodding his approval.

For the first time since moving in, Thane regretted knocking down the wall separating the kitchen from the living room. Sensing the impromptu mini make-out session wasn't going to happen, he finally relented and let Levi move out of his arms.

"Hey! It's back on," Luke called out excitedly and quickly turned his laptop back toward the television so Linda could see too.

The segment opened to the host introducing Arik and Chef Ferico. Everyone in his house grew quiet as they turned to watch the show. The only sound came from Levi's boots tapping against the hardwood floor as he headed across the room and came to a stop behind the sofa, standing there facing the television. Levi crossed those brawny arms over his chest, staring at the show's host. Even at such an important moment, Thane's attention remained riveted to Levi. It was always Levi. It would always be Levi. His world centered on his beautiful, engaging, reserved, sexy redhead.

Thane slipped in behind Levi, wrapping both arms around Levi's waist, loving how his guy automatically rested against his chest and angled his head to the side to give Thane a better view of the screen. The heat from Levi's body helped to distract him from the nervous uncertainty he felt about the show.

He inhaled Levi's scent, which calmed him further, and kissed his neck, keeping his eyes on the television as the camera panned out and the shot widened. This moment was pivotal. He couldn't watch, but he couldn't look away either.

What he saw made his heartrate speed up. Levi must have seen it too. His guy gave a side glance toward him, but didn't say a single word, because seriously, what could be said? They watched as a somewhat uncomfortable-looking Kellus stood stiffly next to Arik who again had a mouthful of food and was lifting a bite of whatever he held to Kellus, seemingly unfazed by the cameras, or the small little fact that he was there to sell a product.

"Goddammit."

"Thane," his mother scolded.

"No!" Thane blurted. "I don't think I can watch this. If I had known we could bring a third person, I'd've taken Luke and at least appeared interested in the show in order to sell our damn product."

The HSN host moved to Chef Ferico, asking a question as he finished preparing the last dish. Okay, that was good. Ferico at least brought the conversation and visual back to the organic oils. When the camera again cut away, Thane threw his arm in the air, this time completely releasing Levi as his hands came to rest on his hips. Arik had walked off the set toward another kitchen setup. When the show panned to a wide angle view, Thane watched as Arik swiped a tray of leftover food before coming back to Chef Ferico's station.

"What is he doing?" Thane asked. "What's wrong with him? We went over this whole deal. He knew exactly what to do."

The host, Chef Ferico, and the oils were forgotten as the camera remained focused on Arik. He could hear the production team begin to laugh in the background and his heart sank to the floor. "So much for our venture and making all that money. I should've just done this on my own." Thane sighed.

"No, it's good, Thane. Look at the sales," Erin said sternly, pointing to the corner of the screen. "People are responding."

"Guess he's making it look too good to pass up," Brock added.

Thane watched Arik reach in Chef Ferico's pan and sop up the pineapple-flavored vinegar and oil mixture onto a piece of fruit. He put the bite in his mouth and rolled his eyes, giving an audible groan of delight. Thane's blood pressure skyrocketed before he did finally look at the counter. The units sold were increasing by the thousands.

"Where did Kellus go?" Logan asked.

"I'm certain he took off and is hiding somewhere in the building. He knows he married a crazy man," Thane answered, his eyes locked on the climbing number on the side of the screen as hope slowly began to filter in.

"Arik's a natural and extremely handsome."

Did his mother sound awestruck as she spoke? Oh for God's sake, had she fallen under Arik's spell too? Thane rolled his shoulders as the tension began to ease. He kept an eye on the products-sold counter, refusing to watch anymore of the shit show Arik was putting on. Levi's strong hands slid along his arms and came to a stop when his fingers entwined with Thane's.

"The sales are higher than you guys thought," Levi said quietly then squeezed his hand.

"We didn't ship this much product to them. Arik must have worked something out," Thane said, glancing over at Levi, then back at the counter. HSN would have stopped the sale when the product availability ran out. Instead, both their allotted time slot and product sales were over their contractual agreement.

"Then it's good?"

"It's hard to say, but yeah."

Levi shifted, his handsome face tilted as he bent in and placed a kiss on Thane's lips. "You deserve good."

"We deserve good, Levi." HSN, Arik, and even the numbers scrolling across the television screen were practically forgotten as Levi turned in his arms, coming chest to chest with him. Thane's heartrate sped up again, but for completely different reasons now. Nothing in the world mattered as much as this man. Levi's tentative, encouraging smile brightened.

Laughter erupted in the room, and Thane didn't bother to look over to see what Arik had done to cause such a reaction. Levi's attention was on him—exactly how he liked it—and nothing else mattered.

Nothing but Levi Silva.

He pulled Levi closer and placed his mouth next to Levi's ear. "Have I told you lately that I love you?"

He felt Levi smile. "Not in the last twenty minutes."

"Well, in that case, I need to rectify that." He drew back so he could gaze in his lover's eyes. "I love you, Mr. Silva. I'm so totally head over heels in love with you that I can't ever think of anything but you. You've ruined me."

He grabbed Levi's firm ass cheeks and started moving him backward out of the room toward the empty hall, needing a celebratory make-out session with the man who had completely swept him off his feet more than he needed any well wishes from his friends and family.

"They're kissing again," Luke announced to the room.

"They're always kissing. Just ignore them," Logan replied.

Levi started to turn away, but Thane wasn't ready to let him go just yet. He kept Levi against him as he secured them a more private spot in the hallway.

"Can you feel what you do to me?" Thane growled as he ground his erection against Levi and pinned his lover against the wall. He loved how Levi's eyes darkened and his body molded perfectly to Thane's.

Levi rolled his hips, pressing an equally hard cock against Thane's as Levi's hands slid possessively around him. "I'm afraid it's always gonna be like this with us," Levi whispered, breath ghosting against Thane's cheek in a sultry caress.

Thane leaned in and licked across Levi's lips. He was thrilled and caught off guard when Levi sucked his tongue into his mouth and escalated the kiss, but he pulled back long enough to say, "I sure hope so."

The End

Looking for more Thane and Levi? You'll see them again. Julian's story is coming soon.

Note from the Author

Thank you for reading our books.
Send a quick email and let us know what you thought of
Reservations to kindle@kindlealexander.com. For more
information on future works click sign-up for our new release
newsletter or come friend us on all the major social networking
sites.

http://www.subscribepage.com/s8y4c3_copy

Books by Kindle Alexander

If you enjoyed *Reservations*
then you won't want to miss
Kindle Alexander's bestselling novels:

Painted On My Heart
The Current Between Us (with Bonus Material)
Closet Confession
Secret
Texas Pride
Up in Arms
Always

Nice Guys Series
Double Full
Full Disclosure
Full Domain

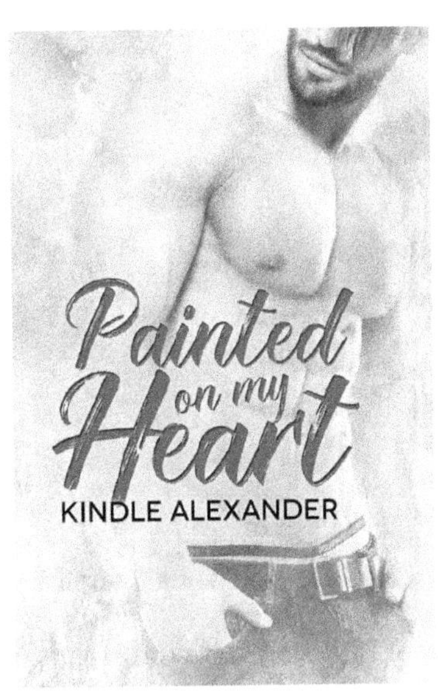

Painted On My Heart
Winner of the 2017 eLit Award Romance category
Winner of the 2017 eLit Award LGBT Fiction category

Artist Kellus Hardin let love and loyalty cloud his past decisions, a mistake he definitely won't make again. Now, lost and alone, he's left to pick up the shattered pieces of his broken heart while facing the truth of his reality.

Arik Layne exudes power, confidence, and determination. But when an encounter with the guarded artist shakes him to the core and alters all his future goals, he finds more than just his heart on the line.

For Kellus, opening himself to love isn't an option.

All Arik wants is to make the artist his.

Can love create a masterpiece when it's painted on your heart?

421

The Current Between Us (with Bonus Material)
Gay/Lesbian Book of the Year, 2014 eLit Awards

Gage Synclair, international, hard-hitting investigative photojournalist, is preparing for the final special report of his career. A story of deception and murder six long years in the making. After spending ten years in some of the worst parts of the world, he's ready to settle life down and open an art gallery in his hometown of Chicago.

Trent Cooper, electrical contractor, is surprised by the last minute request for a fast-paced electrical remodel, little did he know he'd be immediately propositioned by the gallery's owner. Being gay in the construction industry isn't easy, nor is being father to his two young adopted children. Trent keeps his life in separate zones to avoid a short circuit. Will their high-voltage passion break the currents between them forever?

Closet Confession

This version includes Bonus Scenes adding an additional ten thousand words to this edition. Closet Confession was previously released in the *Night Shift Anthology*.

~

Dr. Derek Babineaux is intelligent, dedicated, and one of the best ER physicians in the fast-paced world of critical care at Tulane Medical in New Orleans. Always on top of his game, he's thrown off balance when the newest medical staff member finally unleashes his hidden desires.

Justin Delacroix's job at the inner city's busiest hospital might be just what he needs to ease back into civilian life after a long stint in the military. High-performing shifts make working as a trauma nurse at TMC the perfect way to utilize his skills and quick reaction times. There's only one problem, his attraction for one sexy ER doctor is off the charts, but he has his reasons for not returning Dr. Baby's night shift advances. Or maybe he doesn't.

Always
Book of the Year 2014
Member Choice Awards
~Goodreads MM Romance

Book of the Year 2014
~Sinfully Sexy Book

LGBT Book of the Year
2015 eLit Awards

Born to a prestigious political family, Avery Adams plays as hard as he works. The gorgeous, charismatic attorney is used to getting what he wants, even the frequent one-night stands that earn him his well-deserved playboy reputation. When some of the most prominent men in politics suggest he run for senate, Avery decides the time has come to follow in his grandfather's footsteps. With a strategy in place and the campaign wheels rolling, Avery is ready to jump on the legislative fast track, full steam ahead. But no amount of planning prepares him for the handsome, uptight restaurateur who might derail his political future.

Easy isn't even in the top thousand words to describe Kane Dalton's life after his father, a devout Southern Baptist minister, kicks him out of the family home for questioning his sexual orientation. Despite all the rotten tomatoes life throws his way, Kane makes something of himself. Between owning a thriving upscale Italian restaurant in the heart of downtown Minneapolis and managing his long-term boyfriend, his plate is full. He struggles to get past the teachings of his childhood to fully accept his sexuality and rid himself of the doubts brought on by his religious upbringing. The last thing he needs is the yummy, sophisticated, blond-haired distraction sitting at table thirty-four.

Full Domain
(Nice Guys 3)

Book of the Year, 2016 elit
Awards

Honor, integrity, and loyalty are how Deputy US Marshal Kreed Sinacola lives his life. A former SEAL now employed by the Special Operations Group of the US Marshal Service, Kreed spent most of his life working covert operations and avoiding relationships. Never one to mix business with pleasure, his boundaries blur and his convictions are put to the test when he finally comes face-to-face with the hot computer geek he's been partnered with. Hell-bent on closing the ongoing case for his longtime friend, he pushes past his own limits and uncovers more than he expects.

Aaron Stuart strives for one thing: justice. Young and full of idealism, his highly sought after computer skills land him a position with the National Security Agency. Aaron's biggest hazard at his job is cramped fingers, but all that changes when he is drawn into the middle of a dangerous federal investigation. Aaron gets more than he bargained for when the FBI partners him with a handsome and tempting deputy US marshal. His attraction to the inked up, dark-haired man provides another kind of threat altogether. Aaron tries desperately to place a firewall around his heart and fight his developing feelings, knowing one misstep on his part could ultimately destroy him.

The solution isn't as easy as solving the case, which is treacherous enough as it is. But the growing sexual attraction between them threatens to derail more than just Kreed's personal convictions as he quickly learns temptation and matters of the heart rarely fit easily into the rules he's lived by. Will Kreed be able to convince Aaron to open his heart and face the fact that sometimes the answers aren't always hidden in code?

Full Disclosure (Nice Guys 2)
Book of the Year 2014 ~Sinfully Sexy Book

Deputy United States Marshal Mitch Knox apprehends fugitives for a living. His calm, cool, collected attitude and devastatingly handsome good looks earn him a well-deserved bad boy reputation, both in the field and out. While away on an assignment, he blows off some steam at a notorious Dallas nightclub. Solving the case that has plagued him for months takes a sudden backseat to finding out all there is to know about the gorgeous, shy blond sitting alone at the bar.

Texas State Trooper Cody Turner is moving up the ranks, well on his way to his dream of being a Texas Ranger. While on a two-week mandatory vacation, he plans to relax and help out on his family's farm. Mitch is the last distraction Cody needs, but the tatted up temptation that walks into the bar and steals his baseball cap is too hard to ignore.

As Mitch's case gains nationwide attention, how will he convince the sexy state trooper that giving him a chance won't jeopardize his life's plan...especially when the evil he's tracking brings the hate directly to his doorstep, threatening more than just their careers.

Double Full (Nice Guys 1)

Up and coming football hero, Colt Michaels, makes a Hail Mary pass one night in the college locker room that results in the hottest, sexiest five days of his young life. However, interference after the play has him hiding his past and burying his future in the bottom of a bottle. While Colt seems to have it all, looks can be deceiving especially when you're trapped so far in a closet that you can't see your way out. When ten years of living his expected fast-lane lifestyle lands him engaged to his manipulative Russian supermodel girlfriend, he decides it's time to call a new play.

Jace Montgomery single-handily built the largest all-star cheerleading gym in the world, driven by a need to forget a life-altering encounter with a handsome quarterback a decade ago. His reputation as an excellent coach, hard-nosed business man, and savvy entrepreneur earned him respect in the sometimes catty world of competitive cheerleading. When Jace learns of his ex-lover's plans to marry, his heart executes a barrel roll and his carefully placed resolve tumbles down without a mat to absorb the shock. Can his island escape help him to finally let go of the past and move his life forward?

Secret
Silver Award Book of the Year, 2015 elit Awards

Tristan Wilder, self-made millionaire and devastatingly handsome CEO of Wilder-Nation is on the verge of a very lucrative buyout. With tough negotiations ahead, he's armed with his acquisition pitch, ready to launch the deal of a lifetime. There's just one glitch. The last thing he expects is to fall for the hot business owner he's trying to sway.

Dylan Reeves, computer science engineer and founder of the very successful social media site, Secret, is faced with a life-altering decision. A devoted family man with three kids and a wife, Dylan has been living a secret for years. Fiercely loyal to his convictions, his boundaries blur after meeting the striking owner of the corporation interested in acquiring his company. For the first time in his life, reckless desire consumes him when the gorgeous computer mogul makes an offer he can't refuse.

Texas Pride
Bronze Award Book of the Year, 2014 elit Awards
in both Romance and Gay Fiction

When mega movie star and two time Academy Award winner, Austin Grainger voluntarily gave up his dazzling film career, his adoring fan base thought he'd lost his mind. For Austin, the seclusion of fifteen hundred acres in the middle of Texas sounds like paradise. No more cameras, paparazzi, or overzealous media to hound him every day and night. Little did the sexiest man alive know when one door closes, another usually opens. And Austin's opened by way of a sexy, hot ranch owner right next door.

Kitt Kelly wasn't your average rancher. He's young, well educated and has hidden his sexuality for most of his life. When his long time wet dream materializes as his a new neighbor it threatens everything he holds dear. No way the ranching community would ever accept him if he came out. With every part of his life riding on the edge, can Kitt risk it all for a chance at love or will responsibility to his family heritage cost him his one chance at happiness?

What readers are saying about Kindle Alexander books…

Secret

"INSPIRING, HONEST, BRAVE, RELEVANT—A MUST READ!!!"
~ Natasha is a Book Junkie

"This is a powerful story and truly one of Kindle Alexander's best books."
~ Beyond the Valley of the Books

"Secret tells the story of men who are mature enough to value integrity over pleasure and know that loving each other means caring about the others priorities."
~Indie Bookshelf

Full Disclosure

"In the end… OMG the end… let's just say Mitch and Cody have their happy, one that touched my heart."
~Denise, Shh Mom's Reading

"I give this story five+ perfectly delivered stars."
~Toni FGMAMTC

"Mitch and Cody are perfect and so bloody hot, it made my IPAD melt."

~Jules Swoon Worthy

Double Full

"These two hunky men had me in tears, their love for one
another is magical."
~Jennifer Robbins, Twinsie Talk Book Review

"Kindle Alexander sure can write a red hot sex scene like
nobody else."
~Vickie Leaf, Book Freak

"Without a doubt one of the BEST m/m romances I have ever
read."
~Mandie, Foxylutely Blog

Texas Pride

"I have a severe case of book hangover. Seriously readers – you
need to read this book. Ten stars for me!"
~ Mandie, Foxylutely Blog

"Definitely a great read…I didn't want this sweet story to end."
~Christi Snow, Author